THE SERVANT OF HELAMAN

Other Books by M.D. House

The Barabbas Trilogy (Christian historical fiction)
I Was Called Barabbas
Pillars of Barabbas
The Barabbas Legacy

The Patriot Star Series (science fiction)
Patriot Star

THE SERVANT OF HELAMAN

M.D. HOUSE

CONTENTS

TO RACETRACK
2 MILES
MULEK GATES
TWO VELS CANAL
GARDEN
HELAMAN'S HOUSE
POTTERY SHOP
The Santorem
NAHOM'S HOUSE
ZERAHIR'S HOUSE
ZEDEKIAH
New Hebron
MAIN PRISON
LAW OFFICE
GOLDEN GATES

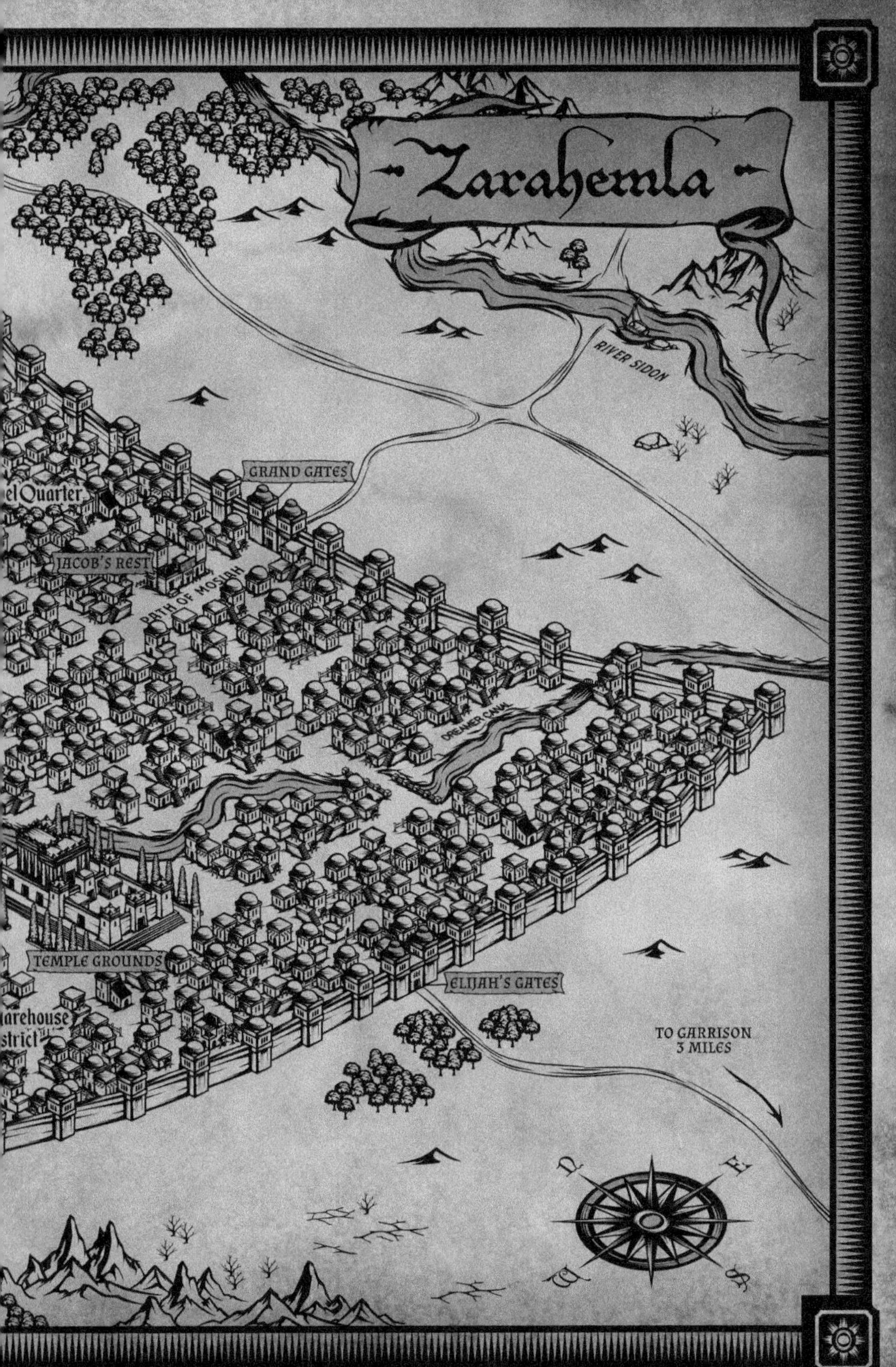

Zarahemla
RIVER SIDON
GRAND GATES
el Quarter
JACOB'S REST
PATH OF MOSIAH
DREAMER CANAL
TEMPLE GROUNDS
ELIJAH'S GATES
arehouse
istrict
TO GARRISON
3 MILES
N
E
W
S

INTRODUCTION
to *The Servant of Helaman*

Very few people have heard of the heroic man called only by the label "the servant of Helaman" in what The Church of Jesus Christ of Latter-day Saints considers ancient scriptural record from the ancient Americas. His name is never revealed, but his briefly chronicled role—from about 52–50 BC—in the thousand-year story of a long-deceased Christian-majority nation is dramatic and inspiring.

Like Barabbas, about whom I've written a full Christian historical fiction trilogy, the servant of Helaman's life has captivated me for quite some time, and what is said about it in the records we have is incredibly thin on details. There are two chapters in the Book of Mormon, Helaman 1 and 2, which contain the entire abbreviated story of the events captured in this novel. I enjoyed the challenge of filling it out and making it feel real, again like the story of Barabbas.

Unlike Barabbas, we can be quite certain that the servant of Helaman was a follower of Christ. Helaman himself was considered a prophet, and also became a civic leader during dangerous political times. We do not know, of course, if the servant of Helaman remained a faithful Christian for the remainder of his life, but that question is open for all of us who call ourselves Christians—we must be ever-vigilant, ever-prayerful, ever-faithful in service and devotion.

I'd like to thank Lance Buckley again for his fabulous work on both the cover and the interior of the book. He wasn't familiar with the characters of the story, or the story itself, but he did some research and blew me away once again with his creative prowess. The map of Zarahemla, capital of the Nephite nation, was created in rough, imagined outline by me, and then professionally by Carlos Valero. For this book, I turned to an editor who *was* familiar with the story, Abbey Huch, whose work significantly refined and improved the text.

The final product will draw you into the lives of these people who were very much like us. The same kinds of temptations and intrigues plagued them, both individually and as a society. The fiery darts of the adversary assaulted them just as they assail us. Our vastly superior technology is mainly fancy wrapping paper, though it acts as an accelerant—for good or ill.

I love this story, which increases my faith and determination to follow the living Christ. I hope you will, too.

M.D. HOUSE
MAY 2022

PROLOGUE

Yea, why do ye build up your secret abominations to get gain, and cause that widows should mourn before the Lord, and also orphans to mourn before the Lord, and also the blood of their fathers and their husbands to cry unto the Lord from the ground, for vengeance upon your heads? Behold, the sword of vengeance hangeth over you; and the time soon cometh that he avengeth the blood of the saints upon you, for he will not suffer their cries any longer.

MORMON 8:40–41

Confidence coursed through Kishkumen's veins as he thought about his disguise. With help from his sister, he had darkened his shoulder-length hair with a root-based pigment. He had used similar tinctures to apply exotic ceremonial markings on his face, hands, arms, and even feet. He had trimmed his beard short except at the very center, which was divided into two thin braids more than a handspan long. A small precious stone had been woven into the end of each braid. The stones were ostentatious, but necessary. Along with the tattoos, they drew eyes—eyes that wouldn't remember much about the features of his face or the nature of his build.

The fine fabric of his clothes, expensively dyed and expertly tailored, soothed his tan skin. He had borrowed them from a trader of exotic garments—without consent, but the owner's loyalties were uncertain. The attire represented a worthy offering to the cause, whether the trader agreed with the cause or not. The comfortable leather sandals were borrowed, too, and they fit him perfectly. He was picky about his footwear, but especially today, when his feet would need to serve him well.

Altogether, Kishkumen felt proud. It wasn't his most elaborate disguise, but it might be his most effective.

He didn't dwell further on his appearance as he sat in the small anteroom with several other merchants and petitioners awaiting their turn to see the chief judge and his advisers in the great Hall of Judgment situated near the center of the mighty city of Zarahemla. He didn't review his plan of action or his several escape routes again, either. He knew it all perfectly, so he didn't have to worry about adrenaline or fear confusing his judgment when the time came. He was experienced in his role, and while he took precautions, he wasn't afraid of death.

Instead, he focused on his motivation, urging the bonfire in his soul to grow, the hungry flames fueled by his fierce desires. The man who should have been the chief judge—the noble Paanchi—had recently been executed for standing firmly and honorably against the coronation of his brother, Pahoran, while his weak-spined, sycophantic brother Pacumeni fawned over the new regime. The high-minded relics of Nephite society had unfairly influenced the election of Pahoran to the judgment seat; they washed out his flaws with endless streams of propaganda, claiming he would carry on the so-called 'righteous' traditions of his father.

There was nothing righteous about them.

Pahoran the Elder had revered and collaborated with the bloodthirsty Captain Moroni, whose arrogant, benighted son now commanded the fearsome but overconfident Nephite armies in his place. Together, Pahoran and Moroni had murdered thousands of innocent patriots who honestly strived to influence the government toward a more peaceful coexistence with the Lamanites and a more tolerant, less restrictive code of laws—untethered to the worship of irrationally vengeful gods. The savage and haughty Nephite leaders had hoisted the maddening and hypocritical 'Standard of Liberty' in every city and village in the land, while incessantly subjecting the people to fevered fancies buttressing their power. They had labeled their victims 'kingmen,' executing them as traitors, both with and without sham trials. The

Nephites would be far better off with a true and noble king than the rotten lot of judges and generals gorging themselves on their labors.

One of those martyrs was Kishkumen's father, another his older brother. But he wasn't as enraged by their deaths as he used to be. His father and brother had died heroes, setting a path for others, like him, to follow. What incensed him now was that the mealy-mouthed, self-righteous Pahoran the Younger occupied the judgment seat and continued to press the cause of the greedy, wealthy Christians on the good people who represented the long-suffering, fair-minded backbone of Nephite success.

Pahoran wouldn't survive the afternoon.

Kishkumen almost let a smile slip. He doubted his expression would look suspicious, but he maintained his character as a shrewd, serious merchant, a stranger to Nephite and Lamanite lands. He had practiced speaking the Nephite language haltingly, as if he hailed from the mountains and coasts far to the northeast. He sometimes considered how those people suffered, too. The Nephites were aggressive traders, their influence oversized. Foreign merchants now used the Nephite language as the lingua franca in most parts of the known world—north, south, east, and west, all the way to either of the unlimited waters.

Someone called his false name, nudging him out of his smoldering reverie. Normally, he felt a brief spike of natural nervousness when the time to kill drew close, but a profound calm settled upon him. He rose, nodded respectfully at the man who held the door open to the audience chamber, and stepped across the threshold.

There he sat: the pompous chief judge of the Nephites, son of a butcher. No wonder so many Nephites had been emigrating the last few years, many of them traveling far to the north. They couldn't abide being subject to such scions of heraldic corruption. Pahoran, looking bored and stupid, lifted a lazy hand to grant Kishkumen leave to approach. The distance to the front of the room measured only twenty paces, but the few moments it took to cross seemed to extend, as if Kishkumen labored under the waters of a swift-flowing river. At the halfway mark, he held out the small, ornate box designed to arouse the greed of the Nephite leaders, the inferno of his determination burning away the imagined current. The gold and gems decorating the top and sides of the box sparkled with reflections of the chandeliers and finely sculpted columns of the well-lit chamber of liars.

He stopped two paces from Pahoran and his advisers, then bowed, his torso nearly parallel to the finely-tiled floor decorated with flamboyant specks of gold, silver, and ziff.

"Oh, mighty ones, I bring spices exotic and medicines new. I present to you as example of benefitting more trade between us." He straightened, pleased at his perfect tone, accent and faulty grammar.

Pahoran nodded with rapacious interest, like a slavering animal, his watery eyes focused on the box. "You may open it."

As Kishkumen lifted the delicate lid, he finally allowed himself a small smile. Then, in the space of two heartbeats, he withdrew the slender dagger hidden in the spices, tossed the box to the side, and lunged for the chief judge. He knew Pahoran's arms would come up, that his body would turn slightly, that a look of shock would paint his face. Kishkumen's knife entered under the ribcage before the first shout, and he waited an extra heartbeat to make sure the thrust moved up to pierce the villain's heart.

He left the knife embedded in the dying body. Spinning away from the judgment seat to his right, he removed his cloak and flung it at the guard who rushed toward him. The guard used his spear to cast the cloak out of the way, as expected, and Kishkumen was under the weapon and past the man before he could bring the sharp edge to bear against him. Instead of heading for the door at the back of the hall, Kishkumen angled for a window, diving head-long through and tucking into a roll as he hit the ground of an inner garden.

He was back on his feet in an instant, letting the sounds around him guide his instincts in choosing the right escape path across the garden, through another part of the building, and out into the streets of the city. As he turned left, he heard running footsteps behind him. Servants and guards had exited the Hall of Judgment using the same entrance he had used earlier, and they had spotted him.

But he was fast. He hadn't met anyone faster. He was still in his prime, and he took his physical training seriously, so he had great endurance to complement his speed. He also had a solid plan. He snaked through the streets, aiming in the general direction of the eastern gates and the river beyond. He knew what his pursuers would think—that he had accomplices with a swift boat, awaiting him along the bank of the great watercourse.

Large irrigation canals traversed the city, though, and when he turned up a familiar narrow alley to race along the back side of a warehouse, he took stock of his first escape option. No people cluttered his vision, and the canal he sought lay just ahead, running perpendicular to his line of travel. The deep water flowed north for a significant distance before curving east to eventually disappear under the unconquered stone walls of the storied Nephite capital—the site of his most recent dispensation of glorious justice. His pursuers already lagged well behind, though he knew they had spread out to find his trail. It wouldn't take them long if he dallied.

He reached the canal and slipped into the water with little sound. Then he took a deep breath and began swimming underwater with the gentle current. He wasn't tired yet. His body felt strong. He knew he could reach a certain secluded garden a short distance beyond the canal's bend to the east with only three or four brief stops for air underneath bridges or amid patches of thick overgrowth along the banks. People rarely swam in the canals this early in the day, and those who did were mostly children, so the risk was low that anyone would see him swimming fully clothed and question him. Once at the garden, he would be out of view of any uncovered windows or streets, and he could leave the canal after recovering the weighted waterproof bag he had secured at its bottom several days earlier. He had placed three other such bags around the city: one in a different canal, one on the roof of a warehouse, and another buried in a different garden.

He reached the secluded garden easily, though by the time he broke the surface of the water for the last time the adrenaline had abated. He quickly changed out of his expensive clothes and sandals and into the common attire stored in the bag, which also contained a plain but well-made and finely sharpened dagger in a simple sheath, along with a small, rough towel to dry his hair and rub the markings off his skin. He wrung out the wet clothes and stuffed them with the towel into the bag, which he tossed back into the water, where it sank quickly. If he didn't retrieve the bag by late summer, when the canals were running low, perhaps someone would find it. But that was an inconsequential worry.

The dye in his hair had completely washed out. With the dagger, he trimmed the ridiculous braids growing out of his chin, shaving the hair close. He kept the two precious stones, placing them in a small pouch he attached to his belt. Then he waited several minutes, listening to the noises of the city. Zarahemla was a huge place, but he was still less than a mile from the Hall of Judgment, which sat like a pregnant and angry sow just a few blocks southeast of the crossroads in the city's center. Sounds of anger and panic occasionally pierced the air loudly enough for him to hear.

Kishkumen smiled for the second time that day, as broadly as the muscles in his face would allow.

CHAPTER 1

*Now ye may suppose that this is foolishness in me; but behold I say unto
you, that by small and simple things are great things brought to pass; and
small means in many instances doth confound the wise. And the Lord
God doth work by means to bring about his great and eternal purposes;
and by very small means the Lord doth confound the wise and bringeth
about the salvation of many souls.*

ALMA 37:6–7

Kihoran, commonly known as Kai when he used his real name, waited patiently as a flock of sheep crossed the narrow road before him, their bleating sporadic and uninterested. They would probably have stopped entirely if the old shepherd and his two well-trained dogs hadn't urged them on. The shepherd dipped his chin in a voiceless apology as he finally crossed the road behind his sheep, the dogs running ahead. Kai nodded back with a smile. He had been gone for six months—a few more minutes wouldn't make any difference.

The night before, he had felt drained—physically and mentally. But the morning had brought new strength now that he was so close to his destination.

Home.

He hadn't always lived in Bountiful, but it was the only place he called home. In a few short miles, he would top a small hill to the northeast of the city, just after the noon hour. He could already picture the beauty and serenity of the most brilliant jewel in the crown of the Nephite nation. Bountiful had become an important crossroads of culture and trade, its reputation still growing rapidly, as Kai could attest from his recent extensive travels. His adoptive parents, Gideon and Ishara, worried Bountiful was becoming too popular, that increased wealth and influence would lead to damaging levels of pride and moral corruption.

Kai was relatively young—having recently turned twenty-one—but he'd already seen a great many places and met literally thousands of people. It was clear to him his parents had a sound basis for their fears: humans were humans, and the fact that most Nephites were professed Christians didn't exempt them from the hard realities of life and human nature. The temptations still came, relentlessly, especially in the midst of great success. Pride was a monster with many heads, feeding on a vast array of lusts.

He had passed few people on this road. Much broader highways existed nearby, some of them finished with stone to handle heavy traffic and large wagons in almost any weather. All the paths around Bountiful were relatively safe, though. The people of Bountiful knew the importance of their city. It had been attacked before, was nearly overrun fifteen years ago by Amalickiah and his ravaging Lamanite armies at the beginning of the Great War, just after Moroni had put down the king-men. Kai's birth parents had been king-men. But that was long in the past, or at least his past. He loved Bountiful. The people were vigilant, the laws strict, the roads and neighborhoods safe. There were far better ways to make a living in such a prosperous city than turning to the dangerous business of banditry.

As he crested the final hill and beheld his beautiful city, his senses suddenly sharpened. Something didn't feel right. His training kicked in, and he instinctively moved off the road into the trees and brush, lifting and placing his feet carefully to avoid noise. He found a good vantage point, well hidden, and spent the next several minutes studying the city's surroundings.

He'd been taught to be patient and observant. Seven years ago, shortly after the legendary Captain Moroni's son, Moronihah, had taken command of the armies, one of Moroni's men had recruited Kai as a scout, and that man had schooled him well. Kai had even met Captain Moroni once, shortly before his lamentably early death, when he served as an adviser to his son. Kai would never forget the experience. Moroni had seemed otherworldly and invincible, yet detailed and thorough—so very thorough.

After observing the area for several minutes, Kai noted nothing obviously amiss. The rolling, forested hills surrounding the city seemed to shrug at his concern. The shepherd had appeared calm, as had others Kai passed on the road. But the people in the city appeared to be moving faster than they normally would—he could tell even from this distance, with the city's outskirts still more than a mile off. He listened for any unusual sounds, but none teased him.

Finally, he rose from his concealed position, feeling slightly silly. He still had an uneasy feeling, but he couldn't identify any immediate danger, so he moved back to the road, not wanting to look suspicious—and even more foolish—by traveling off-road across pastures and fields of grain, corn, fruit trees, and other crops. Summer was nearing its end; the fields had nearly matured. If necessary, he could have easily hidden in most of them. He was no farmer—his blood parents probably were—but he could tell the harvest would be good that year.

He passed a few more people as he neared the city. One of them, a farmer and long-time friend of Gideon and Ishara, recognized him.

"Ho, young Kihoran!" the man said, stopping and smiling broadly. "Welcome home. Your parents will be excited to see you. Was your trip to the east successful? Did you go beyond the mountains?"

Kai grasped forearms with the man and produced a grin, easily slipping into his role as a commercial scout for one of the large merchant groups in Bountiful and Mulek. Though young for such a role in a profession that held little interest for him, he had a knack for it. Commercial scouting offered a good cover that had been carefully cultivated. Moroni himself had conceived the idea of a coordinated spy network and made most of the initial arrangements across the nation. Moronihah had later chosen Kihoran for one of the eastern roles. Men and women scouted and spied to the southeast, south, and west as well. The north was thinly populated, so diplomats or scouts were rarely sent in that direction.

"No, not this time. But I met a visiting Airoack priestess who wanted me to marry her daughter." He laughed, and the older man joined in with a hearty guffaw. Kai remembered names well, but for some reason this man's name took him several seconds to retrieve. Yes, there it was ... Heleorum. "I made some good contacts, and I think the merchants will be pleased."

Heleorum nodded, then gazed out over one of his fields. "We'll have a nice surplus this year. The trade will be good … as long as the peace holds."

Kai's voice turned instantly serious. "Did something happen?" He swallowed in uncharacteristic nervousness. He could almost sense a storm.

Heleorum sighed heavily. "More trouble in Zarahemla. We don't know many details yet, but the chief judge is dead. Murdered."

And there it was. It felt like a mountain had just cracked. The news was devastating, though not entirely unexpected given Nephite history and recent political rumblings. He would need to complete his report and be ready. Almost ten years of mostly uninhibited prosperity had passed since the end of the Great War with the Lamanites, but the peace had grown increasingly uneasy over the last few of those years. Because of the renewed contentions, many people had left, some with the eccentric shipbuilder and explorer Hagoth, some in other groups.

Last year, new dissenters had again stirred up some of the Lamanites, who then attacked the border forts. Moronihah had handily defeated them, but it wasn't clear to Kai why the Lamanites had come in the first place. They had fertile lands of their own, with plenty of trading opportunities. Claims of stolen birthrights were hundreds of years old, and seemed contrived anyway. It bothered Kai that he didn't fully grasp their motives. Some of the other spies and scouts said they understood the reasons behind the attempted invasion, but whenever they tried to explain it to him, his mind went fuzzy. Their answers didn't make sense, though the threat was obviously real. Suddenly he wished he were attached to the main army again. He knew what he did was important, but …

"Kihoran?"

Kai blinked. He had lost himself for a moment. He shouldn't ever do that. But perhaps, he rationalized, such news affecting him so deeply further strengthened his cover, making him appear a frightened common citizen.

"That's awful news," he said with a grave look. "When?"

"It happened more than a week past. We heard just two days ago, when a fast courier arrived." Heleorum laid a calloused hand on Kai's shoulder. "We'll get through this. There are still enough good people in this land who worship the Lord and serve each other. We are under his covenant. He will protect us, though we may pass through some hard times, as before."

Kai blinked again. He had stopped calling such pronouncements blind faith. A deep well of wisdom nurtured Heleorum's words. Gideon and Ishara had assiduously taught Kai to feel such conviction, to seek God's aid. He wasn't good at it yet, though he knew he had received divine assistance on several memorable occasions. He was a scout and spy, after all—paid to be observant and discount nothing.

"I must get home."

Heleorum nodded with understanding and compassion in his eyes. "It's good to see you again, Kihoran, healthy and safe. Please deliver a greeting to your parents."

Kai promised he would as he headed off, his pace quick. He easily maintained the appearance of a worried young Nephite, because he truly was anxious.

And strangely excited.

His sixteen-year-old sister Neva was the first to greet him as he approached the sturdy, wood-framed house, the plaster on its exterior freshly-painted in a light rose color. She had spied him from a side window and came bounding out the door, reaching a full sprint and barely slowing as she jumped into his arms. Her long, black hair billowed around his face as she impacted, and he took two bracing steps backward to catch his balance and hold her off the ground. Her embrace was strong. They shared a special bond, having grown up together in a strange new place. He was her protector, and he relished the role. His fierceness made many young men shy away from her. She didn't seem to mind, though, at least not yet.

She started to sob. After a few moments he set her down gently and pushed himself away so he could see her eyes, dark green to his hazel.

"Is everything okay?" he asked softly.

She nodded, wiping away tears. "I'm sorry, Kai. I didn't think I'd cry this time when you got home. I'm trying to be stronger, like you."

He shook his head. "You *are* strong. Crying has nothing to do with it."

She seemed unconvinced as she stared into his eyes, studying them. Most people told him his eyes revealed little—a trait that made him a good negotiator—but Neva claimed his eyes were wide windows into his soul.

Her gaze sometimes unnerved him. "You look good. It was a successful trip, yes?"

He smiled. "It was. I almost got married."

The shocked look on her face was worth every senine of the deception. Within a second she had figured it out, though, and she slugged him hard in the shoulder. Had she been training with the soldiers? She was getting stronger. It hurt.

"Ouch!" he exclaimed teasingly. "What would you have done if I really *had* gotten married?"

Her stern expression brooked no argument. "You can't marry anyone unless I meet her first. And approve. You *know* that."

He almost chuckled. "I do, and I haven't become fool enough to ignore it."

She studied his eyes a few moments longer, clearly harboring doubts. Then she slugged him again, more softly this time. "And you won't. Come, Mother and Father will want to see you and hear how your trip went. They're both home today."

He still felt slightly uncomfortable whenever Neva called Gideon and Ishara 'Mother' and 'Father.' But he understood. She had no remembrance of their birth parents. She was barely a year old when they were lost. She knew the truth, of course, but to her it was natural to see Gideon and Ishara as her parents. She even reminded him occasionally that she and Kai had been sealed eternally to Gideon and Ishara under God's covenants. She was stronger in the Church than he was, her faith and trust brighter. He loved her for it, even when she pressed him on things—maybe *because* she pressed him on things.

It took a minute for Gideon and Ishara to wrap up their work and join Kai and Neva in the front room of their small but well-maintained home, which lay near the southeastern border of the city. The delay didn't bother Kai. His adoptive parents were skilled and conscientious in their crafts—he a potter and she a seamstress. Neither of them was overly excitable, either, unlike their one blood son, Jevrael, who served in the army. Jevrael was three years older than Kai. Gideon and Ishara had never been able to conceive more children.

They greeted Kai with a fond embrace, Ishara adding the obligatory kiss. She offered to bring him some food, but he politely declined. Or at least he thought he was polite about it. Ishara gave him a stricken look.

"You're gone for six months, traveling the Lord knows how many miles on foot, you look thinner than a baby goat, and my food doesn't appeal to you?"

He thought she was teasing, but even the hint of a smile at the corners of her mouth wasn't enough to convince him, so he tried a safer path.

"Sorry," he said with an appropriately penitent smile, "I just don't want you to trouble yourselves for me." Oops, that wasn't right, either. "I mean, I know it's not really any trouble, but … um, okay, what do you have?"

She couldn't hold back the smile any longer. More than that, she laughed, then embraced him again and squeezed hard, breathing in deeply.

"I'm teasing, my son, but you know there's nothing I wouldn't do for you, nothing you need that I would ever view as a troubling task."

She didn't often make such profound statements, but when she did, Kai took notice. He studied her eyes, and just as Neva could see into his soul, he could pierce his adoptive mother's. She was worried about this assassination, about the welfare of their nation, their city, and their family—primarily their spiritual welfare, to which physical welfare was so often linked. She was a good, kind, perceptive woman—the kind of woman Kai didn't expect to ever find for himself. Of course, he would never say that to her. If he did, she'd flog him with a belt, at least figuratively.

Ishara made them remain seated in the front room while she swished her robes and hurried to the kitchen, where she busied herself. It sounded like she was preparing to kill a fatted calf and prepare a great feast. Gideon pretended not to notice, while Neva cast furtive glances toward the kitchen, clearly wondering if she was expected to help.

Gideon leaned forward in his simply-crafted, lightly-cushioned chair, gazing intently at Kai. "What truth from the east, my son? All we hear are rumors." Gideon and Ishara knew Kai was a spy, and Kai had told Neva just before leaving on this latest mission. She hadn't seemed shocked or worried then, but she looked shaken now.

"I didn't hear anything about the assassination, of course, since it happened so recently," Kai admitted. Gideon's eyebrows rose, so he clarified. "I ran into Master Heleorum on the way in, and he told me. It feels momentous. I could sense the tension from outside the city."

Gideon nodded, his eyes locked on his clasped hands for a moment. "Jevrael has already been sent to join one of the garrisons on the southern border. I've been praying and talking with several of the priests. You don't remember the 'Great Mourning' in the sixteenth year of the Reign of the Judges, since you hadn't been born yet. That followed the bloodiest, deadliest battle in all of Nephite history. For some reason, this assassination feels like it portends something similar, and it harrows my soul."

Kai let his head drop momentarily, a somber chill running down his spine. Jevrael had already left. Things were moving fast. "I've read about the Great Mourning, and Moronihah has talked about it." He glanced at Neva, still a bit uncomfortable about her knowledge of his secret place in the army. "He was only eleven at the time, but he accompanied the main camp with his father, and he helped bury the dead."

Neva shivered, though she hadn't witnessed what he had seen of war. Last year's battle came back to his mind in stark detail. It had been a slaughter. He hadn't directly participated, but he and the other scouts had performed their job well. Moronihah's captains had outmaneuvered and outfought the invading Lamanites, who left a trail of dead and dying for many miles when they retreated.

"Was this the army that followed the people of Ammon out of the old land of Nephi?" asked Neva.

Gideon nodded. "That was the angriest Lamanite army I'd ever heard tell of. They apparently felt like we were 'stealing' their people, in addition to the long list of vain and inaccurate grievances ingrained in Lamanite minds from the time they can walk. The man who wounded me screamed like a demon had possessed him until another Nephite soldier's arrow took him in the throat. I don't know if I would have survived if that arrow wasn't true."

Kai recalled the scars Gideon had shown him from that battle, including a long thick one on his upper right thigh.

Neva leaned forward on her chair. "There was a great battle two years later, when Zerahemnah led the Lamanites in another invasion. You were wounded in that one as well, right Father?" Kai noted the fear in her eyes had been mostly replaced by curiosity and admiration.

Gideon grimaced in remembrance. "It wasn't as bad, but Moroni released me from the army after that battle. And I missed action with the militias in the Great Rebellion started by Amalickiah because I was still recovering. Those were dark times, too, but Moroni put a quick end to it. I wanted so badly to gather to the Title of Liberty he raised at that time—your mother knows. I almost went anyway, sword in one hand, crutch in the other."

"But then there was peace," said Neva.

Gideon smiled nostalgically. "Yes, for a few years. It was such a wonderful time. Everyone was so happy. We worked hard, we were kind to each other, and we were honest. We enjoyed new music, and plays, and dancing, and amazing art. We worshipped God with enthusiasm and studied his word. The Spirit was strong. It almost felt like angels walked the face of the earth with us, constantly.

"The Lamanites were still a danger, of course, so Captain Moroni fortified our cities and increased the strength and skill of our armies. We felt safer than I ever remembered feeling. Some people almost worshipped Moroni."

"He hated that," said Kai absently, surprised he had voiced the thought aloud.

Gideon nodded. "I imagine that's true. Sometimes I forget you once carried reports directly to him or his captains. You've never said much about Moroni's personality, though you've said a lot about Moronihah's."

Kai shrugged. "Moronihah is closer to my age. And his father is a legend."

Gideon chuckled. "Moronihah's fourteen years older than you. He's married and has several children of his own."

"Oh, that reminds me," interjected Neva. "Kai almost got married on this last trip."

Kai didn't know whether to cringe or burst out laughing. Before he could decide for himself, he heard a voice that made him flinch.

"Oh?" said Ishara, entering the room with a large plate heaped with food, including some sizzling boar meat she must have warmed over the coals in their brick oven. Kai's mouth watered. "And why didn't you go through with it?"

She was teasing him ... unless she was admonishing him. He looked at Neva and frowned, but Neva knew he could never really be mad at her. She used that to her advantage, often.

He looked up at Ishara, trying not to appear sheepish. "It was a ruse, set up by a well-connected trader in Airoack. I didn't fall for it."

"A ruse," said Ishara flatly. "You mean an attempt to form some sort of alliance to secure favorable trade. And the young woman went along with it?"

Kai blushed. "Yes, she did."

Ishara laughed, easing some of the tension in the room. "Of course she did. Look at you. Not just how handsome and strong you are, but how intelligent, and witty, and considerate. It's a wonder you haven't married anyone here yet."

The tension returned, and Kai felt the usual embarrassment and annoyance that surfaced whenever the topic of marriage came up.

"I might marry Siarah," he blurted out, surprising himself yet again. Ishara kept chipping away, and now he'd said something he wished he hadn't.

"Oh?" Ishara said with interest, but then shrugged. "If you want to, she's a fine choice. But don't let us pressure you into it."

Was this her way of *increasing* the pressure? Yes, probably, but he was a grown man, and an accomplished spy—a diplomat, too, after a fashion. He decided to exert some control over the conversation, such as he could.

"We haven't spoken seriously about it, and she has other suitors as well. Perhaps that time will come."

Well, he had certainly sounded as dry as most diplomats.

Ishara's eyes narrowed slightly, her gaze boring into him for several long seconds. She didn't frown, but she came close to it. Her voice was patient and compassionate, though.

"Do you love her?"

Kai's diplomacy died. That question, not the silly dances circling it, was the heart of the matter. Did he love Siarah? Did he know what that even meant? He felt attracted to her, for sure. She was beautiful and talented, and his adoptive parents weren't the only ones who had asked him whether he and Siarah would get married someday. Many of the young men he'd grown up with, all of whom were now married, had asked him the same question. To her credit, Siarah didn't pester him about marriage or complain to her friends—at least not that he knew of. She seemed to genuinely like him, and while there were indeed other suitors, she didn't give them much attention. He swallowed as the realization hit him that it was probably time to give her some kind of commitment.

Finally, he nodded, looking first at Ishara, then at Gideon, sparing a glance for Neva as well. "Yes, I think so," he said, trying to affect a confident smile, "but that's none of your business. You brought out food, Mother, and suddenly I'm much hungrier than I thought I was."

It was the first time he had called Ishara 'Mother,' and though he meant it, he also hoped it would make her stop questioning him about marriage … at least for a little while.

Kai may have deflected Ishara's queries temporarily, but he had clearly given her encouragement, too. By midmorning the next day, Siarah appeared at the house, dropping off a delivery of fresh-baked breads and dried apples, with the excuse that her own mother had "made too much."

Neva giggled when she brought Siarah to where Kai sat at their kitchen table and announced her visit. He was examining a scroll on which he had recorded some notes from his trip. In his surprise, he nearly knocked it off the table. He looked askance at Neva, but smiled as he rose and greeted Siarah. He felt anxious about seeing her, but reminded himself that he was a brave scout—a warrior, right?

"Hi, Siarah. The bread smells amazing."

"And I missed you, too," she said, grinning as she handed the basket to Neva and walked over to give Kai a prolonged hug. "You were gone a long time."

Kai winced as he thought about Neva bringing up the young Airoack woman, but blessedly she didn't. Siarah pulled back, keeping her hands around his neck. She had never done that before. Now he was *really* glad Neva hadn't mentioned the Airoack woman. Or had she beforehand? His face warmed.

"It was a success, I hope?" Siarah asked.

"Yes. And I almost made it far enough north to see where some of our people have settled. It's a strange-looking land."

Siarah pursed her lips as she lowered her arms. "I still don't understand why they all left."

"I don't either."

"When do you have to leave again?"

Her tone didn't sound upset. In fact, she seemed calm and in control.

"Soon, I think, because of . . ." He hesitated, though the night before he'd spent some time thinking through how to tell her. He glanced at Neva, who listened intently as she held the basket. "Neva, can you give us some privacy?"

Neva cast him a disappointed look, but then nodded in understanding and headed back toward the front room, still carrying the basket. Kai returned his gaze to Siarah. A nervous curiosity danced in her eyes.

"Can we sit?" he asked. "Just here at the table?"

She nodded and pulled out the closest chair, sitting and turning it to face him as he sat.

"This sounds serious," she said evenly.

Kai frowned, feeling nervous, which probably showed in his expression. "It is. I need to tell you what I really do."

She searched his eyes briefly. "You're not a merchant scout?"

"Yes, I am, sometimes, but mostly I'm a spy and scout for the army."

"Oh," she said. "And that's your big news?"

"Well . . . yes. I thought it was time I told you."

She didn't appear stunned. "Hmmm . . . and why didn't you tell me earlier? Did you think I couldn't handle it? I'm not accusing you," she added quickly, touching his arm, "just asking."

Kai shrugged. "I wasn't sure."

Her eyes narrowed, and then her lips twitched into a smile. "You're sure I can handle it *now*?" She was teasing him, but he didn't mind.

"I never doubted you could handle it, but I can only tell certain people." He realized the implications of what he'd just said, but Siarah didn't launch into a discussion about their future together. Mercifully. He wasn't quite ready for all that.

"It's a dangerous job, I know," she said calmly, resting her hand firmly on his arm. His skin tingled with warmth under her fingers. "But we all have to be strong and do what must be done to protect our people. God will provide where we lack and comfort us when we mourn, if we are faithful."

Kai remembered why he sometimes harbored reservations about Siarah. She was too good for him—too spiritual, too full of faith. He was a warrior. He had seen battle. He hadn't killed anyone yet, but it was only a matter of time. And his faith wasn't nearly as strong. How could he ask someone like her to marry him? Someone who could become like … Ishara. Even if she agreed, would that be good for *her*?

"Um, you're right, I know. He's definitely protected me so far, more than once."

"Really?" She leaned forward, subtle excitement pulsing from her eyes. "Can you tell me about one of those times?"

He wasn't prepared for that question. He had spoken without thinking of anything in particular; it had sounded like the right thing to say. He cast about in his mind for an example. A weak one came, but it was better than nothing.

"Well, last year, just before Moronihah's rout of the Lamanite army, I was scouting along a small river that flowed toward one of our positions. I heard an enemy scout approaching, well before he heard me, and I was able to spot him and keep him in sight to make sure he didn't find us. He seemed like a good scout, too. Luckily, he turned around before he discovered our camp, and I was able to follow him to theirs. It was one of their smaller camps, but Moronihah said the information was extremely helpful."

That was it. It sounded even less impressive than he'd feared.

Siarah nodded intently. "Sometimes our senses are heightened to help us. The Spirit can work in so many ways. He clearly helped you there."

Kai wasn't sure about 'clearly,' but he didn't argue.

"What's Moronihah like?" she asked. "Is he a lot like his father?"

Kai pondered a moment. Moroni had died just four years earlier. He'd gotten sick and apparently recovered, and then suddenly he was gone. Kai hadn't asked Moronihah too many questions about his father. The entire country still mourned Moroni's passing.

"He has big boots to fill, and he knows it," Kai replied. "He's a good chief captain, but I don't know if he'll be as good as his father. He wants to be; he loves the Nephite nation. And I like him. He's a good man."

"Well, I'm glad we have good men like him—and you—to protect us." Siarah's voice had softened, and she had somehow drawn closer without him noticing. Her face hovered mere inches from his, her hand resting now on his chest, radiating heat.

There was no good reason in the world not to kiss her, and so he leaned in.

"Ahem, sorry."

The strange voice made Kai nearly jump out of his chair. He whipped his head toward the doorway, where a sprightly older man leaned his head in. Neva was nowhere in sight.

"The front door was open, and I heard voices," the man said with barely a hint of apology.

"Who are you?" Kai demanded, rising, his voice protectively gruff as he stepped between him and Siarah.

The man stood straight and took a step into the kitchen. "I'm Issachar, from the Merchants Council. We haven't met, but I was sent with a message for you. I was told it was urgent."

Kai knew instantly the message contained new orders, and not from the Merchants Council of Bountiful. "Written or verbal?" he asked.

"Written." The man produced a small scroll, which he handed to Kai. "I'll be off then." He smiled broadly. "Good day, and the Lord bless this house."

He was gone before Kai could say anything more. He listened closely as the man's footfalls drifted away, out of the house and down the street. Kai went to the front door, waited a few seconds, and stepped outside. He noticed nothing suspicious along the street, so he walked around back, circling the house until he was at the front door again. Satisfied, he re-entered and returned to the kitchen table, where Siarah waited, her brow furrowed in puzzlement.

"He was just a courier, right?"

"Probably not. I've seen him before, though I haven't met him. I think he's a spy, too."

"Oh." The gravity of his job seemed to be sinking in.

"Does he really work for the Merchants Council? I mean, as a cover?"

Kai shook his head. "I don't think so, but it wasn't a high-risk deception."

"High-risk deception?"

Kai smiled reassuringly and sat back down. "Tradecraft, I guess." He tried winking at her, though he'd never been good at it. Her eyes focused on the scroll, however.

"Well, I guess I should see what it says." He broke the seal, then carefully unrolled the parchment. He wasn't sure whether he should read it aloud or not, even though Siarah now knew his role. He read the message to himself silently, just in case it contained something highly sensitive.

It did. He had ten days. The travel time would be tight, depending on how fast of a horse they gave him and how much stamina it had. He was given a few contact names, along with a password. The message would go straight into the banked embers of the fireplace once he had it all memorized.

"What does it say?"

He frowned. "I have to leave, today. I'll end up in Zarahemla, which isn't my area, but you can't tell anyone that—not Gideon and Ishara, not Neva, not anyone, okay? I'm sure this has something to do with the assassination. Moronihah is nervous, and he should be if you believe my, um, father." He realized he may as well have read her the note, or most of it, at least. It also struck him that his orders had traveled with the news of the assassination, and Moronihah couldn't have known he was just returning from the east. Lucky timing?

Siarah nodded, staring solemnly at the place where her hand had rested on his chest. "I feel it, too. Something bad is coming."

<hr>

Kai was ready to leave within the hour. He exchanged his unwashed clothes for fresh garments, packed up some hard tack, salted meats, and dried fruits, and filled a new waterskin. He cleaned and oiled his short blades, then added spear and bow to his collection of weapons. Though he would still pose as a merchant scout, he doubted anyone would question a well-armed traveler after the assassination of the chief judge.

Gideon stopped him at the door before he set off to pick up a horse from a stable code-named 'Gate 6' outside the western wall of the city. Kai had already said his goodbyes to Siarah, his mother, and Neva. All three had cried. Gideon didn't. Once in a while, he was known to shed a tear or two, but not this time.

"My son—and you *are* my son—you will be in grave danger. I would take your place if I could, but I realize I can't. Know that your mother and I will pray for you unceasingly. Stay true to your covenants. The Lord will protect you. There is a great work to be done."

He sounded like one of the priests when he became so solemn. His words sent a shiver through Kai.

"I'll be careful … Father. I promise. We'll all get through this."

Gideon gave him a determined smile. "Yes, we will. Thank you for that reassurance, my son. God go with you now. Send word when you can. I'm very proud of you."

Kai embraced him, then set out on swift feet, his feelings an odd mixture of trepidation and excitement, dread and hope.

CHAPTER 2

And if men come unto me I will show unto them their weakness. I give unto men weakness that they may be humble; and my grace is sufficient for all men that humble themselves before me; for if they humble themselves before me, and have faith in me, then will I make weak things become strong unto them.

ETHER 12:27

Nobody greeted Kai at the stables of Gate 6, nestled in a cluster of trees and isolated from the scattered homes around it. In fact, the barn and the nearby house appeared to be unoccupied. But behind the barn, on a long tether, a large bay stallion with a deep chest munched placidly on the grasses of a small pasture, a light saddle strapped to his back. An empty set of saddle bags leaned against the back of the barn, along with a bulging extra waterskin.

Kai wasn't an expert horseman, but he rode horses often enough to be comfortable. He had never visited Gate 6. The place was exceedingly quiet, despite being so close to the borders of the city and its growing walls. The buildings occupied one side of a shallow culvert, which, along with the trees, cut invading sounds considerably. A brook burbled softly close by.

He didn't call out to see if anyone was in the house or barn. His orders had been simple, the arrangements made. He walked up to the bay, who raised his head and considered Kai as if he were making a judgment.

Kai smiled. "Hey, boy. I have no idea what they call you, but thank you for being willing to carry me." His trainers had told him talking to the horses helped. The bay whickered softly, then tossed his head slightly. It seemed like he was anxious to get underway. Kai wouldn't have wanted to be confined to such a quiet, boring place, either. He laughed, patted the stallion on the neck, then went to retrieve the saddle bags and pack them with his things.

Soon he was riding away from the secluded barn, following a narrow trail leading uphill from the culvert, then down and across the brook he had heard. The trees thinned out, and he found himself facing southwest. His eyes scanned the broad plains between Bountiful and Mulek under the midday sun. Jershon, where most of the Ammonites dwelt, lay to the south. The land before him teemed with farms, orchards, and pastures, and was liberally dotted with homes. He thought about stopping in Mulek to seek information; his instructions had directed him to gather what intel he could along the way, but Mulek wouldn't likely be of much benefit. It was too close to Bountiful, and news of the assassination would be brand new there as well. He also felt an urgency to get some miles behind him. Zarahemla seemed to be calling; no place could be as beautiful as Bountiful, but Zarahemla dominated his attention now.

The bay moved easily and powerfully, clearly accustomed to long travel. Kai alternated between walking and trotting him, almost without any prompts. They swallowed miles quickly, angling north of Mulek and merging with one of the major trade roads crisscrossing the nation. By evening they were well beyond Mulek, and Kai stopped at a large village just as the moon made a full appearance through scudding clouds. An inn he had visited before had space, so he made sure the horse was taken care of and then paid for some dinner to eat in his room.

By lamplight, he took out a wax tablet with steel pen and began to plan—not just the waypoints of his journey, but the questions he could ask, the clues he should be looking for to uncover webs of conspiracy. He hadn't lived through the assassination of a senior leader before, and he understood far too little of the politics behind the incident. That lack of knowledge bothered him. A good scout—and especially a good spy—saw *everything*. He needed to know more. He wanted to be useful. And he had a long way to go.

He arose before dawn and saddled up the big bay. He ate a light break-fast from his saddlebags, not wanting to bother the innkeeper or spend the extra senines.

He kept to the same road the entire day, making better time than he had expected and finally stopping at one of the way stations dotting the Nephite empire. It offered water, good provisions for animals, and a strong shelter under which he could bunk. Several wagon drivers had stopped there for the night as well. He gleaned little from them in casual conversation, not even any strong opinions, of which most Nephites had plenty. Though one of them snored loudly, Kai was used to tuning out distractions.

Again he arose early and pursued his journey, expecting to arrive in Lehi by late morning. That would allow him to spend the rest of the day gathering intelligence. He might have been able to learn more in Morianton, given its checkered history, but that would take him too far north.

Unfortunately, he soon encountered a small wagon, driven by an older man and his wife, stopped at the side of the road. An axle had broken, and one of the wheels was damaged. Kai spent several hours helping make the repairs as many other wagons, most of them much larger, passed by in either direction. The couple expressed extreme gratitude, but the delay prevented Kai from reaching Lehi until just before nightfall. The setback could have bothered him, but it had felt good to help. He was calmer, probably due to Ishara's teachings.

Lehi was largely a mystery to him, since he spent most of his time far-ther east. Because the medium-sized city was relatively young—just twenty years old—its walls seemed firmer than those of other cities. They had never been damaged, either. The Lamanites had taken the city during the Great War, but only because the Lehites had strategically withdrawn. Later, the Lamanites had abandoned the city as Captain Moroni, Lehi, and Teancum swept the traitorous Ammoron and his indoctrinated Lamanite armies from the surrounding areas.

Multiple hubs and spokes made the layout unique. Many of the buildings seemed to interlock, boasting small courtyards and waterways that dipped under the streets, forming elaborate garden mazes. Flowing, arched walkways connected several of the larger buildings, and two aqueducts provided the city with water from springs in the hills to the northeast. Kai couldn't discern the purposes of some of the designs, but the architect who had dreamed them up was highly acclaimed. A new section of Bountiful would look quite similar. The lofty architects of Zarahemla paid Lehi little attention, though, or so he had heard.

Multitudes of lamps brightened the city, characteristic of more and more Nephite cities. Light was a sign of prosperity; it meant that both oil and labor were abundant enough to keep so many flames burning through much of the night. Kai decided to take his dinner in the spacious common room of an unusually busy inn. He had rarely eaten a meal with so many people, but he had also rarely heard so many potentially useful conversations going on around him at the same time.

He wore a small purple tab sewn to the collar of his shirt that identified him as one of the merchant profession. He could have worn a thin purple headband as well, as some did. Another man with the same tab on his collar joined him at his table, carrying a plate heaped with steaming food and a large mug of what smelled like strong ale. The man's waist wasn't massive, but if he ate like that every night, it soon would be. He had black hair and a well-trimmed beard and mustache, and he spoke in clipped, eloquent tones.

"Glad to meet a fellow merchant," he announced as he sat. "You look to be young in the vocation. From where do you hail?"

Kai suppressed a smile at the formality. "Bountiful," he replied simply.

"Ah, Jewel of the empire, gateway to the Exotic East. Do you travel much outside the empire?"

"Not really," Kai lied. "Some short trips, but we keep busy enough with all the eastern traders that come to us."

The man bobbed his head cheerfully. "The nation of Nephi is much sought after as a trading partner. Most of my trade in fine jewelry passes across the borders, a great deal of it with the Lamanites, who constantly beg for secrets, by the way." He winked and laughed heartily, cutting off his laughter as he took in his first generous mouthful of food.

This man seems interesting, Kai thought. "Have you traveled very far south beyond the borders?" he asked.

The man raised a hand and nodded as he chewed his food. After swallowing, he said, "Some fine trading routes exist, most of them quite safe.

The Lamanites hate us, but every time they trade with us, they think they're winning, and it makes them feel better. Plus, we manufacture far more goods than they do. They need to trade for them, and we need the raw materials." He winked again as he inhaled another massive forkful.

"I've only been a few miles south of the border. I haven't dared go farther, even in a caravan. And now that the chief judge has been assassinated and soldiers are moving toward the borders ..." He let the words hang, waiting for the man to latch on.

Indeed, the man did, not even waiting to swallow this time. "The Lamanites surely had nothing to do with it." He almost choked, then finally swallowed, grasping for his mug and taking a long draft. "This was manifestly a political hit, an intrigue in the Hall of Judgment. If Pahoran hadn't executed his brother Paanchi, this wouldn't have happened. And now we'll have the dimmest of the three brothers, Pacumeni, as our chief judge, mark my words."

"There are rumors of Lamanite spies conspiring with Pacumeni," Kai said, lowering his voice and leaning forward. He didn't know whether such rumors actually existed.

"No, no," the man said, waving his hand in front of him. "The Lamanites wouldn't dare, not after Captain Moronihah's masterful rout of one of their rogue armies last year."

Kai found it interesting the man labeled it a 'rogue' Lamanite army. And it was clear he didn't know anything useful. Kai already knew there were people who resented Paanchi's execution or viewed it as too harsh, even barbaric. He sat back and laughed. "Yes, you can't believe everything you hear, can you?" He took a drink of water from his own mug. "Just the other day I heard that the northerners discovered the remains of a massive city at least twenty miles in *diameter*, not circumference."

The man nearly spat out some food as he spluttered in mirth. "Was this before or after they caught the fish as tall as an extinct elephant?" His eyes watered, which was strange. What Kai had said wasn't *that* funny. Why was the merchant trying to seem so friendly?

The hairs on the back of his neck began to tingle. And then it hit him: the man was probably an influencer, making a little extra money on the side by quelling rumors and calming anxieties among the people, even if he had to bend the truth to do it.

Kai leaned forward again and took a risk. "Don't worry, our methods are a little different, but we're both trying to prevent the same thing—panic among the people, which isn't good for business."

The mirthful look on the man's face faded as he studied Kai for a moment. He swallowed his food, then nodded. "They're really worried. Where are you contracted from? Bountiful or Mulek?"

"Bountiful."

The man took a sophisticated sip of his ale. "My business is based in Zarahemla, so I received my task from the chief judge's office itself. Two of the high judges share the duties of the office for now. It's pure chaos, as bad as I've ever seen it, but we can't afford another civil war."

He might be useful after all. Kai took another risk. "I'm heading there. I'll make two other stops, but my boss wants me to meet with one of his best trading partners in Zarahemla and assess the situation. The influencing assignment from the Council in Bountiful is an added reason to travel there. And I agree—civil war must be avoided at *all* costs."

The man gave him another long, considering look, and then he spoke decisively. "I am Melekai, of the house of Zohor. I have many friends and close kin in and around Zarahemla. Most of us agree that with the right planning and prodding and preaching, this traumatic event can be turned into a positive for the Nephite people." He lowered his voice. "Our system of elected judges is too unwieldy and inefficient. There is excessive jealousy, infighting, and corruption. It's rumored a group of wise men are prepared to seize power if they can find the right opportunity, and they could bring much-needed stability and security—and additional wealth—to the Nephite empire." He winked again, then added, "Perhaps those who have emigrated north could be convinced to rejoin the empire as well. That would be magnificent."

Melekai had just described a popular dream that ebbed and flowed among the Nephite people: if they had a benevolent king or a group of 'wise' stewards who had complete control, then they could make more progress, increase their wealth, help the poor more effectively, and develop better relations with their enemies. Kai himself had occasionally been tempted by the ideas. But the core of his advanced training with Moronihah's closest commanders and advisers didn't concern spycraft or stealth or the combat arts—it delved into the realities of human nature and the true foundations of progress, which required freedom, eternal truth, common sense, hard work, and sincere charity. Kai had plenty of weaknesses, but thankfully one of his gifts was the ability to believe those concepts, even from a young age.

Melekai was clearly passionate about his beliefs, though, and other people's passions gave Kai his most valuable information. In fact, the man seemed so excited about the prospects of this grand plan that he was willing to confide in a stranger with a shared connection who merely appeared to be supportive. Kai reminded himself again—rehearsing some of his training—that he, too, was susceptible to such passions, so he needed to check himself, especially in novel and disconcerting circumstances.

Kai stared pensively at the tabletop between them, his brow furrowed. Then he surveyed the other occupants of the inn before settling his gaze back on Melekai. He tried to be careful in his word choice.

"I've been thinking lately along those lines. I'd appreciate the opportunity to speak with one of your friends in Zarahemla." He waited, letting his eyes reveal the expectancy he hoped to convey.

After a few moments, Melekai nodded. He was hooked. "There is someone. I can arrange it. He will question you carefully. The situation is … delicate. You understand that."

"I do. Caution and boldness must be balanced."

"Yes. Yes, they must." Melekai's excitement threatened to overtake him again. "If you give me your name, and what quarter of the city you will be staying in, I can get a message to this man, and he will find you. He will call himself either Chorinai or Imrahiel."

Kai nodded, then responded with his undercover name, which he had used so often it seemed almost like his real one. "I am Adonihah. I wasn't born into one of the great houses of Bountiful, but my employer is well respected among many of the Merchants Council there, and I am known by some of them as well. I'll be staying in the Jewel Quarter of the city. I should be there for several weeks."

"Excellent." Melekai seemed deeply pleased, and he leaned back, raising his mug. "You will find your meeting with my friend quite enlightening, I assure you. To progress."

Kai raised his own mug and grinned broadly. "To progress."

Kai departed Lehi the next morning feeling satisfied. He had made a contact and perhaps uncovered a useful thread. He mentally reviewed everything Melekai had told him, examining all the angles as best he could. He would have to be patient and smart to pull that thread. He had been reminded often enough—by circumstances and by his superiors—that one of the most difficult parts of good spycraft was patience.

Six major roads spoked out from Lehi. He set out on the one that would get him to Sidom the quickest, arcing slightly south and passing through the heart of the great and fruitful Plains of the Nephites, one of the envies of the known world, a veritable breadbasket. With a little luck, he would arrive at Sidom within four days. He would have to cross several major rivers, but the high season was long past, and he didn't anticipate many delays at either the bridges or the busy ferry points. He and his horse could easily swim some of the rivers, too, if that unlikely necessity arose.

It turned out he only had to ferry once. Two long, arching bridges had been completed since last he had studied the maps, and more were being built all the time. The developments were mind-boggling. The engineers had discovered new techniques, using materials in different ways. The heartland of the Nephite nation was truly a remarkable place, and despite the number of emigrants who had recently moved northward, it teemed with people, at least relative to most other lands he had traveled. He understood how the reports Lamanite spies took back to their lands could cause great jealousy and lust, but shouldn't those same reports reveal how unlikely it was that such a country could be overthrown? The Nephite armies were better equipped, better fed, better trained, and better positioned. They didn't waste their strength on land-grabbing crusades, focusing instead on well-developed defensive networks, protection for their families, and intelligence of their enemies' strengths, weaknesses, motivations, and movements.

Kai's chest swelled with pride at his part in gathering knowledge of the enemy. But then he reminded himself the chief judge had just been assassinated. Their external enemies couldn't defeat them, but the Nephites were perfectly capable of tearing themselves apart. That thought needled deeply into his mind, introducing a frightening sense of powerlessness. How could he fight something like *that*?

He arrived at Sidom on the evening of the fourth day out of Lehi, as hoped, his mind filled with anticipation and worry. Sidom was a large, established city. It had once sheltered the righteous who had fled from Ammonihah, including the great prophets Alma the Younger and Amulek. But like most major Nephite cities, its politics had become coarse and divisive, many of its people arrogant, perverted, and often unruly and abusive of each other.

He was hopeful he could find another thread or two to pull in Sidom, though perhaps his approach needed to be different than in Lehi. He stopped at a small inn a mile from the city, set back from the road in a stand of trees near a small creek. It wasn't heavily advertised—he and other spies used it when needing to keep a low profile.

The innkeeper, Mistress Havah, didn't seem to remember him, but he didn't buy the act. She remembered everyone. Her mind was as sharp as the words of Jacob, Nephi's brother. She could have risen high in the Nephite hierarchy if she had wanted—and if she were allowed. Mistress Havah was a many-layered mystery, notoriously good at keeping secrets, which made certain kinds of people more comfortable staying with her. She focused on providing shelter, protection, and privacy for what Kai considered a modest price.

Her inn was the most logical place to start.

"Mistress Havah?" he called out after finishing a delicious hot meal.

"Yes?" She appeared in the doorway from the kitchen. Her apron looked freshly laundered and pressed, and her gray-streaked brown hair swept back from her face to gather in a towering rooster tail secured by a handspan of tightly wrapped cloth in bright colors. "Adonihah, is that what you said your name is?"

He smiled as he stood and stepped away from the table. "You knew my name when I walked in the door." He knew she didn't like her ruses to be called out like that, but he was the only guest in the dining room. She raised a hand and rested it on the doorframe, nails clicking a pattern on the wood. He looked around, but no sound emanated from the hallway or the front door. They were indeed alone. Still, he lowered his voice. "I have information . . ." He took a deep breath and looked around again, stepping nearer. "And it's dangerous. It could get me hanged, or worse." Normally, he wouldn't sound so dramatic, but extraordinary times called for extraordinary measures . . . or so he convinced himself.

She didn't blink, but he detected a slight widening of her eyes and a hitch in the pattern of her tapping fingernails. Good.

Kai continued. "I can't stay here, but I know you can be trusted to safeguard information … as a backup only, in case something happens to me."

She thought for a moment. "What would I do with the information if something happens to you, and how would I know?"

He pursed his lips, letting his demeanor grow grave. His orders had asked him to listen for any rumors regarding the chief judge in Sidom, listing Mistress Havah's name as a potential contact, but he took a reverse approach by creating a rumor himself, the bold idea having come to him along the road. "If the chief judge of Sidom is murdered, you will know I have failed. Within a day of that happening, if it does, a man giving the name of Jerameel will arrive and ask for a room for the night. You will give him the sealed scroll I will deliver to you. If the high judge is still alive at this time next year, you can destroy the scroll. It must remain sealed, you understand."

Reminding her of that was highly insulting, but it had the intended effect. In a land already on fire with rumors and fears, she would be somewhat on edge, despite her reputation for calm. He also knew something most people didn't know: Mistress Havah wasn't just a keeper of information. She sought it, too, and was very shrewd in how she obtained and used it. She assiduously kept confidences, yes, but she created ingenious ways to carefully leverage much of what she found. She was a spy, like him, and far more experienced. She might see through his subterfuge, but he needed to make the play. If it failed, he might have burned a bridge. Better that, he thought, than the entire Nephite nation erupting in flames. Besides, Moronihah was his sponsor.

Suddenly, he felt stark terror at the possibility of the Nephite nation's demise, so often prophesied, and his façade cracked. That was perfect, making him seem genuine. Mistress Havah recognized true fear. Perhaps the Lord had just given him a small assist. That's how Gideon, Ishara, Neva, and Siarah would view it.

Mistress Havah's eyes narrowed, and she studied his face for several moments before nodding. "Very well. Throw the scroll on top of the barn as you leave, and one of my men will retrieve it. Where are you heading, if I may ask?"

Kai didn't hesitate in answering. He needed to show he trusted her. "I'll take a room at the *Cunning Curelom*. From there I'll go to a meeting with some associates in the next few days. I can't say where the meeting will take place, or exactly when, because I don't know yet."

"You're leaving right away?"

"Shortly, yes. I need to prepare the parchment and seal it up. For now, it's just in my head."

She nodded curtly. "Take your time. I'll bring you some colored wax and a bowl for warming it over the fire. You have your own seal, I presume?"

"Yes, I do. Thank you, Mistress." He filled his voice with relief, nervousness still mixed in. It sounded convincing to him. He hoped it still sounded convincing to her.

Three hours later, as midnight approached, Kai settled himself behind a small berm topped by a low hedge surrounding a grain field, a mere quarter mile from Mistress Havah's inn. Creating the fake scroll had been easy, but it had taken some time after leaving the inn to make sure he hadn't been followed and then to circle back without being spotted. The bay stallion was smart and well trained, even understanding and executing the command to lie down and stay quiet.

At several points over the next hour he wondered if anything at all would happen—the odds were low—but then he detected movement near the inn—a single man setting out on foot straight to the north, away from the main roads. He groaned inwardly. Whether on horseback or leading a horse on foot, he would struggle to follow the man off the roads in the middle of the night without being seen and heard. He had known that might be the case, though, and he wasn't going to give up the stallion, not this far from Zarahemla.

So, he would have to anticipate the man's path. He watched until the man disappeared from view, memorizing posture and gait while searching his memory of the lands around Sidom. Mistress Havah had surely sent the man. Her allegiances were difficult to pin down, though Kai felt fairly certain she wasn't aligned with the anarchists or the king-men. Then again, he wouldn't place a large bet on it.

He wondered whether Mistress Havah had sent the man north as a diversion. Did she suspect someone might be watching? Kai hesitated as he thought through that possibility. He didn't have time to wait, though, and overthinking a situation could be as dangerous as underthinking it. The man would probably enter the city through the eastern gate, and from there he could go anywhere except the *Cunning Curelom*—Mistress Havah wasn't foolish enough to be so obvious. Even if she were, it wouldn't help Kai. He didn't want her man to follow him; he wanted to know if she sought information from someone else in the city.

If Kai could get through the southern gate quickly enough, he could stable the horse at a different inn and position himself to pick up the man when he entered the city. Without hesitating further, he led his horse quietly away from the vicinity of Mistress Havah's establishment. When he came to the first narrow lane, he mounted and urged the stallion to a near gallop. Their forms sliced through the night toward the main road ringing the city, the cool night air invigorating.

Twenty minutes later, he had positioned himself to observe the inside of the eastern gate from the deep shadows of an alley. He worried he had missed Mistress Havah's agent, and a sense of discouragement grew. But then he spotted the man. It had to be him; the posture and gait were exactly right. He wore a travel cloak and good, sturdy boots, and he didn't seem to be carrying anything. Kai watched him pass beneath one of the night torches placed in intervals along the street, noting the neatly trimmed, dark brown mustache and the thin ocher headband with silver trim that marked the man a member of the educated class. He was older than Kai, but probably not more than thirty.

Kai waited until the agent was at least thirty paces up the nearly deserted street, then peeked out from the alley. The man walked half a block farther and turned right, which happened to be Kai's side of the street. Kai wasn't an expert on the layout of Sidom, but he was somewhat familiar. Instead of following, he headed up the alley in a stealthy jog. If he hurried, he could reach a street crossing with the one the man currently traveled and see if he still followed it. If not, he knew which other street the man would have taken.

He reached the cross street and crouched low in the mouth of the alley, craning his neck so he could see a portion of the intersection to his left. A few seconds later, the man sauntered past, apparently in no hurry. Kai waited a few seconds before straightening and stepping out of the alley, trying to look nonchalant to any curious eyes. He reached the intersection, where he leaned against a wooden building, twisting his head around the corner to follow the agent's progress. The man still walked along the street as it ascended a small hill. He was heading for one of the nicer quarters of the city.

Kai's instincts flared, and he was already pulling back into the cover of the building as the man started to turn his head to look behind him. Kai froze, barely breathing, listening closely for the slightest noise. A city as large as Sidom produced many sounds, even late at night—the occasional window shutter opening or closing, the cry of a baby or small child, a shout, usually in anger at some small thing, or perhaps from a dream. He turned his head as he heard shuffling coming from down his side street. Two men who had taken too much mead approached, their footsteps uneven. They barely glanced at Kai before reaching the intersection and turning left, away from his quarry.

Kai used their emergence from the side street as cover to sneak another look around the corner. The man was nowhere to be seen. He had either continued up the street at a faster pace or turned—or maybe he had reached his destination. Kai knew he was taking another risk, but he headed up the street, keeping his head mostly down and listening intently for any indication of imminent danger. He was a fast runner and a decent fighter, but since a fight would likely delay him from his primary mission of getting to Zarahemla—especially if law officers were summoned or happened by—he would run if it came to that choice, confident of escape.

He reached the top of the street, which leveled off and ran in a straight course for a good distance. The street torches were brighter, fancier, and more closely spaced here, but he still saw no sign of the man. Palatial homes dominated the street, but a few fine shops preened over it as well. Trying to remember how many seconds had passed and where the man could have gotten to at his pace, he decided on another cross street, following as it curved up another portion of the hill. About twenty paces in, he heard something and stopped. It had been a greeting of some sort, coming from around the bend, beyond his view.

He waited a full minute, pretending to search for something in a pouch or pocket. He started walking again just as he noticed a two-man patrol of law officers coming his direction on the other side of the street. He nodded to them respectfully, and they didn't pay him any mind. He questioned himself, though. Why was he following this mysterious man? What was the likelihood of deriving any value from the pursuit? He suddenly felt foolish, overeager. Would his trainers have approved of this mad chase? Probably not. Then again, they had never dealt with the aftermath of the assassination of a chief judge. He told himself risks must be taken, though he still had serious doubts.

He slowed, examining the buildings on both sides of the street as if he were lost. He altered his gait, too, trying to appear slightly inebriated. He noted only two houses with any lights on inside, and he focused on the one to his left in which the lights were dimmer, meaning the source of the light was near the back of the house. That was likely where the man had gone.

The large home had been beautifully crafted of finely milled wood, set back from the street a few paces and surrounded by a stone fence with a sturdy wooden gate held up by thick steel hinges. Kai stopped and bent over to cough, then listened. Yes—a slight rustling came from the space between the fence and the front of the house. That meant at least one guard posted outside—a high level of security. He shuffled along again as if he hadn't heard anything, even mumbling something incoherent to keep up his guise.

When he reached the next intersection, he turned left, where the mansions grew slightly smaller. He didn't want to wander around the richest section of the city much longer—the officers on patrol would be suspicious if they saw him again—but he was curious whether he might be able to get a look at the back of the target house. He had gone only a short distance when he found an alley heading that direction. He hesitated, looking around, feeling suddenly nervous. He almost skipped the alley and moved on, but he took a deep breath and proceeded down it.

As he crept among the deepest shadows, he saw he had been correct that the light inside the house was at the back, and he recognized the same stone fencing. He kept moving, sweeping his eyes left, right and upwards to examine the features of the house and those around it. Perhaps he could access a better vantage point.

He almost didn't detect the pull of the bowstring above him, but his reaction was immediate. He dove forward and rolled, the arrowhead clashing against the stone of the alley behind him. He was instantly back on his feet, sprinting away from the archer. His instincts took over, and he cut to the right, aiming for a narrow space between two houses, hoping no major obstacles would impede him as he tried to break through to the street beyond. He encountered a low fence between the houses near the front, but he got over it easily.

He burst into the street, praying a patrol wasn't happening by, then hoping the opposite. But instead of officers, he encountered two men, both with long cudgels and short knives in hand, racing toward him from the far end of the street to his right. He heard hurried movement behind him as well.

Careening left, he took two steps before realizing he faced a dead end. He couldn't discern any gaps across the street he could escape through, either. The men had him trapped.

He wasn't about to give himself up, though. That initial arrow had been meant to kill. He thought of going back through the gap and confronting whoever came through. But his advantages were speed and quickness, and those were more easily used out in the open—as long as that archer didn't emerge in the next few seconds. He turned and raced toward the two men running at him from the head of the street. They slowed and spread out a few feet as he reached a full sprint. He freed one of his knives from a sheath at his waist, then aimed for the man on the right, who entered a battle stance. But instead of attacking, Kai made a hard feint to his right, pivoted off his right foot and spun past, bringing up his blade to brush blows away as the man swiped at him with his knife. He ducked as he felt the other man closing in, then spun again before regaining his line and dashing away. He heard an unmistakable thunk as an arrow found flesh. He wondered vaguely if he had been hit, but then one of the men screamed.

He veered left, then right, knowing it cost him distance but feeling fearful of those arrows. The farther away he got, the less power and accuracy an arrow would have, so within a few seconds he straightened out again and sprinted for all he was worth, finally reaching the head of the street and turning left, away from the rich neighborhood and the killer guards. He heard brief pursuit, but the men soon realized they couldn't catch him.

Still, he kept running hard until he saw a patrol. He skidded to a stop as they gripped the hilts of their cudgels, backing up a step from him.

"Men fighting!" Kai said breathlessly. "One hit with an arrow, several streets that way." He waved backward, then bent over and put his hands on his knees, huffing loudly.

"Do you know who they are?" asked one of the officers in an annoyed tone.

Kai shook his head. "No, but I think one was upset over a gambling debt."

That would sound plausible enough. The rich gambled as much as the poor did, though generally for entertainment, not from a desire to escape their station with a lucky hit.

"We'll check it out. Go to the officer station three blocks from here. Report what you saw."

Kai nodded as the officers started jogging up the street. He watched them go for a moment, then started out again at a fast pace, initially heading for the officer station, but then changing course to find the stable where he had left his horse. There would be no stay at the *Cunning Curelom*, or anywhere else in Sidom. By midmorning, Mistress Havah would know he had followed one of her men. Whatever she thought, and whichever side she might be on in the country's developing intrigue, he had just lost access to a valuable resource—and perhaps made a dangerous enemy.

Neither his trainers nor Moronihah would be impressed.

CHAPTER 3

*For the natural man is an enemy to God, and has been from the fall of
Adam, and will be, forever and ever, unless he yields to the enticings of
the Holy Spirit, and putteth off the natural man and becometh a saint
through the atonement of Christ the Lord, and becometh as a child,
submissive, meek, humble, patient, full of love, willing to submit to all
things which the Lord seeth fit to inflict upon him, even as a child doth
submit to his father.*

MOSIAH 3:19

The kitchen shined, spotless. It was expansive, even by the standards of
the Nephite elite. But High Judge Zerahir and his wife Lianah used it
heavily, since they still had four children living at home and there were
always a few grandchildren visiting as well. They also hosted many parties,
including important state dinners.

The high judge's family was one of the largest families Arayah had ever seen.
Ara's own family was small, and while not part of the elite of Nephite society,
they were fairly well-off. Her father worked as a lower judge, which was as
far as his talent and connections would take him in the current system. Her
mother had passed two years ago from a wasting sickness. Ara didn't need the
money from working as a housekeeper for a high judge, but the opportunity
to be embedded into such a powerful household had been too much to pass up.

"It looks beautiful, as always," said Lianah from behind her. Ara nearly
jumped, then turned and gave a small curtsy.

"Thank you, mistress," she said humbly. "I will return home for the evening, if that is all right."

"Of course it is, Arayah. And I'm sorry for my husband's outburst earlier today. He's under a lot of stress. You didn't do anything wrong."

"It's okay, mistress. I understand." She dropped her eyes, not wanting to risk revealing the flash of fire behind them. She had never liked High Judge Zerahir. He was rude, demanding, and arrogant. All the high judges were. Lianah was nice enough, and sometimes she showed some spine to her husband, but Ara knew how much she enjoyed being the wife of a high judge. The wealth was incentive enough, but there were other perks—the fancy parties and private theatrical performances, the best tutors for her children, the places of honor at festivals and feasts. Lianah was still an attractive woman in the eyes of other men, too, and Ara could tell she enjoyed teasing them with her untouchable allure. Her husband seemed to find it amusing as well, at least most of the time.

Ara hadn't served food and drinks at one of Zerahir's parties for several weeks—nobody hosted parties at the moment, either because they were afraid of plots against their own lives or because it was too soon to continue celebrating their stranglehold on the wealth of the Nephite people. The downside, of course, was that she couldn't gather intelligence at those parties, where strong drink flowed freely and an attractive young woman could tease many a secret out of a foolish wine bibber. But there were other ways to get information, and she would have a chance tonight.

She walked quickly homeward, passing out of the Santorem—the richest neighborhood of Zarahemla—and through several of the jealous lesser neighborhoods until she entered the area of the city called New Hebron, where her parents had built a house that aspired to be more than modestly prosperous. It was less than a fifth the size of Zerahir and Lianah's, and the fat stone pillars holding up the front portico looked awkwardly out of place in both style and substance, but it was home, and Ara felt safe there.

No sooner had she walked through the door than her father, Nahom, rushed out of his office and grabbed her by the arm, pulling her toward the back of the house.

"Your cousin Kishkumen is here," he said in clipped tones. "He needs to speak to you."

"Kishkumen?" she asked, confused. "Isn't he in Melek?"

"Yes, he was, but he has returned on urgent business."

"How does that involve me?"

"You'll see, my daughter, you'll see."

She pulled back, causing them both to stop. "Father, I'm still not going to marry him."

He looked confused for a moment, then shook his head. "This has nothing to do with that. Come."

He led her through the kitchen to the back room, primarily used for storage. Three chairs had been set up in a rough triangle. Lamplight danced along the windowless walls, and her father shut the door after they entered. Kishkumen was already seated, studying a document, and he didn't bother to rise, barely lifting his head to acknowledge them. He'd been icy even before Ara had denied his advances.

"May I stay?" asked her father respectfully, bowing slightly. Arayah gave him a strange look, but he didn't notice. Something had clearly changed in his relationship with her adopted 'cousin.'

"Yes, Nahom, you may." Kishkumen finally stopped reading and gave them a tolerating expression through dark eyes, letting silence prevail for several seconds, save for some small popping and cracking from the lamps burning impure oil.

She found a chair and sat down, as did her father. Then she waited for Kishkumen to speak.

His eyes bored into her. "You have taken the oaths," he said softly.

She nodded, glancing at her father. They all had. There was work to be done to save Nephite society, and those at the forefront needed to protect each other.

He inclined his head sharply, his thick, nearly blond hair stirring. His voice became red-tongued fire. "You took the first set of oaths. Tonight you will take the second."

Her eyes widened slightly. *The second? How many were there?* She nodded, not daring to object. Kishkumen was supposedly trustworthy. Many reliable people had told her that.

"And then you want me to do something?" she asked. If he commanded her to marry him, she would stab him. She would.

He nodded. "Yes. A change of plans. Nahom tells me you were planning to meet with one of High Judge Zerahir's scribes tonight. The young man desires you, and he might have some useful information."

She lifted her chin slightly, showing her displeasure. He made the meeting sound less seemly than she intended it to be. He was probably jealous.

"But he knows too little," Kishkumen continued. "We need more information, and we need it now. That is why you will sneak into the high judge's house, enter his office, and copy some of his important documents, as many as you can find. If you are caught, you will jump out of that second-story window into the tree that grows near it. I will have friends stationed nearby to cause a diversion and allow you to escape. You are fast and athletic. I've seen you in the city-wide games." His compliment sounded detached, even cold, causing her to shiver.

"Why do you need this information?" she asked through dry lips, unsure whether he would he tell her. She didn't know him well, despite his romantic interest in her. He was also nine years older.

"The government is pursuing some of our friends, and we need to know what they've found out."

"Why would—?" *Oh.* She tried not to appear shocked, but some of the emotion slipped through. As she thought about it, it made more sense. Kishkumen and many of the people he associated with were firebrands, both determined and daring. Somehow they were involved in the chief judge's assassination. But how?

Kishkumen stared disconcertingly at her for several more seconds, then said, "This is why you will take the next set of oaths. Secrecy must be maintained at all costs—otherwise we all hang."

Ara felt deeply unsettled as she traveled back to the high judge's house that night, and it wasn't because she was strapped to the bottom of a city refuse wagon making a run through the area. No, there was something epic—and epically dangerous—happening. Part of her was excited. She wasn't sure how Kishkumen was involved in all of it, but he was clearly connected to the assassination of Pahoran the Younger, a murder she supported wholeheartedly. Another part of her was wary, though. The first set of oaths she had taken was strict. The second was exceptionally intense. Kishkumen had warned her the oaths would be difficult to digest at first, but he promised she would get used to them and even come to embrace them. She hoped so.

The wagon stopped, and she heard two soft raps on one of the sideboards. This was the spot. She quickly untied the rope securing one side of the thick netting that had held her in place, slipped carefully to the ground, and then re-secured the netting before crawling out from under the wagon and into a narrow lane between two great and spacious homes. The men running the refuse wagon moved on, and she was on her own.

They had dropped her less than a block from the high judge's house. Kishkumen had scouted the route beforehand and then meticulously explained the plan to her. He had also made sure she knew how to use the rope and tackling he provided.

It was late—nearly midnight. If tonight was like the last few nights, the high judge would have been up late working, but not this late. He should be in bed by now, the household settled and the guards alert. Ara couldn't sneak past the guards to enter through a door, so she would first go up and across the roof of the neighboring house, quiet as a finch asleep in its nest.

When she arrived, she saw that a ladder had been set up, as promised, hidden in an even narrower lane. She had been assured the inhabitants were away, so nobody would hear her ascending the ladder or crossing the roof. Still, she stayed as silent as possible, not wanting any revealing sounds to carry in the cool night air.

She took her time crossing the roof, making sure each foot placement felt secure, listening for any discordant noise. At the edge of the roof, she assessed the tall deciduous tree growing next to the house and intermingling its branches with the even taller tree near the high judge's house.

She almost turned back. This task was too crazy. Yes, she had been chosen for this mission in part because she was familiar with the layout of Zerahir's office and had a good idea where he kept his most important documents. She was also light, less likely to break a tree branch and fall more than two stories to the ground while trying to bridge the gap between the two roofs. But she'd never done anything so daring—or perhaps foolhardy was the better word.

She believed in the mission, though—the fight against the greedy over-lords of Nephite society—and she had taken the oaths. She shuddered in remembrance. Kishkumen was right; she didn't feel comfortable about the oaths yet. But their cause was valiant, and even though she didn't want to marry Kishkumen, she wanted him and her father to trust her.

She found the thickest limb that wouldn't require her to jump. It reached a point close to her head, and she figured if she could lean forward and grab it with one hand, then rapidly move her hands along it, she could reach a place where the branch would firmly hold her.

She held her breath and raised her arms, preparing to lean forward.

"It's a quiet night. Nothing to report." She froze, barely maintaining her balance on the roof's edge. It sounded like one of the guards from the high judge's house.

"Okay, go home. I've got the watch." Another guard, and she recognized the voice. It came from that young, devilishly handsome man so frustratingly resistant to her occasional flirtations. He had served in Moronihah's army for a time, but she wasn't sure why he didn't anymore. His tone oozed competence, and her nervousness grew. She listened closely, trying to tell where he was. Luckily, his patrol path would encompass the entire grounds.

She heard his footsteps coming nearer, then pausing before receding. She couldn't see anything through the thick foliage of the trees and the darkness of the nearly moonless night, and she trusted he couldn't, either. When she felt confident he was on the other side of the high judge's house, she leaned outward until she could grab the branch, then propelled herself forward, grasping with her other hand and moving hand over hand as fast as she could, knowing she was making some noise. Two seconds later she stopped, her feet finding good purchase on a lower branch while she still held to the one above her head. She slowed her breathing, listening. The guard had not come back yet, and no hint of detection or alarm interrupted her progress.

Ever so slowly, she tiptoed to the middle of the tree, then took a moment to study the web of branches dimly visible ahead of her. Though the tree next to the high judge's house was taller, it didn't have branches this high that were strong or long enough to let her drop lightly onto the roof. She would have to get a few feet lower, where she could then move across both trees to a point that would let her reach out to the edge of the roof with her hands and pull herself up. It wouldn't be easy, and would produce more sound.

She waited an agonizing two minutes until the guard had come and gone again, then made her way carefully down and across to the other tree, then to its center and over to the roofline. Thankfully, the branches were a little stronger than they looked, and she was able to steady herself as she reached up and grabbed the roof's edge. She pulled hard, trying not to scrape against the side of the house too much as she swung her right leg up, catching the rooftop with her heel. She paused briefly, then exerted herself to get her body up and onto the surface of the roof. She rolled onto her back, closing her eyes and catching her breath, listening again.

After a few moments, and she stole silently to one of the three stone chimneys poking up from the roof. She passed her rope around it, feeding both ends through the wooden pulley system Kishkumen had given her. Using a small hook, she attached one end of the rope to a thick leather belt with an iron ring at her waist. Then she sidled carefully toward the back edge of the roof, almost directly over the window to Zerahir's second-story office.

She waited again for the guard to pass out of earshot, then gripped the loose end of the rope with both hands, placed her feet on the roof's edge while facing the chimney, and let herself down slowly, keeping her feet on the wall and utilizing the pulley's assist.

As expected, the window was closed, but the high judge hardly ever locked it. Many of the house's other windows were open at night to let in air, and he had guards, so there was no reason to bother locking second-story windows. She pulled it open slowly, stopping when she heard the slightest of squeaks, then starting again even more slowly. Another large tree hid the window from many angles, but her anxiety had nearly peaked at panic before she had finally opened it far enough to let herself in.

She unhooked the rope, setting the hook carefully on the window ledge and hoping the two lines hanging down from the roof didn't attract the guard's attention. The rope was hard to see in the dark, and the free end didn't hang down much past the window—Kishkumen had calculated the precise length to use.

Once inside, she made sure the door was fully shut, then proceeded to close the heavy drapes over the window and cover the slit at the bottom of the door with a thick cloth she had wrapped around her torso. Satisfied that no light would escape the room, she reached into her small shoulder bag and took out a small candle with a cupped base to capture the melted wax, then lit the wick with her tinder box.

She didn't have to search long for what she wanted. The high judge's desk had two large drawers in it, both of which were always locked. She picked them open easily. She had acquired that skill a long time ago from one of her real cousins. In the second drawer, she found what she wanted—the latest reports on the investigation into the chief judge's assassination. Quickly, she retrieved parchment, pen, and ink from her bag and began copying furiously. There were nearly a dozen documents, some just a page or two, some several pages in length.

She barely registered what she copied, but occasionally something would jump out at her. A high judge under surveillance. Three men arrested for lying to investigators. The first execution of one of the plotters to be announced within the week. Pahoran's brother Pacumeni agreeing to become chief judge, despite the risks, ratification election to come soon. A man of interest named Gadianton who seemed to elude all efforts to firmly implicate him.

She finished, then re-checked both drawers to make sure she hadn't missed anything that looked important. It was then that she focused on the sheaf of parchments sitting on top of the desk. Could Zerahir have left something valuable there? Not likely, but it was possible. She shuffled through the documents, scanning the contents of each page. On the third page she caught the name Moroni, and her eyes locked onto it. She had been taught to hate that name. What was Zerahir—or someone corresponding with him—saying about the late, great captain? She thought it with a sneer, then began reading. It was a letter Zerahir was composing to a wealthy merchant.

Helaman has issued a decree within the Church of Christ, stating that the Christians should uphold the law and the law officers and refrain from searching for targets of retribution. He acknowledges there is corruption in the Nephite government, something his father and Captain Moroni fought hard against, mostly behind the scenes.

He has also appealed to Captain Moronihah to maintain discipline among his troops during the unrest, the military being only a last resort to prevent a violent overthrow of the government. He says Moronihah has agreed, but that he reminded Helaman of Moroni's famous letter to Pahoran the Elder, and the subsequent action demanded by their correspondence.

Ara hated that letter to Pahoran the Elder, which, along with Pahoran's response, sat framed on a wall in the public area of the Hall of Judgment. It was so arrogant and self-righteous, the anger bleeding through devilishly misplaced. The true protectors of the Nephite heritage had taken advantage of Pahoran's vacillating weakness to wrest power from him and place it in the hands of those who could protect the Nephite nation better—and Moroni had gathered an army and slaughtered them. She continued reading.

The Council of High Judges has publicly commended Helaman for his decree, but privately some are worried Helaman is trying to undermine Pacumeni, even though Pacumeni claims to be a Christian, too. I know you are also a Christian, and I welcome any thoughts you may have on the matter.

The rest of that page contained drivel, but the next page was a letter from Helaman to Zerahir.

My dear brother Zerahir, it began, *I am much pained at the death of our brother Pahoran. Like you, I don't believe he was the best governor, but he had many good qualities, he worked hard, and he was learning. The great division that continues to grow among our people, which cost Pahoran his life, troubles me constantly. Truth, compassion, and forbearance are so often abandoned in favor of accusation, acrimony, and vengeance. There are those who believe the only way to unite us again is to burn our system of government by consent to the ground and start over by granting the power of kings to our most educated people, placing them in exclusive control of everything from crop strategies to foreign affairs, with nobody but themselves to keep them in check.*

This is a dangerous and foolish path, as history has so often and decisively proved.

If the Lord himself—or his angels—could govern us, that would be preferable to our arrangement of lower and higher elected judges. But he cannot, because he will not. He honors our agency, which is elemental to our progress. We must struggle and decide for ourselves, else how do we learn the most important lessons of this mortal probation? Without the tests of this probationary state, we cannot begin to imagine the eternal glories of which we are ultimately capable, and if we cannot imagine them, how can we prepare for them?

If we place an unaccountable party of academic and industrial nobles at our head and give them free, unfettered reign, the government of the Nephite nation will quickly devolve into tyranny, which will inevitably lead to anarchy as the tyrants turn on each other and the victims of tyranny rebel. These events will drive us into a never-ending cycle of bloody chaos and fear, worse than what we have already experienced.

The Lord's work is greatly hindered where peace cannot naturally thrive. I know you understand this. I also know you have spoken personally to Gadianton, once a lower judge, now a violent revolutionary. I'm sure he tried to convince you that if he or one of his followers was proposed and ratified as chief judge, he would ensure that peace returned.

Be assured that any peace he delivers can only be short-lived. He has given himself over to the evil one, completely. I have recently excommunicated several members of the Church of Christ who have taken his oaths, who have succumbed to the belief that our Nephite government is beyond hope of salvage and that lasting peace can only be achieved by the iron fist of one like Gadianton who claims his laws will ultimately be more compassionate and just. But those oaths are vile and dark. Their author is Satan himself, and they lead only to cruelty and injustice.

Our laws are not perfect, and many of our judges have become corrupted by the allure of the great power, wealth, and prestige such a heaven-prospered nation as ours offers. Our collective greed leads us on to arrogance and ignorance. Wise King Mosiah and his advisers constructed our system of government under the guidance of the Holy Spirit, and they warned us it would only work effectively if we were a virtuous, faithful people.

I ask you, brother, have we lost such a large portion of our virtue that only a strongman can govern us? Can we only act peaceably if the specter of the sword hangs constantly above our heads? Have we forgotten the great difference between God's guileless plan of freedom and happiness and Lucifer's cunning plan of forced obedience and falsely promised safety? To God the Father and his Glorious Son, each person is precious and possesses unlimited potential, even the man who killed Pahoran, the son of Pahoran, though I fear that man's soul may now be lost because of the choice he made. I pray for him, for he is loved, but destroying the freedom of this people will only hinder their progress and blunt their potential, indeed, even their eternal potential. We must stand boldly against such darkness, with faith in the Lord's promises and constant love for one another.

Please ponder my words. Immerse yourself in the scriptures we have received from our fathers and mothers. Review our long and difficult history. Pray to find wisdom and strength. I welcome your counsel, as I hope you welcome mine, but it is the Spirit we must both urgently seek.

Your brother in faith, until the end,

Helaman

Ara felt something stir inside her. She had never heard Helaman the 'prophet' speak, nor had she studied any of his words. But she had just read a personal letter he had written in confidence, and suddenly she wanted to know more about who he was and what he hoped to accomplish. Was his letter sincere, or was it meant to manipulate one of his adherents into supporting his proposals for policy or law enforcement—or, as some believed, ascension to the throne of chief judge?

She blinked, coming back to her senses. She glanced at her candle. It was nearly a third gone, the cup almost full of wax. She licked her thumb and forefinger and extinguished the flame, then let the wax cool as she tied the copied parchments together with a string and placed them in her bag with her writing implements. She removed the barrier covering the door slit and withdrew the drapes at the window.

After securing the candle, she listened intently for nearly a minute before determining she could safely emerge. It was tricky and awkward to get the rope hooked back to her belt, climb outside, position herself properly against the wall, and close the window. But she did it all with little noise, finally beginning her pull on the free end of the rope, gathering the slack, grateful for the pulley's help. When she reached the roof, she lay on her back again and tried to relax, realizing her heart had been racing. She still didn't hear any signs of discovery from inside or outside the house. There didn't seem to be any access to the roof from the inside anyway, so she felt safe for the moment.

Closing her eyes, she let her breaths come slowly and evenly. She had done it—she had copied highly sensitive documents from the office of a high judge. She had even spied a letter from the Christian church's leader, Helaman, son of the storied Helaman of the invincible stripling warriors—a fable she had stopped believing very early in her life. She would enjoy sharing that bit of information with Kishkumen.

Her breath caught. What exactly *would* she share with him about Helaman? She had detected no plotting for favor in Helaman's words, no proposals for bribes, no obvious propaganda. The letter might be seen as persuasive of the

Christian cause, but to what end? Helaman had given no specifics at all—just trust, and faith, and even a useless prayer for the man who had killed Pahoran. Any good devotee of Nehor knew that man would be fine.

The confusion deepened, and she decided perhaps it was best not to mention that missive to Kishkumen. In fact, she was safer if she didn't—otherwise, he would probably send her right back in the next night, and the night after that, and on until she was caught. She was smart enough to know she would eventually get caught if she kept pressing. That was how life worked.

Having settled the matter in her mind, she finally rose, gathered the rope and pulley, and patiently made her way back to the other house's roof and down to the ground via the ladder. She slinked to the end of the lane, and then settled in to wait.

In about half an hour she spotted an old man pulling two mules down the street, hugging the side where she waited. He wore the prescribed hat from Kishkumen's instructions, and at the correct angle. As he passed by, she stepped out of the lane and grabbed one of the leads, falling into perfect rhythm with his slow, methodical steps. He didn't say anything, didn't even look up at her.

Within minutes, they had exited the exclusive neighborhood and made faster progress toward their destination—not her father's house, but that of another lower judge, a seldom-mentioned acquaintance of her father. She didn't bid the man with the mules farewell as she handed him her lead and diverted to the front door of the house, and he never paused in his movement.

Thirty seconds later Ara sat on a backless bench, facing Kishkumen and her father's acquaintance—who lounged in comfortable chairs—in a dimly lit room. All was quiet except for the sounds of a few insects outside. Kishkumen was clearly trying to hide his excitement. She wondered what odds he had given her of succeeding. He must have had backup plans. She waited for him to begin, but instead it was the judge who spoke first, showing himself to be in charge. She didn't remember his name.

"Did anyone see you that shouldn't have?" he asked, his pointed nose aimed like an arrow at her face.

She shook her head. "No, and nobody followed."

The man glanced at Kishkumen, who nodded. Was he confirming she wasn't lying? The thought kindled a strong feeling of irritation.

"Did you find anything of interest?" His arrogant disregard for her was palpable. Part of her was tempted to say "No" to see what he would do. But she obediently reached into her bag and withdrew the rolled-up sheaf of parchments she had written, handing them to him with a level gaze.

"I was able to access his locked drawers. These are copies of the important documents I found. I put everything back just as it was, and I spilled no wax."

She was angry at herself for somehow wanting to please this smarmy man. She knew she had done well, so she shouldn't need his validation. And yet she craved it, especially with Kishkumen sitting there.

Kishkumen and the man leaned close to each other as they began to peruse the papers. Aside from a few fingers pointed at certain passages and the occasional widened eyes or raised eyebrows, their reactions remained subdued. When they reached the end, they went back to the beginning and read everything again more slowly. She could tell they wanted to comment several times, but they didn't, not in front of her. That was even more infuriating.

Finally, Kishkumen and the man shared a glance, and then the man abruptly got up and left the room, taking the parchments with him, without even a word of thanks. She watched him leave, then looked at Kishkumen. He smiled warmly at her, and it was the most frightening thing that had happened to her that night. She almost blanched.

"You did well, Arayah. You may have saved more than one life tonight."

She wasn't sure how. She tried to remember more of what she had hastily scribbled out, but there were too many holes in what she could recall, too many disparate pieces floating around in her head to make any sense. She chided herself for having been too nervous; she should have gone a little slower and let herself focus on what she transcribed.

She promised herself she wouldn't make that mistake again. And that she would continue to avoid Kishkumen as much as possible.

Kai had ridden his horse hard the last few days, and never once had that amazingly faithful mount complained. He had decided to ask if he could buy the stallion, or keep him somehow, even though he knew that might be selfish. He'd never grown attached to a horse before. He was getting close to giving him a name.

Kai had started growing out his beard again. Mistress Havah knew what he looked like with and without a beard, but he doubted many of her agents did. He had outrun any pursuit anyway, and she didn't know he was headed for Zarahemla.

He approached the magnificent, enormous city in the early afternoon of a beautiful, nearly cloudless day. He paused atop a hill on the east of the River Sidon to survey the Nephite capital, which sat about half a mile from the western bank, the main warehouse district spreading from the docks almost to the city gates. Zarahemla kept growing, and even the eastern bank of the mighty waterway which fueled that growth teemed with inhabitants and buildings of every kind, with the foundations for a wall under construction. The channel was too broad for a bridge, but a dozen massive ferries traveled back and forth at frequent intervals, always making way, of course, for the constant cargo ship traffic moving up and down the river.

The famed stone walls of Zarahemla, gleaming with a yellow and red sheen, seemed impregnable. They stood at least forty feet high and fifteen feet wide at the top, slightly broader at the bottom. It was said they were sunk thirty feet into the ground as well, to prevent effective tunneling, though the water table would generally prevent that anyway. On the east and west, the walls followed a slightly concave curvature, which added to their impressive stature. On the north and south, they were convex. Broad gates allowed entrance at the cardinal points, and Kai counted twenty-five defensive towers on the eastern wall alone.

Zarahemla boasted many tall, impossibly thin towers, most of their colorfully painted spires ending in sharp points aimed at the heavens. Kai wondered how far he would be able to see from the top of the highest spire. At least twenty-five miles, he figured.

He had originally intended to take his horse across the river and stable him at one of the places he knew just to the south of the city. But he had made a good acquaintance a year back, a minor merchant in farm goods who kept a fine home and stable a few miles north of Kai's current position east of the river. That would be a good place for now, and his orders hadn't spelled out when he needed to return the horse. He could make it back to the ferries on foot well before dusk, even if he stayed for a brief visit.

He soon approached the house, connected to a minor road by a long, curving, tree-lined lane. As the structure came into full view, he whistled softly. His friend must have made some fantastic trades lately. He had doubled the size of his home and rebuilt his barn half again as large. The fields beyond lay bursting with the earth's bounty, and in the distance Kai observed two men harvesting wheat. They used a wide wagon fitted with rotating horizontal scythe arms on the front that funneled the cut stalks into wide channels, where one of the men raked them into the bed of the wagon. Three powerful oxen pulled along an already harvested line just to the side of the wagon's path and a significant distance ahead; the other man kept the wagon on its line with a heavy steering mechanism.

Kai dismounted, then tied the reins to a hitching post. Trees surrounded the house, just as he remembered from his quick first visit following last year's major battle, but the roof had been replaced and was more peaked now, with fine wooden shingles that glittered in the mottled light as a breeze tickled the leaves. The home and its surroundings seemed idyllic and peaceful, and suddenly all Kai wanted was for such peace to expand and remain unbroken forever. He couldn't understand why people were always fighting—the Lamanites so easily stirred up to conquest, the Nephites trying to take advantage of each other. Why couldn't they recognize how much God had blessed them? His father, Gideon, was right about the frailty and fickleness of men's minds, the great pride that afflicted so many, and the oft-practiced ignorance toward the Lord's words.

Kai paused, realizing he was starting to understand Gideon's teachings better.

His friend jolted him out of his musings. "Kai, is that you?" he asked, emerging from the front door and taking the two steps to the ground in a single hop, a huge smile on his face.

Kai blinked, somewhat surprised. Was this the same man whose normal demeanor could best be described as respectfully dour? He was a good man, and kind, but not cheery.

"Um, hi Aaron. It's been more than a year." He gestured at the house and fields. "You've been busy."

Aaron ignored the implied query and wrapped Kai in a hug. A hug! Then he backed up a step, still grasping Kai's shoulders. "You look good, Kai. Still not married? Nalani will ask, you know. She was the first to see you coming and is fixing you something to eat. She insisted." He winked.

Kai wasn't sure how to respond. He had only met Aaron's wife once, and she had seemed somewhat reserved. How did she even remember him?

"Oh, well, thank you, but I can't stay long. I need to get to Zarahemla tonight. I was hoping to leave my horse here, though, if I can rent some stable space from you."

Aaron admired Kai's horse for a long moment, then nodded. "Of course. And no charge for feed or anything else, for as long as you need to stable him here. Come, come, you can have a quick bite. We won't keep you long." He put an arm around Kai's shoulders and walked him through the door.

The interior of the home was also more impressive than Kai remembered. Nothing struck him as opulent, but the furniture and fixtures looked new and of high quality. The front room bloomed with color from wall hangings, drapes, rugs, and a large vase of freshly cut flowers. Aaron indicated the largest chair and bid Kai to sit, while he sat in another chair, almost as large, on the opposite wall.

"So," Aaron said, "you're wondering about all the changes."

Kai nodded. After being on a horse for several days straight, the cushioned chair felt wonderful.

"Well, we've been working hard, but that doesn't fully explain it. Things have just kind of ... fallen into place. Conditions for good trades arise. I stumble upon new contacts that lead me to lucrative opportunities. Our health has been good, and the weather has been kind to our crops. Oh, and we were able to purchase several large tracts of land around us for much less than I thought was possible. It's hard to believe. And most of it started when we got baptized as Christians and really began putting our trust in the Lord."

Aaron paused, letting the words hang in the air, smiling confidently. He knew, of course, that Kai was a Christian, though Kai hadn't talked with him much about it. He felt a little guilty about that. He wasn't comfortable talking about his faith, and he didn't want to impose his beliefs on anyone. Deep down, he knew that was mostly an excuse, and Aaron had just proved it to him. He didn't seem to be accusing Kai of keeping the truth from him, however.

"That's, uh, wonderful," said Kai. He felt genuinely happy, but his friend's conversion still seemed strange. He wouldn't have thought Aaron and Nalani would become converts.

Aaron nodded energetically. "It is. And I thank you for your example."

Kai's guilt tripled. He hadn't done anything.

"I know you don't think you helped much, but you did. I watched you carefully, the brief time we were together. The way you treated people, your self-discipline, the courage you showed in defending the Church and its place in Nephite society. You were never arrogant or bombastic about it, as some are. You were just ... solid. That's what I needed to see, and now I understand why."

"Why what?" asked Nalani as she entered the room carrying a plate laden with freshly cut vegetables, dried meats, and dark, rich-smelling bread. She handed the plate to Kai, then sat in a chair next to her husband.

"I was just telling Kai we joined the Lord's church," Aaron answered. "He's pretty surprised." Aaron and Nalani both laughed.

"Well," said Nalani, "The Lord has blessed us, and our children. We were baptized on Aaron's thirtieth birthday, just ten months ago, and I can't count the number of miracles that have occurred since then as we've tried to faithfully keep our new covenants, pay our tithes, give to the poor, and share the gospel with others."

Was this really the same Nalani Kai had met before? She seemed confident, ebullient, and exceedingly content.

"I'm happy for you," said Kai, but he didn't know what else to add, except for, "The kids have been baptized, too, I presume?"

Aaron nodded. "Joseph and Meren, yes. Adonai is too young, of course."

Kai had forgotten the names of the older boy and girl, but because his undercover name was Adonihah, he easily remembered Adonai.

"Well, congratulations." Kai's grin was genuine, growing more so as he studied the plate of food sitting in his hands. For just one person, it was a feast.

"Please, eat," said Nalani. "We had some lunch not too long ago, and it looks like you've been on the road for a while."

Kai didn't want to be rude, so he began eating. The food tasted wonderful, and he was indeed hungry.

"So, you're heading to Zarahemla," said Aaron. "Be careful, my friend. Things feel different there right now, as I'm sure you can imagine."

Kai nodded in agreement, his mouth full.

"We have some friends who were there yesterday," added Nalani. "They heard rumors Pacumeni is the leading candidate to be the new chief judge, with a vote scheduled in two weeks. The couriers to the rest of the country must have been sent out secretly just a few days after … um … it happened … to get it all arranged." She stared at the floor, her face somber.

"And they still haven't found the man who killed Pahoran," remarked Aaron, resting a hand on Nalani's arm. "I don't think the assassin was anyone connected to Pacumeni, which means he could be in danger, too. People are worried. Some are panicking. A few are even leaving the city."

Kai paused as he was about to take another bite. "Why leave the city? The authorities have things under control, don't they?"

Aaron shrugged. "They say they do, and maybe that's true, but when a man can disguise himself and get close enough to the chief judge to murder him … well, it makes people nervous, of course."

"Of course," Kai agreed. "And has Helaman said anything?"

Aaron glanced at Nalani, then answered. "We've heard two official messages from him, but nothing telling us anything specific about the current situation."

"He has asked us to pray harder for our leaders, for our nation, and for its families," added Nalani. "It is good counsel, and specific enough for now. We need to have more faith."

Aaron lifted Nalani's fingers to his lips as he gave her a look Kai seldom saw, except between Gideon and Ishara—deeply respectful, but also embarrassingly intimate in the presence of a visitor.

"Yes, that's true," Aaron admitted. His gaze shifted back to Kai. "Perhaps you can bring us back some additional news. How long do you expect to be in Zarahemla? Oh!" He turned to Nalani again. "By the way, my angel, Kai needs to stable his horse here, and I told him we could take care of it for as long as he needs—is that okay?"

That was another change. The Aaron Kai used to know wouldn't have asked Nalani's permission.

Nalani smiled kindly, nodding at Kai. "Of course, whatever you need. It feels like … well, it feels like you're here on important business, and that the Lord's hand is in it."

Kai blinked, feeling a rush of warmth in his chest. Was his mission truly important? Moronihah had summoned him for a reason, but he was surely assembling many people to perform various tasks amid this crisis. How important would Kai's own role be? Looking into the genuinely friendly and faith-filled eyes of Aaron and Nalani, he determined he would do his very best.

"Well, thank you for your help," he said sincerely, after a brief pause. "I'm just a merchant scout, though, trying to do my job—fairly, of course."

Aaron chuckled, slapping his knee. "Oh, you're no mere merchant scout, my friend. Nalani is right. We expect to see amazing things."

Kai nearly let puzzlement and alarm show in his features. He was sure they didn't know his true role, and Aaron hadn't necessarily implied they did. But why were they so confident?

He would have to figure it out later. At least their food would give him the energy he needed, because it was time to meet his destiny in Zarahemla.

CHAPTER 4

Wherefore, men are free according to the flesh; and all things are given them which are expedient unto man. And they are free to choose liberty and eternal life, through the great Mediator of all men, or to choose captivity and death, according to the captivity and power of the devil; for he seeketh that all men might be miserable like unto himself.

2 NEPHI 2:27

Kai had thought to go straight into the city and find an inn in the Jewel Quarter. He was anxious to see how long it would take Melekai's mysterious friend to find him. But as he left Aaron and Nalani's home, he instead felt a strong desire to visit the large army stronghold three miles to the south of the city. Zarahemla was among the few Nephite cities recently requiring most of the regular army—including many of their families—to be housed outside the walls in times of peace. Kai had friends at the camp, and maybe Moronihah could be found there as well. More likely, though, Moronihah would be somewhere along the Lamanite border or staying the evening at his home in the city with his family.

Kai mulled over his options as he set a fast pace for himself along the road down to the river ferries. If he went to the encampment first, he could immediately send word to Moronihah that he had arrived, though he didn't have much to report yet. If he settled into the city first, under the name of Adonihah, he might come under immediate surveillance, and communication with Moroni could be delayed. He didn't know how extensive Melekai's network in Zarahemla was or how quickly news of his arrival would become known to them.

He decided to avoid that risk and head for the army camp. Most knew him as Kihoran there, though a select few knew his undercover name. It was nearly dark before he stepped off one of the ferries and began his march to the camp carrying his travel pack, to which he had transferred most of what had been in his saddlebags. He felt fresh, so he alternated jogging and walking, rapidly covering the distance. When he arrived at the stone-topped earthen fortifications of the camp, a guard hailed him from one of the wooden towers overlooking the entry passage.

"Ho, Nephite, where are you going?" The man's voice had a timbre like that of a charging bull.

Kai squinted up into the night. A large torch blazed in an iron sconce on the side of the tower, but the guard was mostly obscured behind a pillar, as he should have been. Kai gave a crisp Nephite salute, tapping the fingers of his right hand on forehead and heart.

"I am Kihoran, of the two-seven scouts. I bring a report for the captains."

The second regiment was based a good distance to the south and east, but the seventh scout group of every regiment was far-ranging, helping all the regiments coordinate intelligence.

The guard paused only a second before shouting down, "You may enter!"

Kai passed through the thick wooden gates, then followed the passage between coordinating walls and towers as it wound left, then right, then left again, a narrow killing field for any enemy that breached the gates. When he finally emerged into the main practice yard—which doubled as a broader killing field—he noticed that the number of lights from torches and fires in the central, on-duty area of the camp wasn't even a quarter of what it would normally be. It made sense: Moronihah had been sending troops to the border garrisons, bolstering them against a rumored Lamanite attack. Had he sent too many, though? A determined enemy could come from multiple directions.

He crossed the yard, mostly deserted at that hour, then made his way through the ordered tents, many of which appeared permanently emplaced, some with double walls and small garden patches in front. At full strength, five thousand men and at least three times that many dependents occupied the stronghold, with about five hundred on duty during the nighttime hours.

Near the walls, wooden structures for larger families had sprouted up. Lights shone from many of the windows, which told him most of the families of the men who had been sent to the border had stayed behind. Perhaps they believed the assignments would be short, tensions would soon ease, and the men could return home.

Five large command tents—looking far less portable than last he'd seen them—governed the encampment, one for each group of a thousand men. Each tent bore its own banner beneath the Nephite flag and a modified version of the original Title of Liberty. The tent Kai sought displayed a banner of red and gold in a complex diamond pattern. The Zarahemla scouts operated under that banner, and he hoped to find a few of them in camp.

The two guards at the heavy tent flaps let him pass after he flashed the silver quarter-moon insignia on his collar identifying him as a scout. The spacious tent, which could hold at least fifty people, was divided in two. The front two-thirds sported several long tables set up to facilitate the reading of maps and the writing and receiving of correspondence. Another set of flaps on an inner divider led to the active quarters of the captain in command of this group of a thousand men—the high captain—and his captains over their groups of a hundred.

Two soldiers worked quietly at one of the tables. The rest sat empty. Kai stopped.

"Is the high captain here?"

Only one of the soldiers looked up. The other seemed engrossed in transcribing something.

"No. He's in the city at a meeting. He won't return until tomorrow." The man didn't appear to be any older than Kai. His expression made it clear he wanted to return to his work but didn't want to be rude.

Kai thought a moment. "Are any of the scouts here?"

The soldier furrowed his brow, then nodded. "Yes, a couple, I think. If they're on-duty, they're near the twenty-third cookfire."

"Thank you." Kai reversed his step and exited the tent, passing the guards without a glance. When he had gone a few yards, he started counting the fires that began where the practice yard ended. The Nephite armies numbered their locations in camp, like cookfires, in concentric circles, starting from the east on the outer ring and going toward the northern point first, then jumping to the next smaller circle once the circuit was completed. He tried to count not only the fires that were lit but also the spaces where it appeared they were not. He turned one full circle, then a quarter circle before settling on where he thought twenty-three would be. He marched off in that direction.

He didn't miss by much. He arrived at twenty-five, so he made his way to twenty-three, where half a dozen men sat around the small flames, enjoying the last of their evening meal. As he walked up to them, he saw the two faces he had hoped to find.

"Ho, Lomon and Ajah," he said with a small wave of greeting. The two men on the other side of the fire looked up, then grinned as they recognized Kai. He wondered for the hundredth time how they weren't twins. They were both shorter and leaner than he was, and just as stealthy. They featured the same dancing, mischievous eyes and open faces, which made them terrible spies. They were great scouts, though.

"Kai!" they shouted in unison as they rose. Then Ajah said, "Come, sit at the fire. I'm sure we can find you some grub."

Kai raised a declining hand as he stepped closer. "I already ate," he said with a teasing voice, "and far better than you did."

Lomon laughed. "You mean one of those witches finally enticed you into her house?"

Kai laughed along with them. Lomon liked to talk about witches for some reason Kai and Ajah hadn't figured out.

"No," replied Kai after a moment, "it was a high judge's daughter."

Lomon and Ajah both hooted with laughter, and Kai felt a little stung. After a few seconds, Ajah, still gasping, with tears leaking from his eyes, asked, "Is she a witch?" The other soldiers at the fire couldn't help themselves; they burst into laughter, too.

"I'm glad you soldiers are getting a chance to relax."

Kai knew that voice. Everyone else did, too. The instant silence roared like a tornado. They leaped to their feet, facing their chief captain and saluting.

Moronihah chuckled, his dark eyes flickering in the firelight. "I'm not that frightening, am I?" he asked, arms folded across his chest. Because of his unexpected arrival, he towered over them even more than his tall frame and high position would presuppose. "Well, to the Lamanites I hope I am. But not to you."

Nobody said anything. Kai knew most of the soldiers in the army liked Moronihah, but the chief captain wasn't seen among the troops often. He had a reputation for stern discipline, like his father. The difference was that his father was a legend. Nephite warriors had come to nearly worship Captain Moroni, and for good reason.

After a few more awkward seconds, Moronihah directed his attention to Kai. "You have a scouting report for Captain Benijah, Scout Kihoran?"

"Yes, sir, I do," said Kai smartly, saluting again.

"Very well. I'd like to hear it, too. He's back in his command tent. We decided to return tonight. Walk with me. The rest of you, relax … but keep the talk of witches to a minimum."

Kai couldn't tell whether he was serious or joking about the witches, and he didn't ask. He strode beside the lanky, broad-shouldered chief captain as they marched swiftly toward Captain Benijah's command tent, the same one Kai had visited earlier.

The two guards snapped to attention as Kai and Moronihah approached, then smartly opened the flaps for them to enter. Inside, the two diligent soldiers Kai had talked to had been joined by several others, including some lesser captains. Several conversations happened at once, and Kai couldn't pick up much from any of them. It was clear new orders had been given, though, and the execution planning was underway.

Once those in the room realized Moronihah had entered, all heads turned toward the chief captain.

"Carry on," Moronihah said, then crossed the room to pass through the next set of tent flaps. Kai followed, garnering a few raised eyebrows.

Captain Benijah, a veteran in his late forties with a full head of rare blond hair straight as pine needles, sat behind a large desk, studying some parchments. An aide stood to his left, peering over his shoulder. Benijah rose, and the aide saluted before Moronihah spoke.

"Captain, I need to meet with you and Scout Kihoran for a few minutes."

"Of course," said Benijah, stepping away from his desk while motioning his aide to leave the room. Moronihah went to the vacated chair and sat, glancing only briefly at the documents Benijah had been perusing. Kai stood in front of the desk, hands behind his back.

Moronihah closed his eyes and took a deep breath as he rubbed his temples. His shoulders slumped a little, and Kai felt nervous. He knew the chief captain better than most of the scouts—and many of the officers—and Moronihah had rarely shown such weariness.

Moronihah's eyes opened, and he placed his hands flat on the desk as he leaned back. "Your trip was uneventful?" he asked with a weak smile.

Kai thought a moment before answering. "Not really. Rumors are everywhere, and tensions are rising. I was attacked in Sidom while trying to follow an agent of a spymistress, and I met a merchant in Lehi who has a network of connections here in Zarahemla that bears investigating. Many people are afraid. Even Bountiful is somewhat affected."

Moronihah nodded, then closed his eyes again. He sat motionless for almost a minute, then opened his eyes again and looked at Benijah, then Kai. "The city is a cauldron about to boil over. The search for Pahoran's killer has been hampered by too many people coming forward claiming their neighbors or friends are traitors. The investigators are overworked chasing false leads, and whenever they find a good one, they can't seem to pursue it fast enough. We've caught only three people who knew something of the plot, and they were minor players with little useful information.

"In the meantime, the enemy is attacking on a different front. The nationwide election to select the next chief judge will be concluded within the month. Pacumeni was chosen by the high judges to run, against the private recommendation of Helaman, who hasn't endorsed a candidate publicly, not even himself. Two other prominent men—one a lower judge of the upper tier, the other the wealthiest manufacturer in the nation—also announced their candidacies, and the politicking has become unbearable." He shook his head, sighing.

"I know little of Zarahemla's politics, sir," ventured Kai. "My contacts in the city are few."

Moronihah considered him for a few moments, causing Kai's nervousness to increase. "You're a talented spy, Kihoran. Not experienced yet, but perhaps my most talented. And there is something special about you, something strong that runs deep. I trust very few people, but I trust you." He shook his head. "I can't fully explain it, but my father taught me to pay attention to such feelings."

Kai didn't know how to respond. Should he feel proud or worried? He glanced at Benijah, who studied him carefully.

"We must uncover the plotters," Moronihah continued. "The law officers are trying, but their methods are too … predictable. We need some good spies, maybe even someone who can infiltrate the group who planned the assassination. They're still here, and their plans didn't end with the death of Pahoran. They have a purpose. We have some idea of what that purpose is, but we need more information. And we need names, especially those of the leaders. We have suspicions, but not enough evidence, and we can't hang people on suspicion of treason—that's something King Tubaloth would do." Moronihah took another deep breath. "That's a lot, I know, but we have to start. We have to try."

"I'll do whatever you ask, sir," said Kai, proud that he detected no nervousness in his own voice.

Moronihah smiled wanly. "I know you will. I've witnessed your bravery. But this is … different. It carries more danger than anything you've ever done. There is great corruption in the Nephite government. Our vast wealth drives deadly politics in an endless pit of greed and ambition. My father fought against it. He hated politics and despised politicians. It is said he and Pahoran were good friends, but they really weren't. They … I'm sorry, that's too much information."

Kai blinked. He had never seen Moronihah so unnerved or pessimistic. The seriousness of his assignment settled heavily on him. Strangely, he didn't feel afraid, though. If anything, he was now more determined. Excitement even bubbled up from deep within.

"Sir, I know I can be of service. I want the Nephite nation to remain free for our posterity." He almost stumbled on the last word. He rarely thought about his own posterity, much less used that phrasing. But now that he believed he and Siarah would get married soon, he felt ready—even eager—for the opportunity and responsibility of fatherhood.

Moronihah studied him again, then cocked his head. "You said you were attacked in Sidom. Why, exactly?"

"I took a risk," Kai responded. "A foolish one. I made up a story to Mistress Havah—who, as you know, is a careful dealer in information—about the plot against the governor of Sidom, which was outlined in my orders. After I left, she sent a man to the city, probably to monitor my activities, and I followed him. He didn't like that. Well, he and others. I don't know who they were."

"So you don't know which side she was on—for or against the governor."

Kai shook his head. "No, sir."

"Do you think she might be connected to what is happening here?"

Kai had pondered that. "No, not directly. The man I met in Lehi might be, though. One of his contacts is supposed to find me in the Jewel Quarter. I'm not sure how."

"What did the man in Lehi say his name was?"

"Melekai. I doubt that's his real name."

"And he knows you as Adonihah."

"Yes, sir. So does Mistress Havah."

"Good." Moronihah paused, his expression becoming more pensive. "Did you learn anything else on your trip here? Any rumors regarding Lamanite activity? We know they have agents here, and while most of them are clumsy and easy to detect, I'm sure some aren't."

Kai shrugged. "The rumors aren't much different than they usually are. I haven't seen any indications the Lamanites are planning anything, and I don't think they were involved in the assassination, either."

"Well, it's too early to say *that*." Moronihah removed his hands from the table and folded his arms across his chest.

Kai nodded, feeling foolish. "Yes, you're right. I need to be careful. I noticed this garrison is only at about twenty percent strength, and I know you have good reason for it."

"Yes, the Lamanites are planning something. I feel it, and we have some good intelligence, too. The problem is I can't put my finger on what exactly they intend. I've asked Helaman if he's received any impressions or direct messages from the Lord. He says he hasn't. I haven't, either. It's really bothering me. I'm not sleeping well, and that's odd for me."

Kai swallowed. Moronihah was more discomfited than he had first appeared, a bad sign. Kai needed to get to work. He could help—he knew he could.

"I'll head for the Jewel Quarter tonight, sir. I'll make sure lots of people know I'm there. This friend of Melekai will find me soon, I'm positive, and I'll start making other inquiries as well. I won't let you down, sir."

Moronihah pursed his lips and nodded. "I know you won't. That's the only thing I feel good about right now."

Midnight approached when Kai entered the city of Zarahemla through the Grand Gates facing the river, noting the significant amount of activity, even at that late hour. He had thought about the Elijah Gates on the south side, but they were much less heavily trafficked. Giving his name to one of the gate guards at the Grand Gates likely increased his chances of being found by Melekai's friend quickly. Under the guise of asking directions to a minor shop, Kai told a guard his undercover name. The man, trying to seem alert while clearly bored and sleepy, said he didn't know the shop, but it didn't matter. At least one other guard and several more people heard the conversation.

He arrived at the heart of the Jewel Quarter a short time later and sought out the largest inn he knew of—*Jacob's Rest*. The large, three-story structure occupied half a block along the Path of Mosiah, its first level clad in brown brick, its windows tall and narrow. Two sets of doors ushered guests into the grand common room, and outside each a burly guard lounged conspicuously in a stout chair. Kai would have expected just one guard outside, if any at all under normal circumstances, but he could understand the heightened concern.

He entered and approached one of the innkeepers, stationed behind a tall oak table dispensing food to the servers, who in turn kept the patrons satisfied. Kai was surprised by the size of the crowd at that late hour. He counted at least twenty-five people.

He waited patiently for a break in the action, then addressed the portly man in the belted gray smock. "Pardon me, sir, but I'd like a room. I'll need it for at least two weeks."

The man eyed him up and down, squinting. "You from out of town?"

What an odd question. Weren't most guests from out of town?

"Yes, but not too far away. Noah."

"You here working for one of the candidates?" asked the man gruffly.

Kai gave the man a funny look. "No. Are some of them causing problems? I'm just a merchant scout."

The man scowled, glancing at his purple collar tab as if wondering if it were real. "Yes, some are. A few have even brought their fistfights into the inn. I abhor violence."

Kai nodded in understanding. "Well, I'm glad you're keeping them out. It looks like I chose the right inn. I have a *real* job, and I need to get some sleep."

The man considered him a moment longer, seeming to appreciate his jibe at the political dancers, as they were sometimes called. He scratched at his thinning brown hair and nodded. "Okay, follow me. We'll record it in the ledger and you can pay the first week up front."

Kai almost objected to the steep initial portion, but he followed obediently. The man stepped behind a shorter desk against the far wall and sat down. He opened a ledger and took out a quill.

"Name?"

"Adonihah, son of Jonah. Might I inquire after your name, good sir?" Kai gave his best, most innocent smile.

"Therak," the man responded as he scratched on a parchment. "That'll be three amnors and a senum."

Kai handed him the money. Prices had gone up, but not as much as he'd feared. "Thank you. Which room?"

The man made another note in the ledger. "Second floor, room four." He turned and reached toward the wall behind him, which was decorated with rows of hooks, very few of which had keys hanging from them. He grabbed a key and handed it to Kai. "If you're hungry, the cooks will get you some food. You pay them directly. Prices are posted."

Kai gave a slight bow. "Thank you. Sleep is what I need right now, so I'll turn in. Busy day tomorrow."

Therak grunted a dismissal, and Kai walked away, angling for the stairs at the back of the room as he weaved his way through a few tables. He paused at the bottom of the stairs, an itch at the back of his neck causing him to turn and survey the crowd. He didn't spot anything suspicious or anyone paying him too much attention, so he proceeded up to his room.

Once inside, with the door locked and the solitary lamp lit, he conducted a thorough inspection, starting with the soft-looking bed, then the small table with a large basin and pitcher of water, two narrow benches, the walls, ceiling, and floor, even the two rows of pegs next to the door. Nothing seemed out of the ordinary—there was no apparent access from either of the adjacent rooms, no peepholes or hollow areas he could find. He had expected that—hoped for it, of course—but he had to be careful, especially now that he was in the fast-beating heart of the Nephite nation.

He finally shuttered the lamp and lay down on the bed, staring up into the darkness. He thought of all the places he could go in the morning while faithfully acting the part of a merchant scout. He knew there were spies among the merchant networks in Zarahemla, just as there were in every profession, but he wouldn't reveal himself to either of the two merchant spies he knew about yet. Kai's direct superior, one of Moronihah's lesser captains, had claimed they were both loyal men, but loyalty could be a fickle thing—and not just among spies.

One last thought made him smile before he drifted off to sleep: Moronihah hadn't asked about the horse.

Breakfast was magnificent, partly because Kai hadn't had a hot breakfast in nearly two weeks. Eggs, cured meats warmed in a skillet, a thick porridge with blueberries and nuts, and cool, unfermented ale. With so much food for breakfast, he wouldn't have to eat lunch. The meal was reasonably priced, too, and he made sure to add a tip. A good merchant always did, especially one who wasn't well known in an area.

His first order of business was to visit the massive main market just northeast of the center of the city. Occupying an area several blocks wide, it boasted a sky-piercing, purple-topped tower in its center and a dizzying assortment of shops, either in buildings along the periphery or in permanent tent-like structures organized in diverse clusters. It wasn't quite as chaotic as most markets he'd seen, including a few outside the Nephite nation, but it was plenty active. More than two hundred thousand people now called Zarahemla and its close environs home. The population of the city proper spilled beyond the majestic, impenetrable walls, and many smaller cities hovered close by. Rumors had spread of building a second wall that would allow the city to triple in size inside its protection, but Kai didn't believe it to be a serious proposal yet. Such an extensive wall was a colossal undertaking, and Zarahemla was already reinforced by other fortified cities within a day's fast march.

A few people dressed as Lamanites milled among the crowds, along with some true foreigners. Kai even spotted an Airoack operating a small shop selling jeweler's tools near the eastern edge of the market. He was tempted to drop by if he had time.

His initial target was a merchant who owned a sizeable shop selling cooking wares. He was called Chemish, an old and rare name. Kai had corresponded with him, and he seemed to be a good man. Chemish had never seen Kai's face, and he didn't know Kai's undercover name, either.

As Kai entered the two-story shop, supported by thick wooden pillars running along the sides and down the middle, he surveyed the cookware stylishly displayed around the space. Much of it hung from the ceiling, and Kai had to be careful not to hit his head. Several shoppers browsed the goods, and at least two assistants answered questions or transacted purchases. He didn't see anyone who looked like the merchant. Of course, he had never seen Chemish, either; all he had was a rough description.

He wandered around the merchandise for a time, waiting for one of the assistants to become available. A young woman finally approached, bowing slightly.

"Can I assist you?"

Kai nodded. "Is Master Chemish here today? I am a merchant scout from Bountiful, and my master asked me to meet with him and share some information."

"Of course," said the young woman, bobbing her head. "He's upstairs in his office, working. I think he could see you. Shall I announce you?"

"Yes, thank you. He doesn't know my face, but here—" he pulled a small silver token from a pocket of his tunic "—is my master's token. He will recognize it."

The woman accepted the token. "Perfect. I'll take this to him and tell him you're here. And what is your name?"

Kai almost slipped and gave his real name, the name by which Chemish would know him from their correspondence. It wouldn't have been a good start.

"Adonihah."

"Adonihah. I love that name." She added just the slightest hint of flirtation. He hadn't initially noted the pattern of her bracelets, which signaled she wasn't yet married.

Kai smiled neutrally, pretending not to notice her hint as he backed up a step. She paused only briefly, then went to carry the coin to her master. He had to wait only about a minute before she returned.

"He will see you," she said, her smile even more flirtatious.

"Thank you, um ..."

"Tamar," she said. "You're not from Zarahemla. I can tell by your accent."

"Bountiful."

"Oh, yes, sorry. You already said that." Her eyes sparkled, and Kai almost chuckled nervously. Or maybe he nearly grimaced. Either way, he needed to be about his business.

"Thank you again, Tamar. I will let Chemish know how helpful you were."

She smiled, showing dimples, and added a curtsy. "Don't forget to say goodbye when you leave," she said before turning away and approaching a potential customer.

As he ascended the stairs on one side of the shop, Kai admitted to himself she was cute. She was also an unnecessary distraction. And probably trouble. And what about Siarah?

He was upset with himself by the time he reached the top of the stairs. He stopped to peer down a long, narrow hallway. Only three doors interrupted its progress, closed but for the one nearest the front of the building. He walked briskly to the doorway and turned to look inside. At a large desk facing the windowed front wall sat a middle-aged man in a purple vest and gray robes, his long, black, silver-specked beard tucked underneath the edge of the desk as he reviewed a ledger. He twisted and tilted his head to look up at Kai.

"You are Adonihah?"

Kai stepped fully into the room and bowed. "Yes, Master Chemish. Master Azahir would have sent Kihoran, whom you know, but he was not available. I've only joined Master Azahir recently."

Chemish slid his chair back and rose, accepting Kai's bow with a slight one of his own. He pointed to another chair along the near wall and motioned for Kai to sit.

"How is Azahir these days?" Chemish asked when they were settled, intimating respect for Kai's merchant boss.

"Very well, sir. He has made some profitable recent trades with the Airoacks. Kihoran was involved in some of those."

Chemish nodded, seemingly impressed. "And why did Azahir send you here?"

Kai affected nervousness, as if Chemish's reputation put him off-balance. "He ... has some proposals, arising from some of his recent eastern trading activity. He's going to travel here personally to discuss them with you. I was sent to advise you of his coming and assist with any arrangements you may deem necessary."

"He's coming here? *Now?*"

Kai swallowed and blinked, continuing his feigned nervousness. "Well, he believes things will settle back down quickly, but there might be some opportunity before they do. *We should strike while the witches dance*, he said to me."

Chemish leaned back and laughed heartily. "Ah, my friend Azahir. So astute most of the time, but given to rash moods." He gave a slight shake of his head as he wiped a tear from the corner of his eye. "I will meet with him, of course, but I do not believe things will settle down here soon."

Kai cocked his head, appearing genuinely puzzled. "Why not? The election is already underway, so we'll have a new chief judge in a few weeks, and the officers will catch whoever killed Pahoran. Captain Moronihah has the border secured, too, so the Lamanites can't take advantage of the situation—not that they really could, anyway."

Chemish maintained a broad smile. "Ah, the naïve optimism of youth. You haven't seen all I have, my young friend. And you are not from Zarahemla. The currents here run deep. The waters are swirling fast, with no sign of slowing down."

Kai furrowed his brow and squinted. "How do you know that?" he asked, trying to sound respectful.

Chemish chuckled. "Long experience ... Adonihah, is it?" Kai nodded. "I have many friends here, some in important positions. I also have a few enemies. I try to keep both groups close. The divisions are deepening, the plotting continues, and we're in for a wild ride on an angry bull."

Kai nodded as if he was beginning to understand. "I see. I am sorry to hear that. I confess I don't know much about the capital. Bountiful is, um ... calmer."

Chemish chuckled in agreement. "That it is. But we're all one family, and we have to work together, right? Somehow?"

"Yes, I suppose."

"Well, don't worry too much about what I told you. In the end it will work out, but that end will not come fast, despite what your master believes."

"I see, and I thank you for your wisdom." Kai retrieved a scroll from his pouch and handed it to Chemish. "Here are some of the proposals. I have others to meet with today, but I'm staying at *Jacob's Rest* in the Jewel Quarter. You can send for me if I may be of service."

Chemish nodded. "Thank you, Adonihah. I know you've been instructed not to tell me who else you're meeting with—Azahir is a friend, but he's no fool—but let me advise you to stay away from Jorash and Nezariah."

Kai nodded slowly, looking concerned. "Why those two?"

Chemish waited a few seconds before answering. "They've been keeping some dangerous company. I don't know why. They invited me to a secret meeting once. I refused. Well, I said I would try to attend, then made an excuse for why I couldn't. They knew it for a refusal."

A touch of fear had entered Chemish's voice, sending a chill down Kai's spine. He needed to find a way to approach Jorash and Nezariah, or at least someone near them.

***

The remainder of the day was less eventful. Kai visited several other vendors, all lesser than Chemish, and learned little. Most were willing to broach the subject of politics, and most favored Pacumeni as the next chief judge. Pacumeni and his people had apparently done some effective campaigning, touting his fidelity to Nephite laws and norms, especially as demonstrated after Pahoran had been elected and Pacumeni had graciously accepted the outcome, unlike their traitorous brother Paanchi.

Kai skipped lunch, as intended, and by the time he returned to the inn that evening he was famished. The cooks again exceeded his expectations with a mutton stew rivaling anything Ishara had ever made. He wished he could have tipped the cooks more.

He searched his room again before going to bed, finding nothing, not even any surreptitious messages from Moronihah. None of the innkeepers had said anything to him, either. Of course, he had been there less than a day.

He felt refreshed and excited in the morning, but he suppressed those feelings. His training had repeatedly stressed the need for constant patience. One rash action could spell disaster for oneself, the mission, and even the nation. Sidom proved he still needed to fully internalize that lesson. So he ate his breakfast and calmly planned out his day.

He didn't want to go directly to Jorash or Nezariah or even one of their many assistants or managers. Not right away. He needed to make sure they were under surveillance, though. They might be already, but he would let Moronihah know they bore watching. That meant he would spend the first half of his day meeting with more merchants, keeping cover, but then he would contact someone who could take a secret message to the Nephite chief captain. He knew where to go, and he had the pass phrases.

He returned to the inn at about noon, declining the offer of food from the cooks. Once in his room, he changed into the clothes of a common laborer—a rumpled, long-sleeve, yellowish shirt and brown work breeches with cracking but thick-soled boots from his travel pack. He also had some hair dyes that gave his brown hair a darker sheen. Using a small signal mirror, he skillfully added some tiny lines from a grease pencil to change the appearance of some of his facial features. He was always amazed at how much of a difference the slightest disguise could make to the casual observer. Even the careful observer could sometimes be fooled.

After checking that the hallway outside his room was clear and nobody was ascending the stairs, Kai slipped out and made for the cross hallway leading to the back stairway. He figured there would be guards at the back door where many of the deliveries were made, but they would be watching people coming in, not going out. Of course, that meant when he returned, he'd have to come up with a delivery for the kitchens, ostensibly compliments of some merchant or politician. That cover-up wouldn't be cheap, but he was sure Moronihah would understand.

He sauntered out the back door into the dim sunlight of the broad alley beyond, not even bothering to glance at the two figures sitting on either side of the doorway. He neither appeared nor acted suspicious, and as expected they didn't challenge him as he turned right and kept walking. Within five minutes he was strolling alongside one of the canals, heading for the small warehouse district on the southwest side of the city, a far cry from the main district by the river.

He soon arrived at the warehouse he sought, entering through a narrow door at the rear leading to a tiny office with half-height walls. The man occupying the office jumped to his feet, but it was to yell at some workers to be careful with a stack of crates being lifted with a wooden crane to place on a large wagon.

Kai waited a moment, then cleared his throat.

The man turned and gave him an annoyed expression. "Who are you?"

Kai smiled secretively. "Nobody you would know." He glanced around to make sure others weren't near enough to overhear. "But we have a common friend. His name is Zoram, and I need to get him a message."

The man paused, looking him up and down. Kai understood the hesitation. He was new to this man—especially in his minor disguise.

"How urgent is this?" the man finally asked, seeming to accept Kai as genuine.

"The sons of Helaman turned back and saved the rest of the army."

The man nodded, humming for a moment. The phrase Kai had given indicated the highest level of urgency and that his mission came from Moronihah himself. "Will you write it or tell it?" the man asked.

"I wrote it." Kai reached into a pocket and retrieved a small tube with parchment inside, sealed at the ends with thick wax. "It's coded, of course, and the code is new." It wasn't a new code, but it never hurt to take small precautions.

"Very well," said the man, seeming more respectful now. "Do you need anything else?"

Kai had anticipated the question. His next request was a gamble, but worth the risk. "There is a man who calls himself Melekai. I met him in Lehi. He says he is a merchant with many powerful friends. I need to know who he really is."

The man nodded slowly, thinking. "I don't recognize the name, but I can make some inquiries."

"Take great care. It is a dangerous search."

"Understood."

"Thank you, brother." Kai didn't usually end a covert conversation that way, but the situation seemed to call for it. The man nodded, and Kai left, retracing his steps for a time before striking west toward the Golden Gates. The Santorem—the richest neighborhood in Zarahemla—perched commandingly on a broad hill in the northwest section of the city that afforded majestic views of the sunsets and the wild lands to the west. He wondered whether a common workman would be able to navigate the streets of that prestigious district in the late afternoon, given everything going on.

He had a sudden urge to see the temple, though, which occupied the tallest hill in the city. The structure lay somewhat east and north of the warehouse district, so he backtracked. He had seen the temple only once up close, briefly, several years ago. It was the largest Nephite temple, and while he had never seen Jerusalem, and probably never would, he knew that this structure closely matched the descriptions of Solomon's temple given on the brass plates of scripture.

A few minutes later he ascended a tree-covered path carved into the northeast side of the hill. When he neared the peak, the trees opened up on his right to grant a view of the front and side of the temple through the pillars forming the borders of its expansive courtyard. The tall, impossibly ornate temple doors faced east, like Solomon's, guarded by two massive columns. The white limestone exterior gave off a slightly golden sheen, contrasting with the darker stone of the courtyard. The surrounding grounds were beautifully, precisely dressed. A long series of wide steps fanned out from the eastern entrance of the courtyard, descending nearly to the bottom of the hill's eastern slope. When filled, those steps could hold at least five thousand people.

After Kai crossed into the courtyard and had a clear view of the front doors and columns, he stopped, taking in the altar of sacrifice on his right and the molten sea on his left. The priests stayed busy, but they performed fewer blood sacrifices than what was normal hundreds of years ago. Kai wasn't sure why fewer sacrifices were required now, only that the prophets had decreed it, having received instructions from the Lord. Many priests and teachers, including the prophet Helaman himself, proclaimed the Lord's earthly mission would begin soon, though they never gave an exact year. When his mission was completed, the sacrifices would cease altogether. The uncertainty of the timing felt frustrating sometimes. Kai thought he and his fellow Christians could prepare better if they knew when the Messiah was coming.

He didn't dwell long on the topic. Instead, he let himself feel the peace of the temple, the Lord's own house. He couldn't deny sensing something special whenever he was near a temple, even though he couldn't go past those magnificent doors yet. Some people could, besides the priests, and the restrictions were changing to allow even more people to enter. Ishara almost always wept whenever she talked about the temple and the hope it represented for their family, not just on Earth but in the eternities.

He only gave himself a few minutes to bask in the light and warmth of the temple and its grounds, and then he retraced his steps once more, eager to see how his disguise as a common-class worker would fare in the Santorem after nobody on the temple grounds had given him a second glance.

Once he arrived, he didn't have to wait long to find out. Two officers approached him soon after he began ascending the first street in the posh area. The scowls on their faces told him most of what he needed to know.

"Citizen, where is your business?"

Kai halted, giving them a puzzled and embarrassed look after glancing around. "Oh. I was heading for my mother's favorite bakery, near the northern walls. I must have been daydreaming. I thought I was two streets over. Sorry, I'll turn around."

The officers seemed surprised at his compliant apology. He supposed most people would have at least given the officers an angry frown before turning around. One of them was about to say something when a young woman interrupted, descending the street at a fast clip. She wore commoners' clothes, too, though much cleaner and in bold colors.

"Hi, officers. I overheard the conversation. I've seen him before, and he's no trouble. I'll make sure he doesn't get lost." She winked at them, which seemed to befuddle them further. They obviously recognized her, and she was pretty. Very pretty. The officer who wore a marriage band on his forearm blushed slightly and looked away. The other finally recovered his wits and spoke.

"Thank you. That's … it's much appreciated."

"No problem," she said with a light laugh. Then she looked at Kai. "I know you know where you're going, but I'd like to see this bakery."

Kai didn't blush, but he was confused. Why was this strange woman interested in talking to him?

"Sure. I can take you there." He waved at the retreating officers and headed back down the street. She caught up and walked next to him.

"What's your name?" she asked in a lilting voice.

"Adonai," he answered, not wanting to use his normal cover name.

"So you're a lord of some kind?" Her tone was teasing.

Kai had a quick comeback. "Don't I look it?" He sneaked a look at her, catching her smile. He noticed her violet eyes for the first time, too. They were striking.

She tittered. "Some lords go out in disguise, like you."

He stumbled to a stop. Then he chastened himself for showing surprise. Where was his cool head? Trying to recover, he asked, "You think I could look like a lord? Talk like one, too?"

She didn't offer an immediate answer. She had paused a pace ahead, considering him as a fox might a plump chicken.

"I don't think you're a common workman," she finally said. "Let me see your hands."

He took a step toward her and obediently extended his hands, showing palms covered in roughened skin and a few callouses. He did his fair share of physical work, and he was suddenly glad of it.

She tilted her head and pursed her lips. "Oh. Well, then, why did someone draw those subtle grease lines on your face? It's pretty remarkable work."

He couldn't deny her discovery—he could only deflect it. "I do a little reconnaissance work for one of the business owners. Petty stuff. I'm not sure why he asks me to do most of it."

She laughed again, and his heart fluttered. Her laugh was infectious, and he couldn't stop himself from at least smiling. She returned to his side and put her arm through his at the elbow, causing him to involuntarily crook it. She was expertly flirtatious, that was certain. But why flirt with *him*?

"I do some of that myself," she whispered, pulling on him to start them walking again. "It's kind of fun, even if it's a little risky sometimes." They reached the first intersection and turned left, moving in perfect unison.

"You *like* spying?" he asked, injecting some incredulity into his voice. "I do it only for the extra money."

There was that laugh again. *My goodness*, he thought.

"Yes, I do," she announced proudly. "I don't do it for money. My father's a judge—not a high judge, of course. I've gathered some interesting tidbits for him, including some really embarrassing ones. He's good at using those to our advantage." She nodded as if such mischief were perfectly justifiable.

He didn't respond, and after a few more seconds of walking, she asked, "Were you really going to a bakery?"

It was his turn to laugh. "No. I wanted to see something in the Santorem, but I obviously didn't have a good plan."

"No," she teased, "you didn't. Good thing I was there. By the way, I don't think I've ever seen you. I know this is a big city, but …"

"I mainly work in the warehouses by the river, and my family lives out on a farm."

"Oh, so you got off work early today."

"I had a day off."

"That's rare."

He nodded. "Yes, very. I might actually become a farmer."

She didn't laugh this time. She giggled. "You, a *farmer*?"

"You don't know anything about me," he said defensively.

"Maybe," she conceded, "but it just doesn't feel right for you."

"Oh, so you're one of those prophetesses? Or maybe a soothsayer?"

"Ha ha, no! And what's the difference?"

They crossed Zedekiah Street, the main road leading to the Mulek Gates in the north wall, and kept going. People flowed past them in a muted blur. Kai finally steered her toward a building along the street and stopped.

"Sorry, I need to get going," he apologized. "I have to find another way into the Santorem tonight. Just briefly. Thank you for your help." He lowered his arm and stepped sideways, disengaging hers, which she let drop.

She had a pensive look on her face. "I can get you in, even at night, easily."

He barely arrested his jaw before it dropped. She could? But no, he didn't *need* to go. Why was he letting her manipulate him?

"How?"

She shrugged. "My father knows people."

She knew he was disguised, and she obviously played her own game. Kai wondered what else she knew and whether she might be linked to Melekai's friend somehow. If she was, he didn't want to let them dictate everything.

"Okay," he said after a few more seconds. "Meet me here after the fifth evening bell sounds."

"Almost midnight. Ooh, mysterious. Okay, I'll be ready."

"Good. Thank you." He looked up and down the busy street, then found an opening and took a step.

"Wait. You never asked me my name." He froze, then turned back.

"Oh, I didn't. Yeah, I guess that's right." He felt his cheeks warm a little. "What *is* your name?"

"Raven."

"Raven," he replied flatly. It obviously wasn't her real name.

"Well, is your real name Adonai?"

"Of course," he lied. "Why wouldn't it be?"

"I don't believe you," she said, laughing. Then she stepped forward, grabbed him by the upper arm with both hands, and gave him a kiss on the cheek—in broad daylight, in front of dozens of people! "But I'll see you tonight."

Kai walked away, his eyes fogging a bit as he angled across the street. He took the next cross street, then zig-zagged for a time to make sure he wasn't being followed. When he was close to *Jacob's Rest*, he stopped by a large shop and picked up a basket of various foodstuffs. It got him past the guards at the back of the inn. He set the basket down near the kitchens without alerting the cooks, then ascended to his room. He opened and closed the door slowly, not wanting to produce a strong air current. He then inspected the various pieces of parchment he had placed at various spots on the floor.

None of them had been moved. Good. He could sleep well, especially since he had no intention of meeting up with that mysterious woman who had called herself Raven. She was tempting, but he knew of a man who had been killed by letting seemingly innocent temptations lure him to disaster. If Melekai's friend wanted to make serious contact with him, he would have to find a better way than a flirtatious young tart.

CHAPTER 5

And now, behold, who can stand against the works of the Lord? Who can deny his sayings? Who will rise up against the almighty power of the Lord? Who will despise the works of the Lord? Who will despise the children of Christ? Behold, all ye who are despisers of the works of the Lord, for ye shall wonder and perish.

MORMON 9:26

Kai woke early, feeling hopeful about the prospects of the day ahead. But he tempered his enthusiasm again—this time by reminding himself how dangerous the game of judges had become in Zarahemla and how worried Captain Moronihah was about it.

He felt a small twinge of unease at standing up Raven, since she might be an agent of Melekai's friend, but that feeling passed quickly as he ate breakfast. He had almost finished when a man wearing a cheery smile and the green tabard of a reputable clothing manufacturer approached his table with a full plate of food and asked, "May I sit with you? I really don't like eating alone."

Kai kept his eyebrows from rising as he politely motioned the man to the chair across from him. "Please, yes." He wouldn't turn down a conversation. Minor information was better than none. Of course, he didn't have time to waste, either, so he'd have to determine quickly whether the man was worth talking to.

"I'm Sam," said the man, who looked to be in his early thirties. "I don't have a room here, but I really like the food. My wife passed away recently, and we weren't able to have any children, and I don't want my aging mother cooking for me, and … well, I guess I *could* cook … that is, I *can* cook, but I don't always have time … and the food is really good here, right?"

The man spoke like a wagon hurtling downhill with no brakes and nobody to steer it. Thankfully, he took a large bite of his food. Kai almost smiled.

"I'm sorry about your wife," he said solemnly.

Sam nodded, looking glum for a moment but then brightening again as he swallowed. "She was a good woman. I was lucky to be with her. People die all the time, and I never pretend it can't happen to me at any moment. She has a wonderful family, too, and I'm still close to them. They live outside the city a few miles. My parents are here in the city, and our family tree has deep roots in Zarahemla. I'm a full Mulekite, and even have some princes and princesses in my ancestry. We have some of their stories written in their own hand, though their language had become confusing. It's fascinating to think about what they lived like hundreds of years ago, don't you think?"

Bite two entered Sam's mouth. He chewed as fast as he spoke, so Kai responded at once.

"I'm not sure where I'm from. I was an orphan, and I'm new to Zarahemla, and it feels like the city is about to explode."

There. Hopefully that comment would elicit a response telling him whether he was wasting his time with this man.

Sam nodded as he swallowed. Despite the serious topic, his tone was still light when he reacted. "We'll get through this. There are bad people everywhere, but also a lot of good people. In fact, one of them asked me to give you a message. You're Adonihah, right?"

Kai's breath caught, his senses heightened. Had his contact at the warehouse already heard back from Moronihah, or was it something else?

"Yes, but a message for *me*?" he asked, feigning surprise. "I'm just a merchant scout, and I'm not expecting any messages today."

Sam had already swallowed his third bite. He smiled as another forkful poised before the gauntlet of his teeth. "I think you're more than a merchant scout. You have potential. I can see it. I can even *smell* it." The response wasn't just odd—it was alarming. Kai felt like Sam was laying a trap, but he continued to play along.

"Well, thank you. What is the message, and who is it from?"

Sam squinted at the table, thinking hard, cheeks bulging. His answer came out somewhat muffled. "Well, now that I think about it, he didn't give me his name. He said he was a merchant and that he was terribly busy and didn't have time to come to this inn, but he gave me your description and offered to pay for my breakfast if I delivered—" he paused to reach into a pocket of his shirt "—this to you." He handed Kai a rolled-up parchment, unsealed. "Don't worry, I didn't look at it."

Kai took the parchment and began reading, convinced Sam knew exactly what it said.

Greetings, Master Adonihah,

I am a friend of Melekai, whom you recently met. He gave you high marks and recommended we speak about some opportunities to work together. I can meet you at the ninth bell of the day. I own a small pottery shop across the street from where you left the young woman yesterday.

Imrahiel

A shock traveled up Kai's spine and along his limbs. He wasn't sure it didn't show at least slightly.

"Is everything all right?" asked Sam.

Kai made up a story, useless as it might be. "I don't know. That merchant is a friend of another merchant I know, who also knows my adopted family. There is news about my sister, who has been sick. I might have to leave Zarahemla."

Assuming Sam wasn't an innocent, random message carrier, but rather in the direct employ of this man named Imrahiel, he would report Kai's fabricated response. Kai hoped he could somehow use the subterfuge to his advantage. He could almost hear Gideon urging him to pray, and he decided to heed that advice.

He excused himself, leaving Sam to finish his breakfast alone so he could spend some time in his room, seeking the Lord's guidance as he planned and tried to apply all the instruction he had received in his training. One seemingly inspired thought eventually came, but he instantly doubted it. The idea was incredibly risky. The more he pondered, however, the more it felt like the right path given his newly precarious position. After all, he wasn't sure how anyone had followed him or even noticed he had left the inn in disguise, nor did he know the extent of Imrahiel's network.

A little while later, he left the inn, heading to the market to make a few more contacts. He tried to ensure no one followed him, and he thought he was successful, but he couldn't be sure any longer. He talked with a cloth merchant, a wine seller, a blacksmith, a luxury artificer, two tailors, and three food merchants, one of whom had introduced a new drying and preservation process that greatly extended the amount of time many foods could last. From Kai's perspective as a merchant scout *and* an army scout, longer-lasting food was a compelling prospect.

He grew anxious as the time for the midafternoon meeting with Imrahiel drew close. He felt like he had prepared as well as he could, but he had never swum in waters so deep or broad. To calm his nerves, he made his last stop at a confectioner's tent. He didn't intend to ask any questions or tease out more leads; he just wanted to try something new. He rarely ate anything sweet, though he had tried some exotic sugary treats in his travels.

"What's your latest concoction?" he asked the proprietor, perusing the many kinds of sweets displayed on multi-tiered tables in boxes and bins of various volumes. The candies came in all sizes, shapes, and colors, and they smelled heavenly.

The middle-aged woman looked him up and down, seemingly noting his youth and fit frame. She thought for a moment, then nodded and clucked, reaching for a greenish, oblong candy near the center of her displays. She grabbed one and showed it to him.

"Sweets are fun," she said, "but you look like you take your entertainment seriously. You'll like this. It's more nutritious. Beets and carrots are ground in, and I don't boil the mixture too long or too hot. I sell a lot of these to the soldiers." She cocked her head, as if her last comment were a question.

"Oh," he replied. "I'm a merchant scout, but it looks delicious. I've seen something similar in the Oniheda Alliance. That was my longest trip, and I could've used some of this on the way back." He smiled, taking the candy from her hand. "How much for a dozen of these?"

"A shiblum."

He thought the price a little high, but he didn't have time to negotiate, so he fished a coin from the bag at his belt and paid her. As she busied herself gathering twelve of the new sweets and wrapping them in a thin cloth, he found he couldn't help but ask her a question, and one that was bolder than what he usually started with.

"Do you think civil war is coming?"

She paused while tying the cloth up with a string, then finished before looking up at him.

"Yes, I do." The answer was surprisingly straightforward.

"Why do you say that?"

"We're too corrupt, especially at the top. And our leaders don't seem to be learning anything."

Kai remembered Gideon saying much the same thing on occasion.

"The most powerful families are too entrenched," she continued, sounding melancholy. "Not even another major war with the Lamanites could dislodge them. Some of those elite families even *like* war, because it distracts people from all that has been unfairly taken from them. When the Lord finally comes, those greedy families will wonder and weep." She sounded more like Gideon by the second.

"How do you know I'm a Christian?" he asked softly. He liked the conversation, somber as it was. At the back of his mind, though, he remembered how often he had changed the subject or walked away when Gideon engaged such topics.

She froze him in place with an intense stare that softened after a moment. "I see it. I feel it, too. That doesn't always happen."

Kai's eyebrows rose. Usually people assumed he *wasn't* a Christian upon first meeting him. "When do you think the Messiah will come?" he asked.

She shook her head. "I don't know for sure. You might live to see it, but I won't. And I hope God takes me before we see another civil war, though that is a vain hope. Today, I sell sweets. Tomorrow, I don't know. My husband is gone. I've lost two sons to war, and the other left several years ago. I had one daughter who survived to adulthood. She disappeared, too—with a Lamanite. I don't even know which side of the border they're on. I'm alone.

I have some friends, though, and the Lord's Church, and fair health. I have a good life. But the next life will be better."

Kai wasn't sure what to say. He didn't know why the woman had opened up to him like that. Maybe he reminded her of one of her sons. He felt sympathy for her. He had lost friends in battle, had even carried the sorrowful news to the parents of one of those sons. But he couldn't tell her that.

"I'm sorry for your losses," he said, feeling it sincerely. "A great many have sacrificed for our right to govern ourselves as a free people. I know God recognizes all those sacrifices." He had paraphrased part of a recent speech by Moronihah. It resonated strongly in the moment.

Her eyes glistened as she looked deeply into his eyes. She nodded in melancholy thoughtfulness. "You said you were a merchant scout. You didn't say you hadn't been a soldier, though. You've seen battle."

He glanced away, toward the side of her tent. He couldn't deny it. But he couldn't confirm it, either, for fear of revealing too much about himself. He returned his gaze to her and smiled soberly. "I have to go. I have an important meeting." He wanted to add that the meeting could determine whether a civil war happened or not, but that ascribed too much importance to himself, so he held his tongue. He reached out his hand, into which she placed the cloth bag of sweets.

"I hope those are useful," she said. "Thank you for stopping at my tent."

A lump grew in his throat as he bid her goodbye and turned away, heading up the street toward his rendezvous, wondering at the unexpected experience. He had just wanted to buy some sweets to calm his nerves. But instead, merely talking with the woman had relaxed him considerably. Perhaps he had wasted a shiblum. Or maybe he had made a very good bargain.

A few minutes before the ninth bell, Kai arrived at Imrahiel's pottery shop, a prosperous and expensive affair by the looks of the merchandise and décor. Polished stone formed the floor, while the walls were plastered smooth and painted, window coverings providing an elegant touch. He didn't notice anyone else in the shop at first glance, but there were nooks and corners he couldn't see. So he pretended to browse, admiring some of the wares. He didn't dare touch anything. He recognized a few pieces from other nations—Airoack, Oniheda, Menwor, Tica, Hamidia, even Nianda, far to the west. Such distant, difficult trade was rare, transacted only for highly valuable items.

He paused to examine a shallow washing bowl—or perhaps, for the wealthy, a standing piece simply for show. The flowing pink, green, and orange patterns glistened with specks of what appeared to be pure gold, protected by a thick, clear glaze. The bowl looked heavy, too. He heard someone approaching on slippered feet and turned to see a young man in a cream-colored uniform with copper accents. "Is there something I can help you find?" he asked respectfully.

Kai pointed at the bowl. "How much is this?" He couldn't help himself. He was curious.

"That piece is from the eastern coast by the great ocean. One of a kind, brilliantly crafted, and quite strong."

Kai nodded. The young man hadn't said the price, probably because he wasn't sure Kai could pay. Kai supposed the right kind of clientele for such a shop wouldn't ask the price first, anyway.

"It's very nice," said Kai, turning away from the young man and strolling down a short aisle to examine several other pieces, including matching bowl and pitcher sets, some large serving plates, and a few smoking pipes.

The young man followed him. "Are you looking for anything in particular?"

Kai spun, startling the young man. That was always fun to do in a fancy shop with fragile wares and potential spies. "No," he said evenly. "What are *you* looking for?"

The young man's mouth moved silently for a moment, and then some sound emerged, weakly. "I am just trying to help, sir."

Kai smiled, easing the tension. "Sorry, I know you are. I'm here to meet someone. My name is Adonihah."

The young man stared for a moment, then gestured in the direction of a back corner. "We have some chairs in the back if you'd like to wait."

"Very good, thank you." Kai started walking that way, paying no more attention to the fine pottery. He rounded the corner of a tall display and spotted the small sitting area. Three fine chairs graced the space, one already occupied by a bald, gray-bearded man in a stout green coat, crisp white shirt, and purple breeches secured with a shiny leather belt. His black leather shoes looked expensive, and he wore three rings, all made of gold, two with inlaid precious stones. He smiled and stood as Kai approached. Kai wondered whether the young man had known the man was already here. If not, where had he come from? A door led out back, but Kai hadn't heard it open, nor noticed a resulting breeze.

"Master Adonihah," the bearded man said in a respectful but clearly superior tone. "Welcome. Thank you for coming. Please, sit. Moren will not bother us. I instructed him to close the shop and leave for a while once you arrived." He gestured to the chair across from him.

"I am no master, but thank you," Kai replied, then sat down, the man following suit. "You are Imrahiel?" He glanced to his right to make sure the young man had truly left.

The man steepled his fingers under his chin, his elbows resting on the high armrests of his luxurious chair. He stared intently at Kai for several moments, a small, knowing smile tickling the corners of his mouth. "I am, and you are elusive," he finally answered.

"You found me easily enough."

"Ah, but you are more than we expected. Why go out in disguise? And why approach the Santorem that way?"

"Some things are learned indirectly. A great trader gets all the information he can."

Imrahiel's eyes narrowed. "So why didn't you come back to meet Raven?"

Kai shrugged. "It was too easy. I didn't know her, and therefore I didn't trust her. She's pretty, though."

Imrahiel chuckled. "That she is. And valuable." His look grew more serious. "We are in a great struggle for the heart and soul of this people." He paused, letting those heavy words hang ominously in the air.

Kai nodded slowly, reflecting Imrahiel's somber mien. "We're too divided, and there's too much war."

"Yes. So many conflicts caused by uncontrolled passions and ignorant fancies. A discipline must be imposed. Without it, we will destroy ourselves."

Kai let the silence brood for several seconds, trying to appear deep in thought. It wasn't difficult; he *was* thinking hard. He was speaking with a king-man, he was sure of it. Moroni had defeated the king-men decisively fifteen years ago, but their ideology persisted, their adherents multiplying. Kai himself knew many who felt tempted by their ideas, even among the soldiers in Moronihah's army. The ideology didn't appeal much to him, though he tried to be vigilant and understand its influence among the people.

Imrahiel was testing him, so Kai decided to be straightforward. "You're a king-man," he said neutrally.

Imrahiel's steepled fingers came down to interlock and rest across his slight paunch. "If I were, would that bother you?"

And here was the gambit. Kai felt a spike of uncertainty before he responded. "I'm a spy in Moronihah's army. Does that bother *you*?"

He wondered whether he had been too bold, especially with his question. Imrahiel was his elder, an experienced and wealthy man. Probably ruthless, too. Kai had spoken to him as an equal, in an environment he didn't control.

"Perhaps," said Imrahiel calmly. Kai couldn't tell if he was surprised or offended. "And perhaps not. Melekai recommended you. He is a good judge of character."

That seemed a stretch. He had spoken with Melekai only briefly. He had asked Melekai for this interview, though, after essentially expressing an interest in the cause of the king-men.

"Perhaps a test is in order," added Imrahiel, steepling his fingers under his chin again.

"Maybe," responded Kai. "But I'm not desperate to become part of a secret group. I just want to help people see the truth, which is why I accept influencer assignments. And I keep my country safe by serving in the army."

Imrahiel nodded. "That is laudable. We need true patriots. But *I* need to know you are indeed a true patriot."

"I need to know the same of you," countered Kai, continuing his bold streak.

Imrahiel's eyebrows rose slightly, cracking his façade. Kai thought he should feel worried, but he didn't. Somehow, he knew the conversation was going the right direction.

"What do you know about Chemish?" Imrahiel asked. "You visited him your first day here."

"He works sometimes with my master, Azahir, from Bountiful. He is smart and successful, and he also seems to be aligned with the high judges. He told me to be careful of the currents in Zarahemla."

"Oh?"

"That shouldn't surprise you."

"No. No, it doesn't. And men like Chemish are the primary cause of some of those currents. How well do you know Moronihah?"

"I've met him. Most of my assignments are lower level, though."

"And? What do you think of him?"

Kai thought for a moment. He needed to be precise in his subterfuge. "He's a good soldier. The men like him, but not like they loved his father. He resents that a little, I think. He's not as strategically or tactically sound as his father, either. And he seems more loyal to Helaman than to the government."

Imrahiel narrowed his eyes, dropping his hands. He seemed to be impressed by Kai's observations. "How many of the high judges do you know?"

"I know who some of them are, but I don't know any of them personally."

"Are you a Christian?"

"I was baptized a Christian when I was young."

"And?"

Kai shrugged. "I have my doubts."

Imrahiel leaned forward, lowering his chin to increase the effect of his steady gaze. "Skepticism can be healthy. It is good to fully understand what we support, and why."

"I know a lot of good Christians."

"So do I. It is their leaders I suspect."

Kai nodded. "That's fair. But I'm skeptical of you, too. Why am I here? I told you I don't want to join a secret group, especially not one plotting against the Nephite nation."

"Why would you suspect me of that?"

"I don't know. Should I?"

Kai could tell Imrahiel was getting a little frustrated with him. He probably wasn't used to being challenged. He needed to give him some reassurance.

"I'm sorry," said Kai, waving a hand in front of him. "I'm a little on edge, and I didn't sleep well last night. Some of the rumors of Lamanite activity are getting to me. I'm trying to find out more. We know they have agents here."

Imrahiel studied him intensely, but with more curiosity than frustration. "You suspected I might be an agent working for the Lamanites?"

Kai nodded. "Yes," he said simply.

"And do you believe I am now?"

"Probably not."

Imrahiel huffed. "Good. Well, this is a fascinating conversation. And I have to say, I'm impressed by your demeanor. You're perceptive, and you show no fear. I could use your help."

"In what way?"

There was another pause, as if Imrahiel tested a decision in his mind. "With Raven. She is valuable, as I said, but I fear she is becoming sympathetic with one of the high judges, one who is trying to foist Pacumeni on us as the next chief judge. We can't allow that to happen."

"I agree with that," said Kai, injecting a small dose of earnestness into his voice. "There are better alternatives. Pacumeni's primary qualification is his name."

"Indeed. I would like you to take Raven up on her offer to get you into the Santorem at night. I can tell you the route she walks home in the evening, and you can arrange a chance encounter. You can apologize—make up an excuse—for not meeting her last night. And don't tell her we met. She likes you. I could tell by her body language when you were together. I myself watched from here. She will let slip some things to you—things that will tell me if her loyalty and true patriotism are wavering. I will pay you, of course."

Kai breathed deeply, taking in the instructions. Imrahiel's proposal was a start, and not an insanely dangerous one. "Okay. I can meet her later today, but we can't go tonight. I'm scheduled to deliver a report to Moronihah, in person, at the camp."

Imrahiel's eyebrows rose higher than they had before. He seemed both impressed and suspicious. "Your assignment here is obviously *not* low level."

Kai worried he had just slipped up. "It is, but Moronihah is extremely worried about another Lamanite invasion. I'm not the only one assigned to investigate this issue."

Imrahiel stared at the wall behind Kai, pensive. "Well, perhaps we will be able to ease his mind, if we do this right. You help me with Raven, and I will see what I can find out about Lamanite activity. I have a few contacts I can tap who might be useful."

Kai tried to appear relieved. "That would be good. We need to keep this nation safe."

"Yes," agreed Imrahiel, eyes locking back onto Kai, "we do, and it will not be easy."

Two hours later, Kai ambled down Lehi Street, heading west toward Zedekiah Street, squinting in the late afternoon sun and pausing occasionally to browse various foods offered by vendors. It was the last hour of the day. He'd skipped lunch again, and while he'd eaten a couple of the green candies, he was hungry for something substantive. The interview with Imrahiel had been short but intense. He felt like his mind had run fifty miles with a heavy pack.

Lehi Street was a major thoroughfare, always bustling with people. It bounded the main market on the north, running parallel to the Path of Mosiah which connected the Grand Gates in the eastern wall of the city with the Golden Gates on the west. The Path of Mosiah crossed at right angles in the center of the city with Zedekiah Street, which traveled north to south from the Mulek Gates to Elijah's Gates, also known as the Gates of Fire.

Every kind of food or item could be purchased somewhere along the length of Lehi Street, but none of the finer shops would offer their goods in such a noisy, chaotic environment. Kai felt at home on such a street. It pulsed with the heartblood that sustained the city, which in turn sustained the nation. Perhaps that was an overstatement—there were many great Nephite cities, each a power in its own right, though Zarahemla was definitely the center of their orbits.

He paused at a vendor selling meat pies from a small wagon with a threadbare tarp stretched overhead, held up on one side by two skinny posts. The man was thin, too, his hands thickly calloused, his black hair tied carefully behind his neck. He had a small oven of stacked bricks set up on the ground next to his wagon, and he let passersby watch him make his product. Several freshly baked pies were laid out across the tailgate of the wagon, which faced the street. The rear half of the wagon bed held supplies, its front half framed over and covered as a tiny living quarters for the man. Kai wondered if the baker ever moved from this location. He couldn't see a mule or horse nearby that might pull his wagon.

The man looked up and smiled as Kai admired the delicious-smelling pies. Symbols drawn on the edge of the tailgate signified the different types of filling—chicken, mutton, beef, pheasant, even wild buffalo—and their prices. Beef was what he craved at the moment. He reached into his money pouch and paid the man for a beef pie, then grabbed it off the tailgate. It was still quite warm, which made Kai's mouth water even more. It was hefty, too, meaning the man hadn't skimped on the main ingredients. He thanked the man and took a couple steps beyond the wagon before indulging in the first bite.

Juice threatened to drip down his chin before he caught it with a loud slurp. The pie tasted amazing; he would have to remember that vendor. Nobody noticed his sloppy eating, of course; there was too much activity and noise around him. He moved slowly, enjoying his meal but keeping his focus sharp, scanning the mixing crowds. He approached the cross street Raven would turn down, and the approximate time Imrahiel had given had almost arrived.

When he reached the corner he turned south, finally pausing a few feet down the street and leaning against a post supporting an awning. He looked farther down that street, which quickly gave way to houses. A hump in the road represented a bridge over one of the canals, its sides bordered with stone railings. There weren't as many people moving up and down this street, but they moved with a purpose. More people seemed to be in a hurry in Zarahemla than in Bountiful. They seemed almost frenetic.

Looking back toward Lehi Street and taking another bite, he settled in to watch for Raven. He was naturally good at remembering faces, and he was sure he could recognize her, even at a distance. He was about halfway finished with his pie when a voice from behind startled him.

"It almost looks like you're waiting for someone."

He jumped, nearly dropping the rest of the pie, causing a rivulet of juice to flow down his hand and onto his arm.

When he turned to look behind him, there she was. Raven. He had noticed someone in his peripheral vision walking under the awning along Lehi Street but coming from the opposite direction he had expected. She must have passed through the building to get behind him. Hopefully that was another lesson learned. Kai wondered if she had known he would be there—he couldn't discount that possibility.

"Ahh …" He glanced at the juice running down his arm, then stared back at her. "Hey. Um … sorry, you startled me."

She examined the remains of his pie, now slightly crushed and still dripping. "Is it good?" She didn't sound angry.

He considered the mess in his hands. "Um, yes, it is. One of the best I've had."

"Can I have a bite?"

What? She wanted a bite? Without thinking, he held the pie out so she could easily reach it. She touched his fingers with one hand as she kept her hair back with the other, delicately taking a nibble of the pie. She licked her lips to clean off the juice as she straightened and chewed slowly.

"Mmm … that's really good. Where did you get it?"

"Close by. I don't know the vendor, but I'll remember where he is."

"It's weird we ran into each other again." She took in his attire. "You're not dressed as a common laborer today, and you're not wearing any makeup. This is another disguise, right? You do 'reconnaissance' work for more than one business owner?" She smiled flirtatiously.

Kai swallowed, unsure why he felt nervous. "Yes. In fact, I don't do much day laboring anymore. This is better business. People are always spying on each other, and they pay good money for it."

She gave him a considering, almost suspicious look. "Only to those who are good at it. Why are you hanging around outside a soothsayer's shop?"

Kai twisted, searching for anything signaling the type of shop. He finally spotted a symbol carved and painted into the bottom right corner of a shutter—an eye with a white pupil and black iris, beams of light bursting outward all around it. His vaunted skills at observation had failed him twice in the same day. Of course, it didn't matter what kind of shop he had stopped at. She was playing with him.

"Ah, I missed that," he admitted. "Guess I need more practice. You're familiar with this shop?" Now the teasing was aimed back at her.

Her mouth twitched. "Yes, I've been in there. Do you have a problem with that?"

He smiled, flirting back without even thinking. "Not at all. So what did you learn about your future?"

She grinned impishly, reaching up a hand to pat him lightly on the cheek. "Nothing you would understand, even though it might involve a master spy like you."

He suddenly realized he liked flirting with Raven, even though it was meaningless. Maybe that was part of why he liked it. But it was time to get to his mission.

"So, um, I'm sorry I didn't meet you last night. One of my employers had another task for me, and I couldn't refuse."

Her lips curved into an expression that implied she didn't believe him. "That's all right. I don't get stood up very often, but when I do it's *fantastic*." She clearly meant that to hurt a little.

"How about tomorrow night?" he asked, a little more earnestly than intended.

She stared at him for several seconds, eyes probing. Kai started to get uncomfortable.

"Okay," she suddenly answered, her face relaxing into a broad smile, "tomorrow, same time as today, same place as before. But you know the penalty if you don't show up." She ran a finger across her throat.

He almost laughed at the drama. "I'll be there, don't worry," he said, pretending to be cowed by her threat. It was all part of the game. He started to turn away when she stopped him with a hand on his shoulder.

"You never mentioned who you were waiting for."

Kai let his eyes flash mischievously. "I don't know. Maybe you." With that, he turned and walked briskly back to Lehi Street, hoping he could mark that exchange as one of his very few—almost non-existent—victories when talking with an attractive young woman. It was probably a vain and foolish belief.

Kai knew he would be followed when he traveled to the army camp that night—Imrahiel seemed the fastidious type in his approach to everything. So he didn't want to appear overly familiar to the guards, especially with his real name, since that could be reported by passing 'strangers' on the road back to Imrahiel. As he approached the outer gates, he glanced up at one of the indiscernible men in the tower, raised a hand high, and said loudly, "My name is Adonihah. I've been summoned by Captain Benijah. I'll wait while you check."

Some of the Nephite soldiers given guard duty in a place as secure as Zarahemla weren't the brightest, but they weren't dumb, either. The soldier acknowledged his request without comment or greeting and descended the ladder from the tower to relay the message and receive orders. Kai waited patiently. He would have felt lonely but for the other guards chatting softly about something he couldn't quite make out … and the unseen eyes he was certain watched from the darkness behind him, or perhaps from the occasional traveler along the road.

A few minutes later the guard returned and announced Kai could pass. The heavy gates opened slightly, and he slipped through. The same guard met him as he reached the practice area.

"Captain Benijah wasn't expecting you, but he said to let you through. He's waiting in his tent. You know where that is?"

Kai nodded, thanking the soldier, who saluted and returned to his post. He looked young, probably barely of age to serve. He wouldn't have seen any battles. Kai took a mental inventory as he walked among the tents and cookfires, estimating that most of the soldiers guarding Zarahemla were young and inexperienced, since the veterans were needed at the borders.

Kai went straight to the captain's tent, and the lone guard at the entrance waved him in.

Captain Benijah looked up from his chair, where he had been reading a bound sheaf of parchment. It appeared ancient, maybe scriptural. Kai saluted.

"You're lucky I was here tonight, Kihoran. That young man was confused. He said he didn't recognize your face. He's brand new, still a baby."

Kai gave a slight nod. "Yes, sir. Thank you, sir. I have news for Captain Moronihah. Do you know where he is? I didn't want to approach his house in the city to see if he was there."

"Well," said the captain, scratching his clean-shaven jawline, "he's not here, and you wouldn't have found him at his home, either. He headed for the border this morning. He took the rest of the scouts with him."

Kai tried not to frown, especially at all the scouts being gone. It didn't feel right. "I can give you this message, then," he began, limiting how much he said, even though he knew Moronihah trusted Benijah. "I sent a communication through one of our channels regarding two of the major merchants in Zarahemla—Jorash and Nezariah. Any actions resulting from that message should be halted. It's too dangerous."

"Has the channel been compromised?" asked Benijah, setting aside the parchment book, eyebrows raised.

"Probably. I can't say for sure, but I met today with a mysterious man who had successfully arranged for me to be followed around the city, even when I was in disguise. He seems extremely thorough, and his network must be extensive."

"This is the contact the man in Lehi told you about?"

"Yes, sir. Melekai said he would call himself Chorinai or Imrahiel. He introduced himself to me—by written message—as Imrahiel."

"Interesting. How does this Imrahiel think you can help him?"

Kai shrugged uncomfortably. "Well, I told him I was a spy for the army." He had just said more than he had intended.

Only Benijah's left eyebrow rose this time. "Oh?" He paused, eyes narrowing in thought. "And you figure they probably saw you make contact with the channel." He sat back in his chair, then whistled softly. "You're doubly fortunate I was here tonight. I'm not sure we could trust any of the other captains here with this information. Do you understand what I'm saying?"

Kai swallowed involuntarily as the thunderclap hit. It shouldn't have surprised him that some of the less experienced or less qualified captains might be disloyal. "Yes, sir." He suddenly wondered if he was speaking too loudly, but he knew the area around the captain's tent was broad—someone would have to position themselves next to the tent's double walls to hear them. But the guard …

"Don't worry about Dan," the captain reassured him, reading his expression. "I trust him more than any other man in this camp, save Moronihah when he's here. Dan was one of Helaman's two thousand. Some of his wounds still pain him, but his faith remains strong. He's glad to have made the sacrifice."

Benijah's confidence made Kai feel somewhat better. He had met several of the famed stripling warriors. It was hard to fully believe some of the stories about them. They were a key reason the Nephite nation still existed. Most of them had left the army and returned to their homes, taken up trades, and started families. About five hundred of the original two thousand and sixty remained in the army, but only a handful had accepted rank advancements to captain. Most were lower-level officers, but they provided significant stiffening to the backbone of the army. In addition, between fifty and a hundred new young Ammonites joined the army every year, though they usually stayed for just a few years. Instead of keeping them together, Moronihah had spread the Ammonites among all his armies. He viewed them as a leavening agent, and last year's great battle seemed to have proven him wise.

Benijah took a deep breath. "You're still worried. I can understand that. You're embedded in a dangerous game. Zarahemla has become a regrettably treacherous place." His voice had become thick with disdain, but also infused with sadness. "I fear the city is ripe for destruction. How can the Lord continue to look upon her abominations and be patient? He is merciful, but he is also just. And he keeps his promises."

Suddenly he stood. "I sense goodness in you, Kihoran. Guard it with your life. Now, I have work to do tonight. I need to get a message to Moronihah. We need more men here. Something is coming. I can feel it. There may be another uprising of king-men, and we aren't strong enough— in numbers or conviction—to handle that. Moronihah and I discussed the issue before he left, and I agreed with his decision to keep our troop numbers here as they are, but your coming tonight has renewed my fears. Go, find out what you can. Be careful, but be bold, too. Take Dan with you to the city tonight. He'll proceed to Helaman's house, as Helaman requested just today."

Kai saluted again, feeling the urgency radiating from Benijah. He spun and exited the tent, then found himself face-to-face with Dan, a tall, burly man who stood solidly at attention. His gold-specked almond eyes glinted in the flickering torchlight, which also accented the midnight-blue headband holding his dark brown hair in place. His uniform didn't boast any elaborate decorations, but it didn't need to.

"You heard?" Kai asked.

"Some of it," Dan answered. "He spoke louder when he said I would accompany you to the city, meaning for me to hear. I'll summon a replacement, and we can go. Wait here."

With that, Dan jogged off into the semi-darkness toward the first tents on the north side of the camp. Within a minute he returned, another soldier with a tall spear following. The man looked to be about thirty, like Dan.

"This is Saric," Dan said to Kai. "Saric, this is Adonihah. He's one of our scouts—the last left in the city."

Saric held out an arm. "Well blessed. If you're the last scout, you'll be busy."

Kai forced a laugh, grasping the man's proffered forearm. "And I'm asking for a raise." Saric laughed back. Kai didn't tell him he wasn't doing any scouting for the garrison, that they were essentially blind, and he felt a spike of fear at the thought. A good army should have trained scouts operating continuously. Of course, they were in Zarahemla, far from the restless border with the Lamanites. Also, the primary threat was from within the city, not without, and the city had its own force of law officers. Kai could understand why Moronihah wanted his armies focused where they were needed most, though he shared Benijah's concern about a full-scale uprising of king-men that could overwhelm them.

Kai and Dan bid Saric goodnight and began walking through the camp toward the main entrance. As they crossed the barren practice yard, Dan turned to him and said, "I remember when Helaman the Elder accepted me and my brothers and agreed to lead us. This assignment feels the same, but this time, it's for you. You have something important to do." He said it so assuredly and matter-of-factly—and without breaking stride—that Kai wondered whether he'd heard correctly. He didn't know how to respond, but he'd never conversed one-on-one with a member of the two thousand. It was a golden opportunity.

"What was your first battle like?" he asked.

Dan scrunched his shoulders. "Honestly, I don't remember many details. It was late afternoon. The Lamanites had stopped pursuing us, and Helaman gave us a choice. We knew Captain Antipus might be in trouble. We were nervous, but we were also determined. So, instead of setting up a defense, we went back ... and that's where things get fuzzy. I remember bits and pieces, but some of my movements seemed automatic, instinctive. I was trained, of course, but I wasn't trained *that* well. I don't remember how many Lamanites fell to my sword and spear, but I remember wishing I could have met each of them under different circumstances and expressed to them how surely I knew their Savior loved them as much as he loved me. I suppose they'll eventually have the opportunity to know that truth."

Kai nearly stopped dead in his tracks at that incredible answer, which left him speechless for a while.

Soon, they passed through the outer gates and joined the road heading toward the city.

"It's really true that none of you died in that battle?" Kai asked soberly. He had always marveled at the tale, which had already achieved legendary status. Perhaps he doubted, while at the same time wanting badly for the miracle to be true.

Dan nodded. "Yes, it's true. Miracles are real, my friend, and that surely was one of them. Antipus died, along with eight hundred of his men. We killed more than twice that number of Lamanites, and we took so many prisoners we worried we could never keep control of them. They feared us, though, me and my young brothers. Some thought we were demons."

Despite the darkness, Kai caught the hint of a smile at that misconception. "Were you wounded?"

Dan shook his head. "No, not in that battle. But later I was, several times. Some days are okay. Others are excruciating. But I get through it. And I wouldn't trade my pain away if it meant my adopted homeland wasn't free."

"God could heal you, though, if he wanted to."

Dan seemed to consider that. "Yes, he could. I've asked him to. Maybe someday he will. I still learn from this pain, though, and he knows that. I trust him. That sounds strange to some people."

It did, even to Kai, who counted himself a believer in Christ and had been taught by a faith-filled man like Gideon.

"You have a lot of fai—"

Dan's arm snapped up, his hand signaling a halt. Kai froze, then swiveled his head. In the next instant Dan drew his sword and handed it to Kai, who only carried a knife. Then Dan turned, readying his spear. Kai heard the slightest of sounds, a stretching . . .

"Move!" Kai yelled as he threw a shoulder into Dan, who stumbled to the side but didn't fall. An arrow hissed through the air, thunking into a low embankment. "This way!" Kai darted into the trees and brush that hid at least one phantom archer. He and Dan would be better concealed by foliage and darkness, and the archer wouldn't expect them to charge. They stopped by the trunk of a large tree, and Dan made some hand signals that they should retreat a few yards, then split up and try to encircle whoever had attacked them. He waited for Kai to agree before sprinting away.

While Dan peeled back along the road, Kai plunged deeper into the trees and down a slight slope, circling back toward the approximate origin of the arrow. When he felt close he stopped, crouching and listening. He couldn't hear Dan, so he must have stopped as well.

Kai's heartbeats came fast, but his hearing was good despite the thuds in his chest. He detected someone trying to descend silently from a tree. The person couldn't be more than twenty yards away. Was there anyone else? Feet touched the ground, and Kai picked up movement from a slightly different direction. Yes, a partner. It sounded like they were heading for the river. Kai waited a few seconds longer, then took a different route toward the river, moving furtively but swiftly.

As he neared the water's edge he stopped, waiting. Would they come north, in the direction of the city? After a few seconds, it appeared the answer was no, so Kai headed downriver, pausing every few seconds to listen. He heard them, faintly, moving steadily along a lightly graveled path popular with fishermen. He could get ahead of them if he moved fast enough, but the brush sometimes extended all the way to the water, and he would make far too much noise. Frustrated, he halted, then thought of something different. He raced back up the slope from the riverbank, and when he had nearly reached the road, Dan popped out from behind a tree and nearly stopped his heart. Dan held a finger to his lips, then pointed at the road before directing his finger south, the question on his face. Kai nodded affirmation, also indicating their quarry was walking, not running.

Together they hurried for the road, picking up more speed when they reached it. Soon they passed near the outer gates of the encampment, and the guards barely had time to call out in confusion, Dan signaling back a call for reinforcements. As they accelerated to a sprint, Kai wondered how long Dan would be able to run, given his nagging injuries. But he was taller than Kai, with longer legs, and he didn't seem to be laboring overmuch in keeping up.

They must have run at least two miles—after moderating their pace slightly—before Dan called a halt. They were both breathing hard. Kai's lungs and legs burned. Ten seconds later, Dan led them down the hill toward the river at a fast walk, their bodies finally catching up on the air they needed, their breaths slowing. When they reached a dense thicket along the fisherman's path, Dan stopped and went to one knee. Kai followed suit a few yards away.

A minute later they heard two sets of footsteps, moving along at a fast march. When the travelers were almost upon them, Kai looked at Dan and held up three fingers, counting down.

Two.

One.

They sprang from their concealment just ten feet from two men armed with bows and long knives, dressed in short robes tied at the waist. The man nearest Kai fumbled as he tried to raise his bow and grab an arrow from his quiver. With one quick swing of Dan's sword, Kai knocked the bow from his hand, cracking it. The other man stood frozen, staring at the tip of Dan's spear hovering three feet from his belly. He had dropped his bow.

"Run and you die," Kai warned.

The man whose bow he had struck seemed to ponder the decision. Kai tensed, ready to lunge and strike, but then the man relaxed, arms dropping limply to his sides.

"Now, unsheathe your knives, throw them behind you, and sit, legs crossed," Kai ordered. The men did as commanded, the one near Dan more quickly. Without being asked, Dan took up position behind them with his spear.

"Why did you try to kill me?" growled Kai softly.

"A man paid us," said the docile one immediately. That earned him a look of venomous scorn from his partner. Kai focused on the scornful one.

"You knew where I was, but you didn't know a soldier would be with me when I left. Very few people knew where I would be tonight. Who paid you?"

The man narrowed his eyes and defiantly lifted his chin. Kai glanced at Dan and calmly said, "Right shoulder."

A split second later the man yelped in pain as Dan's steel spearhead glinted in the moonlight and sunk itself a full inch into the flesh on the back of his shoulder, then retracted. The man reached for the wound with his other hand, teeth clenched in pain.

"Don't worry," said Kai in a voice of mock soothing. "That's all we'll do unless you really want a fight. We're going for a walk." He looked at the other man "You, remove the rope from your waist and tie your partner's hands behind his back. We'll tend to his wound in a minute."

The man instantly complied as his angry, bleeding partner alternated between snarling and grimacing in pain. After finishing the knot, the man looked up obediently. Kai hesitated. He had seen a prisoner act compliant before, only to attack when it wasn't expected.

"Good, now both of you, lie down on your stomachs." After a series of groans and curses from the injured man, they were prone. Kai walked to his side and removed the rope belt around his waist, tossing it to Dan. Then he stood and placed his foot on the man's back while resting the tip of his sword on the back of the cooperative man's thigh.

"You want to do the honors?" Kai asked Dan.

Dan nodded, then set his spear down behind him before approaching and placing a knee in the compliant man's back while he tied his hands. Then he checked the first man's knots to make sure they were secure. They were a little loose, so he tightened them.

As Dan stood, more footsteps approached at a run down the slope. A voice called out, and Kai relaxed. Backup had arrived.

Three men burst through the nearest trees, spears at the ready, stopping when they saw Dan and Kai were in control. Then Dan started giving orders.

"We need a three-point escort, thirty yards across. Keep your eyes and ears open. These two men are assassins, sent to kill our only scout. We're taking them back to camp. One is slightly wounded, but isn't bleeding badly. I'll bandage him up when we get there."

"We can't take them to the camp," said Kai. "Someone powerful paid them. We need to keep them somewhere else for a while and get a message to Captain Benijah. Which of these three men do you trust the most?"

The three glanced at each other, seeming both confused and a little uncomfortable. One of them finally spoke to Dan. "You can trust me. What is the message?"

Dan stared at him a moment, then motioned him to walk with him a short distance, where they conversed softly for almost a minute. Then the man started jogging back up the hill. The other two soldiers stood at attention, awaiting orders as Dan returned.

"I know a place we can take these men," he told Kai. "It's secluded, and back trails will help us avoid the occasional night traveler on the roads. It will take a while, but it's worth it."

After ordering the other two soldiers to gather the discarded weapons and use the fisherman's trail to return to camp, Dan took the lead as they marched upslope. Kai brought up the rear, carrying Dan's spear, having given him back his sword. They crossed the road, entering tall grasses and brush, but soon Dan aimed them down a narrow trail heading generally southwest. As they walked, Kai prepared his line of questioning for the two men, his mind still spinning with the implications of what had just happened. Imrahiel had given him an assignment earlier that day ... had he changed his mind and now wanted Kai dead? That seemed the most likely scenario, and Kai cursed himself for telling Imrahiel he would be meeting directly with Moronihah after claiming to be a low-level spy. What an amateur mistake! It was still possible someone else had hired the assassins—another faction, maybe, or even Lamanite operatives—but that was highly improbable. He had blundered ... and nearly gotten himself and Dan killed for it.

Less than an hour later they arrived at a farmhouse surrounded on three sides by large trees which deepened the darkness. Freshly harvested farmland extended the other direction, expanding outward. The house appeared modest but well-maintained. It also felt peaceful, prompting some guilt about bringing two decidedly hostile men into it. Dan stepped up to the door and knocked softly with a distinct pattern.

About ten seconds later the door cracked inward a few inches. Kai heard whispers, and then the door opened further. Dan turned to Kai and motioned.

"Bring them in."

Inside, a single lamp had been lit, resting on a rectangular table with benches along the sides. Kai sat the two prisoners on one side of the table, then positioned himself across from them. Dan chose to remain standing next to the older man who had answered the door. The man was tall, like

Dan, and even stouter, as farmers tended to be. Kai looked from the older man to Dan, and Dan nodded, indicating his trust. Kai could hardly ask the farmer to leave his own house, but his questioning would be different … and certainly less useful … if the man didn't have Dan's full confidence.

"You haven't dressed my injury," complained the wounded man irritably, his face and voice flushed with pain.

Kai glared at him. "You don't trust we will?"

"No."

"Then I guess you'll have to worry about infection. You aren't bleeding to death."

The man scowled.

"But let's start with your friend. Normally, I'd talk with you separately first, but we'll do that later. How much were you paid?" He stared at the nervous man. Both men were a few years older than Kai, but this one looked younger than the other.

"A full onti of silver to split between us, because of the risk."

"What risk? Your job was to put an arrow in a man's back at night as he walked alone on the road."

The man swallowed, then shrugged. "The man who paid us said you were dangerous. He was right." Maybe he was trying to curry favor, or maybe he was being honest. It was hard to tell.

"Do you know the man who paid you?"

Kai heard the small kick under the table—a warning from the younger man's partner.

"I …" the man began, looking nervously at the table. His hands were still tied behind his back. "I'm not sure."

"Yes, you are." Kai looked at the wounded man. "Kick him again, and I kick you. Your friend here is far safer with us than with you. We can find him someplace safe. You can't."

The smugness in the man's eyes claimed he saw what Kai was trying to do. "There isn't any place you can take him that we won't find him."

Kai smiled. "We? You'll be tried by a military tribunal in the morning and hanged. It might even happen here. I have that authority." That wasn't quite true, but if Benijah came … "You won't get a chance to tell anyone anything. Your masters will know you failed, and that you both disappeared, maybe buried in the currents of the Sidon. That's it. Now," he returned his attention to his main target, "what does this man call himself, and where did he meet you?"

The man stared at the table for several seconds, as if memorizing the grain of the wood. He clearly felt terror, which by itself gave Kai valuable information about who he was dealing with. Dan took a deliberately noisy step closer, and the man winced. "He … he said his name was Zemek. There's a secluded garden near one of the canals. We met him there."

"Which canal?"

"The Dreamer."

"No, that's not the one. He didn't give you many details about me, apparently. I doubt he said his name was Zemek, either."

Now the younger man was truly terrified. Kai had insinuated this was an internecine fight, that he was just as cruel as the people this man thought he was working for, and that he knew them.

"Try again," Kai prompted, leaning forward.

The man licked his lips. "It might have been Two Veils."

Kai nodded. "Hmm … I know that garden. Sloppy choice." He had no idea where such a garden might be. He was starting to enjoy the interrogation too much, but it felt like he was getting somewhere. "Where did he direct you to report back? And don't try lying this time." Kai kicked the other man in the knee, hard, then glared at him. "And don't kick him."

The younger man sneaked a peek at his seething companion. His fear of Kai had clearly grown. Then he confessed, "There's a tailor's shop, near the Santorem, owned by a man named Helam. The building connected to it used to be a house—it's now a storage facility used by the tailor and a few others. Before daybreak we're supposed to meet him there and give proof we succeeded."

"Proof?" Kai was curious.

"Um …" The man looked away for a moment, then down at the table again. "Your right hand, the one with the birthmark."

It was a light birthmark, barely noticeable unless someone saw him up close. Imrahiel had, but so had various merchants and shop owners over the last few days.

"Hmmm …" Kai mused, "so if you take your partner's hand back, it won't work." He turned to the wounded man, who stared back malevolently. He was obviously far more indoctrinated and calloused. Kai held his gaze for several seconds, then looked back at the songbird.

"Who does the man you called Zemek report to? Have you seen anyone else with him before, including at Helam's shop?"

The man shook his head. "I don't know. And he's usually alone. Sometimes a young boy will come, to act as a runner if he needs something communicated quickly. And that's … that's all I know." Kai believed him, but he had one more question.

"Have you killed for him before?"

The man swallowed. "No, I haven't." He nodded to his left. "But he has."

"Yeah, I figured," said Kai, thinking. It had to have been Imrahiel. What should he do about it, though? He couldn't retreat to his scout role in the army and give up on the mission—it was too important. Could he play these events against Imrahiel somehow?

He suddenly realized how exhausted he felt. The adrenaline had dissipated long ago, and he wouldn't soon get any useful information from the wounded assassin. Since he was determined to stay in the game, he needed to get back to his room at the inn, and it was a long walk.

He looked at Dan. "Can you patch up our friend and keep these two here until I can get word to the captain on this location? I need to get back to the city tonight." The younger man's eyes widened at the mention of a captain, his shoulders drooping.

Dan nodded. "I already sent the location to him with the other soldier. I will go to Helaman's in the morning, but my brothers and uncles will guard them well. God go with you, brother. He makes you a hard target." His knowing smile gave Kai some additional confidence that he was making the right choice to step back into the shaken hornets' nest.

CHAPTER 6

O then despise not, and wonder not, but hearken unto the words of the Lord, and ask the Father in the name of Jesus for what things soever ye shall stand in need. Doubt not, but be believing, and begin as in times of old, and come unto the Lord with all your heart, and work out your own salvation with fear and trembling before him.

MORMON 9:27

The first bell of the day was only two hours off by the time Kai reached Jacob's Rest. He felt like old Father Jacob must have felt after wrestling with an angel. The difference was that at the end of that wrestle, Jacob had spoken his true name, despite his fears of being discovered by Esau's men. Kai still worked under an assumed name, and not a particularly effective one, either. His plans were a shambles, and he gambled his life by returning to the city. Perhaps that made him brave, like his ancient forebear. Or maybe it further exposed his foolishness.

Each day presented more evidence of how corrupt and dangerous Zarahemla had become. Almost getting killed strengthened that perspective greatly. So he made sure his door was securely locked, placing a chair in front of it to alert him if someone tried to enter. After checking his window, he let himself sleep deeply, though part of him felt reckless for doing so.

He woke after just four hours, primarily because a gnawing hunger attacked. The night's activities had drained his strength. Eating four more of the green candies had helped, but only a little. After happily noting he was still alive and that the chair hadn't moved, he refreshed himself by washing his face and hands. Then he walked casually downstairs to enjoy a full breakfast. He observed the room carefully as he ate, but he didn't notice anyone paying him undue attention. Surely Imrahiel had someone watching for him, especially since the assassins hadn't returned as expected. And Kai still had both his hands.

After a deeply satisfying meal, he shouted his thanks to the cooks as he stepped out the door and started for the main market. He had some follow-up visits to make to a few of the vendors, and he wanted to keep up appearances for Imrahiel's spies. Just another normal day for a fake merchant scout.

Time passed painfully slow, though. Compared to the last twenty-four hours, everything he did, every conversation he had, seemed mundane. He knew the sharpness of the prior day's events would dull over time, but getting there would be mentally arduous. What made it worse was his intense curiosity about the upcoming appointment with Raven. Would she actually meet him? Would he be ambushed again? The wait was barely tolerable.

At long last, when his thoughts had become large stickweed blossoms pressing against the inside of his skull, the time arrived to find the building across from the fine pottery shop—which he could accurately label 'Imrahiel's Lair' now—and meet his fate. Normally, he would mock himself for being so dramatic, but not today.

He arrived a few minutes early and leaned against the building to wait, glancing only occasionally at the pottery shop, wondering if Imrahiel lurked inside. Nobody had seemed threatening so far, but it was late afternoon, the streets filled with too many potential witnesses.

The eleventh bell of the day sounded. No Raven yet. He sat down, settling in. A fanatical law officer might question him about loitering, but the chances of that were small until darkness began to descend.

The warm afternoon sun beat directly upon him, but he was confident he could remain patient and alert.

"Hey, wake up, sleepyhead." A stiff, two-fingered poke in his upper arm accompanied the voice. His eyes snapped open, and as he regained consciousness a flood of humiliation crashed over him. Raven's voice, Raven's fingers. And she was laughing. He didn't even know when he had dozed off, or for how long. He awkwardly got to his feet, brushing off his rump. He blushed furiously, but at least he was still alive.

"I'm here," were his first words, hastily considered.

"I see that," said Raven, moving closer. She smelled of jasmine. "I wasn't sure you'd show, man-who-calls-himself-Adonai."

He smiled self-consciously, frozen between the urge to step away and the desire to edge closer. His eyes were wide open, but his mind still felt sluggish. He needed to right the ship, so he gestured up the street.

"Do we go now, or do we need to wait a little while? And it's Adonihah."

She quirked an eyebrow. "So, you're your own son. Adonihah, son of Adonai. Nicely done." She twirled, hooking him by the elbow and pulling him into the street. "Now is perfect. I haven't been to the Santorem yet today. My employer wanted me to come in the evening instead, to help him prepare for a dinner party. Some very important people will be there, apparently. You can come, if you like."

"What?" he said, perplexed. "I'm not invited to a dinner party at a noble's house. In fact, I've *never* been invited to one of those."

"No, silly," she said with a simper. "You can help serve the meal. I'll vouch for you. They won't mind the extra help. And they like me ... unlike you."

Unlike him what? "Are you saying you don't think I like you?"

"Do you?" She turned her head to consider him as they walked, her violet eyes competing with the jasmine perfume for alluring impact.

He swallowed. What would Siarah think if he said yes? He'd flirted as a spy before, but this felt different, in part because he worried about the real answer.

"Hmmm ..." He frowned slightly, trying to deflect. "Well, you seem nice."

She skipped a step, nearly stopping. "I seem *nice*?" A look of hurt and incredulity painted her face. He couldn't tell how much of her expression was real, though.

He coughed, trying to think. She could still be a valuable contact, if she didn't try to kill him. "Yes. Very nice. I mean, I don't really know anything about you. You're beautiful, but—"

"That's a little better." Her smile returned as she resumed their previous pace. Then she tilted her head, staring at him. They almost ran into an old man trying to get his cart across an intersection. "But what?"

Why did women always ask deeper questions? Kai wondered why it mattered whether he liked her or not. Was she toying with him for sport?

Or was she just incredibly vain? She *was* beautiful. She probably received a lot of attention from a host of potential suitors.

"But nothing," he said after a moment. "I like you, okay?" Would that be enough? He didn't really want to play this game. She seemed to sense it and backed off, if only a little.

"Well, I'm glad," she said, "because if you didn't like me, it would be harder to trust me."

He nodded. "True, I suppose." Her comment sounded ominous, given her link to Imrahiel.

They passed the entrance to the Santorem, which seemed even grander than it had the other day. As they walked up the main street, a different pair of officers nodded politely at them—or rather, at Raven. Less than a hundred yards later two private guards did the same. Raven started humming until they got to the first major cross street.

"So, where do you want to go first?" she asked. "We don't have to be at my employer's manor for another hour. You said there was something you wanted to see."

"Yes," Kai responded, making something up. "One of my employers wants to know whether one of his biggest trading customers still lives here, as he claims. He suspects the customer overextended last year and that his creditors seized his assets, including a house here in the Santorem."

"Ah," she said, "but wouldn't the property office have a public record of homes that had been seized? They wouldn't give you the name, maybe, but you'd know which house, right?"

It was a valid question, so Kai had to think quickly. "This is a highly secretive, well-connected man. The records don't show anything, but my employer is still suspicious." He shrugged. "And I don't really care. He's paying me. I'll take it."

She laughed lightly. "Yes, I would, too. All these nobles are secretive, and it's hilarious sometimes to watch them pretend everything is perfect when it's so obvious they're putting on a show. I actually burst out laughing once in front of an obnoxiously rich man and his wife shopping for gaudy rugs; I had to make a quick excuse."

Would Raven laugh if she found out who he really was? Probably not. And *he* didn't pretend for show.

She stopped. "Okay, which way?"

He pointed left, and they continued in that direction. At the second street he turned right, at random, and she followed, staying by his side but not holding his arm any longer. He pretended to scan the houses on either side of the street, nodding greetings to the few people they encountered, including another set of private guards. Three quarters of the way down the street, he turned to Raven and said in a low voice, "Next house on the right, with the gray shingles."

She didn't look immediately, which meant she was at least decent at surveillance and keeping up covers. She slowed her pace though, and when they were in front of the house, she halted, pretending she had gotten a pebble in her shoe. She voiced loud annoyance as she stooped to take it off, adding a lengthy display of shaking it out and making sure nothing else inside would threaten her tender flesh. Kai was able to alternately glance at her and cast his eyes around, taking note of the unknown house. It wasn't one of largest, but it certainly fit the style and opulence of the neighborhood. The exterior was clad in both brick and richly stained wood, enhanced by large, ornate windows. The double doors were broad enough for a small carriage to pass through, and he spied at least two lamps already lit inside, though the sunlight had only recently begun to fade.

Raven replaced her shoe, then slapped him on the chest in another burst of flirtation. "There, all fixed. Did you see what you wanted?"

Kai nodded, not looking again at the house, and they started walking again, her arm once again in his. "We still have plenty of time," she said. "There are some nice shops here, including a few where you can sit down and enjoy a meal. We should eat before we have to ... you know ... serve fancy food to other people and watch *them* eat."

"Lead the way."

After two more turns, she led them to a narrow, two-story building set back from the street a few yards. It sported a beautiful garden out front, featuring tall flowers in reds, golds, and purples among various bushes, some of which yielded different kinds of vegetables and spices. Narrow trees bordered either side of the garden, matching those running down the center of the street. They were as healthy and well-pruned as any trees Kai had ever seen.

Raven pulled Kai inside, then pointed at a small square table with two chairs, set against a side window. "We can sit there. I know the owner. I'll ask him to bring us a simple meal—we're not rich like they are." She waved her thumb toward a man and a woman at a different table. The woman noticed her and frowned. A group of three men sat at another table, but they were deep in conversation.

An open archway stood at the back of the room, and Raven rapped on the side of it, waiting until a wispy-haired man with a bushy mustache emerged. He recognized her and smiled. It seemed everyone in the area knew Raven. They spoke for a few seconds, and then she returned to the table, where Kai still stood.

"You don't have to wait for me to sit," she said, smiling in a teasing way, but she still sat first.

Kai took his seat without responding. He had determined he needed to hold his tongue—unless asking her something that could provide useful information.

"I can pay," offered Kai, instantly breaking his new rule.

She winked. "No need. It goes on my employer's tab. As long as it's reasonable, it's no problem. Of course, there's two of us, but you'll be helping tonight, remember?" Kai was sure he was being played. But for what? Maybe she was working with Imrahiel to get rid of him a different way. That thought settled in him with a bone-deep chill.

"Who's you're employer?"

Her eyes twinkled with fake intensity as she sized up the question. "Well, I guess I can tell you now, since we'll be there soon. It's High Judge Zerahir. He was Pahoran's biggest ally. He seems like a nice enough man on the surface, and he works hard to keep up appearances, but he's a hungry lion underneath, and he loses his temper a lot when he's at home."

"Aren't they all hungry lions?" offered Kai.

She laughed. "Yeah, probably. It's hard to tell which ones have the sharpest claws, though."

Kai nodded in agreement.

"I like his wife," Raven added. "She treats us all well. It's why I've stayed so long."

Imrahiel had mentioned she was perhaps becoming sympathetic with a high judge. What a prize for him to have someone on the house staff of a powerful man like Zerahir. Did he have more than one person there? Kai nodded again, then noticed the owner bringing them two plates of food along with two mugs on a large serving platter.

"That was fast," he said as the man laid down their plates.

The man smirked slightly. "This is easy food to prepare."

It was true: each dull plate held some vegetables, a thick slice of bread, and a small chunk of meat, cooked simply and with few spices. These were not the fancy plates the man created for his wealthy customers.

Raven seemed happy, though, and she attacked her food with vigor using the incongruous-looking silver fork on her wooden plate, not even glancing at the man as he placed the mugs and left. Kai thought about commenting on her dining etiquette, but decided against it. He began eating at a more moderate pace, though the amount he put in his mouth each time was twice what she did. She must have been hungry, because she didn't try to talk while she ate. When she finished, she produced a small napkin from a pocket in her skirt, then delicately dabbed at the corners of her mouth, as if she were a high-born noble and had just completed her meal in a stately manner, instead of the mad rush he had just witnessed.

He coughed to cover a laugh, and she narrowed her eyes. "What?"

"Nothing. You like food. That's normal."

"Ha ha, funny. I haven't eaten all day. I had too much to do. I don't get many days off."

He acted appropriately chided, but then another teasing smile broke through of its own accord. "Sorry, I understand. I've had a busy day, too."

"Oh? Finding decent clothes to wear for me? I like what you picked out."

He glanced down at his clothes, in plain tans and browns. They were nothing special, though they weren't as dull as the laborer's outfit he had worn when she'd first seen him. "Thank you," he replied as if she hadn't mocked him. "I can't afford anything fancy."

"Well, you and I have that in common," she said in a dulcet croon. "So, should we head for the high judge's? I'll explain the basics of what we have to do tonight as we walk."

He wasn't sure he was ready. He was likely walking into another trap. But he told himself he would be careful, and if he spotted anything developing he would be the aggressor and look for a quick escape. That wasn't easy to do on foreign territory, but represented his only option short of abandoning the mission.

They entered through the back of the sprawling manor, having seen at least three guards as they passed through the outer gates, then an inner gate, and finally the servants' entrance. The guards appeared competent, and he wondered with concern whether the high judge himself could somehow be working with Imrahiel. Or at least pretending to. If either case were true, Kai's chances of surviving the night had just dropped considerably.

They proceeded to the large main kitchen, a beehive of activity generating an array of amazing smells that made their just-eaten meal seem extremely bland. The air was warm, too, despite several open windows. Two giant cooking hearths dominated one wall, both blazing at full output.

"Hi, Artus," Raven said to a middle-aged man carving strips of cooked mutton into precise chunks. "This is Adonihah. He's going to help serve tonight."

The man looked up blankly, glanced at Kai, said "Hi," and returned to his work, having barely skipped a beat.

"He's grumbly sometimes," Raven explained. She kept to the side of the kitchen opposite the hearths, stopping near a middle-aged woman mixing a salad in a very large bowl. "Keriah, this is Adonihah—Doni for short. He's helping me tonight."

Doni? Kai hated the awful nickname. She was punishing him.

The woman gave Raven a patronizing smile. "That's nice, dear. I'm sure he'll be useful." Her eyes swept across Kai before she returned to work. She could have been Artus's sister. Or maybe they were married. Kai didn't ask as Raven started moving again. She didn't stop until they had left the kitchen through another doorway. They walked down a short hallway, and then she opened a door to lead him into another room. One young man occupied the room, his shirt off.

"Oops," said Raven. "I always do that. Sorry, Raphem." She turned to Kai. "You can change into your uniform here, Doni. There should be an extra one that fits you. Raphie can show you." Without giving Kai a chance to respond, she bounced out the door to disappear down the hall.

Kai carefully inspected the room. There were no other doors, only a small window high up in the wall. Boxy wooden drawers stood stacked against the two side walls, and two benches occupied the middle.

"Did she call you *Doni*?" asked Raphem.

Kai nearly grimaced. "Yes, she did."

"Did you pick that?"

"Nope."

The young man smiled. "Well, she's something. I didn't pick Raphie, either. I pity the man who tries to figure her out. It sure ain't gonna be me."

Kai gave a short laugh. "You're wise. So, where do I find a uniform?"

Raphem had pulled on a puffy-sleeved shirt with broad blue- and cream-colored vertical stripes. His breeches were black and fit him snugly. He walked barefoot across the room to one of the drawers sitting at about chest level. He pulled out shirt and breeches and handed them to Kai. "These should fit. The lower drawers have thin stockings and soft shoes—they don't want our footsteps being too loud, of course." He winked.

"Thanks," Kai said, taking the clothes and wondering about the fancy stockings. He made sure to close the door before dressing, but he noted it didn't have a lock. Raven could 'accidentally' pop in at any time. His bigger worry was that he wouldn't be able to hide his knife in the uniform unless he strapped it to his forearm. And he couldn't do that with someone watching. Raven was smart to make him weaponless. Kai wondered what would happen if he just withdrew. He tried to think of an excuse to leave.

After a few moments of indecision, he decided to stay and see it through. He was curious what the dinner party would be like, anyway. Who would be there, and what might they say when not paying attention to servants within hearing? Of course, whatever intelligence he might gather would be useless if he were dead by the end of the night.

He had barely gotten the uniform on when Raven opened the door and stepped in, following another young man who had come to change. "Sorry," she said again. Raphem was lacing up his shoes. He just smiled and shook his head without looking up.

Her act made Kai more suspicious by the second. She had done this before. Who else had been a victim of a trap laid by Raven? Maybe Imrahiel had already set him up a second time. Well, this would technically be the backup plan, since the other assassins had failed. He wondered whether Captain Benijah had made it to the farmhouse yet.

"You almost ready?" she asked. Kai was amazed at how quickly she had changed. Her blouse was diagonally striped in orange and yellow, her skirt a shimmering lime green topped by a wide leather belt dyed a deep crimson. She had a bright orange scarf in her hair, too, to hold her black locks back from her shoulders, which were partially bare.

"Two minutes," he said. She smiled and nodded as she left, leaving the door open again.

He shook his head, copying Raphem, then examined himself in the polished steel mirror pegged to the wall near the door. The uniform wasn't so bad. He had worn more exotic things on some of his eastern missions. He quickly found stockings and shoes—the stockings a shockingly expensive and non-dingy white—aiming to be out of the room before Raven returned again. He deposited his street clothes in a different drawer after asking Raphem what to do with them, reluctantly leaving behind his precious knife. In such an opulent mansion, and working near the kitchens, there would hopefully be plenty of items he could improvise as weapons.

He had just followed Raphem out of the room when Raven almost ran into him.

"Okay, here we go. This'll be fun." She grinned giddily and patted his cheek. Then she grabbed his hand and led them back toward the kitchens, where the serving staff had lined up against the wall opposite the hearths, awaiting the signal from the chief servant to proceed with the first course of the meal. Kai was surprised the guests had already arrived. He hadn't heard much activity beyond the kitchens, although it was an exceptionally large house.

They stood waiting for at least fifteen minutes, watching as the dozen or so cooks made the final preparations. A few items covered with cloth were placed near the hearth to stay warm for later. Other dishes went into a chiller.

It had to be the last of the ice, and they must have packed it thick in a deep cellar to survive the summer so it could be used now.

Finally, a floppy-haired man wearing a bulbous maroon hat and a long black cloak over his white shirt and voluminous blue breeches entered the room, looking both regal and harried.

"Hear now, be sharp everyone. We've had a few additions to the party, including Master Pacumeni and His Eminence, High Priest Helaman." A few gasps followed, mainly from the cooks. Kai felt Raven stiffen next to him. Excellent—something unexpected to throw off Imrahiel's plans. Pacumeni and Helaman would both have their own guards. Kai had never heard Helaman called 'His Eminence,' and he wondered how Helaman might react to that title. Kai had never met him, though he'd seen drawings and paintings depicting him. He was only five years older than Kai.

"We must be *perfect* tonight," the man continued, glaring sternly around the room. His eyes settled on Kai for a moment, and then he looked with intense inquisitiveness at Raven. He seemed about to comment, but then he clapped his hands, raising his voice. "Two minutes! First dish in two minutes!" He whirled and left the room, expertly flourishing his cloak.

Kai turned to Raven, who had relaxed. "This *will* be fun," he whispered. "I've never been within a mile of this many powerful people gathered in one place."

She elbowed him in the ribs. "Don't tease me. I shouldn't have brought you. Liram won't fire me, but I might not be getting any more free meals." She seemed highly displeased by that.

Soon they marched out of the kitchen carrying small serving trays with the first dish: marbled bread infused with some sort of pudding, accompanied by impossibly thin slices of melon wrapped around steamed carrots. Kai had a hard time imagining how those flavors would work together. He supposed his unrefined taste explained why he wasn't a chef or an obscenely wealthy man.

He tried to mimic the way the other servants carried their trays into the magnificent dining room—some holding just one plate, like him, and some two—then prepared to model their precise actions as they began to set plates in front of the guests. They moved in a line, each person exiting the room after delivering their plates. A quick count told him there were twenty-one people seated around an impossibly large table. He had seen big tables before, but this one looked extremely heavy, too. It must have been assembled in at least five pieces.

He brought his mind back to task in time to serve the next person around the table, roughly opposite of where Helaman and Pacumeni sat at either arm of the man who could only be the high judge. Zerahir was narrow-shouldered and broad-waisted, with a wide nose under glassy brown eyes and straight brown hair. To Kai, he didn't look like a high judge, but he certainly dressed like one. He even wore one of the stylish new hats with a fluffy tassel that toppled over the brim.

Pacumeni was dressed much the same, but without the hat. Helaman was different, just as Kai—and his father Gideon—would have expected. His simple brown cloak hung on the back of his chair, and he wore a tai-lored white tunic with medium-length sleeves. His slightly curly brown hair was thick, his beard short and well-trimmed. Unlike everyone else at the table—including the half-dozen women—no rings decorated his fingers. Instead, he bore a simple brass marriage band around his right forearm. Kai couldn't decide whether this man of just twenty-six years of age really looked like the prophet—the leader of all the Christians throughout the lands of the Nephites. Helaman's uncle Shiblon had died the year before and transferred the mantle to him. Or, as Gideon would say, the Lord had transferred the mantle.

Helaman didn't appear intimidated by the company, or even out of place. His parents would have trained him in etiquette, of course. He chatted amia-bly with the man on his left as he waited for everyone to be served. He noticed Kai staring at him, and his light brown eyes locked onto Kai's. At the same moment, Kai heard a soft hiss from the exit. He realized he had stopped after placing his plate, so he started moving again. There were two more servants behind him. Kai knew he had caused a noticeable holdup, and now Raven would be in even more trouble ... but perhaps he in less, unintentionally.

When he finally exited the room, he expected to be accosted by Raven or the maroon-hatted chief servant, Liram. Instead, Raven came up beside him as they walked toward the kitchens to await their orders regarding the second dish.

"Why did you stare at Helaman?" she asked. She seemed calmer than expected.

"I'm sorry," he said, shrugging. "I'd never seen him before. He's so young."

"So? You're younger, I'm guessing."

"Yeah, but the Christians call him their prophet. Shouldn't the prophet be someone older, more experienced?"

It was Raven's turn to shrug. "I don't know. I read something he wrote once, to . . ." She trailed off, then continued. "Well, it wasn't what I expected. I didn't know how to interpret it. He's a smart one, at least. And smart people are the cleverest in their deceptions."

"Unless they're too proud," said Kai. "Arrogance makes people do really stupid things."

"Yeah, I guess that's true. And smart isn't the same as well educated, anyway." They had reached the kitchen, where they joined the line along the wall again to wait.

Nearly twenty minutes passed before Liram made his next appearance. The dinner group must have been enjoying a long discussion. And, frustratingly, Kai couldn't hear a word of it.

Liram clapped his hands, as before. "Get the second course ready. We will serve the plates all together this time, not in a course around the table. And you," he pointed an admonishing finger at Kai, "what is your name?"

"Adonihah," Kai answered with a deep bow.

"You've done this before, yes?"

"Of course," Kai lied. Well, it wasn't quite a lie. He *had* done it before. Twenty minutes ago.

"Well, gather your wits, boy. We're not gawking at the guests."

"Yes, master," Kai replied before straightening.

Liram frowned, then expanded his scowl to everyone else in the room before flourishing his cloak again as he left. All eyes then fell upon on Kai.

"What did you *do*?" asked Artus.

Kai was about to respond when Raven spoke. "He was curious about Helaman, who gave him a funny look. I probably would have paused, too. And if you worry about Doni, you'll mess up yourself. So don't."

"I'm sorry," added Kai. "It won't happen again."

Amid a few grumbled murmurs, the cooks finished the second dish—meats, dates, and small potatoes. Some of the meats were wrapped in leaves Kai didn't recognize. As the servants marched out of the room with the plates, Kai was careful to maintain the right distance from the person ahead of him. When they entered the room, they all took places around the table. The man who had led the line was clearly the head server, because everyone waited for him to nod before laying the plates before the guests. Kai was a fraction of a second late, since he was mimicking the others, but it wasn't noticeable. He didn't even glance at Helaman this time, though his mind itched to sneak another look. Once the plates were placed, the head server turned and walked sedately toward the exit door, the group smartly uncurling from around the table as the line formed and extended out of the room.

Raven was right behind Kai this time. "Good job," she whispered just after they had passed through the doorway.

He glanced back at her. "Were you nervous I'd mess it up again?"

She laid a hand on his shoulder. "No. Well, maybe."

He laughed softly but still got a "Shhh!" from somewhere up ahead in the line. He almost laughed louder, then regained his senses. He wasn't there to flirt, or pretend to flirt, or whatever he was doing with this woman who had likely lured him there to be killed.

They returned to the kitchen and lined up yet again. The process was almost as boring as an extended surveillance. And he *still* wasn't learning anything.

"What's the third course?" Kai asked after a couple of minutes to break the monotony.

One of the older cooks glared at him, turning from her preparation of some sort of pie. "It's dessert, you lemuelberry," she snapped. "Mistress Lianah allows no more than three courses. I'm sure Raven told you that." She didn't look at Raven, but it was clearly an accusation.

"Oh, right," said Kai. "Yeah, I forgot. She told me. But why only three?"

Raven tensed next to him again. She probably wished he would stop asking questions.

The same woman stared at him a moment as if he were a dumb animal. "'Cause she wants, and that's enough for you."

"She thinks it makes her look humbler," said Raphem. "I don't know if it does, but some of the other ladies of high society say it's pathetic behind her back. I like it, personally. How many different types of food does a person need at one sitting?"

Kai saw a few slight smiles and nods from the other cooks and servers, but the woman just switched her glare to Raphem for a moment, huffed as if he wasn't worth responding to, and returned to her work.

Kai was about to inquire about some of the high-society women when a guard walked in through the back door, short spear in hand.

"Which one of you is Adonihah?"

Kai sized up the man. He had a confident air about him, and he looked experienced. He wasn't one of the guards Kai had seen when he and Raven passed through the grounds to enter the manor. So was this the play? Take him out back? Separate him from the others? Helaman's guards were probably all inside. Pacumeni's also. He should have thought of that.

"I am," Kai said, taking a step forward and raising a hand. The guard's eyes snapped to him. They were hard to read, but they definitely weren't friendly.

"Come with me, by order of High Judge Zerahir." He turned and walked out, expecting Kai to follow, which he did. He wished he could somehow swipe a knife as he left the kitchen, even a small one, but that was impossible. As soon as they had exited, another guard materialized, falling in behind and staying a few paces back. Kai didn't recognize this guard, either, and his senses were alert for the slightest threatening movement, from ahead or behind. Before reaching the back door of the manor, the first guard turned to ascend a staircase—the one servants would use to service the second floor. Kai found it odd—going out back or down into a cellar made more sense.

At the top of the staircase, they turned right, toward the front of the manor. For half the length of the hallway there were doors on either side, but then it opened up, giving way to railings on the left side. A cross hallway led off at that point, too, and when Kai was able to view the open area, he found himself looking over the grand central foyer, which featured a wide, straight staircase in the middle. Two opulent hanging lamps graced either side of the foyer, each capable of holding at least a dozen bright flames encased by small glass panels in intricate wire framing.

They proceeded to the last door off the hallway. The first guard opened it, then stepped aside and motioned for Kai to enter. Kai figured it would be a small room, where they could easily overpower him in a confined space. If he could jump the railing and avoid breaking an ankle in the landing, he could escape through the front door.

He hesitated and gave the guard a quizzical look. "Why was I summoned? Nobody even knows me here."

"Precisely," said the guard behind him. The first guard didn't change his expression. "We just have a few questions for you." He motioned again for Kai to enter.

As convinced as part of him was that an ambush awaited, he didn't feel that impression from either of the guards. So, continuing to appear innocent while maintaining full alertness, he crossed the threshold.

The room was much larger than expected, appointed with the finest furniture and decorations for honored guests. Smooth paneling of a dark wood lined the walls, and several plush rugs covered much of the floor.

The front of the room had been arranged as a sitting area near a large window overlooking the now mostly dark street. In a thickly-cushioned chair, positioned in the corner facing Kai, sat Helaman. A third guard stood about ten feet away, his eyes conducting a quick study. It didn't matter how many guards there were, though; Kai felt instant, joyous relief in Helaman's presence.

Helaman remained seated as the first guard ushered Kai to a chair on the other side of the window, at least ten feet from Helaman. The man then stationed himself in the corner a few feet behind Kai. The second escort closed the door and remained outside in the hallway.

After several seconds, Helaman spoke. "High Judge Zerahir said he had never seen you before, and I noticed you watching me. Why?"

Kai swallowed, trying not to appear nervous. "I wasn't originally planning to be here tonight, and I didn't think you'd be here, either. It is an honor to meet you, though."

Helaman's face showed some surprise, and he glanced at the guard standing behind Kai. Kai could almost feel the man frown. Helaman returned his gaze to Kai.

"Why *are* you here?"

Kai couldn't tell him it was top secret and therefore he couldn't say. He was talking to *Helaman*.

"I presume you have full trust in these two guards?" asked Kai carefully.

Helaman blinked, then clasped his hands and settled them comfortably in his lap. "I do."

Kai nodded. "Good. My name is not Adonihah. It's Kihoran, and I'm from Bountiful. I joined the army seven years ago as a scout novice. I do more than scouting now. After Pahoran was assassinated, Moronihah asked me to come to Zarahemla. A dangerous game is still being played here, as I'm sure you know. And that's all I feel comfortable saying right now. I'm sorry."

Helaman considered that information for nearly a full minute. His eyes had shown only a hint of additional surprise. Of course, he already knew how treacherous the waters were.

"Assuming you're telling the truth, why does Moronihah trust you?"

Kai frowned slightly. "I'm not sure. I'm good at my job, and I don't think I've ever let him down, but I'm not the most skilled or experienced person he has. I'm honest with him, though, and he and I both know how important it is to preserve the freedom of this nation."

Helaman turned his head to stare out the window, breathing deeply. "If this nation isn't worthy of being preserved, then it shouldn't be. After the vast providence we've been gifted, we still reject the word of God, and even his love. It's hard to believe sometimes how foolish we can be."

Kai felt the pure melancholy in his voice. He cast his eyes toward the floor, having no response.

"You are a Christian, I presume?" asked Helaman.

How did he answer that question in the presence of the prophet of the Lord? Was he, truly? He had been baptized, and had tried to be faithful and obedient to the statutes and ordinances. He had no serious doubts that Helaman, and many great leaders before him, were prophets and prophetesses.

"I am," replied Kai, raising his eyes and feeling his conviction grow a bit in saying it with such firm feeling in front of the prophet. "And I will die one. I'm not as knowledgeable as most. I can't do miracles or anything. But I will defend the cause of the Christians to the last drop of my blood."

Helaman considered him a moment and then nodded soberly, seeming at least ten years older than he was. "I hope that's true of both of us. But don't presume you can't do miracles. You have probably already taken part in many, and there will be more opportunities—that I can promise."

"How do we know he's telling the truth?" said the guard behind Kai.

Helaman took another deep breath. "I feel like he is, but you're right. We should be careful." He focused again on Kai. "Kihoran, can you tell us anything else?"

Kai knew he must. "Captain Benijah can vouch for me, since Moronihah has just left. I met one of Benijah's guards, too, who said he sometimes serves in your house. His name is Dan. He was one of the two thousand led by your father."

Helaman's eyes widened slightly. "You know Dan?"

"Yes. I met him last night after speaking with Captain Benijah. He knows me only as Adonihah, though."

Kai felt the guard shift behind him.

"What is it?" asked Helaman, looking again at the guard.

"Dan was supposed to report at the house last night, but he never showed."

Helaman's eyes snapped back to Kai, suspicion suddenly evident. "Where did he go after you met him?"

Gravity leaked into Kai's voice, and he couldn't withhold anything now. "We intended to come to the city, but two men ambushed us along the road. We captured them, and they're at a secure location. Captain Benijah may have already interrogated them. I don't know if Dan returned to the camp. He told me he would be coming to your house today."

"You expect us to believe that?" said the guard.

"No, I probably don't," Kai replied, not daring to turn his head. "But it's true." He maintained eye contact with Helaman, hoping the truth would be evident in his eyes.

"You said you didn't expect to be here tonight," continued the guard. "How did you get in?" It was a little unnerving to be questioned from behind, but he felt no fear.

"A young woman who calls herself Raven. She was right behind me in the last serving line."

Helaman and the guard shared a brief look. "I presume the name 'Raven' isn't on the list of approved servants."

"No, it is not," confirmed the guard.

"Find out her real name," Helaman ordered. "Send Emer right now." The other guard in the room immediately strode to the door, opened it, and had a brief conversation with the guard outside. In the meantime, Helaman's attention returned to Kai. "She's your … target?"

Kai nodded. "She clearly has some connections, but I don't know how high up they go. I believe one of those connections sent the assassins last night."

Helaman whistled. "And you still accompanied her here?"

"Yes, sir. I had to try. A chief judge was murdered, and the assassin hasn't been caught."

Helaman nodded slowly and solemnly, studying the floor for a few moments. "Despite our best efforts, we keep running into roadblocks. Where are you staying?"

"*Jacob's Rest*, in the Jewel Quarter."

Helaman hummed. "A decent choice. The cooks there are as good as I remember?"

"Better, probably. I'm eating well. I'm not spending too much of the treasury's money, either."

Helaman laughed suddenly, which seemed odd and yet completely ordinary. Couldn't a prophet laugh?

"I believe you, Kihoran. I think I spend far too much of the treasury's money—the people's money—myself. The cost of my personal security alone has doubled since the assassination."

"There are wicked people who would stop at nothing to eliminate you."

"And there are people who would sacrifice their lives to save me, though I hope I never have to accept such a sacrifice. Unfortunately, it has always been so in our great eternal battle against the ambitious and diabolical former Son of the Morning."

Kai was no expert on the scriptures, though he was sure he'd heard that term used to refer to Satan before.

"I believe you to be sincere, Kihoran," Helaman continued after another brief pause. "My guards will check out your story, of course, because … well, that's what they do. I could have one of them tail you back to the inn tonight if you wish."

Kai shook his head. "Too risky. But you could send one ahead to the inn for a meal to make sure I get there. If I don't, Captain Benijah should be notified … and Raven should be questioned."

Just as he finished, the guard named Emer entered the room and shut the door.

"I have her name, sir."

Helaman cocked his head. "Who is she?"

"Her name is Arayah. She is the younger daughter of Nahom, a lower judge in the city. She has been employed here for about nine months and receives high marks for her work from Lady Lianah."

Helaman narrowed his eyes in thought. "Thank you, Emer. Nobody else need know we inquired. You spoke only with Lady Lianah about this, correct?"

"Yes, sir."

"Good. I will speak with her before I leave. Shortly before that, you will go to *Jacob's Rest*, enjoy a meal, and await this young man's arrival." He gestured at Kai, and Emer gave a sharp nod before retreating through the door.

Helaman looked at Kai. "So, now you know her name. Does that help you?"

Kai nodded and smiled. "And the name of her father. Yes, it does. Thank you. Hopefully this can accelerate things. I'll have to be careful, though."

"Of course. Now, you should return to the kitchens. I think the service is done, but there are always a few late requests from guests, especially among people who enjoy far too much food than they could possibly need." He sighed. "You can tell the other servants my guards questioned you, but everything is okay. Which is true."

"For now," added the guard behind Kai.

Kai ignored that, though it sent a slight chill down his spine. "Thank you, sir," he said to Helaman, making as if to rise. "So … I'm free to go now?"

Helaman laughed again. "Yes. It pains me I had to question you in the first place. But such are the times in which we live. And it was useful, besides. Thank you, Brother Kihoran."

Kai rose and thanked him again, a lump forming in his throat at the prophet's warm use of the word 'brother' to address him. He acknowledged each of the two guards before walking to the door. After opening it carefully, he quietly stepped through. He descended the back stairs and went to the changing room first, to get out of the uniform. When he arrived back at the kitchens, the cooks were busy fulfilling some special requests that had just come from a few of the guests, just as Helaman had predicted. Half the serving staff were still there, including Raven. The look on her face was a tortured mixture of worry and relief. Real or faked, he couldn't tell.

"What happened?" she asked immediately, not trying to be quiet, her eyes widening as she took in his change of clothes. "Am I going to be fired for bringing you here?" She waved a hand around the room. "That's what everyone is betting." He sensed more than nervousness in her tone. She seemed genuinely afraid, which he could understand. Since she was in Imrahiel's secret employ, getting fired from a job in a key high judge's household would be terrible for her.

"Well, they all lost," said Kai with a relaxed chuckle. "Helaman's guards just wanted to make sure I checked out, since I wasn't on the original list of servants for tonight. His inclusion in this dinner was last minute, so nobody could have known. And these are dangerous times, right?"

Relief flooded her eyes.

"I take it dessert went well?"

She let out a quick breath. "Yes, without a hitch, though we all noticed Helaman had already left. I guess he doesn't like desserts. We're just mopping up now—that is, fulfilling the remaining guests' whimsical requests. Nothing unusual about that."

"Okay, well, I think I'll just leave now."

Keriah, who was working on some sort of pastry dish, raised an eyebrow. "Without getting paid for your work tonight? Mistress Lianah wouldn't hear of it."

Kai laughed. "It's okay. I was just doing this to help a friend." He glanced at Raven, who seemed a little shocked. "She can collect the payment for me and then split it up among the rest of you. I did make a silly mistake, after all."

Keriah appeared confused for a moment, but she just shook her head and kept working.

"Thanks for letting me help," Kai said to Raven as he started toward the rear door of the kitchen. "Good night."

A second later he heard, "Wait!" as Raven rushed to catch up with him. Then she turned to the others. "Let Mistress Lianah know I wasn't feeling well and Adonihah walked me home, okay? She'll understand."

It was Keriah who nodded and shooed them out, smiling slightly. She might have winked, too, but Kai wasn't sure.

The guards gave them no problems, and when they were on the street, Raven took his arm again, letting him lead.

"I'm sorry," she finally said. "I didn't know Pacumeni and Helaman would be there."

"It's okay. It was interesting. I learned a lot." Indeed he had.

"I think Zerahir's up to something," Raven said. He waited for her to elaborate, but she didn't.

"What do you mean?" he finally asked. "Everyone in this city is up to something. Including you and me."

She didn't look at him, and her tone remained serious. "Yeah, but we're nothing. We're not even garden snakes compared to these leviathans."

Kai shrugged in the soft moonlight. "Hasn't it always been that way? People in power are born into it, and they make sure the rest of us stay in our place. When they fight with each other—which is almost constantly— we're the ones who get the most bloodied. Take the assassination of Pahoran. It has already led to more conflict, more commoners dead. I was orphaned because of such in-fighting."

He had taken a risk by talking about his personal life, but he wanted to see how she would react. He hadn't taken a position for or against any faction, just against the violence factionalism caused.

She walked in silence for a while. As they approached the entrance to the Santorem, she said softly, "My father believes we just need to put the right people in charge. The smartest people, not the ones with the right lineage."

Kai nodded but kept pressing. "Who chooses *them*? How do we know they're the smartest? And what does being smart have to do with caring about people?"

She tugged him left down the first street outside the Santorem. After a few seconds, she said, "Don't let my father hear you say that. He'll assume you want the common people to keep selecting our leaders. How can you and I know who is best to vote for? It's the richest and most powerful who can afford the best influencers and construct the most elaborate, believable lies." She sounded bitter.

Kai pondered her statement. He was getting somewhere . . . if, that is, he wasn't about to be murdered by Raven and Imrahiel's friends. He abruptly pulled her to the right down another street, making sure she wasn't the one dictating the route. She didn't pull back, just asked, "Where are you going?"

"I want to see something," he said. "I can't tell you what it is, though. I have too many bosses."

"Ooh, you're so mysterious, but okay." The flirtatious Raven was back, at least partly. Her willingness to follow him didn't preclude them from being tailed, but it meant if he were going to be attacked, he would at least have some warning—and he had his knife back.

After a few blocks and several turns, he stopped and faced her. "All right, done. So how do we get to your house from here?"

"My, aren't you forward," she said coyly, fluttering her eyes in the light from a streetlamp. She still wore her garish serving uniform. Had she even noticed?

"But you asked me to walk you ho—"

"I'm teasing, silly. I didn't really ask you, though. I just said you would, and you didn't object." She winked, then pulled him forward by the elbow. "And we just happen to be very close to my house." She giggled, walking faster. Kai's heart froze for a moment as he realized the ambush could be set near her house. Was that why she hadn't objected to him leading the way?

Two minutes later she stopped, pointing. "There it is. Home sweet home."

Kai looked around warily before focusing on where she had indicated. The house was nice. It wasn't large, but it had two stories, and through the narrow gap between houses Kai spied what appeared in the dimness to be a little garden in the back.

"Well, it's a fine home. And, um, thank you for an interesting evening." He smiled, then started to turn, senses alert for anything unusual.

She latched onto his wrist, and he was proud of himself for not jerking it away.

"Do you want to come inside and meet my father? My mother passed away a couple of years ago."

"Oh, I'm sorry. And sure, I guess so. Will he be up? It's pretty late."

She smiled. "Knowing him, yes, he will be. And he'll be curious why I brought someone home. I never do that."

Kai had no idea if she was telling the truth, and his senses heightened further. He was about to change his mind and refuse, but before he knew it she had whisked him inside, closing the door gently behind them.

The front room was modestly appointed, though he couldn't see much in the meager light. An archway to his right led to another room, perhaps a dining room. A lamp flickered at the back of the house, and she led him down a narrow hallway toward it. The stairs were probably off the kitchen in the back, which was common. Only two doors led off the hallway, one on either side. She signaled toward the left door as they passed.

"That's my room. It's small. My little brother sleeps across the hall. My father and older sister have rooms upstairs. There's a privy attached to the kitchen down here, and another upstairs. They both connect to the sewers, but sometimes the sewers in this area get backed up. It's not pretty."

She had stopped in the kitchen, a twin in size and shape with the front room they'd entered. "My aunt usually helps with the cooking," she continued. "I work a lot, and my sister is … well, she's *not* a cook."

The stairs were at the side of the kitchen, as expected, and Kai soon heard steps descending—just one pair of feet, and not in a hurry.

A refined-looking man with dark hair emerged after reaching the bottom of the stairs, wearing a dull gray sleeping robe and soft slippers. He looked to be in his early forties, but there was no sign of graying in his hair or narrow beard and mustache. His face was thin, his eyes a bright hazel. He cocked an eyebrow as he saw Kai, then looked at Raven questioningly. "You have brought someone home, daughter?" It was clear he was really asking *why* and *whom*.

Raven gave a slight bow. "This is Adonihah, Father. He's a merchant scout from Bountiful, here on business, and we met in the market when I was shopping for some things for Lady Lianah. High Judge Zerahir had an important dinner tonight. Helaman and Pacumeni were there. Adonihah helped serve, as a favor."

"Oh?" Her father's face instantly perked up, and Kai knew it had nothing to do with him. "You must tell me all about it. Later, though." He looked at

Kai, turning himself to face him. "Welcome to Zarahemla, young man. My name is Nahom. You seem young to be a merchant scout so far from home."

Kai thought the comment insincere and condescending, but perhaps her father was just trying to unnerve him. Given he was still alive, he was okay with that.

"My master just lost one of his older scouts to a competitor," Kai replied. "I'm still learning, and it's my first trip to Zarahemla. The city is even bigger than I thought."

Nahom smiled, but the grin didn't reach his eyes.

"Where are you staying?"

Oh, here we go again, thought Kai. "*Jacob's Rest*, in the Jewel Quarter. Just for a couple of weeks, though."

Nahom nodded, as if pleased Kai would be leaving the city soon. "So, what did you think of the high judge's house?"

Kai was about to answer when a soft knock sounded on the kitchen door. Nahom's eyes widened slightly, and then he extended an arm toward Raven to usher her and Kai back toward the front of the house. "Please take your young man to the front, and don't let him stay lo—"

He was interrupted as the kitchen door opened, admitting a man in a long, dark-gray cloak. He was taller and leaner than Kai, his hair nearly blond and his eyes dark. He was probably close to thirty years old.

The man froze momentarily when he noticed Kai. He flashed an angry look at Nahom, ignoring Raven completely. But then he regained his composure and bowed slightly.

"Forgive me for intruding, Master Nahom, but I bring important news regarding one of the cases currently before you."

"I was just leaving," said Kai. "It was nice to meet you, Master Nahom, and your daughter as well. I'll let my master in Bountiful know I was well received." He bowed to both Nahom and the newcomer, then retreated down the hallway, Raven following him all the way outside, where they stopped after a few steps.

"I shouldn't have brought you here," she said, sincere worry permeating her voice. "I'm sorry. That man you just saw, he's ..."

"He's what?"

"Well, he wanted to marry me, but I adamantly refused, and … well, I think he's a little bit unstable mentally, and I … oh, what a mess. I'm sorry, truly."

Why was she so earnest in apologizing? Kai found it odd at first, but then he realized she had just inadvertently led him to a clue regarding the evil plaguing the city. And she knew it.

"What's his name?"

"His name?" She looked flummoxed. "I … can't tell you his name. I'm sorry, again."

Kai was certain he could remember the blond man's face and find out more about him. Perhaps this encounter would ultimately lead him to Pahoran's assassin. Oh, how he hoped so. He'd never wanted anything so badly in his life.

CHAPTER 7

But before ye seek for riches, seek ye for the kingdom of God. And after ye
have obtained a hope in Christ ye shall obtain riches, if ye seek them; and
ye will seek them for the intent to do good—to clothe the naked, and to
feed the hungry, and to liberate the captive, and administer relief to the
sick and the afflicted.

JACOB 2:18-19

When Kai entered the common room of Jacob's Rest, he spotted Helaman's guard alone at a table with a half-eaten plate of food. He didn't let his gaze rest on Emer as he ambled toward the stairs, though a sense of gratitude suffused him. Once he was safely in his room, it fully registered that the day had ended and he was still alive. He had spent much of the last twenty-four hours assuming he would have to fight again for that survival, but nothing truly threatening had happened. Maybe Benijah had extracted additional information from the assassins and acted quickly to protect him. He was intensely curious to find out.

He paced his room for at least two hours, reviewing everything that had happened. He had some solid leads. He had made a good ally in Dan and felt deeply honored to personally know one of the two thousand. And he had met Helaman, the young prophet. After reliving their conversation at least a dozen times, he knew he had experienced something profound, even transforming. But he didn't know what it meant, nor why Helaman had let him go so easily. If Kai had been in Helaman's place, the questioning would likely have continued much longer.

It was well past midnight before he took to his bed, and even then, he lay awake for another hour or two. His mind should have been exhausted, but it kept racing like a frightened rat trapped in a barrel. When he finally grew drowsy, his thoughts turned to Raven—or rather, Arayah—and then Siarah. Foolish fancies frolicked in his mind. Two different roads. Two sets of possibilities. By the time he fell asleep, his conscious mind had dismissed the fear that Arayah was trying to kill him, though his unconscious mind still proved difficult to convince.

Kai went downstairs early, a long stretch of uninterrupted sleep having eluded him. His first surprise was seeing Emer seated with another man at one of the tables, neither in a guard's uniform. They certainly made him feel safer, but they also potentially jeopardized his mission. Imrahiel's spies would eventually notice that some of Helaman's guards were watching Kai, and he didn't know how Imrahiel would interpret that.

But there wasn't anything he could do about Emer at the moment, so he requested breakfast from the cooks and sat down to wait. He had brought some parchment and an expensive lead stylus, like some of the merchants now used, to continue some notes he had been working on in his room.

His food came, and as he ate he recorded everything he had experienced the past two weeks, searching for any details or connections he might have missed. For example, why had Melekai chosen to sit with him at the inn in Lehi? Was it because he was young and wore a merchant pin? Had he appeared persuadable? Why had Mistress Havah immediately sent one of her men into Sidom? Was that man one of those who had attacked him there? Were the two captured assassins military trained? They seemed to be, though no two soldiers could be expected to stand against one of the two thousand. And what had Kai said in his conversation with Imrahiel that would have caused him to send those assassins the very same day? He thought he knew, but was he right?

He ate slowly as he thought, and the combination of his deep concentration and the security Emer provided caused him to let his guard down.

He didn't notice that three men had approached and now stood to his left. When one of them spoke, he nearly jumped out of his seat.

"Master Adonihah, you have been summoned by the judges for questioning regarding the disappearance of one of the army's soldiers." The man said it loudly enough that most of the quarter-full room could hear.

Kai studied the officer for a moment. The man clearly had many years of service under his belt. "I'm not sure what you're talking about," he said calmly, "or how I can help, but okay. Where are we going?"

"Central office. You need not be restrained if you agree to come quietly."

Kai glanced at Emer, whose face was painted with curiosity. Then he rose, keeping his hands in plain sight. "Can I just grab my notes here?"

The officer nodded, and his two companions spread out to form a triangle around him, as if he were dangerous or might try to escape. Kai didn't risk another look at Emer. Imrahiel's spies were probably going insane trying to figure out the scene.

The four of them emerged onto the street, then walked briskly among the light crowds. The sun was up, but not strong yet. Kai figured it wouldn't do any good to question his escort, so they continued in silence for several minutes until they reached the majestic three-story stone structure that housed the central law offices of the city. A larger two-story edifice surrounded by stout fencing squatted next to it. The city's main prison reached two levels below the ground as well—any deeper and it would constantly flood.

Two guards kept careful watch at the entrance to the law offices. They glanced at Kai curiously as he was led inside, perhaps because he was surrounded by three officers and yet not restrained. He had never been on this side of Nephite justice. He presumed he would be led to a thick-doored stone cell somewhere. Hopefully, he wouldn't have to wait longer than a few hours to be questioned.

But instead, the officers marched him up two flights of stairs to the top floor, where the senior officers and investigators had offices. They directed him into one of those offices, a spartan affair with a simple desk and five chairs, then asked him to sit along one wall. Two of the men took position outside the door, leaving it open, while the other one, instead of staying with Kai, left for some other part of the building. They had let him keep his parchment and stylus, and they hadn't searched him for anything else, which meant they had inexplicably allowed an armed man onto the third floor of the central law offices.

Ten minutes later, Captain Benijah stepped through the doorway.

"Adonihah," he said, winking, "welcome. I hope you weren't too worried about why you were brought here."

As Benijah closed the door and took a seat behind the small desk, Kai shook his head. "No, not really. I was curious, of course. But why *am* I here? And where are Dan and the two assassins?"

Benijah set his arms on the desk, leaning forward. "We've had some fascinating conversations with our two guests. Dan decided against going to Helaman's house right away. He continues to remain with them, and we've created a story that Dan himself went missing. Only his wife and children—and Helaman now, of course—know the truth. His family have placed themselves in quarantine, claiming they're very ill."

Kai thought about that for a moment. It seemed like a smart idea, but what did it have to do with him?

"So why did you bring me in for questioning by linking me with his disappearance?"

Benijah nodded, frowning. "I thought long and hard about this. You're in serious danger, Kihoran. I know you understand that, but I just spoke with Helaman this morning. You were at High Judge Zerahir's house last night. There are at least two spies in his household we're watching closely. You left with someone else, went to her house. That was good. You may have found a third spy, and we now have Nahom's house under surveillance. But it's too hot now. You've done an amazing job in an extremely short period of time. I'm astounded, quite frankly. But now I need to get you out of here, keep you safe. In fact, I think Moronihah would never forgive me if I didn't."

"Wait," said Kai, feeling flustered. "I have to *leave*? There are leads to follow. I'm making real progress. I know it's dangerous, but that's what I signed up for, and my life isn't worth more than anyone else's. What if ... what if you kept me in prison for a few days, and then let me go? You could spread another rumor that the law officers think I was involved, but nothing can be proven. That would make our enemies think, and maybe buy me some more time. It might even *endear* me to them."

Benijah appeared to consider the idea for a moment, but Kai could tell it was just for show. He smiled. "I know this might disappoint you. But it wasn't my recommendation. It was Helaman's."

Kai leaned forward abruptly, disappointment overcoming his deep respect. "So what. He doesn't have any authority over the military—or over the law officers."

Benijah maintained patience, though it was clear Kai had just drawn him to the edge. "True. But as the prophet, he has authority with *me*. I asked him the same questions you're asking. He listened. And then he told me it was necessary to get you out of here. I trust him on that. You should, too."

Frustration boiled inside him, but he didn't have an adequate response. *Listen to the prophet* was what Gideon and Ishara always preached. Benijah was telling him the same thing, and Kai knew the man wouldn't budge. So, he would have to accept the change of plans, but he let his objections show unmistakably on his face. After a few seconds his jaw hurt from gritting his teeth so hard.

"All right," he finally said, looking out the window at the Zarahemla skyline, refusing to meet Benijah's gaze. He knew his behavior was childish, but he was angry. "Where am I going?"

Benijah waited a few seconds to respond. "I don't need to know that. Nobody does. But it must be at least fifty miles from here, and you'll be there at least four months. Then you can send a message to me, and I'll respond. You can be angry, soldier, but you will obey orders. Dan isn't too happy, either, but he knows how to obey orders—especially from someone he knows he can trust."

That comment stung. Kai nodded in embarrassment, returning his gaze to the captain. "I'm sorry, sir. How do I leave Zarahemla without being seen?"

"In a refuse wagon tonight ... driving it, not buried in it." He leaned back and grinned, spreading his hands in mock apology. "It's still not a pleasant duty, but it'll work. You'll be in disguise, too. We'll circulate the story that you're in prison, awaiting further questioning. I've chosen only men I can reasonably trust to know anything about this."

Kai nodded. "Thank you, sir. And I trust you. But I think the number of people we can truly count on dwindles by the hour."

Despite his many travels and his upbringing near a rural area, Kai had never driven a wagon. Luckily, and unexpectedly, he didn't have to drive that night. He found himself with an experienced wagon driver, a gnarled older man missing at least two teeth and smelling almost as bad as the load they hauled. The trash dump sat to the northwest, so after exiting the city they followed the main road north for a few miles until it forked. At that point, Kai bid the driver good night and hopped off, disappearing into the brush while clutching his travel pack, which had been retrieved from his room at the inn by none other than Emer.

He knew some small ferries operated a few miles farther north, and Benijah had advised him not to use the main ferries near the city. But he was also a good swimmer, and there was always deadwood available along the shore that could provide additional buoyancy and some protection from the river's undertows. He didn't need to cross the river in a straight line, anyway. He just needed to reach the opposite bank so he could make for Aaron and Nalani's house—and his horse. So he chose to swim.

The water wasn't too chilly, and both the wind and the current were calm. The crossing took about twenty minutes in the moonlit darkness, after which he set out at a slow jog up the bank and toward the road. Within another hour he had arrived at the house, his clothes nearly dry. He figured the fifth bell of the night approached, but light danced dimly in the home's interior, so somebody was still up. He knocked softly on the front door, taking a step back to wait, prepared to bed down under the trees for the night.

In a few moments, the door cracked open and an eye peered out. Then the door opened wide, revealing Aaron's face, split by a wide grin.

"Kai, you're back, and so soon! You look . . . well, a little bedraggled. Come in, come in. Can we get you something to eat?"

"Thanks, Aaron, I'm fine. And full. In fact, I've probably been eating *too* well." He patted his stomach for emphasis. "I just came to get my horse, and then I'm off on another assignment."

"Oh? Where to?" Aaron grabbed a small lamp and stepped outside, closing the door behind him. Then he started walking briskly toward the barn, Kai keeping pace.

"Melek," said Kai, though that wasn't his intended destination.

"Melek. I don't think I've ever been there. I hear it's nice … and much calmer than Zarahemla." He chuckled. "Did your business go well?"

"There were a few surprises, but overall I feel like it went very well. My master will be pleased, I think."

Aaron turned and smiled, not breaking stride. "That's great. You're a good man, and a hard worker. And smart. I see great things in your future, Kihoran of Bountiful."

Kai shrugged and mumbled a thank you as they approached the outer barn doors. Aaron swung them open and led them inside, pausing to hang the lamp on a large nail.

"I've been keeping him in the barn sometimes," Aaron explained, "especially at night. He's a highly valuable horse, and … well, I trust most of my neighbors, but not all of them."

Kai appreciated his friend's diligence. "Thank you, sincerely. And I can pay you for keeping him and feeding him."

Aaron waved the suggestion away as he proceeded deeper into the barn. "No, no, it was no trouble at all. We didn't have him long. Besides, and I hope you don't mind, I've bred him with three of my mares, so I probably owe *you*. In fact, if at least two of them conceive, you can have one of the foals. Honestly, I couldn't find a better sire than your horse. Maybe you can bring him by again … say, about this time next year? I'll pay you up front. And it looks like he's only about six years old, so he could sire a lot of fine horseflesh."

Kai chuckled. "That's fine, as long as I can make it work. I can't tell you where I'll be next year, or when I could come by, unfortunately."

Aaron stopped and slapped him on the shoulder. "I know, my friend. But I'll hope for it." He pointed. "Here's his stall. The saddle is right there on the post. I need to get back inside and help Nalani with the kids, who are having a hard time sleeping tonight for some reason. Don't worry, it has nothing to do with you; we've been fighting them for a couple of hours. I wish you could stay, actually. Are you sure you can't?"

Kai nodded. "I'm sure. In fact, I'm already running late. But thank you again, and I'm hoping for that foal you just promised." He smiled and tried to wink. His skill hadn't improved.

Aaron gave him a quick hug—another new behavior—then grasped his shoulders. "Travel safe, Kai, and take care of that horse." He laughed—a rich, hearty laugh full of comfort and contentment. Aaron really had made a good life here. Kai was happy for him.

"I will. Say hi to Nalani and the kids for me."

"For sure. Goodbye, and God bless you."

After Kai had picked up the saddle and led the stallion out of the barn, Aaron took the lamp and retreated toward the house, shouting back another benison. Kai then set to preparing his horse for travel. He set a new goal, too: the horse would have a name by the time he reached his destination.

The city of Gideon, almost due south, was only half as far from Zarahemla as Melek, and it met Benijah's fifty-mile requirement. Barely. Even traveling unhurried, Kai arrived in less than two days. He had passed through Gideon only once before. Situated along a tall bluff on the east of the river Sidon, it commanded impressive views of the fertile countryside and thick forests nearby. He noted the taller hills surrounding the larger area, which the locals called the Valley of Gideon. Being from the east, the hills were small, so it didn't look like much of a valley to him.

Gideon still carried a strong reputation as a hotbed of anti-Nehor sentiment. By and large, the Gideonites exhibited strong loyalty to Christ's Church, much more so than many of their brethren and sisters in Zarahemla. They were also fiercely independent, producing some of the finest soldiers in the army.

Nehor the Strong had been in his prime when he killed the aging namesake of the city, who had dared stand up to his vainglorious preaching. Following a trial before Chief Judge Alma the Younger, Nehor had been hanged on the hill Manti. That was during the first year of the reign of the judges, eighteen years before Kai was born. Almost forty years after Gideon's murder, the people still paid him high reverence because of his vital assistance to Alma the Elder and King Limhi in leading a great number of the people of God out of captivity. The fact that he had spared the grotesquely selfish and cruel King Noah when the Lamanites invaded Lehi-Nephi only seemed to burnish the luster of his reputation. The monument the Gideonites had built in the center of the city to honor him had recently been expanded, the news of the project traveling across the nation. The tower at its center had nearly doubled in height and was now surrounded by a circle of houses and shops forming the inner ring of a grand new marketplace. Access to the tower, which offered guided tours, was controlled by members of his family, who lived in some of the surrounding houses.

Kai passed through the marketplace in the late afternoon, noting the difference in the atmosphere. It wasn't as crowded or frenetic as the main market in Zarahemla, and buyers and sellers alike seemed happier. That was the magic of good, honest, voluntary exchange, especially when people felt they could trust each other.

The city of Gideon was growing, especially outside the walls; Kai had witnessed large numbers of homes under construction as he rode in. The land to the east of Gideon sloped gently downward, and the area was fast filling with people. While some parts of the Nephite nation shrank—especially with the recent emigrations northward—Gideon flourished.

He hadn't forgotten to name the stallion before passing through the city's tall gates. The name Vyim—which in its old Hebrew form invoked a sense of enduring trust—had come to him suddenly when the city first came into view, and it seemed wholly appropriate.

Kai knew who he wanted to contact first. Shemnilom was an old priest with an infectious laugh and a shockingly full head of brilliant white hair. He was also one of the best spies in the entire nation. He didn't do much field work himself any longer, but his web of contacts continued to produce astounding results. Kai had met him twice—once in Bountiful, and once near Zarahemla. Moronihah held Shemnilom in awe. So had his father Moroni.

Kai had learned that Shemnilom spent most of his time in one of the synagogues near the heart of the city. His sons and daughters largely provided for him now, or at least they thought they did. His spymaster pay was quite comfortable, and much of that money went to helping people in trouble— for all kinds of reasons—get back on their feet. Shemnilom hadn't told Kai that secret, of course. Moronihah had let it slip once, then made Kai swear he would never tell Shemnilom nor anyone else. Kai smiled at the memory.

After securing Vyim outside the synagogue—which was at least a hundred years old, from a time when the city hadn't been called Gideon—Kai found the wizened priest in his office at the back. Shemnilom's hearing was still sharp, so he was already standing, waiting for Kai to step through his open doorway.

Recognition dawned on his face. "Kihoran," he said, smiling broadly, eyes twinkling. "It's been almost two years, has it not?"

Kai was amazed at his memory. "Yes, Master Shemnilom. But this time I'm under orders to stay hidden for a time. I just came from Zarahemla."

Shemnilom gave a sympathetic frown. "Ah, that old viper's nest. I've lost two spies there in the last year—one defected, the other is dead. And I'm having a devil of a time trying to get actionable information on the shadowy group pulling most of the anti-government strings there. I thought I was close to identifying some of the big fish, filleting them, and getting them into the frying pan … but that was when one of my spies turned up dead, floating down the river with an arrow through his throat."

Kai almost reached for his own neck. Shemnilom didn't need to know how close he had come to dying the same way, at least not yet. Or maybe he already knew; Kai wouldn't be surprised.

"Anyway," Shemnilom continued, "I presume you were in Zarahemla on a mission from Moronihah? And you discovered some things—or some people—that got you into serious danger? Well, you're welcome to stay here as long as you like. In fact, I have a room in the synagogue where you can sleep, and I live close by with my youngest son and his family, though he's about to be a grandfather, too. Which means I've journeyed past 'old.'" He winked, with genuine mirth in his eyes. "But sit for a minute, please." He motioned Kai toward a chair, and they both sat.

"So," said Shemnilom, "we're in the stew now, aren't we? The chief judge has been murdered, rumors are flying every which way about who did it, and Moronihah is preparing for another invasion by the Lamanites—who, by the way, probably had nothing to do with the assassination but sure as the north star are trying to take advantage of it. And Zarahemla—along with a few other cities—is about to explode like a bad melon. Exciting times, my young friend, exciting times."

Kai gave him a sickly smile. "You don't sound too worried."

Shemnilom laughed. He actually *laughed*. The outburst seemed incongruous in the situation and yet somehow natural.

"Perspective, my son, perspective. When you've seen as much as I have, you know the Lord plays the long game and outsmarts all of us combined. I stopped trying to outthink him a long time ago, and I finally learned to trust him, too. Most of the time, anyway … I guess I'm still working on it." His smile didn't diminish in the slightest. "This life is an important test, and all he asks is that we do our best—with his help, mind you—and then eventually we go on to the next step. I'm not afraid of that next step. In fact, some days I welcome it. It will be nice to see my parents again." He chuckled, and Kai's smile became grim.

"Maybe I'll join you. I don't want to spend the next fifty years living under tyrants, whether they're Lamanites or Nephites."

Shemnilom nodded, his grin slowly fading. He leaned forward, placing his arms on his tiny desk. His eyes filled with wisdom and compassion. "I know, son, but I'm going to let you in on a little secret. This people will continue to pass through stiff trials, but it will be many decades before it gets as bad as you fear, and then only for a relatively short time. The Messiah is coming to the earth soon. I can't say when exactly, but perhaps in your lifetime. Certainly not in mine. Sometime after he comes, he will make his promised atonement for our sins—which is the sole reason for our eternal hope. And then he will visit his people here. Right here, in this land, as has been foretold. Such miracles the people will see then. But we see many miracles now, too. We just don't notice them as much as we should."

Kai had heard the prophecies. He had even seen some of them fulfilled. But the promised future events were still uncertain in his mind. When exactly *would* the Messiah come, and how would his coming affect Kai's life and the things he did with it? He found it impossible to piece everything together on his own. That was why he was willing to follow faithful, strong-minded men like Moroni and his son Moronihah. Like Shemnilom and his father Gideon, too.

"Why are we so stubborn?" Kai asked, staring at one of the wobbly-looking legs of the desk, which threatened to buckle with the old priest leaning forward on it.

"We're human," responded Shemnilom, "and we live on a fallen earth that doesn't yield the necessities of life easily. We achieve varying degrees of success controlling our physical passions and taming the land, but we're always jealous of each other, and constantly tempted by the adversary and his multitudes of disciples. We're also children of divine heritage, and such royal progeny can indeed be arrogant. We think we know better, and we want other people to acknowledge we know better. We want followers, people who will do—and even think—what we tell them, often by force, and we pretend that is what defines success."

He paused, growing more solemn. "Some people give themselves over completely to Lucifer's enticements and false promises. They will do anything to win—quite literally anything, including murdering and enslaving others—while actively rebelling against God or aggressively ignoring him. God doesn't ask us to do 'whatever it takes' to achieve good goals. He will never prompt us to lie, cheat, steal, or kill, even if our ultimate intentions seem good to us … unless necessary to directly blunt the hand of the evil one under the Spirit's direction, as we must do sometimes with our spying. Do you remember Ammonihah?"

Kai had always been intrigued by the story of Ammonihah. The infamous Nephite city had been utterly destroyed almost thirty years ago. It remained uninhabited. "The city's leaders murdered the innocent wives and children of the Christian men they had forced to flee the city," Kai responded. "Then they kept Alma and Amulek captive until God destroyed the prison—with the city's chief judge inside—and led the prophets out. Less than a year later, the Lamanites razed the city, killing everyone. For some people, that fear of the Lord's wrath alone keeps them in line."

"Yes," said Shemnilom, "but making an example of the fruits of Ammonihah's treachery wasn't the Lord's primary purpose."

Kai's eyebrows rose. "What was it, then?"

Shemnilom sat back, crossing his hands on his stomach. "What happened when High Priest Alma was rejected in Ammonihah the first time, and he left?"

Kai thought back to his studies. "An angel instructed him to return, so he could find Amulek and try again to call the people to repentance."

"Yes, that was certainly part of it, though Alma didn't know Amulek yet. But what was the first reason the angel gave for commanding him to go back?"

"Um …" Kai stumbled, but Shemnilom didn't leave him flailing for an answer.

"The angel said the leaders of Ammonihah were studying to destroy the freedom of the Lord's people, of the entire Nephite nation. The Lord, through Alma and Amulek, gave them a final chance to divert from that dark and violent path, which they rejected, and then he took care of the threat. The people were ardent Nehors, by the way, some of them more ruthless than Nehor himself."

"The cult of Nehor is still alive and well," noted Kai.

"Yes, but they're more fragmented now, and strong places of moral and political sanity exist, like this city, and like Bountiful. People across the nation notice how well we do here. We are blessed, and they know it. Some of the really bad ones fear it."

"But some don't."

"True. The people who killed Pahoran don't fear God's wrath. They either believe God doesn't exist or that he favors *them* in their quest to impose—by deception, fear, and violence—a 'new, benevolent order' of things. For most of them the motivation is primarily greed and lust for power, but for some few … well, they think they've somehow risen above the human condition, as if they're now demigods who can lead us all to a future of no want and zero conflict, provided we give them control of every aspect of our lives, down to our very thoughts. It's naïve, putrid nonsense, and always has been. You can't force humans to improve their condition. You can only teach them truthfully, encourage them to cooperate, and open them up to God's influence."

Kai hadn't expected to receive such an intense lecture, but he deeply respected Shemnilom. He had been offered sanctuary, a place to lie low, in a city where he felt safe, with the added benefit of some powerful mentoring. Perhaps he could rest a bit, too. He doubted he would let himself, though.

<hr>

The first day of Kai's 'rest' was emotionally excruciating. Myriad thoughts crashed into each other at breakneck speed, over and over, and he couldn't banish any of them. First and foremost, it pained him that he had been removed from the game, at least for the time being. He had told Benijah everything he knew, and while he hoped others could pick up the various trails he had left and find some success, not being involved at all left him thrashing in a dark void.

Shemnilom seemed to understand. Kai could only imagine the things the aged priest had experienced in his life—events far more difficult than anything Kai had yet faced. The perceptive spymaster didn't ask whether Kai wanted to talk about how he felt, but he did make sure he was available if Kai chose to open a discussion.

Some intense physical training got Kai through the first day, especially a long run to the nearest village to the south and back. A narrow footpath wound down the southern edge of the bluffs, offering a welcome challenge in both directions.

The active garrison in Gideon was tiny—no more than a hundred men. However, most of the city's strength resided in its militia, and Kai learned they conducted regular drills and training exercises, except on the Sabbath. Shemnilom gained him a favorable introduction, and Kai enjoyed participating in their training, quickly noting the many skilled fighters he could learn from. Some had experience in multiple battles, including the defeat of the Lamanites the prior year. Three hundred of the men of Gideon had mustered for that conflict, in addition to the Gideonites in the regular army, and only one had been lost.

By the time the third week rolled around, Kai felt calmer, mostly. He still longed for news from Zarahemla—especially anything stemming from the groundwork he'd laid—and he pestered Shemnilom constantly. The long-suffering priest usually nodded in understanding, enjoining patience. Benijah hadn't instructed Shemnilom not to let Kai in on what was going on, but Shemnilom himself still awaited news.

On the fourth day of that week, a messenger arrived at the synagogue with some parchments for Shemnilom. Ostensibly, the young man only delivered messages and instructions from the Church of Christ. But Shemnilom let Kai know the young man carried intelligence from time to time as well, as he had that day. Unfortunately, Kai had to wait several agonizing hours for Shemnilom to review all the documents first. Normally, Kai could handle waiting, but current circumstances enhanced the severity of the test. Eventually, after full dark had fallen, Shemnilom called Kai into his office and asked him to shut the door.

"So, how are things in Zarahemla?" Kai blurted as he inadvertently slammed the door and then sat.

Shemnilom rubbed his temples. "Still relatively quiet. Perhaps too quiet. Most of the targets we've been tracking have gone to ground for a while. They don't seem to be doing much. Of course, the election is next week—or rather, that's when the first results will start arriving in Zarahemla to be tallied, a little later than anticipated, and then the citizens of Zarahemla will cast their ballots. It seems pretty certain Pacumeni will be the next chief judge. Helaman could easily have the position if he wanted it, and some have tried to convince him to take it, but I know he doesn't want to return to the practice of the Church's high priest also being the chief judge."

The news was anti-climactic. Boring beyond belief. Kai couldn't decide how that made him feel—a sense of emptiness and lack of purpose remained, drumming a steady beat in the back of his mind. Maybe Shemnilom wasn't telling him something.

"Any word on Dan?"

Shemnilom quirked an eyebrow.

"Dan is one of Benijah's guards—and Helaman's. He made the arrangements to sequester the assassins."

"Ah, yes, sorry. No, nothing about Dan, or about the assassins. I assume they're still being held in the same place. Benijah can't risk transferring them to one of the prisons. They've 'disappeared,' after all, and I'm sure that's giving certain people serious pause. It's a good play."

"And nothing on Raven—er, Arayah, and her father Nahom?"

Shemnilom shook his head. "She's still working at High Judge Zerahir's home, and her father continues performing his duties as a lower judge, but they haven't been doing anything suspicious. I'm sorry, Kihoran, there just isn't much happening. We'll have to wait a bit longer. You're here for a few months, anyway. Perhaps the timing is perfect."

Kai nodded as if he agreed, but he was sure Shemnilom discerned his deep disappointment. He desperately wanted to be doing something useful, and at the same time he was growing upset with his own impatience. He'd been proud of himself for waiting wisely in previous situations, like his last trip east. But now he felt anxious and unsettled almost constantly. He knew he needed to change. To grow up. To be more faithful and persevering. Shemnilom made no further comments, just clapped him on the shoulder and dismissed him.

He slept fitfully that night, but somehow woke rested. Shemnilom told him during breakfast at his son's home that he wanted Kai to review a sermon he planned to give on the coming Sabbath, so he could have a different perspective on it. Kai knew he was just offering him busy work, but he accepted.

He also invited Kai to travel with him to two villages that day, so he could deliver food to a few people in need and leave the members of the church some messages he had written out. Kai agreed to go, but as they began their ride out of the city, he felt a little self-conscious. Shemnilom rode a hybrid animal that looked to be more mule than horse, while Kai towered over him on Vyim, whose coat gleamed in the scattered sunlight lancing through scudding clouds. Shemnilom seemed perfectly content with the circumstances, however.

The walls of Gideon weren't nearly as magnificent as those protecting Zarahemla. They didn't stand as high or wide, and they looked utilitarian instead of grand. They seemed sturdy enough, though, and the few men who manned them as hardy as could be found anywhere. Kai and Shemnilom traveled due east at first, along a minor road that climbed and fell across low hills, keeping to a fairly straight course. Farms dressed much of the landscape as far as Kai could see. There were some cattle, too, but not many. Most of those ran farther south.

Scattered clouds remained throughout the morning as they journeyed to their first stop—the village of Esther's Rock. Kai couldn't see any large rock formations in the vicinity, so he presumed the name was metaphorical. They stopped before a modest home near the large well in the center of the village.

After dismounting, Shemnilom retrieved two large bundles from the panniers on the back of his half-mule. He smiled at Kai. "Pimli is one of our teachers. He helps care for the Lord's flock here. He does some trading, like you, but he also has a small farm about half a mile away. We'll drop this food and clothing off with him or his wife, and they'll make sure it gets to the families who need it. He's the one who sent me the request."

They approached the door and knocked. A few moments later a dark-eyed, auburn-haired woman with a wide green apron opened the door. She beamed. "Brother Shemnilom, you're here. That was fast. Come in, please."

As she ushered them in, Shemnilom introduced Kai, using a cover. "Sarah, this is a visitor from Lehi. His name is Coren. He's staying with me while he trains with the men of Gideon. He wants to be a soldier."

Sarah looked at Kai with admiration. "Thank you, young man, um ..."

"Coren," Kai said, smiling.

"Yes, Coren. Sorry, my mind is always a bit frazzled with four kids running around. Luckily, two of them are napping right now."

Kai didn't ask where the other two were, but he could hear the laughter and shouts of many children somewhere in the distance outside.

"Where shall we put these?" asked Shemnilom as he held out the bundles of food and clothing.

"Here," said Sarah, extending her arms. "I'll take them to the back." She hesitated, giving him an uncertain look. "But don't leave yet. You have time to chat for a few minutes, right?"

"Sure we do," said Shemnilom with a warm laugh. "We'll wait right here."

There were only two chairs in the room, so Kai and Shemnilom sat on cushions. Sarah returned quickly, taking one of the chairs. Her eyes fluttered as they focused on Shemnilom. She seemed nervous.

"I'm sorry Pimli isn't here. He went to help Joren with some of his cows, even though ... well, he knows nothing about cows, but I think it was an issue with a fence, so he figured he could help."

"Don't worry about that," said Shemnilom with a reassuring wink. "We'd just as soon talk to you as him anyway. How are the children doing? And your parents? I understand they were ill recently."

Sarah blushed slightly, then answered. "My parents are fine now. It was nothing serious, and the doctor was in the area and gave them a new medicine, which nipped the illness right in the bud. It was amazing. I don't remember which herbs he said were in it. One of them was callum, I think."

"And the children are healthy?"

"Yes, yes, they're doing well." She blushed again. Kai wasn't sure why. She obviously had a high regard for Shemnilom, so perhaps she felt awed by his aura of celebrity.

"Good. What are they praying for these days ... the older two?"

That seemed an odd question. Well, to Kai it did. Sarah didn't seem fazed by it.

"Well, they're ten and eight, both baptized, as you know, and they come up with some insightful things." She smiled. "Kyrion prays for all the seeds the farmers will plant in the spring. He names the different types of seeds, and sometimes he names the farmers. Abish prays that everyone will be kind and help each other. She names a lot of people, too, especially if she knows about some … um … difficult situations. It's a wonder to hear them pray, sometimes. I wish I had their simple faith."

Shemnilom grinned broadly. "Well, some of that faith is their own, but much of it comes from their mother and father. You're more faithful than you realize. Life is filled with so many challenges that it's often hard to recognize how well we're doing in God's eyes. He only asks that we do our best as he tries to teach us, though. He promised us the opportunity to become like him, and he's fulfilling that promise every day. Keep praying with those wonderful children. Study the scriptures with them, too. Work hard with them, and have fun, too. You will help each other succeed—not just for the next life, but for this one as well."

"Thank you, Brother Shemnilom," Sarah said humbly. Her nervousness returned, stronger. "But there's one other thing. I …" She hesitated, glancing at Kai, then the floor, then Shemnilom, then the floor again as tears welled up in her eyes and streamed down her cheeks. "I have been unfaithful to … to my husband. And now …" She took a deep, shuddering breath, wiping away a few of the tears. "I am with child, and I know not if that child is Pimli's." She burst into more tears, which quickly became great, heaving sobs.

Kai blinked, stunned and distinctly uncomfortable. He looked at Shemnilom, whose face twisted in sorrow, his eyes radiating deep compassion.

"Sarah," Shemnilom said softly several times before she got her sobbing under control. She gazed at him while soaking up tears with her apron. "Sarah, this is serious. I know you know that. But there is a path through this that leads to forgiveness, happiness, and peace. That path will require honesty—which you've started to demonstrate today—humility, and hard work."

"But … but the Law of Moses." Stark terror pulsed in her eyes.

Shemnilom gave her a tender smile. "The Law of Moses points us to Christ and prepares us for his higher law. I fear you've been listening to the literalists again. Sister Sarah, I can't say how everything will work out, just that your Heavenly Father loves you very much and will help you. He *will* help you. He is disappointed, but not angry. I will help you, too, along with some of the sisters. Have you talked to any of them?"

She shook her head. "No, just you."

"All right. Well, please speak with Sister Dinah. She has been called to assist in these kinds of situations, and she has much experience and a compassionate heart. I'd like to ask you a few questions first, and I'll request that young Coren here step outside and care for our horses while we talk."

She bobbed her head, seeming somewhat numb but at least calmer. "Okay."

Kai took the cue and immediately got up, bowing to Sarah before leaving. The room felt heavy, and yet light had already begun to fill the space. Kai could sense it. She had just released a great burden, though more challenges would come.

He had completely brushed down Vyim and the half-mule before Shemnilom emerged from the house. His expression was one of melancholy mixed with hope. Kai didn't say anything, just followed the kind priest's lead as he mounted and turned up the street. Kai knew they would head north from Esther's Rock to their second destination. It was shaping up to be a long day. But at least this visit gave him something to ponder.

"Such is the sacred opportunity of ministering to each other," Shemnilom said solemnly as they passed the last house in the village. "Most of the sorrow in the world doesn't come from our mortal frailties or natural disasters—it arises from the ever-abundant harvest of sin and betrayal." He breathed deeply, and then his face brightened somewhat. "Fortunately, we have a Savior who will absorb the sins of those who truly follow him. Without him ... well, this world would be a much darker place. In fact, I wouldn't want to live here at all, and neither would you."

CHAPTER 8

Where was Adonihah? That was Arayah's primary concern as she made her way home after successfully infiltrating High Judge Zerahir's study for the second time after a long pause in her active spying endeavors. She had made sure nobody followed her, and the strange men who had been surreptitiously watching her father's house for many weeks seemed to have gone away. It was almost the ninth hour of the night, and while the days had grown shorter, the sun would still rise within the next three hours. She had served for another of Zerahir's dinner parties the prior evening, which had reminded her forcefully again of Adonihah. He had disappeared nearly three months ago. Had his master called him back to Bountiful? Or—she tried not to think about it—had her father and his friends done something to get him to leave, one way or another? Her father had seemed so upset when Adonihah had seen Kishkumen, though Kishkumen hadn't even been named. Could that be part of it? If so, why?

Her father had recently reassured her that the men and women he had started meeting with again after a short period of dormancy were non-violent. They were just trying to make things better, he explained—get the right people in place in the government, make sure proper order was maintained.

She no longer harbored much trust in her father.

None of the documents she had found and copied that night named Nahom, or even Imrahiel, but they were explosive, and she could connect the dots with other things she had recently learned. Three months ago, the Nephite government had discovered reliable intelligence that uprisings were being planned in Zarahemla, Noah, and Sidom. The timing was said to be uncertain, but the events would be coordinated. Further, the reports revealed that the aim was to hold those cities hostage with a demand that the Nephite leadership agree to form a 'unity' government with Tubaloth, king of the Lamanites, who claimed new dangers from the south and west of his kingdom threatened his people.

Such activities weren't unprecedented, of course, except for the fact that three major cities would allegedly rebel simultaneously. But Ara had discovered a new twist. Documents in Zerahir's locked drawer claimed the existence of new evidence that the earlier reports were planted as a ruse to get Moronihah to strengthen the interior at the expense of the border cities. As far as she could tell from high-level correspondence, Moronihah and the high judges had never trusted the earlier reports in the first place. So, despite Moronihah's reportedly growing unease at leaving the garrisons in Zarahemla and other major interior cities so weakened, the vast bulk of the armies remained along the border.

Ara now realized those earlier reports were *not* a ruse. She had overheard her father talking with Kishkumen a little too loudly one night shortly after Adonihah disappeared. What he'd said hadn't made much sense at the time, and she hadn't caught all of it, but now she understood. Imrahiel and others had planted the new evidence to make certain Moronihah didn't bring some of his troops back from the border. It was a sinister, clever game, taking advantage of haughty Nephite predispositions. Without a doubt, what Kishkumen and the others were planning would be incredibly violent, not peaceful, as her father claimed.

Ara believed the national government in Zarahemla desperately needed to be reformed, but causing a new civil war couldn't be the answer, could it? Did her father truly believe such dreadful conflict necessary? She knew Kishkumen did. She also knew Kishkumen would become incredibly powerful if their plan succeeded. Then she wouldn't be given a choice about marrying him.

That dire destiny caused her to think even more longingly about Adonihah. Was he gone forever? Had she really had any chance with him anyway? He didn't seem as susceptible to her charms as others. He was smarter, steadier, more in control. She liked that. But she wondered if he had felt any real interest in her.

Without thinking, she nearly kicked a cat walking by. The animal picked up its pace, somehow sensing the potential danger, and she growled at it to confirm its fear of her. A few minutes later, she paused at the front door of her house, trying to calm the jumble of confused and angry thoughts. She needed sleep, but part of her wished her father were awake and she could confront him.

Opening and closing the door as quietly as possible, she tiptoed through the front room and down the hall to her bedroom. The house slumbered, dark and silent. She was tempted to slam her bedroom door to vent her frustration, but she resisted, instead closing it gently and finding her bed in the near-total darkness. She lay down, not even bothering to wash her face or clean her teeth, much less brush her hair.

She thought sleep would come quickly after such a long day. It didn't. She reviewed everything in her mind again, this time including a new letter to Zerahir from the Christian leader, Helaman. She remembered the first letter she had seen from him, and the strong impression that he wasn't scheming for power or fomenting hatred and resentment. Based on both letters, he didn't seem naïve, either. In the new missive, he had cautioned Zerahir about Gadianton—one of her father's friends who was a constant public thorn in the government's side. Gadianton had run for chief judge in the election, but he had also tried to convince the high judges to simply install him as such. Her father had let that fact slip recently. What enticements had Gadianton offered for that position, and how had he expected to fulfill them?

Despite the disagreeable topic, reading that second letter from Helaman to Zerahir had sent warm currents flowing up and down her spine, filling her bosom. Something in the way Helaman talked about God sang to her soul in a way she had never felt before. On the other hand, the warnings Helaman had given to Zerahir gave her chills, leaving her mind darkened under a heavy cloak of dread.

She hadn't copied the letter, but she remembered one phrase distinctly. *Brother Zerahir, the Lord will soon call on the faithful to leave Zarahemla.* Helaman had added that the process would need to be orderly and that he would soon send him his plans.

She knew the number of Christians in Zarahemla had been declining, but they still made up a significant portion of the population. Suddenly it struck her that Helaman hadn't said "the Christians." Instead, he had spoken of "the faithful." Were they the same thing in Christian parlance, or did 'the faithful' refer to a more specific group? Would some Christians refuse the order from their prophet to leave mighty Zarahemla? Would Helaman ask them to leave permanently? Though she knew far too little of how Christians thought about such things, she knew there were bad Christians, just as there were bad people in every group.

The question was *why*. Why would the Christian prophet ask his followers to abandon Zarahemla? What did he know? And how would he determine the timing? Would God really tell him?

She struggled with that last question until it finally put her to sleep.

It was late morning before Ara left her room to find some breakfast. Her father had departed a few hours earlier, according to her sister, who didn't know if he'd gone to the court buildings or somewhere else. That was probably for the better. Ara needed more time to think before she tried to pin him down with her concerns. In the meantime, she needed to deliver the intel she had gathered, using a special courier to avoid surveillance, and then return to Zerahir's later to serve yet another dinner party. Two nights in three. The parties had become more frequent, the list of prominent people having attended at least one of Zerahir's events growing. But she didn't yet know why he held them so often now.

On a rebellious whim, she decided to be bold and take her copied documents directly to Imrahiel, rather than to one of his or Kishkumen's couriers/henchmen. That's how she thought of their people now. Most of them looked and acted mean—godless even. And she was no longer convinced Imrahiel or Kishkumen even had souls.

She knew she would find Imrahiel at the pottery shop that day, since that's where the courier would have delivered her information, and she went in through the front rather than the rear to appear less suspicious. If anyone happened to ask, she would say Mistress Lianah had bidden her to browse for a new decorative piece for her house.

Moren was the first to greet her inside the shop. She knew he was clueless regarding Imrahiel's true nature. He always seemed happy, and she hoped he could stay that way.

"I need to talk to Master Imrahiel," she said, chin lifted slightly. She strongly suspected that wasn't his real name, but she had only known him by that name. Perhaps it could be considered his real name now—even his shop clients knew him as Imrahiel.

Moren bowed. "I'll let him know. You look pretty today." He turned and walked smoothly toward the back and up the stairs before she could respond. Moren was sweet on her, but he was too young, and annoyingly shy. It was nice of him to say, though, especially since she didn't look her best.

She continued to the small sitting room in the back corner of the building and sat down to wait. She felt confident she wouldn't have to wait long—Imrahiel would be anxious to get his hands on some new information, especially after the authorities had effectively shut down most of his clandestine activities for almost three months.

She was right. Imrahiel soon appeared, taking his customary sumptuous chair, sitting back, steepling his fingers, and gazing at her with those predatory eyes, a slight smile tickling his lips. He wore gray and blue today, but the three gaudy rings were the same.

"So," he said, without any greeting, "you were successful, I presume?"

She nodded as she retrieved the documents from her satchel. "Yes, Master Imrahiel. Here they are. The government knows something big is coming. The leaders must be nervous, because they're falling for conspiracy theories."

Imrahiel ignored her words, taking the documents and beginning to peruse them. He kept a straight face, making it impossible to discern what he thought about each one. After a few minutes, he looked up. "Excellent. Well done. But why did you bring these to me personally? Those weren't the instructions."

Ara swallowed. "This is critical information that should be as secure as possible. I made up an excuse that Mistress Lianah sent me to look for a new pottery piece. It's plausible."

He nodded, but she couldn't tell whether he accepted her explanation or not.

"I understand there is another dinner party at Zerahir's this evening?" he said after a few disquieting moments.

"Yes, master, there is." Imrahiel must know one of the invitees.

"I will need that full guest list."

"Yes, I will bring it tomorrow." She wondered why he couldn't request it of the invitee he knew. Perhaps it was someone he was grooming, and he couldn't ask directly.

"Very good. Now tell me, are you ready?"

"Um ... ready for what?"

Imrahiel's eyes darkened as he smiled wickedly. "For what comes next. Pacumeni has already proven to be the spineless, selfish chief judge we expected him to be, but it won't matter. We're ready. I need to know I can count on you."

"Yes, master, you can. I trust you. Just tell me what I need to do."

"Soon, my clever Raven. Very soon. Stay close to Zerahir and his family. The orders will come."

Her spine felt permanently chilled. It was clear something terrible was about to happen to Pacumeni, and probably Zerahir, too. She didn't particularly care about such high-minded men, but she wasn't heartless, and this sounded like the prelude to the bloody cataclysm she feared. She could also end up being implicated. Was that part of the plan? Was she being set up to take a fall? She would have to make her own plans—find a way to survive what was coming. She determinedly avoided swallowing or otherwise appearing nervous.

"I am ready," she said, injecting as much confidence and loyalty into her voice as she could.

Imrahiel's smile softened slightly, and then he nodded. "Good. Just remember, we'll have to do some hard things in the short term, but the rewards will be great. Remember your oaths. You may go now."

She rose, bowed, and then strode quickly out of the store, forgetting all about pretending to examine new works of expensive pottery for Mistress Lianah.

All throughout the dinner at Zerahir's home, she wavered in her mind between cornering her father regarding a proposed unification with the Lamanites and trying to forget about it. It was growing more difficult to perform her role in their shadowy group of professed Nephite patriots obediently.

By the time she arrived home that night, she was too tired to think about the issue. As it turned out, though, she found her father reading in the front parlor when she walked through the door. He looked up with what almost seemed like concern. For whom, though?

"You spoke to Imrahiel today. He commended you on the information you gathered."

She nodded and mumbled, letting her father see how tired she was, hoping the conversation would end right there. She knew it wouldn't.

"He sensed some doubt from you. It is dangerous to question the cause."

She shook her head, letting annoyance lace her reply. "I don't doubt the cause. I told him that. And I was exhausted. What did he expect?" She plopped down in a chair, adopting the air of an unfairly treated teenager, which she had done many times in that house.

Her father frowned. "He expects us all to play our parts. And he can't afford any weak links or loose lips. Your friend Adonihah tried to talk to the wrong people, claiming you were a spy, and he had to be removed."

She came fully awake. Anger flared. She couldn't help that it showed. "What did you do to him?"

Her father's face set firmly. "He will not be returning to Zarahemla. That is all you need to know." It probably meant they'd sent him out of the city, then ambushed and killed him. It was one of Imrahiel's favorite methods of dealing with dissenters or other threats. When it involved people she believed were terrible, she was able to set it aside. But Adonihah?

She had to be careful with her next words, though her fury hadn't abated. "Fine. He doesn't matter, not compared to the payoff at the end of this. But I have to ask one thing." She felt proud she sounded so convincing.

"What is that?"

"Are you sure it's wise to pursue unification with the Lamanites? Their hatred of us runs long and deep."

He squinted, no doubt wondering how much she knew, and how she knew it. "That's not for you to worry about."

"Don't *you* worry about it?" she asked in challenge.

He paused, probably thinking of a way to get her to back down. He loved her; she knew that. And she used that love to her advantage, often. After a few seconds he took a deep breath.

"I did at first," he admitted, surprising her. "We have battled for so long. Countless people have died, including innocent women and children. It seems impossible that our two nations could come together as one. But how else can we stop the continuous cycle of bloodshed and anguish? We can share the government among us and begin to build bridges of common purpose and understanding. If we could live in peace for an extended period of time, we could become the greatest nation the world has ever seen, greater even than the Jaredites once were."

Of course there were benefits to the Nephites and Lamanites living in continual peace and combining the management of their internal and external affairs. She'd heard that argument many times, and it made sense. But how would an alliance work? Not just in theory, but in practice? She was no philosopher, but she had studied some history and knew how people behaved. She had a hard time ignoring that stark understanding, even for a goal so noble.

"Do you really believe it can work?" she asked softly, making sure her voice sounded sincere.

He nodded, a fervent hope rising in his eyes. "Yes, my daughter. Yes, I do. And I wish your mother were here to see it. She dreamed of such a transformational event."

Ara doubted that was an accurate depiction of her late mother's feelings on the subject, but she didn't argue. She felt certain her father would defend her loyalty with Imrahiel, which meant she was safe—for now.

Kai had impressed several of the senior Gideon militiamen, having trained with them for almost four months. His martial combat skills had improved considerably, his growing confidence a product of being humbled many times by the skill and experience of the men of Gideon. Shemnilom came and watched him sometimes, as did several young, unmarried women. He had evolved into more than a novelty, becoming a celebrity of sorts in certain circles. He could picture some fathers who weren't too keen on the attention their daughters paid him. And he didn't try to encourage it!

He came up with an idea to both break away for a bit and give back a little, and the leader of the militia, a steel pillar of a man named Jeruzim—Jeru for short—liked it. Jeru assigned two of his men to the exercise involving long-range scouting, which the Gideonite militia had rarely been tasked to perform. Both men were farmers who could spend a few days away from their fields with the planting season still a few weeks off, and they had their own horses, too.

So, on a cool, early morning in the last month of the year, Kai rode out to meet the two men at the south gates of the city, Vyim carrying two light packs with travel rations. The men sat their own horses easily, and both looked to be fine mounts, though it was clear neither was built for speed. Long-legged Vyim, with his thick cannons and fetlocks, was fast while still being hardy.

"Good morning," said Kai in warm greeting.

"You're early," said Phinben. "Gideon may not produce the finest scouts in the army, but that's because scouts like to sleep in." He grinned at his companion, who bore the rare, obscure name of Zeus, after the ancient Greek god of Mount Lykaion. Most Nephites didn't know anything about the ancient Greeks, and nobody would have mistaken this Zeus for a god, not with his pudgy, slightly pear-shaped frame and wild shock of greasy black hair. Zeus could ride a horse, though. Jeru claimed he was the best natural horseman he'd ever seen.

Kai had heard the same kind of banter before, and he knew how to answer it. "Scouts work while the infantry sleeps, and sleep when the infantry works, so we don't get a lot of rest."

Both men laughed, and Kai smiled. He liked these two. But then, there wasn't a member of the Gideon militia he *didn't* like.

"You ready to see what a long-range scout mission looks like?" he asked, turning Vyim toward the southeast. A minor road angled that direction.

Phinben smiled. "Don't worry. We'll keep up with that fancy horse of yours."

Kai urged Vyim forward, then cast a taunt back. "Well, we'll see how sore your backsides are by the end of the day. You remember the rotations we talked about?"

"Yes," replied Zeus. "We'll follow your commands. And my backside welcomes the challenge." He gave a hearty whoop, but Phinben didn't join in; Kai guessed he didn't spend much time in the saddle. Kai, however, had been making sure Vyim got plenty of exercise.

They followed the minor road for several miles, and then Kai gave the first signal with arm and hand. They struck eastward off the road, spreading out both abreast and along their line of travel, like the top half of an arrowhead launched toward its target.

Then began their rotation. Kai, at the tip of the arrow, trotted Vyim forward, distancing himself about a quarter mile from the others until he found a spot of ground with decent cover and a good view of the countryside ahead. Then he stopped, surveying the landscape. At his signal, the others continued forward, Zeus starting to trot his horse when he was even with Kai's position. He would find the next vantage point and similarly signal. Then Phinben would take the lead, completing the flip of the arrowhead when he found another good observation post. At his signal, Kai would catch up and take the lead again while Zeus also moved up.

It was a gray day, but with little in the way of precipitation. They made good time during the morning, covering a lot of ground. In the afternoon, Kai planned to show them a different pattern that would take them in wide sweeps around their line of travel. They would proceed more slowly toward their destination, but they would scout a much wider swath of territory along the way.

They paused for a lunch of dry travel rations and water near a broad bend in a stream between two low hills. Since they were in Nephite lands, Kai didn't worry about posting a sentry atop one of the hills.

It turned out to be a good thing they hadn't set a guard. As Kai led them away from the stream and up the hill to the north at a slow walk on their horses, Vyim suddenly stopped. He didn't make a sound, but he wouldn't move, and Kai knew what that meant—he had smelled something out of place. Intrigued, Kai signaled the others to be quiet as he dismounted and crept toward the top of the hill on foot, acting out a real scouting mission. The brush was moderately thick, with a few scattered trees that became scarcer as he reached the crest. The wind was in his face, northern winds being most common that time of year.

He was on his belly when he viewed what lay on the other side. He squinted, making out two men about two hundred yards away. They were enjoying a meal just inside the edge of a stand of trees. Their mounts stood placidly nearby, and Kai studied their markings and tack. He couldn't be sure, but the horses looked to be from the far south of the country, near the borders with the Lamanites. They bore light streaks and spots across their shoulders and flanks, and the leather of their bridles and saddles was dark. He couldn't see any heavy saddle bags, so the men weren't traders. And while there were farms and villages nearby, journeying so lightly off the roads seemed odd. He wondered whether the men were hunters who just hadn't had any luck yet.

He decided to treat the situation as a test—one that shouldn't scare these two mysterious travelers too badly. Part of him reasoned the experiment would give him a chance to show Phinben and Zeus what a scout group should do when encountering—and potentially surprising—an enemy scouting party. The other part of him admitted he also wanted to impress his friends.

He inched his way backward until he could safely turn and walk down the hill. His party was well out of earshot, and downwind, but he was still careful. When he got back to Phinben and Zeus, he explained the approach they would take. Kai himself would be the distraction—the other two would spring the trap.

He walked Vyim back toward the west, having noted on their way in a small culvert that would hide him for a while. The other two headed east, also leading their horses. There wasn't as much natural cover in that direction, so Kai would wait an extra five minutes once he was in position. He could spend that time observing the two strangers, which is what he would have done in a real situation. He would also have been alert for any other scouts nearby, though he didn't worry about that on this practice run.

By the time he could see the men again, they had re-secured small travel packs to their saddles and were getting ready to mount up. Kai realized his plan probably wouldn't work ... which was often how it played out in real life. Still, he was curious to find out who the men were, so he mounted Vyim, nudging him to a fast trot after they emerged from the culvert. Within seconds the men heard and spotted him, but instead of pausing to watch him approach, they jumped into their saddles, turned their horses, and fast-trotted the opposite direction, disappearing into the trees. Kai hadn't expected that reaction, so he urged Vyim to greater speed. He heard the two men accelerate as well, breaking free of the tree line on the other side and forcing their mounts to a gallop. Vyim more than matched their speed after passing through the grove, and Kai began to close the distance.

Then, just before the men could enter another patch of trees, Zeus and Phinben bounded out of those trees on their mounts, about thirty yards apart but each angling straight at the horsemen. Phinben shouted toward Kai. "Bow! Bow! Contact enemy!"

That wasn't a scout signal—it was an infantry command. Kai's mind hitched for a moment, but then accepted the shocking news—Phinben had just informed him the two men were Lamanites, which meant they must be long-range scouts. The irony washed over him as he hugged Vyim tighter with his knees and unhooked his bow from behind the saddle. He nocked an arrow, his mind and body executing the trained motions smoothly. The men had hesitated upon seeing Phinben and Zeus, unsure which way to go. One yelled to the other—Kai could clearly hear the Lamanite dialect—and they turned their horses to aim for the gap between Kai and Zeus.

But Kai had covered a lot of ground. The men were no more than thirty yards away. He loosed, and so steady was Vyim that the arrow nearly hit the lead Lamanite in the upper back, still grazing his arm and causing him to shout in pain. Another arrow, from Zeus, who was even closer, took the second Lamanite in the shoulder. The man screamed and almost lost control of his horse. Leaving that man for the others, Kai aimed Vyim for the lead Lamanite and his mount. Vyim vaulted forward as if he had just been released from a bow himself. The man freed a short sword, glancing back with some panic as Kai approached, but Kai kept Vyim a few yards back and nocked another arrow.

"Drop your sword and slow your mount!" Kai ordered. It appeared the man might continue his attempt at escape, but it had surely dawned on him that Vyim outclassed his steed by a fair margin and that Kai was pretty good with a bow. He'd also already lost his companion.

He started to slow, and Kai made sure he and Vyim stayed far enough away that the man couldn't suddenly turn his horse and close with them. He hadn't dropped the sword yet.

"The sword!" Kai yelled as the horses slowed to a walk. The man took on a pained expression as he turned to look back again, then finally dropped his sword in the tall grass before coming to a halt. Kai kept his eyes on the man while listening to what transpired behind him. Phinben and Zeus had gotten control of the other Lamanite, who was seriously wounded. He heard the man scream again as they removed the arrow so they could dress the wound.

"Now dismount," said Kai. "On the right side." That was the side of the horse in full view of Kai.

The man reluctantly slid off his horse, glancing at his upper left arm, which showed blood where Kai's arrow had sliced through flesh. Then he stood calmly, holding the reins. He was slightly shorter than Kai, with darker hair and eyes.

"Your name," said Kai, resting his bow on his knee with an arrow still nocked.

"Caman," said the man flatly, chin held high.

"You're a long way from home, Caman. And you're a long-range army scout. Why are you here?" He didn't expect to get a straight answer.

"Our king believes you are planning to attack us. We are sending patrols to see how many troops have gathered from the interior. You already have large armies massed at the border."

Kai calmly stared at him, trying to decide how plausible that excuse sounded. It wasn't bad. After the major battle more than a year ago, and with the assassination of Chief Judge Pahoran, the Lamanites would logically worry about any concentration of Nephite troops on their border. And yet, the Nephites hadn't ever struck into Lamanite territory, save for some small hit-and-run raids to disrupt supplies and communications or to create diversions. Never to take territory or conduct a major offensive. Why would the Lamanites think that had changed?

Kai challenged him on it. "King Tubaloth is Ammoron's son. He knows the Nephites aren't aggressors. In fact, the only reason Tubaloth is alive is because Moroni didn't pursue your armies into the heart of the original land of Nephi. He could have. He was angry enough. You would have been decimated."

"Then maybe he was a fool," said Caman smugly.

"A fool who made all your leaders look like fools. What does that make *them*?"

The man worked his mouth angrily for a moment but couldn't come up with a response.

Kai blinked as the truth hit him, like an arrow with head of ice and fletching of fire. "You're probing avenues of attack into the Nephite heartland, bypassing the heavily fortified border cities."

The man froze for just a moment before recovering, and that was all the proof Kai needed. He didn't even listen to the man's half-mumbled response.

"On the ground, face down," he ordered, raising his bow. The man complied, and then Kai dismounted. Every good scout carried rope, and he put a knee in the man's back as he tied his hands behind him, then his feet. They would untie his feet to get him back on his horse for transport.

Kai mounted Vyim and urged him to a gallop toward where Phinben and Zeus still administered to the other scout. Vyim skidded to a halt mere feet away.

"They're scouting attack routes into the center of the nation, meaning to bypass the border cities," Kai announced.

"That's suicide," said Zeus, shaking his head.

"I caught the other one—he calls himself Caman—in the lie," replied Kai, turning his head to take a glance in Caman's direction. The man hadn't moved. "And it's the only thing that makes sense. I've never seen a long-range Lamanite scout this far north, and no other scout I know has, either. We're weak in the center. Can you imagine the damage they could cause if they succeeded? Even if we eventually beat them?"

Phinben and Zeus looked at each other, their faces becoming deadly serious. Phinben responded first. "You might be right. You have the fastest horse. Get to Gideon. Spread the word. I don't know where Moronihah is, but someone from Gideon should be able to get a message to him. Captain Benijah in Zarahemla should know about this, too, along with Helaman."

"I'll go there after stopping at Gideon," said Kai. He'd been feeling a growing urgency to get back to Zarahemla anyway. Even if the prescribed time hadn't quite passed, this discovery was a valid reason to return.

"Good. Go now. We'll take care of these two."

Kai knew they would. He turned Vyim, sensing that the stallion instinctively understood his need to travel fast. Kai barely had to encourage him before he bolted forward, reaching a dead gallop in just a few strides. That speed was dangerous away from the roads, so Kai slowed him a bit. He also made sure he gave him plenty of water and enough short intervals of walking between runs. He hadn't truly tested his horse's endurance yet, but he was about to.

***

Kai's news lit a wildfire in Gideon. At least fifty messengers scattered in every direction, including no fewer than twelve directed by Shemnilom, who knew where Moronihah was likely to be. Kai made sure Vyim was fed well and had a few hours of rest, but then he set out before midnight for Zarahemla at the same rapid pace, knowing if he pushed he could be there before morning.

When he arrived at the outer gates of the army camp's fortifications, the sun had just peeked over the eastern horizon.

"Kihoran of the two-seven scouts!" he shouted. "I have an urgent message for Captain Benijah!"

The guards, who looked new and barely old enough to hold a spear, paused a moment to confer before deciding to let him pass. At least they didn't make him wait while sending a runner, although a few more minutes wouldn't have mattered.

Horses generally weren't ridden through the camp, except sometimes in the practice yard, but Kai rode Vyim all the way to Benijah's tent door at a slow gallop, two guards stepping forward and lowering spears as Vyim came to a halt and Kai sprung from his back to land in front of them.

"I have urgent intelligence for the captain," said Kai, resting a hand on Vyim's heaving shoulder. Vyim was heavily lathered, but he was steady. What a marvelous animal. One of the guards seemed to recognize Kai, and he and the other soldier relaxed. They didn't motion him inside, though.

"He's meeting with several of his captains," said one.

"Good. They'll want to hear this, too," insisted Kai. "It involves newly discovered Lamanite activity, *inside* our borders, east by southeast of Gideon."

The guards glanced at each other, eyes widening. Kai had originally intended to tell only Benijah, but it didn't matter if others knew. They would all find out soon enough. The guard who had spoken disappeared inside the tent, returning a few seconds later.

"They'll hear your report," he said. Kai thanked him, passed him Vyim's reins, and then entered the tent, crossing into the active command quarters to find a group of eight captains seated, with Benijah standing before them.

"Come," said Benijah, waving him to the front of the group. "Give us your news, Scout Kihoran." He stepped to the side a pace as Kai approached. Kai didn't turn to the face the captains, though. He spoke directly to Benijah.

"I did a long-range patrol training yesterday with two members of the Gideon militia. We traveled southeast and then east for only half a day on horseback before discovering two long-range Lamanite scouts. They tried to escape, but we captured them. They're being questioned right now. Riders have been sent to the border garrisons and all the major cities in the area. Moronihah will be aware soon, if he isn't already."

Benijah nodded slowly, face grave. "It's rare to find a Lamanite patrol that far north, even during wartime. We can presume they weren't lost."

"No, sir, they were not."

"Do you know where they crossed the border?"

"No, sir, but further questioning might reveal that. I'm confident they were scouting an attack route into the heartland to bypass the border garrisons."

Benijah's jaw muscles twitched. "They would like nothing more than to strike at our soft belly. They must know we would crush them in the end, though. Who would agree to lead such a reckless campaign?" He held up a hand to forestall an answer. "Never mind. They've surprised us with maniacal foolishness before. We can't afford to be naïve about it. Tubaloth constantly swears to his people he will someday drink Moronihah's blood, just as his uncle swore to drink Moroni's. We should take his intentions seriously. What else?"

Kai was caught flat-footed. "Well, um, that's all I know right now, sir. They wouldn't be sending long-range scouts unless they were planning something imminent. We need to warn everyone and get some scouts down to the land of Nephi as well."

"Are you volunteering?" asked Benijah.

"Yes, sir, I'll go," said Kai.

Benijah nodded. "Thank you, soldier. We'll discuss it. You can rest here in the camp. And I want to speak with you privately tonight about the Gideon militia."

Kai knew their discussion wouldn't concern the militia. He was anxious to sing its praises, but he was even more interested in updates from the investigations in the city. It felt like he had been gone a year, not a mere four months. He saluted, then turned and left, retrieving Vyim to lead him to one of the stables near the walls. After that, he had an entire day to kill, and no orders that precisely confined him to camp. A thought blossomed. He was certain he could come up with a disguise good enough to get him in and out of Zarahemla without Imrahiel or one of his agents noticing. He would even use crutches, and he would leave camp the back way, through the small postern.

With Vyim cared for, Kai made a visit to the camp quartermaster, who oversaw a small warehouse of goods against the north wall. Kai needed an eye patch, which he would accentuate with bandages wrapped around his head, along with crutches, a plain cloak, and a bag of apples he would drop off for Vyim before leaving. When the man asked for authorization, Kai told him Benijah was his commanding officer and that a rider had suffered an unfortunate encounter with a low tree branch while traveling during the night, which was true—he himself had, but it was a small branch. The man barely raised an eyebrow, and he dutifully recorded the requisition and its purpose.

Half an hour later, having jogged most of the way from the camp's walls carrying a small pack on his back, Kai approached the western gates of the city, the least busy of the four cardinal gates. He shuffled forward on his crutches, glancing at the guards with his uncovered eye as he passed beneath the towering city walls.

His first destination was the warehouse where he had made contact with another of Moronihah's spies. He watched people closely—including the law officers—as he went, trying to gauge moods, noting odd behaviors. Excitement at being back in Zarahemla coursed in his veins, more so than expected. He felt alive and somehow useful again.

As he neared the warehouse and scouted out a spot to rest, he assessed whether anyone was watching him, but all seemed normal. He hadn't noticed anything strange on his route from the gates to the warehouse, either. But he couldn't quite tell if people were acting normal because they were *trying* to act normal, or if he was letting his imagination take too many liberties.

He sat against the wall of a smaller warehouse across the street for at least twenty minutes before he noticed any real activity. A large wagon arrived, loaded with barrels and boxes and a few items covered in tarps. As was usual with such sizeable shipments, the wagon carried two drivers to help with the unloading, and they brought the conveyance to a halt as the massive front doors of the warehouse slid open on nearly soundless tracked wheels. Only prosperous warehouses boasted such a feature.

Once the wagon was inside, the doors closed. Kai hadn't noted anything interesting, and he hadn't spotted the man he'd met with before—no, wait, was that him? He squinted toward a man approaching from far up the street. He seemed to have the same hair, facial features, and build, though he couldn't be sure yet. Kai looked away for a few moments, then tilted his head back and closed his eyes. The man would see Kai as he approached, but he would likely dismiss him.

The sound of another wagon coming up the street from the opposite direction masked any sound of the man's approach. Several other people traveled the street as well. Kai opened his eyes and brought his head forward, pretending to be interested in the wagon. He watched it slowly pass by, then caught view of the man—definitely his contact—as he turned down an alley at the side of the warehouse. Kai had come down that same alley several months ago, but from the north. He leaned back and shut his eyes again, listening closely for a few seconds before finally rising, taking a small drink from his waterskin, and following after the second wagon on his crutches.

As he passed the alley, he pretended to stumble, catching a glimpse of the narrow passage as he righted himself. A man approached from the other end, and Kai almost staggered for real. It was the tall, nearly blond man he had seen in Arayah's kitchen, wearing a minor disguise. Kai didn't stare, despite the intense desire to confirm his eyes hadn't lied. Who was he? Why was he here? He must be linked somehow to Imrahiel. If so, there were multiple possibilities, none of them good. His strong desire to leave the army camp and come to the city suddenly seemed like inspiration.

He kept shuffling along, a little faster now, taking a left at the next street, then another left to approach the north end of the alley. It was risky, but he might be able to get away with pretending to rest again while keeping a lookout.

Setting up across the street under the awning of a blacksmith, he sipped more water and waited, trying to think of a way to get closer. Perhaps he could start down the alley and find access to a rooftop tall enough to give him a clear view. He was still studying his surroundings and weighing options when a man screamed, followed by a door slamming. A few seconds later, the man from Arayah's kitchen burst from the mouth of the alley. He was fast, about as fast as any man Kai had seen, his footfalls light on the street as he crossed and turned up another alley. By the time a man emerged from the alley in pursuit, the blond man was already gone, and the pursuer had no idea which way to go. He would never have caught him anyway, not with those short, pudgy legs. The man stopped, eyes darting around in frustration and anger, then squeezed his hair in his hands as a look of intense pain washed over his face. He seemed to recover himself, then headed back down the alley at a run. Something had happened—something bad. And Kai had a good guess what it was. He had spotted blood on one hand of the man from Arayah's kitchen as he sped by.

Law officers would flock to the scene shortly, so Kai needed to move. People in the street already shouted at each other, trying to determine what was happening. Kai wished there were a way to get a message quickly to Benijah, but the only resource he knew of for such a thing was a man who might now be dead himself. Kai wouldn't be able to notify the captain unless he personally went to the camp or the law offices, but that was out of the question. He couldn't afford to become part of an official investigation.

As he started shuffling down the street, he had an idea of where he should go next. The new location was even riskier, and he didn't dare play the stop-and-rest routine there. But he had to have a look—two if he felt comfortable.

Almost an hour later—it was painful to move so slowly—he had reached the street that was home to Imrahiel's high-end pottery shop. He tried to seem purposeful, moving in a straight line. The traffic was much greater, but people tended to move around him, not wanting to get in the way of a man on crutches who had only one good eye. He'd have to remember this disguise—it had its drawbacks, but it came with definite advantages as well.

He was casually examining a random shop to his right when someone brushed by closely on his left, moving in the same direction.

"I know it's you," came a feminine whisper. "Follow."

He nearly tripped, barely keeping his composure, staring at the back of the woman who had just spoken to him. By her walk and the flow of her hair, he knew instantly it was Arayah, the sharp-eyed Raven. When had she had spotted him, and how had she recognized him? He hadn't noticed her … yet again.

She moved at a casual pace, not much faster than his, and she didn't look back. She was just another Nephite on an errand she had done hundreds of times, paying no attention to people she was accustomed to seeing. He wondered whether he should take the first cross street, ditch the crutches and eye patch in an alley, and lose her. But his curiosity intensified. Where would she lead him, and why would she want to talk to him? Why even bother making contact?

She turned left at the next street, then right a couple blocks down. He fell farther behind, but he knew she would find a way to let him keep up. She stopped in a tiny shop beneath a just-as-tiny home as if she had eyed something interesting. She even bought some ribbons to make the ploy look legitimate. He smiled at that for some reason as he continued by.

Soon enough, she overtook him again, this time on his right, whispering as she slowed to re-examine her purchase. "Next left, then the first right, then the second alley on your left." After she continued past the next left, waving to a random passerby, he obeyed her instructions. When he finally emerged from the alley to which she had directed him, he found himself in a small, unkempt garden behind a large brick house, situated along a canal running perpendicular to the alley. A high stone fence bordered one side of the garden, ascending the outer canal bank and running almost to the edge of the water. Along the other side of the garden, a line of thick, interlaced trees marched from where he stood, ending at a narrow path beside the canal. Arayah emerged from that path moments later, motioning him to step into the garden and out of view of anyone on the street.

The garden obviously belonged to someone who meant it to be private, though there was no gate. What if they were spotted? Did Arayah know the people who lived in the house, or was it abandoned?

"Why did you come back?" she asked, voice just above a whisper. He detected both anger and relief. "My father said you had left and wouldn't return. He refused to give me specifics."

"How did you know it was me?" he responded. "I don't look anything like myself. I'm not even walking properly."

She shrugged, and suddenly her anger evaporated. "I know your eyes, and your cheekbones. Oh, and your ears, or at least the one not covered by bandages."

"My ears," he said flatly.

"Yes, is that so strange?" He had no idea. Who studied ears that closely?

"Why did you want me to follow you?"

"So we could talk. I couldn't believe it was you, and I ..." She took a deep breath, squaring her shoulders as if to firm her resolve. "I have something I need to tell you. Um ... wait!" Her hand came to her mouth. "Do you actually *need* those crutches? Did something happen? I just assumed ..."

He smiled, setting the crutches down and standing straight while removing the eye patch.

"Well, I didn't fool *you*—again. I wonder how many others I didn't fool."

"Who were you trying to fool?"

Kai shook his head. "It doesn't matter. You were going to tell me something?"

"Not until you answer my question." It sounded like a delay tactic, but she put her hands on her hips for emphasis.

Kai stared at her a moment before answering. He needed an effective yet neutral answer. "Certain people would be unhappy to see me back in the city."

She blinked. "Like my father?"

He paused again, then admitted, "Including your father, yes."

"And Imrahiel."

Kai's eyes widened slightly. He hadn't expected her to go there. "Imrahiel?" He tried—too late—to make it appear he'd never heard the name.

"I wondered," she said. "You just confirmed it." Indeed he had, and he felt frustrated with himself.

"Well, now I can tell you even more than I thought I could," she said.

Wait, what? Kai thought in disbelief.

She turned and took a few more steps into the garden, angling toward the canal, trampling on some unruly weeds. Kai followed. Then she stopped and faced him again. "My father and Imrahiel are part of a group trying to overthrow the city."

Kai already knew that, and she clearly noticed his lack of surprise.

"You knew?" she asked.

He nodded.

She thought for a moment, and he witnessed resolve hardening in her eyes. "Did you know they plan to hold the city—and two other major cities— for ransom to force a unity government with the Lamanites?"

Now *that* revelation momentarily stuck his mind in thick mud. Arayah's father and Imrahiel—and others like them—colluding with King Tubaloth? Kai's brain slowly began functioning again. Of course they were. It had been done before. His birth parents had supposedly been involved in the last attempt to force a change in the government outside of the election process. They had communicated with the Lamanites, too, but not *beforehand.*

"They killed Pahoran, didn't they," he said. "And they've been seeding rumors the Lamanites are about to attack the border."

Arayah stared at him, seeming slightly shocked. "I . . . I don't know about the chief judge's murder, but . . . you could be right. And yes, they've been aiming to weaken the defenses of Zarahemla."

"Which other cities do they plan to attack?" Kai looked around, nervous that anyone might overhear. Curtains covered all the back windows of the house, and the door was closed. But he grabbed her elbow and pulled her closer to the canal, anyway. On the other side of the waterway crouched the long back wall of a nondescript building with no windows, just some narrow horizontal slits near the top.

"Noah and Sidom. They seeded that information with several high-level aides in the Hall of Judgment. Then they planted information that it was all a ruse meant to draw Moronihah's forces back to the interior, away from the border. They used *all* their resources on those efforts."

The air seemed to thicken around Kai. Three major cities, including the capital.

"Clever. They've fooled the high judges—and Moronihah. How do they plan to take over the cities?" he asked.

She shook her head. "I don't know, but they could be gathering somewhere."

"Or the Lamanites are coming, bypassing the border cities." Kai watched intently for her reaction to that suggestion. It appeared she hadn't thought seriously about the possibility. Most Nephites couldn't.

"But how . . ." she trailed off, and then it seemed to hit her. "They'll come in small bands, then re-group. It will still be risky. What if they're spotted?"

"They'll have to kill or capture anyone who spies them," said Kai bluntly. "I just helped seize two of their long-range scouts, southeast of Gideon. They're coming. I'm just not sure from which direction. Moronihah is being notified."

Arayah put her hand to her mouth again for a moment, then dropped it. "You're with them."

"With who?"

"The government."

Kai cocked his head. "What if I am? Does that make me an enemy?"

She swallowed, then gazed into the garden. "A few months ago, I would have said yes. Now I'm not so sure."

"And I'm supposed to believe that?"

Her eyes snapped back to him. "Yes. My real name is Arayah, but most people call me Ara. I've been spying on High Judge Zerahir for my father and Imrahiel. I've copied several highly sensitive documents from Zerahir's study. Some of those have made me think. And I met you. My father and his friends are . . ." She swallowed again, then looked down with a heavy sigh. "They're not good people. I used to think they were—part of me still wants to believe—but they aren't. They're ruthless, and I can see the greed in their eyes. They lust for control, not to make life better for everyone, even though that's what they constantly preach. I think my father started out wanting to improve society, but he's been corrupted, too."

Her confession sounded impressive, even heartfelt. But Kai couldn't afford to fall for convincing carols from pretty young women.

Just then they heard voices arguing near the mouth of the alley. Kai caught a few words: "… man on crutches … alone … officers …"

Kai grabbed Ara's elbow again. "We have to get out of here." She didn't appear as alarmed as he felt, but she agreed with a curt nod.

"We can't take the path by the canal; we'll cross their line of sight," she noted.

"And they might be watching the other street. I hope you don't mind getting wet, then." He motioned toward the canal, lowering his voice but adding urgency. "Quickly."

They ascended the outer bank as swiftly and quietly as they could, then descended. Kai slipped into the bracingly cool water first, Ara following without any hesitation, her skirt billowing up around her until she pushed it down and it became soaked. The spring season meant the waters had already begun to rise from their low point, so while this canal—Two Veils, if he remembered right—was one of the broad ones, the water was already more than waist deep, though the current was still mild. Kai pointed downward, and when she nodded, he submerged completely, kicking off the bottom of the canal against the current, in the direction of the footbridge beyond the end of the stone fence. Luckily, they were in a relatively secluded section of the city, and nobody was crossing the bridge at the moment.

He tried to stay well under the water's surface, since a splash could give them away. On the second stroke with his arms, his right hand brushed something that felt incongruously like a bag. He paused, instinctively grabbing it. It wasn't too heavy, and so he kept swimming. He soon passed under the bridge, and when he reached the other side, he emerged carefully from the water, trying not to take too loud of a breath. After determining nobody was around, he waded across the canal and climbed the far bank, which led him to a small yard behind another home—actually three homes in a row, meaning they would have to pass by several windows before finding a break to get to a street.

Ara emerged from the water and followed silently, just as he heard men entering the garden they had vacated. They had increased in number. They discovered the crutches and eye patch, and another loud argument ensued. Somebody had already been sent to fetch law officers, and he clearly heard the word "vagrant." He smiled at that; he felt like one in truth.

As he aimed for a gap between buildings, Ara hissed softly from behind him. She motioned toward the middle house, then walked casually toward the door. Kai hesitated, but decided to follow. Did she intend to knock and make up a story? What if the men overheard?

But no—she opened the unlocked door and went inside. Kai quickened his pace, following her through the doorway. A bronze-skinned, thick-bodied old woman in the kitchen gazed questioningly at them as Ara held a finger to her lips. After a moment, the woman crossed her arms and directed a stare of patient remonstration at Ara. Kai quickly understood that Ara was no stranger ... and he wasn't the first man this old woman had seen tagging along with her.

Ara pointed toward the front room, and the woman motioned them forward, sparing another inquisitive glance at Kai, seeming to measure him in an instant. Ara found a chair, indicating another one for Kai. When the old woman had sat, she spoke first.

"Ara, my dear, I'd love to hear how you ended up in the canal with a man, acting like someone is chasing you." She tapped her fingers on her knees, and Kai would have paid an artist good money to capture the expression on her face. He suppressed a smile.

"This is Adonihah," said Ara. "He's with the army."

Kai raised an eyebrow toward Ara. He hadn't told her that outright, though she could have inferred it. And the fewer people who knew, the better.

Ara's eyes stayed fixed on the old woman, who peered closely at Kai, then back at Ara. "That doesn't answer my question, dear." Again, that face. He would have paid *two* artists.

Ara took a deep breath, her mien determined, as if she refused to be lectured or cowed. "There are people in the city who don't want him here," she said, "including my father."

The woman's eyes narrowed, and her fingers stopped tapping. The room became eerily quiet.

"And how is your father these days?" she asked gently.

"Not well," replied Ara. "Not since my mother passed. It's gotten worse." She didn't say what 'it' was, but Kai had a guess.

"And this young man knows something about it?"

Ara nodded. "Yes."

"How did you meet him?"

Ara glanced at Kai. "We met randomly a few months ago, and he helped me serve a dinner party at the house of one of the high judges. Then he disappeared—army business. He just came back today."

"And the canal?"

"Law officers were coming," she explained with her hands spread before her. "His mission is secret, and they would compromise it."

The old woman nodded as if Ara's explanation made all the sense in the world to her. She turned again to Kai.

"Is this all true?"

Kai nodded. "Yes, ma'am. I can't say much more, though."

"You don't have to," she responded, her tone as kind as any he'd ever heard. "I can see it in your eyes. Something big is coming. Something terrible. Tell me, would you recommend that an old woman leave the city for a time and visit her son in the country?"

Kai stared out the front window for a moment, feeling something inside move from the back of his head and into his chest. It was the Spirit, he was certain. He returned his gaze to her. "Yes, I would, and as soon as possible."

She nodded, and her fingers started tapping again. "You will take care of Ara?"

Kai looked at Ara. "I think she can take care of herself, but I'll help if I'm needed." Ara smiled in thanks, and he returned his gaze to the woman. "I have to return to the camp tonight, and from there I'm not sure where I'm going. Can I ask your name?"

The old woman smiled at him as if he were now a close acquaintance or even a relative. "I am Naome. I used to care for Ara's mother when she was a little girl, then later her children, including Ara. My husband has passed, but I have two surviving children—a son and a daughter. One other son was killed in battle, and another daughter was taken captive by the Lamanites several years ago, during the Great War. I haven't heard from her since."

Kai nodded somberly. Her story was all too common. Many Nephite families had similar tales to tell. Like Naome, most seemed proud they had been called upon to give so much.

"Thank you for your sacrifice," Kai said, but he worried his words sounded empty.

Naome didn't seem to think so. She smiled gratefully. "And thank you for yours, young man. Trying times are coming for you." Abruptly, she got up. "But at least I can make sure you leave here on a full stomach. It will be at least an hour, so make yourself at home." With that she headed back to the kitchen.

Kai looked at Ara, who smiled.

"I like her," said Kai in a low voice. "She seems like a good friend of your family."

Her expression suddenly darkened. "My father hates her," she muttered. Kai raised an eyebrow, and she continued. "My mother always confided in her, and my father didn't like it. Naome was always talking about spiritual things, too, and that annoyed him. She only took care of me when my mother brought us kids here so she could go off on errands by herself, usually without my father knowing."

"How did your mother die?"

Ara's shoulders sagged. "She got very sick. The doctors tried everything. None of the medicines worked. She wasted away, right before my eyes. She was scared at first, but I remember at the end she wasn't. She seemed at peace. I don't understand why, and part of me has been angry at her for a long time for giving up on us. It's childish, I know."

Kai had nothing to offer, so he kept his mouth shut. After a few moments he changed the subject back to their immediate situation.

"Why that garden? You've been there?"

"Yes. The family who used to live in the house . . . well, the man is a long-time friend of my father's. I think he still owns it and rents it out sometimes." She glanced at the bag Kai had carried in with him, and he followed her gaze. He had set it on the stone floor, and water had pooled around it. Naome hadn't asked about the bag, though she must have noticed it.

"What is that?" Ara asked.

Kai picked it up, letting water drip for a few seconds before setting it on his lap. "I don't know. It was at the bottom of the canal. It seems waterproof, and it's weighted." He untied the knot holding it closed, then expanded the opening. The first thing he pulled out was a shirt, slightly damp and mildewy. He knew instantly the cloth was expensive, and when he held it up with both hands, he noted the exotic, foreign cut. In fact, he'd seen shirts like it before and had even sold some inside Nephite territory. It had been dyed a light yellow, but was starting to bleed. Ara reached out a hand and he gave it to her, then pulled a pair of expensive breeches from the bag, dyed a rich blue, with hems at the bottom tightened by fine leather straps. It had loops for a belt, which he also found inside the bag. The belt matched the exquisitely crafted sandals sitting on top of a deep brown cloak at the bottom, along with a small, dark-smeared towel.

After Ara had examined each item, she asked the obvious question. "Who would hide these at the bottom of a canal?"

Kai stared at her for a long moment, his face serious. "An assassin."

CHAPTER 9

Wherefore, brethren, seek not to counsel the Lord, but to take counsel from his hand. For behold, ye yourselves know that he counseleth in wisdom, and in justice, and in great mercy, over all his works.

JACOB 4:10

Kai dropped the bag with the assassin's discarded clothes onto Benijah's desk in the command tent.

"The clothes of Pahoran's assassin," he announced.

Benijah, sitting in his chair, raised his eyebrows as he opened the bag and began to extract the contents. At the breeches he paused, then set them aside and took out the cloak. He looked up at Kai, his eyes wide. "This is what the assassin was wearing."

Kai hadn't seen the detailed reports, but from what he had heard, he had already been certain. It couldn't be a coincidence.

"This might give us a lead, but I'm not sure," continued Benijah, sounding excited. "Someone either sold these or had them stolen, and we can begin to make inquiries."

"Yes, but I think I have something better. I found the bag hidden in a canal near a small garden. The house probably belongs to a friend of Arayah's father, Nahom, who is part of Imrahiel's group. The name of the owner of the house is Hadrim, but he doesn't live there. Perhaps the city records will show where he lives."

Benijah stood up, his face cast in wonderment. "How did you get this information?"

Kai shook his head. "I don't really know. Well, I do, but I can't explain it. I wore a disguise into the city. Ara still recognized me. I hadn't been looking for her. She wanted to talk, and she led us to this garden. Then we heard some men talking about getting law officers to check out a vagrant—which was me, of course—and we got out of there."

Benijah was still taking that in when Kai added, "I have other news, too. Our agent in the Old Warehouse District—the one who often relays messages—I think he was attacked today, maybe killed. I caught a glimpse of the attacker, but I wasn't sure what to do. I'm sorry about that. He was fast, but maybe I could have caught him. I've seen him before, by the way, at Nahom's house. Did you get any reports?"

Benijah looked both thoughtful and concerned as he resumed his seat. "You somehow stumbled upon that mess as well? At the right time?"

Kai still felt a little stunned by the coincidence himself. But surely Benijah didn't suspect he was involved in any way ... did he?

"I was in the area for more than an hour, sir, listening and looking for anything that might be off, any rumor I could trace. And then ... well, it happened."

Benijah nodded, leaning back with his hands behind his head, eyes scanning the roof of the tent.

"And there's more, sir, though I'm not sure how to verify it."

Benijah's eyebrows nearly reached that roof as he straightened, lowering his hands. "In the *same day* you returned from Gideon?"

Kai could understand his hesitation, but he was becoming annoyed by the captain's disbelief. "Imrahiel is coordinating with others, including the Lamanites. They plan to take three cities, then demand a unity government. Zarahemla, Noah, and Sidom are the targets. Those scouts we found make more sense now. The attack has to be imminent, and it's *not* a ruse."

Benijah set his jaw as his gaze pierced Kai. After a few uncomfortable seconds, he said, "I'm still awaiting more information on that. I should have it in the next day or two. In the meantime, you may stay in the city and see if you can find out more."

It seemed an abrupt dismissal, and it was Kai's turn to be suspicious.

"What about the scouting mission into the lands of the Lamanites … um, sir?"

"On hold for the moment. Let's focus here for now. Moronihah has other scouts he can send, anyway, in whatever directions he deems best."

"But we might not have much ti—"

"You brought me information, and you have your orders. Is there a problem?"

Kai shook his head. "No, sir."

"Good." Benijah stood. "You are dismissed, soldier. Report back here four days from now."

Kai saluted and left, knots twisting in his stomach. The Lamanites were about to invade. He was sure of it. Ara's father was involved. He'd found some leads on Pahoran's killer, but now Benijah suspected him of … something. Benijah would at least follow up on the leads, though, which was good. It struck him as cosmically odd that suddenly he didn't want to go back to the city; he yearned to be part of the scouting missions to the land of Nephi to ascertain new Lamanite troop movements, supply lines, and communications. He knew he could figure out their planned infiltration lanes, if given a little time.

He decided not to stay the night in the camp, but to retrieve Vyim and head to the city, even though it was late. He wouldn't go in disguise. Time was short, and he needed to poke the hornets' nest harder. He would return to *Jacob's Rest*, and he would make sure Imrahiel knew it.

The innkeeper on duty expressed surprised at seeing Kai again. He had been told, he related, that Adonihah had returned to Bountiful, his business having been transacted. Kai made up a story about an unexpected trading opportunity with a new seller who had come to Zarahemla from far to the southeast of the lands of the Nephites—a rare find his master wanted to capture as soon as possible. His master would have come himself, but he had been sick lately.

The man accepted the story, probably not caring one way or the other, and he gave Kai the same room he had stayed in before, at Kai's request. He then made sour mention of the fact that Helaman had called a large conference of the Christians in the area but didn't want to hold it at the temple hill in Zarahemla, where such gatherings normally convened. Instead, he had arranged for it to take place in Gideon. That meant, of course, that *Jacob's Rest* would lose out on a lot of business a regional Christian conference would normally bring.

In reciprocal fashion, Kai didn't care about the inn's perceived plight. He was curious, though, about the timing.

"Do you know the date of the conference?"

The innkeeper shook his head in obvious disgust. "That's the other nonsensical thing. It's on the second day of the new year. In the *morning*. The Christians planning to attend will leave during the day of the New Year festival, which means none of them will be coming here for food and drink. The festival is one of our busiest days of the year … but not *this* year."

"When did Helaman make the announcement?"

The man scrunched his brow. "I think it was just over two weeks ago." He surprised Kai with a throaty chuckle. "I know a good many Christians who are none too happy about it. Some think Helaman is a foolish child letting the power get to his head. I'd have to agree with that!" He shook his head mockingly, then focused on his ledger. "So, two weeks again? Is that what you're intending? You didn't stay the full two weeks last time, so you have some credit."

Kai affirmed it, though something made him think the length of his stay wouldn't matter. Why had Helaman called the conference on such an odd day, and not in Zarahemla? He couldn't have known two weeks ago about Imrahiel and the Lamanites, could he? Yes, of course he could have, and in more than one way.

Kai bid the innkeeper good night and went to his room. He did the same checks as before, and it was secure. Even so, a long time passed before he fell asleep.

Breakfast tasted every bit as good as he remembered. He felt spoiled again, especially since he should have been on his way toward the border and beyond, living off the land and a few slim rations, trying to scope out the Lamanites' plans.

But he might as well make the best of it, and his first visit of the day would be to the hornets' nest—Imrahiel's fine pottery shop. He hoped Imrahiel himself would be there.

He took a meandering route, not feeling like he should be in any hurry. The last day of the year was two days hence. Traffic moved a little slower. Like the people in Bountiful normally did, the people of Zarahemla seemed to be saving up some energy for the New Year's Day celebrations. They would surely be happy to see year forty of the Reign of the Judges end, given the brazen assassination of their chief judge just a year after another brief but major conflict with the Lamanites. The celebrations would be a time for joyful peace, healing, and gratitude. Or at least entertaining distraction. Little did the people know what was coming, and though Kai realized it was big, he still understood far too little himself.

The pottery shop was deserted except for the young man he had spoken with before.

"Is Master Imrahiel here?" asked Kai as the young man approached.

He gave a quick nod. "Yes, he is upstairs. Do you have an appointment?"

"Yes, I do," Kai lied. "My name is Adonihah."

Kai waited near the front while the young man retreated to the back of the shop and up the stairs. He returned a minute later.

"Master Adonihah, sir, he will see you in the sitting room in a few minutes. You can wait for him there." The young man bowed and moved to the side, and Kai took his time walking to the sitting area. He remained standing until Imrahiel appeared a few minutes later. Then he sat as Imrahiel took a seat in his large armchair.

Kai waited for him to speak. He knew Imrahiel expected him to defer, and Kai didn't want to overly annoy him—not given the ploy he was about to try.

"So, you've returned. I was surprised and a bit dismayed that you left without saying goodbye." The lie was smooth, if a bit arrogant.

Kai tried to appear regretful. "I'm sorry. I would have if I could. I was called away suddenly by the army. Most of the captains are nearly frantic about the Lamanites, so I went on some scouting missions. I'm lucky to still be alive."

"Oh?" said Imrahiel, resting his elbows on the chair arms and steepling his bejeweled fingers in front of him—in pure curiosity, not concern. "What happened?"

"Well," said Kai, faking nervousness, "the scouting missions went fine. But two men tried to kill me shortly before I received those orders. I didn't think they were assassins—just bandits—but when I told Moronihah about it, he was convinced they were assassins, probably commissioned by one of the high judges."

"Not surprising. You've seen him recently?" Imrahiel hadn't batted an eyelash when Kai mentioned assassins or high judges, but Moronihah's named perked his ears up. "Where is he?"

"He's still at the border, traveling among the garrisons. I spoke with him about two weeks ago."

Imrahiel nodded slowly. "Good. That makes us all feel safer." The chill accompanying his words penetrated Kai's chest. "So why did he send you back?"

Kai amplified his nervous demeanor. "He said I'd done a good job scouting, but that I needed to return and keep digging. He wasn't specific, and it almost seemed like … well, like I was meant to be bait. He's not as popular as his father, and he knows he has enemies. He has at least one other spy in the city, and that man was supposed to deliver some additional instructions to me today. He didn't, probably because Moronihah didn't actually tell him to."

"Hmmm …" Kai was certain Imrahiel knew about the man from Nahom's kitchen, and the attack on Kai's contact, but his eyes didn't reveal anything. "Do you believe he has lost trust in you, to treat you like this?"

"I don't know. He's under a lot of stress. I thought he still trusted me, even after we talked, but something Captain Benijah said when I reported back—" he frowned deeply, making sure to show a strong flash of frustration "—reinforced the feeling that something wasn't right, and I'm worried I'm just a disposable tool in one of their schemes."

Imrahiel leaned forward. "What did the captain say?" Kai smiled inwardly. Imrahiel was hooked.

"He said my loyalty would be tested, and he made it sound like it already *had* been, and that I had at least partly failed."

"And what did you say to that?"

"Nothing. What could I say? I know he's frustrated my meetings with you didn't bear him useful fruit. He doesn't like you, by the way."

Imrahiel started to chuckle, then cut it short, his face turning to stone. "I'm well aware of that. But I'm not worried about what Captain Benijah thinks of me. I know he's sent some clumsy oafs to watch me from time to time. He sent you, too. He's both corrupt and stupid. What was his response to hearing of someone trying to kill you?"

Kai pretended not to take offense, like an obedient subject. "Unlike Moronihah, he dismissed the assassins as bandits who thought I would be an easy target."

"You clearly weren't. What happened to the assassins?" Imrahiel likely still didn't know the disposition of his two men. That was a beautiful thing.

"We fought. I wounded one of them, and they escaped. They only had a narrow window of time to get the job done, and they didn't plan the attack very well. If a high judge hired them, he probably didn't spend much money."

He thought that insult might rankle Imrahiel, but the king-man just smiled, then dropped his hands. "It sounds like you need something from me."

Kai swallowed, continuing to affect nervousness. "I could use some protection, and I can earn it. I met Helaman at that dinner party I'm sure Raven told you about, and he seemed to like me. I also know one of his guards. In fact, there's a chance I could become one of his guards, too. I could leave the army. Then I could get you more valuable intel. I know Helaman isn't officially part of the government, but he still has a lot of influence, right?"

Imrahiel pursed his lips. "That's true. But Moroni and Benijah have Helaman's ear. If they suspect you—"

"Then I'll know for sure, and I'll figure out something else. I'm resource-ful." He was proud of what sounded to him like the perfect touch of eager confidence in his tone.

Imrahiel studied him for a full minute. Kai stared back, maintaining a determined but respectful mien. Finally, Imrahiel broke the silence. "I will think more on your potential usefulness ... *if* you can become part of Helaman's guard. Where are you staying?"

"*Jacob's Rest*, like before." Kai was certain Imrahiel already knew that.

"Good. I'll keep the inn under surveillance. You should be safe there. Make contact with your guard friend. You might help Raven as well. I know you can find her. There's a strong link between Zerahir and Helaman, and we need to keep working on that. Now—" Imrahiel stood, pointing a finger at Kai's chest "—if you're going to work more closely with me, or at least attempt to, I'm going to need you to take an oath."

Kai nodded. His crazy plan had worked. He was in.

Kai's growing unease about the Lamanite and rebel plans gave him a sharp sense of urgency. Immediately upon leaving Imrahiel's shop, he returned to Jacob's Rest, retrieved Vyim, and went for a ride outside the city walls. In fact, he circumnavigated them, searching for anything suspicious. Then he set off cross country to find the woods and the house where the assassins had been held. Benijah hadn't said anything about not visiting the house, and nobody was following him, so Kai felt justified investigating.

It was a short ride, since Vyim wanted to go fast. They arrived at about the noon hour, the sun strong overhead. Just outside, he spotted a man repairing harnesses for the upcoming plowing and planting. He looked like he could be Dan's brother. He wore a simple gray headband to catch the sweat.

"Good day," Kai said in greeting before dismounting. He didn't bother tying Vyim to anything; he knew the horse would stay.

"Do I know you?" asked the man, setting his tools down, straightening, and turning to fully face Kai. He didn't seem concerned, but he had a prepared look about him.

"No. My name is Kihoran. I was here with Dan a few months ago. We brought two prisoners. Are they still here?"

The man relaxed slightly, shaking his head. "They were taken elsewhere."

Kai wasn't surprised, but he had hoped to find Dan. "And is Dan back at the camp or in the city?"

"He's in the city right now, I think."

"He's your brother or cousin?"

"Cousin."

"So, you're one of the two thousand as well?" The man looked the right age.

"I am. My name is Lehi."

"Well, it's an honor to meet you. We might need you all again soon." Kai had tried to make the comment sound like a joke, but Lehi cracked only a slight smile.

"We're ready. Moronihah knows that, and so does Helaman. We're scattered across the nation, but we can gather quickly."

As soon as Lehi mentioned gathering, Kai remembered Helaman's call for a conference. "You know Helaman called a special conference in Gideon, right? Are you going?"

"Yes," replied Lehi, nodding firmly. "We'll be there. In fact, I think most of the two thousand will come, even those who don't live in this region. Unfortunately, I know of some saints who don't want to miss the New Year celebrations and will therefore skip this conference. We're encouraging everyone to attend. It's a minor sacrifice, and it feels right."

Something stirred in Kai. It *did* seem right. "I've just come from Gideon. I trained with their militia. They're some of the best soldiers in the nation."

Lehi gave a full smile this time. "I remember. Yes, they are." The smile faded quickly. "And I hope they're ready."

"For what?" Did Lehi know something more?

"For whatever's coming."

Kai returned to the city, unable to shake the shards of doom lodged in his heart by Lehi's warning. Was there something he could do to stop the overthrow of Zarahemla? He'd alerted Captain Benijah, and returning to camp to reinforce the warning would just make him look more suspicious. He needed to talk to Dan and Ara. He resolved to find Dan first, which meant he would have to visit Helaman's residence in the Santorem, though he'd never been there.

Approaching the Santorem on horseback gave Kai a slightly different perspective of the neighborhood. And Vyim was such a fine horse that the perception of onlookers changed as well. Even the private guards acknowledged Kai with a nod or a gesture, and when he asked one of them to direct him to the house of Helaman, the man was only too happy to help.

A short time later, Kai approached the manor. It wasn't as large or ornate as that of High Judge Zerahir, but it appeared immaculately kept, and it was well guarded. He dismounted before the front gate, looping Vyim's reins over a small iron railing meant for the purpose. Two guards maintained posts just inside the gate. One of them addressed Kai through the bars.

"Do you have business here?"

"I'd like to speak with Dan, if he's here," replied Kai in a respectful tone.

"Your name?"

"Adonihah." He had almost said Kihoran, because Dan knew his real name, but he needed to be Adonihah here, especially if Imrahiel already had a spy in the household.

"I'll let him know. Wait here." He whispered a few words to the other guard, then strode through the topiary gardens toward the side of the house, where he disappeared. Kai stepped away from the gate, standing near Vyim.

A few minutes later, the gate swung open and Dan emerged. He wore a crisp uniform of black and tan, like the outside guards, with thick leather bracers on his forearms. He carried a cudgel in his hand and a long knife at his waist.

He gave Kai a long, considering look. Benijah must have spoken to him.

"Is there somewhere private we can talk?" asked Kai.

Dan nodded. "Yes. Follow me." He led Kai through the gate, then to the right along a path through the gardens until they reached a small open area with two stone benches. Dan sat on one, indicating the other for Kai.

"I just came from speaking with your cousin Lehi."

Dan blinked. "Why did you go there?"

"Something big is happening, Dan. Lehi knows it. Helaman clearly knows it, too. Why else would he call a conference on the day after the New Year festival, in Gideon, not here?"

Dan stared at him. "I don't know. But Benijah says *you* seem to know too much."

Kai gave an exasperated huff. "I don't know *enough*. That's why I went to the house, hoping to find you or see the two assassins. I've infiltrated the group trying to overthrow the government in Zarahemla. They even gave me their first oath."

Dan tensed. "Why would you tell me this?"

"Because Benijah might not listen right now. And because a man name Imrahiel, one of the ringleaders of this evil band—who despises Benijah, by the way—ordered me to get close to Helaman's household. I told him I had a contact. That would be you. So we're talking. And Imrahiel will know within a few hours that we talked. He has spies everywhere. Maybe even here."

Dan took his time processing the information, eyes focused firmly on Kai. Finally, he asked, "What do you suggest I do?" It was as much a challenge as a query, and Kai could understand his hesitancy.

"Find a few guards you really trust, and make sure at least two of you are near Helaman at all times. That's my suggestion. In a few weeks, maybe when you and Benijah feel like you can trust me fully again, I want to become part of the guard detail. Helaman and I have met, at High Judge Zerahir's home, and I think *he* trusts me."

Dan raised his eyebrows, and Kai lifted a hand to forestall an objection. "I know this sounds strange, but I also know something awful is about to happen. It's been building ... and I don't think we're ready."

Dan leaned forward, dipping his head to stare at the ground. Kai remained quiet, letting him think.

Finally, Dan looked up. "I told Benijah I thought the assassins had spooked you, and that you served the Gadiantons now."

"The who?" He'd heard the name, but not the term.

"That's who leads them. A man name Gadianton, a wealthy lawyer and activist who used to support the king-men. We're confident of it now. We just don't have enough hard evidence to arrest him for anything yet."

Kai thought for a moment. "There's a young woman I met. She and her father are involved in some way, through Imrahiel. I've told Benijah about them. Her father's name is Nahom. I'm going to find her today. Maybe I can figure out a way to learn something more. I'm worried the rebels—or these Gadiantons—will strike during the church's conference in Gideon."

Dan's eyes narrowed. "Have you heard something specific?"

Kai shook his head. "No, but what better time for an attack? Even some of the garrison will go to the conference, I'm sure, if only to provide extra protection for Helaman."

"I don't think Benijah will allow that," said Dan, but he sounded unconvinced, which probably meant Benijah was indeed planning to have some of the garrison attend the conference.

"Either way," said Kai, "the garrison is far weaker than normal."

"Are you coming to the conference?"

"No. I have work to do here. I can't … I mean, I think I would enjoy it, but I can't leave." Kai was again surprised at his own change of mind. First he longed to return to Zarahemla, then he was anxious to leave, and now he was determined to stay? Actually, he didn't have much of a choice—he needed to report to Benijah the evening of the New Year festivities. So unless he traveled during the night to get to Gideon on orders from Benijah, he would remain in Zarahemla.

Dan studied him a few moments longer. "I do believe something bad is coming, and I certainly hope you're not involved in it."

Kai took his meaning, and he didn't protest. Instead, he asked, "Do you have any contacts among Pacumeni's guards?"

Dan shook his head. "No, but as chief judge, Pacumeni selects his own guards. I know Benijah has sent a few extra men, too."

"Do you think Helaman can send Pacumeni a warning? I know it will be almost impossible politically for Pacumeni to leave the city right now, but he's a Christian, and if Helaman can't persuade him to leave, maybe he can convince him to increase his protection detail."

Dan smiled for the first time during their conversation. To Kai, it felt like a minor victory. "I'm sure Helaman has warned him. There isn't anything more to do."

Kai returned the smile, somewhat grimly. "You're right. I'll see you when you get back." He stood and reached out his arm. Dan rose and clasped it.

"Be safe, Kihoran."

"Be safe, Dan."

Dan escorted him back outside the gate, where Kai mounted and turned Vyim down the street in the direction of Zerahir's house. He would just ride by, slowly. Perhaps Ara, through some coincidence, would be working at the front of the house and happen to see him. If not, he would go to *Jacob's Rest* and return on foot in the late afternoon to a main street where he could catch her on her way home. He noted with some unease that his desire to see her exceeded the need to deliver a message.

It turned out Ara did spot him, and she burst out the door just before he reached the next house. He spun Vyim toward her.

"Adonihah!" she exclaimed, coming to a stop near his left boot. "What are you doing here?" Her eyes widened as she admired Vyim, running a hand down his neck. "And where did you get such a *magnificent* horse?"

"I'm borrowing him. His name is Vyim, and he's faster than the prairie winds."

"He looks it," she agreed, then looked back up at him. "But why are you here? Everyone is going to talk."

"About what?" he asked innocently.

"About *us!*" she said, slapping him on the boot. Kai's heart skipped a beat. The way she'd said it made it sound like it was her greatest wish that everyone did indeed talk about them.

Kai tried to laugh it off. "Well, tell them I just invited you to dinner. Just don't tell them where. Can you meet me at *Jacob's Rest* after you leave today?"

"Yes," she said. "I've heard the food is very good there."

"It is."

"Okay, then. I'll see if I can leave a little earlier than normal. Mistress Lianah might even encourage it." She gave a coy smile, then whisked her skirt around as she turned and headed back toward the house.

Kai sat watching as she re-entered the manor. She turned with a wave and a smile before disappearing through the door and closing it. A guard, patrolling the front gardens, gazed at Kai quizzically for a moment, but then continued on his way. Kai closed his eyes. Had he taken on more than he could handle? He was grateful Siarah was all the way across the land in Bountiful. What would she think, even though it was part of his mission? The situation was more confusing than anything Imrahiel could throw at him, but at least he had a few hours to think.

Kai was already seated at one of the more secluded tables in the dining room when Ara arrived. She had changed her clothes and now wore a full dress, light and dark blue with some yellow accents. It didn't look overly formal, but it accentuated her figure. Kai couldn't help but stare a moment, and he guessed every other man in the establishment copied him. Ara ignored them all, focusing on Kai as she stepped sedately over to his table. He rose before she arrived, then hurried to pull out her chair and help her be seated.

"You look amazing," he said as he returned to his seat. He was being honest.

She tilted her head slightly, a demure smile appearing. She had put on some makeup—not much, but it highlighted her eyes and cheekbones. She had pinned her hair up in places, too, following one of the new styles.

"Thank you," she said primly. "You look like you could use a bath, but I won't complain." She surveyed the room, a broader smile teasing her lips.

Kai didn't know what to say. He clearly hadn't taken this dinner as seriously as she had. At least, not in the same way. Though he couldn't deny she was alluring, she was also a spy—and for the wrong side, at least partially.

Her gaze paused on a couple two tables over. More particularly, their plates of steaming food. She glanced at Kai. "The food looks expensive."

Kai shrugged slightly. "I usually only eat breakfast here, but don't worry about it." Her attitude seemed a little strange. When he had first met her, he had thought her one of the common working class, but then he learned her father was a judge, and even lower judges tended to be well-to-do. Maybe her father was miserly with his money, and she had to pay for everything herself. Or maybe he gambled. Gambling ruined a great many men. That and drinking. And infidelity, which often accompanied both.

"Okay, well, why don't you pick something out for me and tell the cooks," she said. "I chose for both of us last time."

"Last time was free," he reminded her.

"And your point is what?" she replied, slightly-darkened eyebrows raised.

He chuckled, raising his hands in surrender. "Nothing. Your choice last time was brilliant." Before she could respond to that jibe, he was up and moving away from the table, toward the cooks. One of them, a large, middle-aged woman, smiled as he approached.

"What's the best thing on your menu tonight?" he asked.

"Ah, it's beef tips braised in a tangy sauce with eastern legumes and a bread pudding with raisins that will make you squeal like a pig."

Kai's mouth watered at the description. "Wonderful. Two plates, please, and two mugs of your best mead."

The woman nodded, leaning to her left to get a look at Ara sitting at the table. Then she gave Kai a knowing grin. "She's a doll. We'll make sure she's impressed." She winked as Kai blushed. Then he returned to the table, walking slowly to let his face recover.

"Don't tell me what you ordered," she said as he sat. "I want to be surprised."

Kai smiled. "The cooks promised to impress you." He hadn't planned on saying that.

She laughed. "I think it's *you* they're trying to impress." She suddenly switched topics, saving him from figuring out how to respond. "What are you planning to do for the celebration?"

He shook his head. "I don't know. I've never been in Zarahemla for the New Year festival, and I missed the last three festivals in Bountiful since I was traveling."

"You like to dance, though, right?" she asked.

"Oh … well," Kai stuttered, "I mean … I guess so, but … I'm not good at it."

She snorted … elegantly. "All men say that. I don't know why. It's silly." Her chiding expression lasted only a moment, her face brightening. "Everybody dances during the New Year celebrations, and there's so much food, from everywhere. Some of it's even free … well, except at the inns, which tend to raise their prices. It's amazing. I'm sure they do something similar in Bountiful."

Kai nodded. "Yeah, pretty much. They have a lot of races, too, and wrestling contests and baking competitions."

"Here, too!" Ara's eyes brightened further. "You should enter one of the wrestling contests. The men usually take their shirts off."

He blinked, feeling the blush return. She was flirting as she always did, but he hadn't been as affected by it before. Maybe it was her dress, and her makeup, and her hair. And was that perfume?

He tried to recover with what he hoped was a sly, confident smile, but it felt weak. "And you'll be entering one of the baking contests, right?"

She laughed, lightly slapping the table. "No, of course not. I bake like I sew—badly. I'll enter one of the races—on your horse!" It sounded like she was joking, but Kai couldn't tell for sure.

Kai laughed along with her, finding his responses becoming less forced. "If he'll let you. He's picky."

"Oh?" she said. "Like you?" She paused, staring intently at him, her slight smile daring him to come up with a suitable answer.

He was saved by one of the servers arriving and setting their plates in front of them. The young man placed two tall, thin mugs from his serving platter onto the table as well. "Enjoy your meal," he said with a slight bow before retreating.

Kai stared at the steaming food. The smells nearly overcame him. He looked up at Ara, who spent a little longer gazing at her plate. She smiled finally, meeting Kai's eyes. "This is incredible. Thank you, Adonihah." Then she lifted her fine silver fork and began eating, slowly and properly, unlike the way she had devoured her meal at the restaurant in the Santorem. He could tell she savored every bite. It reminded him of how much pure joy his sister Neva usually expressed, even in the simple things, which made him happy. He sternly reminded himself he wasn't in Zarahemla to protect Ara, though—at least, not just her. He was there to defend the Nephite nation and the cause of freedom.

When he finished his food, and she was nearly done, he decided to ask his first serious question. He had thought hard about what it should be, and he lowered his voice, checking to make sure nobody was close enough to overhear, though the lively room provided a good amount of background noise; a small band was even setting up to perform.

"So, what do you think the Lamanites will do when they have control of the city?"

She frowned slightly as she swallowed a bite. Then she took a leisurely sip of her mead. "I think they'll be a little harsh at first, but then things will get back to normal, especially once a unity government is agreed upon."

Kai narrowed his eyes. The answer didn't match their last conversation. "That's what your father thinks. What do *you* think?"

She forked another bite, pausing. "I think it won't work out how the Lamanites have planned it. I'm worried. Maybe even terrified. There, you happy? I already told you I didn't like this topic." She took her next bite, adding a small smile that showed she wasn't truly angry at the question.

He launched into the next one. "Why do you think Helaman called the Christians to a conference in Gideon to be held the day after the New Year festival? Do you think he knows something?"

She nodded as she finished that bite. "I think he's concerned, yes, but I have no idea whether his conference has anything to do with the planned overthrow. I've never understood the Christians well. But Helaman seems like a good guy. He's kind of cute, too. Too bad he's married." She flashed her most flirtatious smile yet, then quickly put more food in her mouth.

Kai rested his arms on the table and clasped his hands, leaning closer. "Do you think the assassin will go after Pacumeni?"

She sat up straighter, wiping the corners of her mouth with a napkin. Then she shook her head. "No. Pacumeni didn't have his brother Paanchi hanged. Pahoran did that. In fact, Pacumeni will probably make a good puppet for those setting up the unity government. My father doesn't like Pacumeni, but I haven't gotten the sense he wishes him dead … or rather, believes he *needs* to be dead."

"Are you sure Pacumeni's not part of the unity government plot?"

"Pretty sure. I've seen some messages coming to Zerahir. Pacumeni doesn't seem to be worried about anything except being assassinated like his brother. He's paranoid about it."

Kai scrunched his brow. "I can imagine." He paused, then took a risk. "I spoke to Imrahiel and asked for his protection. I told him Captain Benijah of the garrison here is using me as bait for some scheme among the high judges. Imrahiel agreed, but asked me to get close to Helaman, which I think I can do. I even took an oath."

Ara froze, then blinked once, twice, a third time. Her skin took on a bluish cast, as if she couldn't breathe. "You swore the first oath?" she asked in an icy whisper.

"There's more than one?"

She squeezed her eyes shut. "There are at least four. I've taken the first two." Her eyes popped open, revealing stark terror. "They'll punish you severely you if you break your oaths, even kill you if they think it's necessary. They'll do it without hesitation, Adonihah. You shouldn't have taken that oath." Her intensity was startling, but he had no regrets.

"I had to. I need to know more about what's going on. And by the way, aren't you breaking your oaths by speaking to me this way? Or are you spying on me for Imrahiel?"

She stared silently at him for several seconds. Both umbrage and fear danced chaotically behind her eyes. "No," she said finally, "I'm not spying on you, though he asked me to. Did you think this was all a show?" Anger leaked into her voice.

"He asked me to spy on *you*," Kai responded calmly, "shortly after I first arrived here. He was worried your devotion to the cause was slipping. I'm not surprised he asked you to spy on me, too."

She continued to study him, until it became distinctly uncomfortable. Then she said, "What's really going on in that crazy head of yours, Adonihah? Do you think I'm your enemy?" She swallowed, suddenly appearing anxious about his answer.

"I just need to know where you stand."

She gave an exasperated shake of her head, raising her hands, palms up. "I don't *know* where I stand, Adonihah. Do you know where *you* stand?"

He waited a few moments to answer, then nodded. "I do. It has become clearer to me over the last few months. Before I came to Zarahemla, and then traveled to Gideon, I was just an obedient soldier. But now I see why I need to be doing what I'm doing, and those reasons center on God like they should, finally. I follow his prophet, Helaman. As long as he supports the Nephite government, I will fight to protect it." Those words sounded strange coming out of his mouth. He was astonished he had articulated them so well. He truly wouldn't have been able to do so six months ago.

Ara seemed stunned. Her eyes went slightly wide, her jaw slack. Her voice became a low whisper. "So you're really a *Christian*? Imrahiel believes you left that religion."

"Yes, I am," he said, proud at how firmly he felt it. This certainty of belief was new territory for him.

Suddenly she reached her left hand across the table and grasped his right hand. He almost retracted it out of shock, even wondering if a dagger would appear in her other hand.

"Can you teach me about it?" she asked, seeming sincere. Kai's mind spun. Was this a trick?

"Um ... sure, I guess so. Do you really want to know?" His gaze flicked to her right hand, which still sat innocently on the table.

Her nod carried great energy. "Yes. When I was secretly copying documents for Imrahiel at the high judge's house, I found two letters from

Helaman to Zerahir." She reached for his other hand, then squeezed both. "The letters weren't what I expected. Helaman is not a politician. I can't find any hint of selfishness in his words. And these were *private* letters to a trusted confidant. I was already starting to doubt 'the cause' because of the sheer cruelty I saw growing in my father, but those letters accelerated my uncertainty. They *sang* to me, Adonihah."

Kai sat flummoxed for several seconds. Could she be making all of this up? He glanced down at her hands grasping his. Her grip was still tight. He looked into her eyes again, trying to measure her sincerity. She was a skilled spy, so how could he trust what he thought he saw there? And then there was the request itself, which caused its own tremor of nervousness. He had never spoken in depth with anyone about his beliefs. He didn't know enough to adequately teach someone else, did he? What could he say? Where would he start? He didn't even have any copies of the scriptural writings with him, and he hadn't memorized much.

He leaned back a little, letting her maintain the hold on his hands. "I'm not the best teacher," he began, "but I'll try. I can get advice from some priests, too—maybe not ones here in Zarahemla, since Imrahiel would notice, but in some nearby towns, or in Gideon. I know a great priest there."

"We could take a trip there," she said with obvious excitement. "I'm sure your horse could carry us both." An idea flashed in her eyes, and she smiled broadly. "We could go to that conference in Gideon. We can enjoy the New Year celebrations in Zarahemla in the morning, then leave for Gideon in the afternoon. We might not be able to find an inn with a room there, but that's okay. We can sleep out under the stars."

The conversation had become uncomfortably personal, but that wasn't why Kai shook his head. "I have to remain here. There's too much to do. I report to Captain Benijah the night of the celebrations, and I'm guessing he'll ask me to stay anyway."

Disappointment clouded her face for a moment, but then she shook it off, her expression cheery. "That's okay. We'll both stay here … um … together?" Her eyes darted to the stairwell.

He knew exactly what she was asking. "No, I'm sorry," he said, gently breaking her grip. "I can't do that."

Confusion and hurt ruled her features momentarily, but then her eyes went wide, and she blushed deeply. "Oh, Adonihah, I'm sorry. You're a Christian. Of course. I've just thought for so long you weren't one, that somehow I … well, I—"

"Don't worry about it," he said, waving a hand in front of him. "Seriously, don't." There was more to it, of course, but he wasn't going to bring up Siarah.

After the server had removed their plates, Ara made Kai promise he would meet her at the third bell of the first day of the new year to enjoy some of the festival together. Kai wasn't sure what Imrahiel would think of his two questionable spies spending the day together, but maybe he'd be happy, since one might expose the other and get him some valuable intel at the same time. Kai's resentment of the man grew two sizes just thinking about it.

Ara wanted to keep talking, so they spent the next three hours at the table. She peppered him with questions about his family and his upbringing, often launching into stories of her own life, especially experiences from when her mother was alive. Kai knew what it was like to lose a parent—to lose both parents—though the specific memories had dulled. Ara had an animated way of speaking when she felt comfortable, and she related some surprisingly personal—though not inappropriate—things. He started out hesitant, but he opened up as the conversation progressed.

Finally, as one of the hour bells rang, she said, "I'm sorry, I need to go now. My father is expecting me. But I'll be here for the celebrations, okay?"

Kai nodded. "It's a date."

"Good." She rose and smoothed out her dress. Kai stood, too. She smiled at him and hesitated, then waved as she turned and started walking away. What had she been about to do? Kiss him? What would he have done if she had tried? He wasn't exactly sure. But he had wondered several times that night what it would be like to kiss her, and that thought made him feel a confused form of awful.

He spent a few more minutes at the table, thinking about their conversation, having requested another mug of mead. When he eventually got to his room, he noticed a letter had been slid under the door. He did a quick check, out of habit, but everything was in its place. Intensely curious, he stooped to pick it up, noting the feminine handwriting on the outside of the parchment, which had been folded flat and sealed with a small bit of red wax. He thought he recognized the flow of the script. He broke the seal and unfolded the parchment, remembering to close his door with his foot as he took another step into the room. He sat on the edge of the bed as he began to read. Awe and guilt struck him at the same time.

The letter was from Siarah. Before leaving Bountiful, he had told her he went by the undercover name of Adonihah most of the time. But she couldn't have known he was at *Jacob's Rest* … unless she had arranged for someone to find out where he was staying, which wouldn't have been too difficult.

He paused, feeling the parchment in his hands. She had written him a letter, which she hadn't done before. Why did that feel so special, and so intimate? She didn't have to write him; he certainly hadn't written her. That cued only part of the guilt. He would be spending the New Year festival with another woman, someone who clearly liked him and was beautiful and interesting. He could argue to himself the entire night that spending time with Ara was part of his mission, but it seemed like an excuse.

After struggling a few more moments to make sense of his thoughts, he started over.

Dear Adonihah,

I know you've been gone many times before, but this time seems the longest. I also know your job is important. The murder of the chief judge is such a horrible, evil thing. We received news not long ago that Pacumeni has become the new chief judge. We hear many rumors, too, some of them truly frightening.

I worry about you in Zarahemla. It doesn't seem like it's safe there. I know I don't have any say—you must follow your orders—but if there's a way for you to get out of the city, please take it. I've prayed about your safety, night and day, and this is the answer I've been getting. I pray for Helaman, too, and the other church leaders. Just when it feels like we're entering a time of peace, the threat of cruel and devastating war rises again.

I know the Lord, our Savior Jesus Christ, who will come to the earth soon, is watching over you. I know he is, and not just because I've pleaded for your safety. He has a purpose for you. I feel that, deeply. I hope you feel that in your prayers, too.

Things are calm in Bountiful, besides anxiety over all the rumors. My family is doing well. Yours, too. I just had dinner last night with your parents and sister. We had a wonderful time. Gideon and Ishara are such good people, and Neva misses you almost as much as I do. She is an amazing young woman, full of faith and optimism. I wish I was more like her!

The clothing I make continues to sell well, especially the children's clothes. I enjoy making them the most, and I suppose that comes out in my designs and handiwork. I someday wish to be able to make clothes for my own children … for our children. I hope that's not too forward.

I love you, Ҡ Adonihah. You are amazing. I pray for you always. Please be careful.
With warmest regards,
Siarah

Kai stared at the letter for a full minute. Then he read it again. His heart warmed within him. He had always felt loved by Gideon and Ishara, even though he wasn't their biological son. This emotion, though, was new, different, and amazing. Siarah loved him. It didn't matter that she was one of the most sought-after young women in Bountiful. She had given her heart to Kai, and with her, he was truly no longer an orphan.

CHAPTER 10

*O ye pollutions, ye hypocrites, ye teachers, who sell yourselves for that
which will canker, why have ye polluted the holy church of God? Why are
ye ashamed to take upon you the name of Christ? Why do ye not think
that greater is the value of an endless happiness than that misery which
never dies—because of the praise of the world?*

MORMON 8:38

The first-day festivities in Zarahemla were as grand as anything Kai had
ever seen—not just in other cities but in other nations. The Nephites
of the capital city did their best to put the entire world to shame with
assiduously detailed planning and exorbitant expense. People traveled many
miles to join the parties in Zarahemla; some even shunned the grand celebrations in other large Nephite cities, as if embarking on a holy pilgrimage.
Nothing held a candle to the capital.

Kai and Ara began their day watching the races at the large track two
miles north of the city. Workers had labored for several weeks preparing
the track with a fresh bed of finely crushed stone, layered over with a clay-
heavy soil and compacted. The circuit of the track measured at least a mile,
and spread thirty feet wide all along its length. Other workers—artisans,
mostly—had made repairs and adjustments to the large-scale replica of the
city of Zarahemla that occupied the area inside the track. The model included
walls, roads, and the River Sidon, with real water pumped along its course
by a mule-driven water wheel and returned underground to cycle through.

He'd never seen the famed replica before, its outer walls standing half as tall as a man. People walked around inside the miniature city, feeling like giants as they observed the painstaking details the artisans had created, including new buildings and bridges, additions to houses or shops, and even house flags that had changed over the past year.

Large, permanent seating structures of quarried stone and thick timbers stood on three sides of the track—west, north, and south—and Ara explained that at least a thousand new seats had been added over the last year. A multitude of large, colorful pennants of varied designs marched along the tops of the stadium structures. The most notable was a stylized version of Moroni's famed Title of Liberty. Kai wondered if Moroni would appreciate the bold, new colors and precisely formed lettering. Moronihah had never mentioned what he thought of the 'updated' design, but it was becoming increasingly popular throughout the nation as a decoration. Hopefully, it still provided some real inspiration, too.

The track hosted multiple kinds of races, some occurring at the same time. Horses could be ridden on the outside half of the track while people raced on foot on the inner half. Having humans running in close proximity to horses was insanity, in Kai's opinion, even though it was a reality sometimes in the army. The most grueling races were the seven-lap events, meant to signify the seven times the Israelites circled the city of Jericho on the seventh day of their siege. At the end of the seventh lap around the track, the trumpets blew loudly, and the fans in the stands pretended to fall back into their seats, or into each other, laughing and cheering as they imagined the walls of Jericho tumbling down so their ancestors could conquer the city. It would have made more sense to Kai if they had built a replica of the city of Jericho in the middle, with mechanisms to make the walls fall, but the people of Zarahemla seemed to love the symbolism of their own walls continuing to stand while everyone outside the circumference of the track fell.

After watching a few races, Ara asked to return to the city for lunch—or what she called 'feast of a thousand different bites.' Kai knew what she meant, and he suspected he would tire of trying so many free samples. But as they progressed among the hundreds of food vendors set up for the festivities, he found he enjoyed taking just a small bite of something from each shop or stand. He wasn't a picky eater, nor was he accustomed to fancy foods, so by about the twentieth vendor he worried he had spoiled himself permanently.

After several more delectable bites, he begged for a halt. Ara laughed and then took him to the wrestling matches. She didn't press him to enter any of the contests, as she had threatened to do, but he noticed her glancing occasionally away from the contestants toward him—and more specifically, his chest. He wasn't used to feeling so self-conscious. His chest was the strong chest of a military man who kept in fighting shape, but it wasn't anything special.

After less than an hour, she grew bored of the wrestling, so they found their way to one of the outdoor theaters set up on the major streets. Actors had developed and rehearsed short plays, which they performed to thunderous applause and a light rain of coins thrown toward the stage after each performance.

The first play they watched was the story of Abish, the Lamanite woman who had gathered her people to hear from Ammon and witness the miracle of King Lamoni's revival about four decades ago in the Land of Ishmael, far to the south. Her good intentions had nearly gotten Ammon killed. The performance contained a great deal of dramatic fainting—including the protracted death throes of the brother of the man Ammon had slain with his sword at the waters of Sebus—along with vociferous arguments and wails of despair, followed by joyous celebrations. A short encore commenced, featuring the confrontation between Ammon and Lamoni's father, King Laman, in which Ammon overpowered but spared the king, showing both martial ability and clever magnanimity in gaining autonomy for Lamoni and his people, who became the core of the Ammonites. Dan's parents might have been from Ishmael.

The next performance they viewed was the episode of Nephi's broken bow. The man who played Nephi was a hulking monster, and although they had obviously rigged the metal prop bow to break in the opening scene, Kai could picture the man snapping a real steel bow in half. The actor exaggerated his emotional reactions to the devastating loss of his hunting tool, and his fierce bulk made the drama seem even more incongruous.

At the happy conclusion of that show—Nephi having found food for his family after constructing a new bow out of wood and receiving instructions from the Lord on where to hunt—Ara and Kai wandered over to a different stage on another street. They stopped at several more food vendors along the way, catching the tail end of a play about the final, calamitous battle of the Jaredites, replete with an actor playing Shiz donning a cloth that covered his head and blended in with the floor of the stage, thereby making him look headless. After he did a wobbly, partial push-up and collapsed, the actor playing Coriantumr made a sweeping, victorious flourish with his wooden sword, leaned heavily on it, and then crashed to the stage himself, the impact amplified by someone behind the short curtain slamming two large pieces of wood together. This play had a narrator, too, who voiced the part of the prophet Ether, recounting the many warnings from the Lord he had given to Coriantumr and his people.

That performance was followed by another involving a headless villain at the end—the infamous Laban of Jerusalem, jealous and wicked one-time keeper of the brass plates of Jewish scripture, which had given the Nephite nation its rich historical and linguistic traditions as a branch of the house of Israel.

Afterward, they wandered away to search out more food vendors. Ara now focused on sweets.

"There aren't nearly as many people here as normal," she commented with a small sigh as they strolled along.

"Many Christians have already left for Gideon," noted Kai unnecessarily.

She creased her brow. "Why did Helaman have to call the conference for tomorrow again? I love the large crowds we usually get for the major festivals, but especially this one. It doesn't feel the same."

"This is more people than I've ever seen at a festival," Kai offered.

"Well, you're a country bumpkin from Bountiful," she teased as she took his arm. "I shouldn't complain, though. I've never had as good a companion for *any* of the festivals." She gazed up at him, eyes sparkling. He chuckled, trying to play along without doing it *too* well. And without that note from Siarah, he wondered whether he would be acting at all.

"You have low standards," he joked.

"Well, be glad I at least have *some* standards," she quipped.

He wasn't sure how to take that comment, but he laughed anyway, and she continued pulling him along, from vendor to vendor, stage to stage, until they arrived at the great plaza in the center of the city as the sun was setting. Musicians played various types of music: some Nephite, some foreign, some ancient. People had started to dance, too. Ara shrieked in delight as the musicians launched into a new song, grabbing Kai's hand and pulling him out into the plaza among the dancing couples.

He wasn't a great dancer, because he'd never danced much, but he did have the ability to feel the beating heart of the music and translate it to his limbs. Ishara had always told him that with a little training he could be a fine dancer. And it wasn't that he didn't enjoy dancing; he had just never found much occasion for it. Luckily, Ara was patient and didn't tease him too much. He spent the first hour watching other men closely, trying to understand and mimic their movements. But there were so many different types of dances; how did anyone learn them all? Ara laughed when he asked her that question. She seemed to know the steps and flourishes for each and every dance, and she even helped him with the parts specific to the men. She must spend a great deal of time dancing, he decided.

They twirled and skipped around the plaza for another two hours, with only a few breaks. The frolicking crowd increased as the evening deepened, hundreds of lamps strung on ropes around the plaza lighting up the night. He had to admit it was an amazing scene. He had never thought he could have so much fun dancing and listening to music.

As the third bell of the evening neared, Kai knew he needed to be heading for the army encampment. When Ara called another break, he let her know. She understood, of course—but she told him he had to meet her the next day at the place where they had eaten in the Santorem. He promised he would try, but that it depended on his orders. She accepted that condition, then gave him a smoldering kiss on the cheek. She said she would keep dancing for a while, with a smile that conveyed she was trying to make him jealous. Part of him *was* envious, though that made him feel like a lecher.

He spent the brisk walk to the inn trying to refocus his thoughts and prepare his report for Captain Benijah. A lot was happening, and he was becoming more deeply enmeshed in the conspiracies swirling through the great city of Zarahemla, which many Nephites called the heaven-favored capital of the world, even considering Jerusalem. After witnessing the festival that day, he found it hard to argue against that opinion.

Vyim seemed anxious to travel, and he wanted to run, so Kai gave him free rein. Vyim's energetic pace made the trip to the encampment exceedingly short, leaving Kai less time to rehearse. He felt nervous. He hated that Benijah didn't fully trust him, and he wasn't sure how he could change the captain's suspicions about him.

When he announced himself at the outer gates, the guards waved him in immediately. That was either great or awful news, but their specific behavior didn't give anything away. He dismounted after crossing the practice yard this time, leading Vyim to one of the stables first, as was proper. In truth, the longer it took him, the better.

When he finally approached the command tent, he felt mostly ready to see Benijah. He recognized both guards, and they ushered him inside. In the first room, three captains conversing around a small table stood when he entered. Their faces were impassive, but it jarred him that they had stood. The flaps to the next room parted, and Benijah stepped out, rolling up a piece of parchment and placing it in a small tube. He looked at Kai.

"Welcome, Kihoran," he said, his tone completely unremarkable. Another great or awful sign. He turned to one of the captains at the table and handed him the tube. "Get this to Gideon—tonight. Take three of your best men."

The man saluted, then hurried out of the tent.

Benijah addressed Kai and the two remaining captains. "Come into the command room." He turned and passed back through the flaps. Kai let the captains precede him.

Benijah seated himself behind a new, larger desk. Six other chairs faced it. Kai and the captains sat and waited for Benijah to speak first.

Benijah brought his arms up onto the wooden surface, clasping his hands and settling his eyes on Kai. He appeared both thoughtful and solemn. "An attempt was made on Helaman's life last night. One of our soldiers had chosen to stay a double-shift and was able to help stop it. One guard was killed. Helaman, thankfully, was uninjured. There were two assassins. One died, and the other was taken. We haven't yet been able to ascertain the surviving assassin's name. He may not be from Zarahemla."

Kai could barely breathe. He was convinced Imrahiel was somehow involved, which made him seethe with anger. He glanced at the two captains, who stared solemnly at the table. They weren't asking any questions, which meant they already knew.

"Was Dan there?" he asked Benijah.

"Yes. He was the soldier who remained. He said he stayed because of you."

"He wasn't killed, was he?" asked Kai, concern spiking.

"No, thankfully. Nor was he hurt. Can you tell me why you gave him that warning? Did you have specific intelligence?"

Kai shook his head. "No, nothing specific, not even about Helaman. I had a strong feeling, though. Dan told me the group I've been trying to infiltrate is called the Gadiantons. It's becoming clear to me how evil they are—and how determined to overthrow the government and install their chosen people at the head of an all-powerful oligarchy. And I . . . well, I have, I think, earned some trust from them, though they haven't told me about Gadianton yet. I was invited to take their first oath."

Benijah narrowed his gaze, then observed the two captains for a moment before addressing Kai. "Did you take that oath?"

"Yes, sir. I do not intend to keep it, though. It's a false oath, and vile."

Benijah nodded pensively, his eyes clouded. "We had someone inside a few months ago. He disappeared. You'll need to be exceedingly careful, and not just for your own safety. If they ask you to take the second oath, don't do it."

"Sir? Why?" Ara had already issued the same warning, but hadn't offered any specifics on the oath itself.

"Because then they'll probably ask you to hurt or even kill someone, possibly someone innocent. It's not worth it."

"Even if we can save the nation?"

Benijah's mien turned more serious. "Take the long view, Kai. You are valuable as a scout and a spy, but to the Lord you are most valuable as a covenant member of his Church, and as a literal child of God. Knowingly killing innocent people would imperil your soul, and blunt—perhaps even sever—your eternal progress. We don't gather intelligence that way."

"But what if I was just following orders? I wouldn't necessarily know the person was innocent of any real crimes or not." He knew instantly what he'd said was ridiculous, and he almost cringed.

Benijah clearly discerned Kai's discomfort, giving him a tight smile. "There are two problems with that. One, you would be following the orders of people you know for certain have evil intent. And two, God can always accomplish his work without resorting to lying, cheating, stealing, or killing innocent people. If we can't have faith in that, then we don't understand enough about who God is and why he does what he does, and we don't *deserve* to prevail."

Kai pondered that assessment, feeling the truth of it settle in his mind as it never had before. He had wrestled with similar moral scenarios in the past. Some of his trainers had given comparable explanations, but their reasoning had been difficult to understand when applied to the real situations in which he often found himself. Benijah had articulated it clearly.

The captain leaned farther forward. "I know it's hard to comprehend sometimes, but trust me. I know it's real."

Kai nodded, then took a deep breath and asked, "Do you trust *me*, sir?" He hadn't intended to ask the question so directly, but it seemed right.

Benijah sat back, his face becoming pensive again. "I think so. More importantly, though, Helaman trusts you. I briefed him early this morning before he left for Gideon. He knows everything. Chief Judge Pacumeni, too. You did a good thing. Keep searching for more information on the Gadiantons, but be careful—and again, don't take that second oath."

Helaman had told Benijah he trusted Kai. Contemplating that gave him an incredibly warm feeling and a rush of pride. Some small doubts crept in, though. Did Helaman really mean what he'd said? And had Kai truly earned that trust?

He was tempted to ride for Gideon, but he decided to return to Zarahemla, partly because he was anxious to do more to justify Helaman's trust in him. So many questions raced through his mind. Had what he'd told Dan really helped save Helaman's life? If so, what more could he figure out? What plots could he uncover? Which Gadiantons could he expose with enough evidence to convict them? He felt a strange thrill at the possibilities, despite the dangers. He knew he wasn't invincible, but for that night, at least, he felt close to it.

Unexpectedly, *Jacob's Rest* brimmed with customers, despite most of the Christians being gone. He overheard one of the innkeepers joking that having the Christian conference elsewhere had turned out to be a *good* thing; people had poured in from other towns, and they were willing to buy more alcohol at higher prices. The inn was making a killing off people who felt less inhibited with fewer Christians around.

Kai pondered that irony as he climbed the staircase to the second floor and entered his room. It was getting late—already past the fifth night bell— but he knew customers would remain well past midnight. He suddenly felt fully spent, both mentally and physically. The day's many festivities— especially the dancing—and his overall sense of anxiety made him rejoice in the prospect of sleep. He wanted to be up early, though, his determination toward the mission rejecting his body's suggested plan to sleep in.

He had just awakened and was washing his face when he heard the trumpets. He froze, listening intently for the call to repeat. They blared again, their message unmistakable: the gates were closing, emergency order. How often had that happened in Zarahemla? A few times, maybe, but it had to be rare. He quickly dressed, belting on his short sword and grabbing his bow. By the time he opened his door, he heard another set of trumpet blasts. The call to arms. It repeated three times, the third as he skidded to a stop in front of the stable doors behind the inn. He raced inside, saddled Vyim in record time, then rode for the Grand Gates on the eastern side of the city.

Sure enough, the gates stood closed, and he spotted nervous guards atop the wall. They weren't gazing east, though—they stared toward the west. He wheeled Vyim in that direction, grateful there were few people outside despite the trumpets. The last bell of the night hadn't sounded yet, and the dawning sunlight was just beginning to make things clear.

He marveled again at Vyim's speed. On smooth roads he was lightning. Maybe that should have been his name. He could have won every race the day before at the track. Soon Kai approached the Golden Gates. Far more soldiers—and a few militiamen—had gathered on the walls above those gates, and Kai hailed an officer still on the street.

"What is the threat?" he shouted, imbuing his voice with authority, knowing Vyim enhanced it.

The man paused only a moment before answering. "Army approaching from the west. We have no scouts in that direction, but it appears to be Lamanites, moving fast."

Kai's gut twisted, his mind reeling, dread pounding at his chest. Vyim pulled at the reins, rearing and spinning in a full circle.

"Where's the garrison?" Kai asked. He saw far too few soldiers inside the walls.

The officer shook his head, obviously trying to force down panic. "There's no time to get them all inside. They're mustering now to march here and defend the gates. We'll bring in as many as we can, and we'll provide cover from above. The militia is being gathered, too, but many of those men are in Gideon, including every single one of Helaman's two thousand who live nearby."

"How large is the Lamanite army?" Kai's mind had stuck momentarily, amazed at how woefully unprepared the Lamanites had caught them.

"Big, but we don't know exactly how big. They're close, but the trees hide a lot of them."

"Open the postern," Kai ordered. "I'm a scout. I'll see what I can find out and get the information to Captain Benijah."

The officer turned and ordered a soldier to open the interior side of the postern gate, several paces north of the main gate. Kai urged Vyim toward it, then dismounted to lead him through, another soldier preceding him to remove the locks and reinforcements from the exterior gate so he could exit. Once outside, Kai remounted and kicked Vyim into a full gallop to the northwest, trying to get around the front edge of the advancing Lamanites to better assess their numbers. They were no more than three miles away now, about the same distance from the city to the garrison. He knew they would have a few horses and that some might give chase, but he wasn't worried. Vyim was fresh, and the Lamanites' mounts had obviously traveled much of the night.

Kai quickly discovered that the Lamanite front extended farther north than he had initially perceived, so he slowed Vyim and turned to race back toward the south, encouraging every bit of speed Vyim had so he could reach the mustering Nephite garrison. Nephite troops ran toward the city from the encampment at a run, aiming for the area in front of the Golden Gates where they could hastily set a defensive line while getting as many soldiers inside as possible.

Kai spotted the garrison's banner held by a man riding next to Benijah, who himself rode a gray and black steed. A path opened for Kai to approach, and without any further direction Vyim pulled up hard to stop directly in front of the captain.

"I can't see the northern edge, sir! This is a massive army."

Benijah's face turned grimmer. "See what you can to the south and west."

"We can't keep them out of the city," said Kai. "But we might hold inside the garrison walls—at least until help arrives."

"I will not give up Zarahemla without a fight. We'll arm everyone inside if we have to. Go. Now."

Kai didn't see much benefit in that. It was already clear they were vastly outnumbered. He was about to suggest he gather a few other horsemen and find a way to harry the Lamanites' flanks, or trick them into thinking reinforcements would soon appear, but Benijah had moved on, shouting orders to several of his captains, who hastened to obey. So Kai obeyed, too, noting again with a depressed feeling how few Nephite men remained in the garrison. They were maybe a thousand strong, and very young. He estimated the Lamanite king had somehow gathered at least twenty thousand men and deposited them near the gates of Zarahemla, as if dropped out of the sky.

He rode Vyim hard, and soon revised his assessment. The Lamanite lines extended a great distance, and were extremely deep. There had to be at least fifty thousand troops. Zarahemla had no chance. The walls of the garrison wouldn't have helped much, either, not at fifty-to-one.

Unless … unless the Lord intervened. He could, Kai knew. He had before. Hope filled him as he swung east, then north, aiming for the main road that would take him to the Grand Gates on the east side of the city. When he arrived, Vyim's flanks and shoulders glistened. Kai shouted up at the soldiers on the wall. "Open the postern! I'm a scout from two-seven, under Benijah's orders."

One of the guards peered at him carefully, then turned and shouted down at some others. Soon the outer door opened, and Kai dismounted to lead Vyim through. Once inside, he remounted, heading back across the city, finally stopping at the stairs leading to the top of the wall near the Golden Gates. He vaulted off Vyim's back, then raced up the steps, carrying his bow and a full quiver. Several militiamen followed, bleary-eyed from the night's celebrations. A few of them looked like they could barely walk, much less hold a sword, but fear would loosen their blood soon enough.

The Lamanites were close now, and they had slowed. Kai expected they would stop, and some new Zoramite or Amalekite general would come forward and shout a demand for surrender through a large bull's horn. It made sense for the Lamanites to wait, anticipating capitulation. The Zarahemla garrison was vastly outnumbered, and most of the Nephite soldiers weren't even inside the strong walls of the city. Even if they were, a force of fifty thousand men was more than enough to breach the Nephite defenses.

But the Lamanites didn't stop. As Benijah and his meager force began to organize a few paces from the gates, with only a shallow ditch for cover, horns sounded up and down the Lamanite lines. Kai knew what they meant, and he anxiously scanned the horizon, hoping to see a miracle. But the skies were clear—the Lord hadn't sent tornadoes to help them. The earth didn't buckle and rupture under the enemy, either, as it had for the armies of Enoch. *Why?* Kai cried within himself. *Now would be the time!*

The Lamanites charged, and Kai's hopes crumbled beneath their pounding feet and blood-curdling yells. Benijah and his men were doomed unless they surrendered. Kai knew they wouldn't.

After another silent prayer, he set aside his despair and nocked an arrow, letting his training take over. The top of the wall featured a ledge to protect his legs as he stood and fired at the onrushing horde, just after Benijah's men began to engage. He selected his targets carefully and made sure his aim was precise, knowing that for a couple of seconds each time he fired, he was blind to whatever missiles might be coming at him.

He hit his first mark, a captain, square in the chest, though the man's armor prevented the arrow from penetrating deeply. He missed his second target, then hit his third and fourth, causing serious wounds. He paused briefly, taking stock. The bristling spear wall of the Nephites held for the moment, but it couldn't endure long, not even with the storm of arrows flying from the top of the wall. Would a Nephite army arrive, maybe from the north or south? Was *that* the miracle? Would Moronihah himself lead an army to their rescue?

Hope dared to flare in Kai's chest until he spied a group of Lamanites with overlarge bows. He had seen such bows before. Instead of using arrows, they utilized long hooked shafts attached to ropes. Dozens of these archers spread out along the wall for hundreds of yards. They began launching, hooks sailing over the top of the wall, trailing their ropes. Some of the hooks didn't catch, but most did, and then men with special gloves began climbing the ropes, placing their feet on the slightly outward-sloping surface of the wall. Lamanite archers with regular bows, along with slingers, moved closer to protect the climbers, some of whom had already fallen victim to Nephite arrows. Kai had witnessed the deadly sound of the Lamanites' long slings, but he had never heard so many of them singing at once, accented by the staccato of hundreds of snapping bowstrings.

Nephites on the wall began to fall, struck by stones and arrows. As Kai ducked, he saw a portion of the Nephite defensive line below shatter. Crouching, he slung his bow over his shoulder, and then began running south along the wall, drawing his sword and hacking at ropes. He severed more than a dozen before Lamanites started to top the wall ahead of him. Instead of retreating, he charged, cutting down one man with a feint and a vicious slash across both thighs, then pushing another back over the wall before several others formed a group and rushed toward him. He retreated, knowing that holding the top of the wall was now impossible. He reached the stairs and ran down, narrowly avoiding a dagger thrown from above.

Shortly after touching the ground, he jumped on Vyim and sped down one of the streets of the city, heading east. Soon he heard shouts and clashes ahead, near the eastern walls, meaning the Lamanites had surrounded the city already and were breaching the walls in all directions. The situation was disastrous, hopeless. And still no horns announced the approach of a Nephite army. The city was lost. He turned south, toward the warehouse district, searching for a place to lay low until reinforcements arrived and he could rejoin the fight. Perhaps he could even sabotage the Lamanites from the inside.

A few people swirled around him in a panic, but most huddled inside their homes. He heard screams and shouts, even some prayers thrown heavenward. Occasionally he spotted a small group of men carrying various types of weapons, most of which needed sharpening, oiling, or restringing, but the men were rudderless; they didn't know where to go or what to do. He also noted a ragged line of unarmed people—men, women, and a few children—hurrying in the direction of the temple. He wondered if they were Christians who regretted their decision to skip Helaman's conference; either way, he hoped they would find some sort of refuge on the temple grounds. He sorely wished he had decided to go to Gideon, and taken Ara with him.

He reached the warehouse, proceeding to the sizeable barn next to it. He found the owner of the barn inside, trying to calm frightened animals, mostly horses. Kai startled the man as he entered, then raised a hand in peace. "I need a place for my horse, just temporarily. The city is falling."

The man stared dumbly at him for a moment, then indicated a stall farther down. "You can put him in there. Is it the Lamanites?"

At first Kai thought the question silly, but he supposed it wouldn't be to a citizen of Zarahemla. He nodded. "I don't know how they got so many men past the border unnoticed, but they did. I'm going to find a way out of here as soon as I can, so I can carry intelligence to Captain Moronihah."

The man pointed upward. "There's a loft up there. It'll hide you, hopefully."

Kai nodded his thanks, then walked Vyim over to settle him in the stall. A thin layer of straw topped the hardened dirt, and at Kai's command, Vyim lay on his side, closing his eyes as if he were pretending to sleep. Then again, maybe he wasn't pretending. He had run hard.

Kai climbed to the loft, finding additional straw and some hay. There were also several large wooden boxes he could reposition to form a small, protective cubby. The boxes were full and hard to move, but soon he rested comfortably, speculating on how quickly the entire city would fall, how many people would die, and when the nearby Nephite garrisons could respond. He also asked himself if he should have fought to the death, as Benijah and his men likely had.

That thought bothered him so much he got up and explored the loft further. He crouched near the small window looking down on the street, studying the limited view it afforded. He spied a short portion of the southern wall in the near distance through a break in the buildings, but besides that, he could see only the street and a few structures, including one thin tower capped by a bright yellow flag hanging nearly limp. A three-story manufactory rose just a short distance away across the street, its upper floor probably residential. He could hopefully see and learn more from there.

Leaving the safety of the loft would go against everything he had learned in his training, but he had a nagging desire to investigate. He climbed down, noting that the barn's owner had left, as expected. He checked up and down the street, realizing that the sounds of battle were subsiding. The city's last gasp neared. Hopefully, Benijah and some of his men had surrendered and were still alive. He jogged down the street toward the three-story building, ducking into the alley next to it. He tried the first door he saw, and it opened. Inside, he found two flights of stairs leading up to the third floor. He quickly ascended, encountering a heavy wooden door where the stairs ended. He was surprised to find that door unlocked as well. Upon opening it, he discovered a small room occupied by several women and children. They also seemed startled the door hadn't been locked. One of the women gasped, looking accusingly at another.

Kai held a finger to his lips, enjoining silence, then pointed upward, asking the question with his eyes. One of the older boys stood and motioned for Kai to follow. He led him through another door and down a short hallway, then gestured at a square panel in the ceiling.

"Do you have a ladder or chair?" Kai whispered.

The boy disappeared into a room off the hall, then returned with a chair, which he positioned underneath the panel. Kai thanked him, then stood on the chair. After releasing two latches, he swung the access door upward easily, then lifted himself through the opening. He nodded his thanks to the boy before closing the panel, then moved in a walking crouch across the rooftop, which gave an unobstructed view in most directions. He settled in the southeast corner, a low coping around the roof giving him some cover from potential watchers on the city's walls or other buildings. Then he waited, listening.

Several minutes later, he heard a fresh clash of arms. The commotion was near, just to the east. He twisted, peeking his head above the ledge. A large skirmish had erupted, and it seemed to be migrating toward the inside of the southern wall. His eyes scanned back and forth, searching, and then he saw them—a large group of Lamanite soldiers pushing a smaller group of Nephites toward the wall, spears and swords clanging as men screamed and fell.

They reached the wall, and within a few more seconds the remainder of the Nephites had fallen—all but one, the man they had been protecting.

Even from two hundred yards away, Kai could tell that man was Pacumeni, if only by the elaborate robes of state he wore.

From among the Lamanites emerged one of the largest men Kai had ever seen, bulging with muscle. Kai thought he saw knots of rank glinting in the sunlight on the man's shoulder, and he guessed he was a captain or even a general—perhaps the general who led the entire army. His sword was massive, but he held it in one hand with ease.

He didn't quite shout, but his bold voice reverberated off the wall. Kai heard the words clearly enough to understand.

"You have been found guilty, Pacumeni," he pronounced.

"Of what?" pleaded the hapless chief judge, hands held before him, palms up.

"Of treason."

"Treason?"

"Yes, treason. You have stolen the government from those who should rightfully possess it: those of the first birthright. And you have subjected them to your will for hundreds of years."

"Subjected them?" Pacumeni sounded dumbfounded. "We live in peace. We let you live in peace. We even trade with—"

"Silence!" The yell sounded like a peal of thunder. "You give scraps to those who are kings! That changes today." He raised his mighty sword, gripping it in both hands.

Pacumeni's hands reflexively rose higher to guard his head. His voice quavered. "Wait! We already surrendered the city. It's yours, General Coriantumr. And I am not your ruler."

Kai couldn't tell if Coriantumr—whom he had never heard of—smiled, but he imagined he did. He clearly detected the condescending smirk in Coriantumr's voice.

"No. No, you are not." Coriantumr then took a lunging step forward and swung his blade powerfully, smiting Pacumeni against the wall, nearly slicing him in two.

Kai turned away from the grisly scene, and even though he'd seen it from a distance, he wanted to be sick. His stomach lurched as he processed the unimaginable fall of the city and the fact that another chief judge had just been killed. Was this the beginning of the end for the Nephite nation?

Had similar armies shown up at Noah and Sidom, or were Gadianton-led rebels holding those? How had the Lamanites gathered such a large army and gotten it so close to Zarahemla without the Nephite army knowing? It was almost too much to process.

But process it he must. He was trapped, and help might not be coming after all. There was no possible way of riding out of the city on Vyim. He might be able to escape by retrieving some rope from his room at *Jacob's Rest* and scaling down the wall, but that wasn't likely, either. The Lamanites would patrol the walls heavily, at all hours of the day and night. They would well remember some of the stratagems the Nephites had employed against them during the Great War. And, of course, when they found Vyim, they would take him. The stallion would make a fantastic spoil of war for some Lamanite captain, or this General Coriantumr. It pained him to think about that possibility, though not as much as contemplating the likely deaths of brave Benijah and his men.

He didn't tarry on the roof any longer, lest a Lamanite on one of the walls eventually spot him and think him suspicious. He retreated through the roof access and down into the hallway. The chair was still there, as were the women and children in the front room. All the men in the city who hadn't already fallen in the fighting would be rounded up and questioned—except the Gadiantons, who were probably rejoicing, both in the Hall of Judgment and in Pacumeni's home, thanking General Coriantumr and his captains profusely for their swift and complete victory.

As Kai considered the stricken, pleading faces of those women and children, he contemplated where fifty thousand Lamanite soldiers would camp in and around the city, and how they would all be fed without a secure supply line. This attack had been a colossal gamble for them, but now that they held Zarahemla, they could raid all the food stores in the city and for miles around, impoverishing the Nephites and letting them starve. The fall of the city was terrible by itself, but the aftermath would be far worse. He also knew what some of the fifty thousand Lamanite men would do when they grew hungry in other ways, and his soul quailed at the thought.

He had no words of comfort to offer the group before he left. He advised them to stay and remain together, and he promised to return with more information if he could. They gazed upon him as if he were their savior. He most definitely was not.

He sneaked back to the barn, returning to the loft after checking on Vyim. He settled in, mind straining, trying to formulate a plan, hoping again that Nephite armies were close. Surely, people from outlying areas had taken messages to other cities and to the garrisons. But how long would it be until help came? And how would the remaining Nephite leaders respond after discovering three major cities had been taken hostage? The nation was once again without a chief judge, and many of the high judges were trapped in Zarahemla.

Nightfall came, and though Kai's belly rumbled in hunger, he ignored the discomfort. He was thirsty, too, and he knew Vyim must be as well. He crept down from the loft every couple of hours to make sure Vyim knew he was still there, and he didn't get much sleep in between. He listened closely to the sounds of the vanquished city. He heard two Lamanite patrols pass by, but mostly the air was filled with mournful wailing, which would trail off occasionally, then start up again. The howling subsided only with the dawn. Kai supposed the sunrise—coupled with exhaustion—numbed a portion of the people's grief. But he knew that the coming night, after a full day of contemplating what a Lamanite occupation meant, would bring increased lamentations. He could imagine the Lamanite soldiers reveling in the Nephites' suffering. Most Lamanites he had met harbored a visceral disdain for Nephites, viewing them as rich and arrogant, if not downright evil.

At about midday, Kai descended again from the loft. When he felt it was safe, he coaxed Vyim to his feet. He fetched some hay and even found a bucket with some water. He wondered if the owner had left it for him and Vyim, thanking him silently if that were so.

He didn't have a brush, so he used some of the cleaner straw to rub Vyim down thoroughly, whispering softly to him all the while. He wished the barn could remain a haven for them, but he knew it wouldn't. The Lamanites would eventually search every home, barn, shop, warehouse, and other structure in the city, and Kai had no viable plans to prevent their inevitable discovery. He was one against fifty thousand.

He had just finished when he heard a commotion coming from a warehouse a few buildings down—enemy voices shouting that they were taking all the food and supplies they could find, warning residents and workers not to resist. Those Lamanites would arrive at the barn soon. Kai bade Vyim lie down again, which he obediently did, then crouched at the side of the stall, waiting, both sword and knife out and ready.

Lamanites burst into the barn. The owner, who must have returned upon hearing the tumult from up the street, foolishly demanded to know what they were doing. The sound of one of the soldiers striking him in the face followed. One Lamanite gruffly boasted that a large part of the army was continuing their march, and they needed supplies, including cows and horses—anything that could be eaten or ridden and wouldn't slow them down too much. The soldiers then snatched up several horses and two cows near the front of the barn. Kai tensed as he waited for them to search the stalls in the back, but another shout came; more soldiers had arrived, and the captains ordered the men to keep moving, as Coriantumr was anxious to begin the march. The soldiers miraculously left, joining with their companions and moving on down the street.

Kai's pulse didn't slow until they had progressed a good distance, though he worried about the women and children in the manufactory. Fortunately, the Lamanites weren't searching for people. After several more minutes, Kai felt much calmer … and incredibly blessed to still have Vyim.

He finally left the stall, spotting the barn's owner sitting dejectedly on a stool near the open doors, back against the frame, head drooping. Kai approached slowly, noting the redness and swelling in the man's cheek.

"Thank you for not telling them about my horse," he said quietly.

The man registered his presence after a moment, then nodded. "Well, I'm glad for you they didn't take him, but I imagine they'll be back." He stared dejectedly toward the street.

"I'm sorry about your animals," said Kai. "If I can, I'll replace them."

The man turned his head and blinked, giving him a strange expression. He didn't ask Kai how. After a moment, he went back to staring at the street.

"I'm going to do a little scouting," Kai informed him. "My horse will stay quiet. I'll be back soon."

The man nodded, finally seeming to come out of his despondent reverie a little. "Be careful, young man. You look like you know how to take care of yourself, but I've never seen anything like this, and I'll wager you haven't, either."

Kai thanked him again before slipping out and finding the familiar alley leading north. At the first street, he waited until he couldn't see any Lamanite patrols in either direction, then crossed and followed another alley. He patiently moved from alley to alley five more times until he noted a growing buzz indicating men mustering to march. He ducked into a building, ascending to the second floor. An older couple in one of the front rooms didn't make a peep as he gestured for silence and took up position near a window.

From there he had a decent view of the muster, which extended up and down the broad Path of Mosiah. At least three thousand men filled his vision, and within minutes they began marching eastward, joined by fully laden wagons, horses, cows, and other smaller livestock from the side streets. They were indeed taking all or most of the food. Kai couldn't tell what proportion of the Lamanite army was leaving, but the march out of the city took at least half an hour, as Lamanites kept pouring into the line to join the procession.

Finally, the street sat mostly empty, and the city became eerily quiet. Kai asked the couple if there was an interior access to the roof. When they said no, he left the building, scanning for a ladder that would get him to the top. He quickly found one and ascended the wall, crawling toward the front of the roof so he could get a better view of the whole street. In that position, he could also see large sections of the city walls clearly, and what he witnessed puzzled him. The Lamanites seemed to have left only a small force behind. He surmised two reasons for it: first, the Gadiantons could probably handle most of the policing; and second, Coriantumr might have placed a large number of troops in the now-abandoned army fortress to the south. Both were likely true, and Kai began to hope he might be able to find a way out of the city. He needed to find Ara, though—she might be able to help.

He first hazarded a visit to *Jacob's Rest*, entering through the rear door after making a risky dash across the Path of Mosiah. There wasn't much activity inside the inn, except for the handful of cooks and innkeepers who lived onsite engaging in a doleful discussion about where they would find ingredients. Their food stores had been almost completely gutted, the Lamanites leaving barely ten percent of what the inn normally stocked. If they weren't under occupation, they could send wagons to nearby towns and cities to buy additional foodstuffs. But the gates were closed, and they didn't have any wagons left, anyway.

Once Kai got to his room, he gathered up his few things, slinging his pack over his shoulder. He wished he had a back sheath for his short sword, which he had bound between his shoulder blades under his shirt to keep it hidden. He had strapped his knife to the outside of his leg, under his breeches. Neither weapon would be quick to access in a fight, but at least he had them. He was turning to leave when Ara appeared in the doorway, her face flooding with relief as she stepped inside and closed the door.

"Adonihah, you're safe!" She took two quick steps and launched into an embrace, squeezing tightly around his neck. Kai stumbled as he caught her. Her expressiveness no longer surprised him, but everything was happening too fast, and he keenly felt the trauma of the last twenty-four hours.

She loosened her grip, letting her feet touch the floor. Then she grasped his face with both hands and kissed him, pressing hard. His mind fractured, despite his best efforts to prevent it, and he couldn't deny how much he enjoyed that moment of release in such a poignant time of storm and chaos. He wasn't sure how long the kiss lasted, but at some point he opened his eyes, and then she wrapped her arms around his waist and buried her head in his chest.

"I was sure you'd been killed," she whispered, issuing a shuddering sob.

"I'm surprised I wasn't," Kai admitted, allowing his arms to envelop her. "I took out a few Lamanites before escaping the walls and hiding with Vyim, but I need to get out of here. I must get to the army. Captain Benijah is probably dead, and Moronihah could use every bit of information he can get, including the death of Pacumeni, which I witnessed."

"I know about Pacumeni," Ara responded in a somber tone, her voice somewhat muffled. "My father is furious, and I suspect Imrahiel is, too, but not about that. Coriantumr was supposed to keep most of his troops here and send only a few reinforcements to Noah and Sidom. But he took almost his entire army out of Zarahemla, swearing to cause as much destruction as possible while cutting a path through the heart of the nation, all the way to Bountiful." She leaned her head back and looked up at him. "Do you think they could make it that far? I know your family is there." She seemed genuinely concerned.

"That's valuable information," he said after a hard swallow. "Are you absolutely sure?"

She bobbed her head confidently. "My father mentioned it several times last night as he cursed Coriantumr's stupidity."

Kai took a deep breath. "It makes some sense. The Lamanites have set such objectives before. They believe if they can break through to the north countries and dominate there, they can surround and eliminate us entirely. Or enslave us. I'm not sure I understand their reasoning, but they obsess over it."

Ara pressed her head into his chest again and squeezed him tight. "I'll help you get out. You and Vyim. I know you need to do this. I . . . can cause a distraction. I'll bring a few friends, other young women. We'll . . . hmmm . . . we'll demand the gate guards let us through so we can go to the river . . . to swim! They won't be able to resist that. Men love to watch women swim, am I right?" She gazed up at him again, smiling through tears at her terrible idea.

Kai shook his head. "That will put you in danger. Serious danger."

She blinked hard, then gave him a defiant look, the sheen of tears accenting her expression. "We're already in serious danger."

"You'll make yourself a target," Kai insisted.

She released her hold on him and backed up a step, tossing her head. "I'm already a target. Imrahiel and the others thought they could control the Lamanites. Clearly, they can't. Look at me. Am I not a target?" She dared him to disagree.

Kai's heart shuddered as it sank. Unless she hid herself away, she was definitely a mark for ravenous Lamanite soldiers or officers. Before he could object any further, she stepped forward and grabbed his face again, delivering another potent kiss that welcomed thick fog into his mind. Then she moved toward the door. "I'll go gather my friends right now. When do you want us at the gates?" She paused, awaiting his answer.

He blinked a few times, rubbing his chin, realizing he couldn't talk her out of it. "Um . . . two hours from now? I'll be in the . . ." he marked a route in his head ". . . first alley between the second and third streets from the Grand Gates. South side of the Path of Mosiah." Despite his objections, he thought her plan could work. Even if the guards opened just the postern doors, he could ride low on Vyim and get through, hopefully with enough speed that they couldn't stop him. And the sooner he and Ara executed the plan, the better. The remaining Lamanite troops had to be exhausted. They couldn't have established all their security protocols, either; Zarahemla was a big city, and unfamiliar to them. The trick would be getting Vyim from the barn to a spot near the gates. They would have to move from alley to alley, just as he had in getting to *Jacob's Rest*, and that strategy was riskier with a horse, especially one so magnificent. He prayed the plan would work, and that Ara would escape the guards' inevitable reaction.

She gave a firm nod. "Okay, just after the ninth bell. Middle of the afternoon, late in the guards' shift. We'll be ready." She darted out the door, and he heard her hustling along the hall and down the stairs. He stood still for a few more seconds, feeling almost stunned, trying to replay everything that had just happened, even the kiss … or rather, both kisses, though they seemed to merge. He soon refocused on the task at hand, reminding himself sternly that escape was the top priority, followed by the welfare of the Nephite nation. Within the next few hours, he would be either free or dead, and if free, maybe he could help save his country.

CHAPTER 11

*Now this was the faith of these of whom I have spoken; they are young,
and their minds are firm, and they do put their trust in God continually.*

ALMA 57:27

Vyim seemed skittish, mirroring Kai's anticipation and nervousness. Kai again thanked the owner of the barn, who hadn't moved from his stool. The man wished them well, even offering a brief prayer on their behalf. Kai appreciated the man's thoughtfulness, knowing he would need all the help he could get.

Kai had wrapped the buckles and rings of Vyim's tack in cloth so nothing would jangle and expose them to Lamanite patrols as he led him along on foot. At a simple command, Vyim already knew to be as quiet as possible. In fact, Kai had never heard a horse step so softly. It took patience to steal all the way to their destination, avoiding the eyes of watchers on the walls as well, and near the end of the journey, he started to worry they would be too late. But it seemed as if God had paused time—keeping the sun in its place—so Kai and Vyim could get into position. The third bell sounded just as they entered the final alley, the one that would bring them within fifty yards of the gates. Kai focused intently as they moved down the narrow passage, and Vyim somehow became even quieter, following Kai's lead. They neared the exit, but Kai didn't want to get too close. He stopped, then silently mounted to listen and wait.

Two minutes later he heard voices—female voices—calling to the Lamanite guards in tones both pleading and insistent. He recognized Ara's among them, and a ball of anxiety formed in his gut, cold and fiery at the same time. He listened more keenly as the guards responded, the banter continuing for a full minute before he heard the first creak of hinges. Luckily, the sound didn't come from the postern door—they were opening the main gates.

Kai gave Vyim a light squeeze with his heels, and he responded instantly, bounding out of the alley. Kai turned him right, toward the gate, and in three strides he was at a full gallop.

Shouts of surprise erupted from both women and guards. One guard shouted to close the gates, but Kai and Vyim had already attained the threshold, with plenty of room to pass through. They hit the main road and flew south, Kai randomly weaving them along the broad highway, knowing arrows would seek them from the walls. Several whizzed past, one grazing Vyim's left flank. Vyim didn't react to the pain, unless it was to increase his speed a hair more.

Soon they were out of range, but Kai knew he had kicked an anthill around those brave women. They had already started scattering as Kai and Vyim passed through the gates, and he prayed again they would all find safe places to hide; also, that the Lamanites wouldn't link them to his escape. They could easily make the connection if they thought about it. Then again, the men at the gate and along the eastern walls might make a pact to keep quiet about their blunder to avoid trouble from their captains. Kai latched his prayers onto *that* possibility.

He passed the garrison without incident by taking the fisherman's path closer to the river, hidden among trees. For the first several miles, he worried about Lamanite patrols, but he didn't encounter any. No Nephite scouts showed themselves, either, which likely meant help was still distant. Kai decided he would go to Gideon first to seek Shemnilom and Helaman, along with Jeruzim and the other leaders of the Gideon militia. Then he would travel whatever direction they could tell him Moronihah might be found.

He alternately ran and walked Vyim, trying not to overtax him, but Vyim pulled on the reins often and wanted to run farther each time. Kai was able to make him stop twice for water, but Vyim only grudgingly accepted the invitations to rest.

It took just three hours to reach Gideon, and when Kai arrived, he found a beehive of activity. Men poured into the area from outlying towns and farms, all armed and armored for war. As expected, word of the conflict had spread fast. Kai was sure some mounted scouts had already been sent out, though they probably hadn't had a chance to return with their reports yet.

Kai approached the northern gates of the city, trotting a well-lathered Vyim under a dimming sky with few clouds. Kai was sweating, too. It had been a warm day and a hard ride.

"Scout Kihoran of two-seven!" he announced. "I seek Jeruzim!"

The gates almost immediately began to open, and Kai passed through into a citywide scene of ordered urgency. Fletchers busily made arrows, blacksmith hammers clanged nearby, and men drilled and sparred to shouted orders. A young captain jogged over to meet him.

"You're Kihoran?" he asked.

"Yes."

"Follow me. I'll take you to Jeruzim." The man led him east at a fast walk, heading for a structure built against the inside of the wall. He stopped at the entrance, looking up at Kai. "I can make sure your horse is cared for," he said, then pointed to indicate some place farther along the wall. "There's a stable about a hundred yards down. I'll take him there."

"Thank you," said Kai, dismounting and handing him the reins. Vyim seemed to want to object, but he complied.

Upon entering the building, Kai waded into in a loud, steady hum of voices. He found himself in a barracks room, but all the bunked beds had been moved to the sides to clear out a large space for tables laden with maps and surrounded by officers. Couriers stood along the edges of the room. Kai quickly spotted Jeruzim, who saw him at almost the same time. Jeruzim's eyes widened, and he held up a hand to stop whoever was talking to him as he rounded the table and nearly sprinted over to Kai.

He grabbed Kai by the shoulders, then exclaimed, "It is good to see you, Kihoran, alive! You bring news?"

Kai nodded, and Jeruzim took him by the elbow, leading him to the table he had just departed. He gestured around its circumference. "You know many here, but there's no time for formal introductions. These are all our captains, not just the ones from the city proper. A small contingent just arrived from Shem, too. Everyone, this is Kihoran, the brave scout who helped capture the two Lamanite long-range scouts." He turned to Kihoran. "What is the latest from Zarahemla, and how did you get out?"

Kai cleared his throat, feeling more than two dozen eyes boring into him. "As you probably know, the city has fallen. Pacumeni was killed—well, executed—by the Lamanite general, a man named Coriantumr. I saw it happen." A few of the captains shared glances, but no one appeared deeply surprised, and nobody seemed to recognize Coriantumr's name. "They had about fifty thousand men, in my estimation, and I would guess more have infiltrated and will join that main group. Almost all the soldiers left the city this morning, heading east with whatever provisions they could plunder. That made it possible for me to escape past the remaining Lamanite guards, with the help of a few friends and some subterfuge."

The captains began discussing the dire news in anxious tones. All were aghast at the Lamanite numbers and their immediate move into the relatively unprotected Nephite heartland. Their voices grew loud, and some of them gesticulated wildly toward places on the maps.

"Captains!" interrupted Jeruzim. "Let us hear if there is more." They quieted, and he turned again to Kai, signaling for him to continue.

Kai's voice grew even colder than intended. "This attack was coordinated by a rebel group called the Gadiantons—king-men and Nehors, most likely. The Gadiantons started the rumors that the Lamanites were readying to attack the border, and they weaved in other rumors that the Nephite government blamed the Lamanites for the death of Pahoran. With help from the Lamanites, the Gadiantons plan to hold three major cities as ransom to force the Nephite nation into a unity government with King Tubaloth. The other two cities are Noah and Sidom."

Conversation among the captains burst forth again, more frantic now, eyes and fingers darting around the maps. It was Kai who raised his voice this time, so he could finish his report. "The Gadiantons are apparently livid that Coriantumr took almost his entire army out of the city. He was supposed to send a few troops to Noah and Sidom to assist the Gadiantons—who I presume have taken over the governments in those cities—and keep the rest in Zarahemla. But Coriantumr rejected the plan, choosing to conquer and pillage all the way to Bountiful and cut the nation in half. The intelligence on this is good, as it comes from inside the Gadiantons, and I trust the source."

A hush settled over the entire room, everyone focusing their attention on the main table.

"This is devastating," one of the captains noted with a timbre of doom.

Jeruzim raised a finger toward that captain. "Yes, it is, but also to our strategic advantage. Coriantumr doesn't know the terrain along that path as well as we do. We'll send harrying forces to slow him down while we gather our strength. Then we'll surround him. He is a fool. He has delivered himself and all his men into our hands."

That assessment sounded too optimistic to Kai, even though some logic underpinned it. But before their deliberations began again in earnest, Kai turned to Jeruzim and asked, "Where's Moronihah? I need to deliver this news to him, too."

Jeruzim rested a hand on his shoulder. "Messengers have already been sent to request he come to Gideon. I suspect he will, but we don't know. We need you to lead the scouts here while we formulate plans to present to Moronihah."

Lead the scouts? Kai's eyebrows rose, but he didn't object. "Yes, sir. Who do I speak with first?"

"An officer named Fandimr. You can stay here and help us until he returns. I believe he's out on a scouting mission himself right now."

Kai had never attended a senior captain's council. But he recognized he was there to answer questions they might have as they developed their plans—like how the Lamanites were armed, and their troop composition, including cavalry. Kai quickly realized that the captains of Gideon knew little about Nephite troop locations and strongholds beyond a hundred-mile radius of their city. Yes, they knew where the major garrisons and fortifications were located—most citizens did—but troop deployments always fluctuated, even more so in the last several months.

The captains seemed practical, though, by both temperament and experience. They focused on specific preparations to defend the city and the lands round about, on the disposition of their scouts—knowing they desperately needed better information—and on the critical messages being sent to other Nephite cities and garrisons.

They posed a few queries to Kai, predictably specific to the strength and troop types of the Lamanites. One of the captains asked whether Kai had truly witnessed the death of the chief judge, Pacumeni, and so Kai recounted that gruesome story. Solemn moments followed, sorrow and anger swirling in the faces of the men around the table.

"God rest his soul."

Kai nearly jumped as he recognized the voice. He turned to see Helaman standing two paces behind him, flanked by Dan and another guard. Dan nodded respectfully, and then Helaman locked gazes with Kai briefly before walking around the table to take a position directly opposite him.

It was customary, of course, for a prophet of the Lord to join a war council, especially in a faithful place like Gideon. Jeruzim and the other captains would want to know of any inspiration the Lord was willing to provide to his chosen oracle. The captains observed Helaman intently, apparently waiting for him to offer up some suggestion or for Jeruzim to ask him the first question. After a few moments, Helaman directed his attention to Kai again.

"You helped save my life the night before I came here, Kihoran." He again sounded far more mature than his twenty-seven years would suggest.

Kai wasn't sure how to respond. "I don't think I did much," he said, then dropped his eyes to look at one of the maps, which showed a close-up view of the strategic points of defense along the city's walls.

"Well, I do," Helaman affirmed. "The Lord has spared my life twice in the last three days—once through you, and once by sending me here for the conference. He was precise about time and place, and when he's that specific, it's best to listen and do *exactly* as he suggests."

A pause followed as everyone pondered the prophet's words while sparing some slightly incredulous glances for Kai. After a few seconds, Kai lifted his gaze to Helaman, whose eyes had closed. A tear leaked from one eye, and suddenly the prophet threw his arms high in the air, tilting his head up and proclaiming:

"Oh, Zarahemla, how have you fallen? Why did you not listen to your kind, long-suffering Savior, who offered you his healing wings for protection and solace? Why did you lift your head in pride, believing you were invincible? Why did you persecute the saints and grind the faces of the poor in the dust? Why did you so grossly pervert his statutes and judgments? Will you hear your Lord now? Will you humble yourselves and turn your faces toward him? Will you put aside your lusts and obey his commandments? Will you let him rescue you from bondage?"

Kai had never heard a more heartfelt and soul-wrenching plea. He bowed his head, noting all the others had as well. It was a sacred, supernal moment; God's prophet had opened a conduit to heaven for all present to witness.

Silence reigned for a full minute. It seemed like the entire city had stilled, for Kai couldn't hear anything happening outside the building, either. Or perhaps the Spirit of the Lord had insulated them from outside noise for this moment. Kai knew he would never be able to adequately describe the experience and the feelings that accompanied it.

Finally, Helaman spoke again, looking at Jeruzim. "Captain Moronihah will be here soon—perhaps before midnight. You can continue planning for the defense of this city, but it is safe. The Lamanites greatly fear the men of Gideon, just as they feared the men of Teancum—and of Lehi." That name seemed to give Helaman serious pause, but he didn't remark further on it. "I will rejoin your council when Moronihah is here. Thank you, brethren, for your faithful and courageous service to your people in preserving their lives and freedom as children of God."

Helaman then did something his father had been noted for. He slowly worked his way around the table, saying a few words to each man, touching an arm or a shoulder, smiling in glorious confidence. Kai watched in awe. He knew God guided Helaman, and he wondered why he was so blessed to witness it. When Helaman got to him, he grasped Kai just above the elbow.

"You have come a long way, Kihoran," he said softly. "Stay true. There is more for you to do."

And with that, he moved on to the next man, leaving Kai to ponder in sublime peace.

The first wave of scouts from Gideon returned over the next few hours. Their mission had been twofold—gather information on enemy threats, and spread the word to muster to Gideon and its environs. The land around Gideon was already filling up with militiamen and their families. Many received patrol assignments, while others trained with fresh weapons made by the city's tireless weaponsmiths.

Only two of the returning scouts—out of more than twenty, and neither of them Fandimr—questioned why Kai had suddenly been put in charge, but they didn't cause any trouble. Kai received all their reports, asking probing questions to understand more precisely what each had seen and heard. He sent three pairs back out in different directions southward to check on Moronihah's arrival, since they hadn't seen any forward scouts from his army yet. He sent a trio west, instructing them to take two weeks of supplies and travel among the more remote but well-scouted areas of the western borders to understand how the Lamanites might have gotten so many men through unseen. The Gideonites still had long-range scouts out to the north and east, but Kai sent several more pairs back out in those directions on shorter missions, with the additional purpose of assessing refugee needs. He knew the gathering to Gideon would soon include great numbers of displaced and desperate people, who would require significant and immediate assistance.

It felt strange not to be heading out on a mission himself. Part of him even felt guilty. But being trusted by Jeruzim as a leader was satisfying, despite the doubts he had about himself. He wasn't so concerned about his relatively young age—the stripling warriors had taught everyone how effective youth could be—but he didn't have training and experience as a leader. Perhaps, he thought, God wanted to show him—and others through him—that he could indeed do his own work, using tools he selected in his own wisdom.

He didn't have much time to dwell on philosophical or spiritual musings, though. He set about organizing the various pieces of information from the scouts into reports he could give to Jeruzim and his captains—and also to Helaman and Moronihah. In his effort to be thorough, he forgot he had missed dinner, but one of Jeruzim's aides insisted he at least eat something while he worked.

The night was nearly half gone when Kai heard the first trumpets announcing the arrival of a Nephite army. He almost jumped up from the desk he'd been allotted and raced outside, but remembered his reports weren't quite ready. He didn't have much time left. He didn't worry that none of his scouts had reached him first with news of the chief captain's imminent arrival—in fact, he could well guess that Moronihah was plying those scouts for every bit of information they could give him as they marched.

With difficulty, he refocused, completing his report just as the level of activity inside the command center ramped up. Moronihah would arrive soon. He reviewed his several pages of notes and observations, trying to think of anything he had left out or some insight he had missed. He wished he could have had Fandimr review the report, too, but Fandimr had asked to participate in one of the new scouting assignments northward. Kai made a few other notations in the margins of the parchments, then gathered them and stood up from the desk, his backside feeling somewhat numb after sitting in a hard, flat chair for so long. He wasn't used to that.

Only three of the captains stood around the central table in the command center, studying maps with some of their aides, who took notes. One of the aides informed Kai that Jeruzim had left a few minutes ago to greet Moronihah, so Kai paced the perimeter of the room, trying to loosen his legs, listening to the chatter of the couriers speculating on how many men Moronihah had brought with him. It dawned on Kai that they hadn't received any confirmation it was indeed Moronihah arriving—they just knew Helaman had predicted it.

After his second circuit of the room, a thunderous shout of joy erupted from outside. Kai stopped, his head snapping toward the west doorway. The shouting continued, along with furious clapping and a few somewhat ragged and off-key songs—standard army fare. Then Captain Moronihah and Helaman swept into the room, followed by an entourage of high-ranking captains and at least three dozen aides and couriers. Jeruzim entered just behind them, next to Shemnilom, whose eyes burned with a holy fire.

Moronihah strode ahead with his long legs, his dark, wavy hair flaring out behind him. He hadn't noticed Kai yet. Most of his group faded toward the walls. Only Moronihah, Helaman, Jeruzim, and two of the senior captains joined the three Gideonite captains already at the large planning table. Shemnilom came to stand next to Kai as Moronihah began to question Jeruzim and his captains about what they knew so far.

"He's in a righteous fury," whispered Shemnilom. "I almost feel sorry for the Lamanite army."

Kai felt the same passion as their chief captain, and his voice was bitter. "I don't. Captain Benijah is almost surely dead, along with all his men. I didn't get time to confirm it."

Shemnilom bowed his head, closing his eyes. Kai hoped he hadn't sounded scolding—he hadn't seen a hundredth of what Shemnilom had in his life.

"Kihoran, come to the table!" Moronihah barked. The order caused Kai to jerk, his head whipping toward the center of the room. His feet felt like tree roots for a moment.

"Go," said Shemnilom gently, pressing lightly on his back. Kai finally got his limbs working and started toward the group, noticing all eyes in the room turned toward him. He sped up, stopping a few feet from Moronihah and saluting. Then he held out his sheaf of parchment.

Moronihah turned to fully face him, accepting the papers. His voice sounded richer and deeper than usual. "You have done well, Scout Kihoran. Better than I had imagined. I now know why I felt such a strong impression to call you from Bountiful to Zarahemla. I resisted it at first." He looked over his shoulder at Helaman, who tipped his head, then returned his attention to Kai. "These scouting reports will be useful, but I have another assignment for you. Captain Lehi should be receiving a message soon to gather men in Jershon. Those orders don't include where to march them from there, but because of you we know General Coriantumr is aiming straight for Bountiful. You will ride for Jershon with orders for Lehi to stop the Lamanite advance on Bountiful, and you will be one of Lehi's scouts. Take three horses so you can ride more swiftly—including the one you've apparently appropriated for yourself."

Kai caught the slightest hint of a smile in Moronihah's subtle reprimand. He saluted again smartly with a "Yes, sir!" before turning sharply and starting for the door.

"Kihoran!" Helaman's call stopped him, and he turned back. "You were an instrument in the Lord's hands in saving my life," he said loudly for all to hear, some for the second time that night. "Thank you."

Kai bowed in acknowledgement. "It was my duty," he said simply, then turned and aimed for the door again, feeling the uncomfortable weight of all those stares.

It was a relief to break out of the building into open air, and he began jogging toward the stable. He wouldn't ride Vyim first, since Vyim hadn't had a lot of rest. The Gideonites possessed many good, sturdy horses. They weren't as fast as Vyim, but they were fast enough. The keeper of the stables raised his eyebrows at Kai's request for two Gideonite steeds with high endurance, then sent a runner to confirm the order. Kai didn't blame him. The horses were precious, and war was once again upon them.

It felt good to be in the saddle again with a clear, simple purpose. Kai wouldn't have been the head scout around Gideon for long anyway—not with Moronihah arriving and the Nephite armies assembling. He hoped the scouts he had sent to the west found something useful, though. The Nephite captains needed to understand how the Lamanites had executed their bold plan on such a large scale.

Vyim didn't seem happy being riderless, and connected by a rope to the other two horses. Kai was tempted to let him run without the rope, but he wasn't sure how the other horses would react. They had been trained to travel in a rotating line, and he didn't want to upset the rhythm they knew.

Vyim almost appeared to glower when Kai didn't transfer the saddle to him upon switching horses the first time. But he obediently followed, and they continued to eat up ground. Kai kept to the major roads, because they were faster and he wasn't scouting. As they passed towns and villages on the way to Jershon, he could see word of the invasion preceding him. The marshalling of men and supplies was well underway everywhere. Some men shouted questions about where they should go as he flew by. Kai could only yell back that they should await orders—he had no authority to tell them anything else.

He perceived fear in the eyes of many, but less than expected. Mostly, he witnessed determination building, along with anger. He could imagine how most would react if he told them about the scheming of the Gadiantons and the Lamanite king. The news wouldn't necessarily surprise these humble, hardworking rural people—they had seen such plots before—but it would stoke the fires of their wrath higher. The politics and pride of the largest Nephite cities had long been a large thorn in their side. 'Progress' pursued by selfish, underhanded political means never panned out for the common people, regardless of the careful sophistry with which it was presented—inevitably, the powerful just became more powerful.

He spent more time praying in the saddle than he ever had before. He had already felt a shift occurring in his spiritual understanding, a strengthening of his connection to God. He feared the change was partly driven by desperate circumstances, but the impressions were undeniable; his mind was opening up, and he caught glimpses of eternity. He discerned clearer purpose in what he was doing and greater resolve to see it done well. In some ways, the shift seemed subtle, but in others, it was as if he had just scaled a spiritual cliff, standing in amazement at the view from the top.

At some point near the end of his breakneck journey—which took almost four days—a sense of calm reassurance settled over him. He couldn't explain it, but somehow he knew everything was going to be all right, that the Nephites would once again triumph over their embittered, inveterate enemies. That feeling swelled when he first caught sight of Lehi's gathering army, which was larger than he had expected—close to twenty thousand men—and well ordered. Lehi's reputation had been rightfully earned; the Lamanites feared the courageous captain who had crushed so many of their well-laid plans with clever strategies and the indomitable spirit with which he imbued his soldiers.

As Kai entered the burgeoning encampment riding Vyim, he raised a signal flag indicating he had orders from the chief captain of the armies. Hand signals from several officers directed him to Lehi's command tent. When he arrived, three men rushed forward to take care of his horses, and he was ushered immediately inside to see the venerated war leader.

Lehi appeared more fearsome than Kai had imagined. A large man with a muscular build, he sported a curling brown mustache under a completely bald pate. Kai had only seen portraits of the younger Lehi in victorious battle poses from the era of the Great War, which had ended more than ten years ago. While Lehi was in his mid-fifties, he still looked to be in excellent fighting shape, his uniform sharp, his sword arm strong.

One of Lehi's captains exited the tent in a hurry to carry out some command. Two other captains stood with Lehi, awaiting their own orders.

Kai saluted, then held forward his small flag in one hand and a rolled-up scroll in the other. "Sir, I bring orders from Captain Moronihah. I am Kihoran, of the two-seven Scouts."

Lehi turned to face him, blowing out his mustache and tucking his thumbs behind his belt. "Captain Tianmen?"

One of the captains stepped forward to retrieve the flag and the message, then handed the message to Lehi. Kai turned to withdraw, but Lehi's voice held him.

"Hold on, son. You can stay. Let's see where our captain means to aim this spear." Kai turned back, standing at attention as Lehi began to read.

"Hmmm …" Lehi appeared thoughtful after reading the first few words. Several seconds later he looked up at Kai, cocked an eyebrow, and continued reading. Another "hmmm" followed, and soon after, "Idiot." Finally, Lehi addressed his captains. "Well, it appears we have a wild boar to put down, and we have this young man here to thank for telling us where it is."

Kai hadn't realized the orders included anything about him. He bowed respectfully. "Just doing my duty, sir."

"Well, that's a good example for all of us, isn't it." He turned again to his captains. "Set the formations. We start marching in two hours, at the seventh bell. Those still coming in can follow our path and catch up." Both men saluted and raced out of the tent. Kai almost followed, but Lehi motioned him forward with a finger.

When Kai approached, Lehi laid a hand on his shoulder. "You've done good work, son. I recognize a brave man who has followed the Spirit in doing his duty. You have two hours to rest. Get some shut-eye. You're coming with the main body of the army, and I'll have work for you to do. I know the areas around Bountiful well, but so do you." Lehi patted him on the shoulder, hard. He probably hadn't meant to be so forceful—but his hand and arm were just so … large. Then he turned toward a small table with some maps, and Kai knew he was dismissed.

***

The march of Lehi's army started out slow, but Kai did the math in his head. The Lamanites could only move so fast, and while they wouldn't be meeting stiff resistance as they pillaged through the middle of the nation, there would be some fighting. The Lamanites would focus most of their scouting on the line toward Bountiful, and Lehi probably didn't want to get into position too soon and risk some of those forward Lamanite scouts spotting his army and giving Coriantumr time to maneuver.

After the second day of the march, Lehi invited Kai to one of his nightly war councils, in which they discussed the most advantageous areas they could meet the Lamanites in battle and successfully turn them away from Bountiful. At one point, Lehi turned to Kai.

"Scout Kihoran, you know this area as well as most of us, and you've already played a key part in helping us prepare for this conflict. I'd like to hear your thoughts."

Kai doubted he could add anything useful. He'd been listening closely while the members of the council talked, though, and he had one suggestion. "Well," he began, stammering a bit, "if you surprise them, and they know it's you, many of them will panic. And your men, who are all superior warriors, will be fresher, too." He hadn't said that to ingratiate himself with the famous captain; it was simply true. "So, um … I don't think you need to attack them in a place that leaves them an easy retreat. You can rout them and then harry their retreat … um, sir."

Lehi nodded thoughtfully. Then he turned to his captains. "Thoughts? Is this wise advice?"

Several of the captains glanced at Kai, and he could tell a few of them didn't think much of him giving *any* advice, or even being privy to their council. But one of the younger captains spoke up, one who had advocated nearly the same concept Kai had just described.

"I'm convinced that's the best approach. I know two areas that would be perfect for a surprise attack, especially one slightly south of their expected line of travel, which our long-range scouts should be able to confirm for us soon. If we hit them here—" he pointed to a place on a massive map "—they will have just crossed the river, with wide bluffs behind them to slow any retreat. We'll be waiting in the forests on either side of the road here." He pointed again.

"And how do we get them to deviate south a few miles?" asked Lehi.

"By picking off some of their scouts fanning to the north and leaving the ones to the south alone. Coriantumr doesn't want a major confrontation before he reaches Bountiful, so he'll seek the quickest path that minimizes his risk. Of course, we'll have to time our advance into the area ... well, almost perfectly."

Lehi blinked, scowled, blinked again, and then smiled. "I like it. We know we need God's help anyway. Who here doesn't believe the Lord will help us execute a bold plan?"

Kai recognized what was happening. Strong leaders encouraged healthy, open debate among their subordinates—the only way to apply the best thinking to a problem, But when leaders knew what needed to be done, they nudged their people toward it. Sometimes it was more than a nudge.

No objections surfaced, and so Lehi ordered the captains to start drawing up specific plans for placement and maneuver. Then he turned to Kai. "Okay, son, I'm giving you five of my best scouts. You'll handle that northern fan of Lamanite scouts for us. And you'll leave right now."

Feeling stunned yet again, Kai nodded, saluted, and then hustled to retrieve Vyim.

Kai led his group northeast first, aiming to swing in a wide arc around the Lamanites' long-range scouts. He ran his men in a tight pattern to move swiftly while availing themselves of the best vantage points, some of which the Lamanites wouldn't be aware of given their unfamiliarity with the territory. Fortunately, they didn't see any Lamanites, and Kai felt reasonably confident they hadn't missed any, either.

Once they were far enough north of the Lamanites' expected line of travel along the primary road to Bountiful, he drove his group hard to the west, sending one pair at a time to the south to make sure they hadn't overshot, allowing them only a little time to catch up. Those pairs had to work hard, but on a rotating basis. After the first full day, Kai started angling his group southward, expecting they should soon discover the Lamanite army.

It was on the third day—a little later than expected—that they made their first contact with the enemy. They spotted a single scout, and he was sloppy.

He didn't keep to the paths providing the most cover from the direction he was scouting, and he shouted commands at his horse occasionally. Kai was still wary, but not surprised. The Lamanites weren't known for the strength of their scouting units. Coriantumr would use his best scouts for long-range missions, and all of them would be farther east already. The general probably felt confident now, too, thinking he was certain to reach Bountiful before encountering serious Nephite resistance.

If Coriantumr took Bountiful, he would occupy another heavily fortified major city. He would have sliced through the Nephite nation, gaining easier access to the northern countries. But what then? He wasn't leaving large garrisons behind in his wake, was he? Could he even afford to? The only thing that began to make sense in Kai's head—and it had been bothering him for a while—was that Coriantumr would link up with other Lamanite armies who had moved up to take position east of the Nephite borders. Perhaps they would even seek again to ally themselves with cities and nations in that direction. Some people in the east would be eager to see the mighty Nephite nation split open for plunder, even though they distrusted the Lamanites.

That conclusion sent an icy chill down Kai's spine, harrying his thoughts as he and his men set up their ambush for the careless Lamanite scout. The plan was to kill him and take his horse, but suddenly Kai had an idea. If they wanted to influence the movement of Coriantumr's army, then maybe they needed to provide him a more tangible, provable, and immediate cause to worry. The unexplained disappearance of a single scout wouldn't make much impact; Coriantumr might just think he got lost, or even defected, which was known to happen.

Kai broke from his own plan and stepped boldly from the bushes when the scout was still more than fifty yards away.

"Halt!" he shouted, raising his arm. "Archers have you targeted. Do *not* move." The man stopped his horse, searching the trees behind Kai with frightened eyes. "By order of High Captain Lehi, you will surrender yourself, your weapons, and your horse." Kai reached for his belt as if looking for something, and as hoped, the man abruptly wheeled his horse and began fleeing the way he had come.

"Fire!" shouted Kai, hoping the others would let loose, knowing they might kill the man anyway. He reached for his own bow and fired an arrow after the rapidly shrinking man, while shouting orders at phantom units as if he were mobilizing a pursuit. The others did indeed launch, and one arrow caught the man in the thigh, causing him to scream but not unseating him. Perfect.

"What in Baal's breath was that!" shouted Amon, the scout Kai had paired with in their scouting patterns. He emerged from the trees with another arrow nocked, and there was blood in his eyes as he glared at Kai.

"I'm sorry," Kai said. "I had an idea but didn't have time to explain. That bumbling idiot of a scout will return to the main body of Coriantumr's army to report there's a large force to the northeast of them and that they're pursuing him. He'll exaggerate. That's what we want. We can move forward and pick off the scouts Coriantumr sends to confirm, and when *they* don't return, he'll increase speed and veer south. He does *not* want a large confrontation before he gets to Bountiful—especially not with Lehi. There's probably another Lamanite army waiting on the other side of the border."

After delivering his explanation, he stood calmly, staring back at Amon. The others approached, two of them with arrows nocked. One had his sword out.

"Who hit him with the arrow?" Kai asked authoritatively.

"I did," said Amon in a challenging tone.

"That was perfect," said Kai, nodding approval. "He'll be hysterical, and the threat will look real. Now tell me, is there a flaw in my thinking?" He waited several seconds, until Amon relaxed his grip on his bow and shook his head.

"No," Amon finally admitted. "That makes sense. I don't like that it wasn't the plan, though." He scowled at Kai. "I don't even know you, and Lehi put you in command." The others had relaxed, too, and Kai explained further.

"It's my fault for not thinking of it earlier. I should have." He felt that keenly. "But it was the right thing to do. Now let's get moving and set up the ambush for the next scouts. We know that fool took a straight line back to the army—he was panicked and dumb. We should set up east of his path, since the army is still moving."

The others looked at each other, and one by one they nodded, then saluted—even Amon.

Relieved, Kai jogged back through the trees to retrieve Vyim, the others following and mounting up. He led them straight south first, making sure to stay out of any good lines of sight from the west and fanning two men out to the east. When they reached the top of a low, tree-lined hill that ran for a short distance east and west, Kai ordered them to spread out along the western half. From there, they had a clear view of anyone approaching from the south or west. He wasn't all that far from home, and he knew this landscape well. The main road ran five miles to the south, with a lesser road a few miles south of that. Both led to Bountiful.

They waited. Kai suspected it wouldn't be long, and he was right. Less than an hour later, two mounted Lamanite scouts raced out of a line of trees a mile to the southwest, aiming for the hill Kai and his men occupied, perhaps believing they would obtain a good view to the north from there. The view really wasn't that good—too many overlapping hills obscured sightlines northward, but the Lamanites didn't know that. They were a long way from home.

Kai had agreed to let Amon fire the first shot as a calculated concession, so he waited until he heard the first snap of Amon's bowstring before letting loose himself. The Lamanites had gotten very close before Amon fired, and both men ended up with three arrows sprouting from them in quick order. They barely screamed before falling from their horses and hitting the ground hard. The horses turned and galloped away.

Kai surveyed the landscape carefully for a full minute before signaling his group to emerge from cover to check on the scouts they had downed. One of them was already dead with an arrow in his neck. The other had been hit in the chest, stomach, and hip. He would probably die, too, but the process would be long and painful. He was still conscious, wheezing in agony.

Kai knelt beside him. "Your glorious leader has put you all in a very bad place."

The dying man gritted his teeth, then considered Kai without the hatred customary of Lamanite soldiers. "This is a stupid campaign. I never wanted to come. I just want to live—" He groaned loudly, a hand pressing against his bleeding gut. "I want to live in peace, with my wife and children."

Kai frowned, wondering whether he felt sympathy for the man or not. "How many Nephites have you killed who wanted the same thing?"

The man shook his head, eyes squeezed shut in pain. "I haven't … killed any … I even … let one go."

Kai didn't believe him, but didn't need to refute it. "Your army has killed thousands. You've probably taken some women and children prisoners, too, and I can only imagine what you've already done to many of those women." Kai felt less sympathy by the moment. Amon stood just behind him, and Kai could almost feel the fury emanating from him.

"But *I* haven't. I swear. I—" Another sharp pain wracked him. "This is wrong. I know it is." His voice had weakened.

Somehow, Kai started to believe him. Part of him protested loudly that he shouldn't be swayed, that the man was simply begging for his life, willing to say whatever he thought he needed to say. But another part wondered if the man was honest, knowing he was about to die.

"Is a Lamanite army waiting on the other side of Bountiful?"

The man seemed relieved Kai had asked him the question. He gave a slight nod. "Yes. It's . . . it's mixed, with some cities from the east. Those others won't let the army advance until Bountiful is secured. And they'll abandon us—aaaagh!—quickly . . . if it looks like the tide is turning."

Kai almost growled. "Well, the tide is about to turn." The man nodded, grunting, and again he seemed almost relieved. It was a strange reaction.

"And Coriantumr believes Lehi is approaching from the north or northeast?"

The man nodded, eyes squeezing shut as he struggled to breathe properly.

Kai stood and backed up a step. "We'll remove the arrows and dress your wounds, and one of my men will stay to guard you until . . . well, you'll probably die, as will many of your friends. You shouldn't have come. You should have found a way to resist."

The man accepted that pronouncement. Kai ordered two of his scouts to patch him up, then moved off a short distance with Amon and the other two.

"What do you think?" Kai asked them. "Should we scout a different direction? Should we try to get closer to Coriantumr's army, or should we return to Lehi and report?"

"Someone needs to warn Bountiful about that other army," replied Amon.

Kai nodded. "They probably already know, but I agree. You two?" The two other scouts looked at Amon before nodding, but Kai felt only slightly annoyed by their hesitation. "Okay, go now," he ordered. The two saluted, then turned and raced for their horses.

"We should leave two men here with the prisoner," said Amon.

"Agreed. And what about you and me?"

"We should return to Lehi." The look in Amon's eyes said he thought Kai would object. There was still suspicion there. But Kai understood—they were fighting a war.

"Okay, I'll lead," Kai said. "We'll go fast. I hope your horse can keep up."

Amon's horse gamely kept pace, but it was almost dead by the time they encountered two forward scouts of Lehi's army. Those men reported that Lehi's force was growing by the hour, having increased half again in size since Kai and the others had left. Kai ordered one of the forward scouts to give Amon his horse and stay behind to care for Amon's exhausted steed while Kai and Amon rode on. There were no objections, given the urgency of their information.

When Kai and Amon reached the main body of the army, they found Lehi riding at its head on a massive black stallion with thick legs and broad hooves. The beast could have pulled a large wagon by itself, but Kai couldn't make the image come together in his mind. This was a warhorse, complete with flared nostrils and fiery eyes. Lehi must have lifted it directly from a fairy tale.

Kai saluted smartly as he and Amon pulled up and turned their mounts to walk alongside the Nephite general.

"Sir, we made contact," Kai began. "One of their scouts is dead, another dying, a third lightly wounded. We think—or rather, I think—the scout who returned to them is panicked. We made him believe we were the forward elements of an army approaching from the northeast."

Lehi nodded, scanning the horizon as he thought. "So, you still believe the Lamanites want to avoid contact and will take your bait to veer south? We're counting on that."

Kai almost gulped. "I do, sir, yes. It seems they have another army waiting across the border. They've probably already found the secondary road a few miles south of the main road, too. Coriantumr likely has them moving as fast as possible, but we haven't confirmed. I can return, if you wish."

Lehi waved a hand. "I already have scouts out to verify their movements."

Of course he did. Kai felt foolish, but he endeavored to explain the remaining details as they continued riding, Amon adding the occasional comment.

Lehi pondered a few more moments after Kai had finished, then pinned him with a steely gaze and nodded. "Good work, soldier. I believe I would have done the same as you. Coriantumr wants to reach Bountiful before he's challenged. We have a strong garrison there, but he can overwhelm it, especially if he signals the army waiting to the east and they attack it together."

Kai didn't bask in the apparent praise from the esteemed general, and he didn't know what to say.

Lehi turned to one of his captains, riding behind and to his left. "Captain Zimig, execute New Bow. And I want Samat's men on the march to Bountiful within the hour." The captain saluted and peeled away, heading back along the line. Lehi had been prepared for this moment, Kai realized in wonderment. The captain was taking a risk sending part of his army to reinforce Bountiful, but Kai appreciated that, since his family was there. Of course, if Lehi didn't succeed in turning Coriantumr, then it wouldn't make much difference. Kai wondered if Lehi could be contemplating an alternative plan to trap Coriantumr between his army and the walls of Bountiful. How would that work, especially if Bountiful came under attack from both east and west? Kai's sudden doubts must have shown on his face.

"Don't worry, son," said Lehi. "We're picking up the pace now. Within the next twelve hours we'll be in position, and shortly after that we'll hit them—and hit them hard. Amon will return to the scout group now. You're with me."

Kai didn't know if he'd been promoted or not, but it didn't matter. A major battle loomed. He'd only ever been on the peripheries. He'd experienced real combat, but never in the heart of a teeming mass of frenzied men struggling to conquer lest they be killed, like Benijah's ill-fated command. In such a battle, luck was often more important than skill, and if one of your companions made a mistake, it could mean your life. He questioned whether he was ready.

Lehi and his soldiers marched all through the night, which put them exactly where Lehi had said he wanted to be. When the troops were all positioned, Lehi commanded them to get some sleep, save for a few sentries and scouts.

He told Kai they'd have about four hours to rest, though the first skirmish scouts hadn't yet returned.

Kai obeyed the order to rest, and while he hadn't intended to truly sleep, exhaustion overtook him almost immediately after he had lain down near a small thicket. The next thing he knew, one of Lehi's aides was gently shaking his shoulder, prodding him awake. Once Kai's mind registered that he'd been dead asleep, he came fully awake in an instant, sitting up so rapidly he startled the aide, who stepped back and then grinned.

"They're close—about five miles out, on the path you predicted," the aide said.

Who? Kai wondered. *Oh, yes, the Lamanites.* He thanked the man as he got to his feet and brushed himself off. His mind wasn't quite back in full operation yet, but he felt more refreshed than expected. "Where's the high captain?" he asked.

"Over here. Follow me." The man started moving through the woods, heading up a small incline and approaching the western boundary of a forested area. They passed many men in the underbrush along the way. A few still slept, but most were awake, checking weapons and armor.

"Lehi really likes you, you know," the aide said. "There aren't many people he calls 'son.' Most of us are soldier ... or lout." He grinned again at Kai. "That must've been some message from Moronihah."

Kai didn't reply, just gave a self-deprecating shrug. He didn't know what had been in that note, though getting immediate command of a group of scouts attached to the Nephites' most fearsome army said something.

They found Lehi standing next to a thick fir tree, a looking glass held to his eye. Those were new, rare ... and expensive. They were also extremely useful on a battlefield.

"Sir," the aide said, "I have brought Scout Kihoran."

Lehi turned. "Ah, Kihoran. Feeling rested, I hope."

Kai nodded as the aide retreated. "I am, sir. And you?"

He chuckled. "I've never needed much sleep. Don't know why. But I got a couple hours. I'm not too proud to admit that if I'm slow-witted on the battlefield, more of my men will die. I want them to be able to return to their families. I also want the Lamanites to pay dearly for what they've done."

The hard glint in his eye helped Kai further understand why the Lamanites feared him so much.

"Here," he said, giving Kai the looking glass. Kai handled it carefully. He had used one before, briefly, but had never had one requisitioned to him. "You can see the Lamanites crossing the river now. They're about halfway done, and the process will take a few more hours. They're clearly nervous about being attacked from behind . . . and from the northeast." He chuckled softly. "Your ruse was a dandy. I might be able to shout 'Boo!' in a few minutes and send them all scattering."

Kai smiled, but he didn't laugh—that would cause too much noise. He took a step forward to find an unobstructed view, then raised the glass to his right eye. The terrain ahead jumped toward him. Yes, there they were, at the river. The water flowed high, but they had built some pontoon barges pulled across by ropes. Their process seemed decently efficient, Kai had to admit. Coriantumr had also—wait, where was the bridge? The road wasn't a major artery, but it had a bridge. Or it used to have one.

He lowered the glass and looked at Lehi, who nodded knowingly and winked. "You noticed the bridge is out. I sent men ahead to destroy it and make it look like an accident, with the collapse originating on the west side, not the east. Our trick appears to have fooled them, at least enough for our purposes."

"He's starting to fan out his troops, though," Kai observed, "so he knows there's a possibility he'll be attacked."

Lehi nodded. "Yes. Fat lot of good that'll do him. In fact, it might make it easier for us. We'll hit him like Samson wielding that jawbone, son. He'll be cryin' for his mama by nightfall."

Kai nearly laughed again. He liked Lehi, and thanked the Lord they were on the same side. He brought the looking glass back to his eye and observed for a few more seconds until Lehi asked him to return it. Then they retreated farther into the trees.

"Get ready," Lehi said. "We'll launch the assault in the next hour. You'll be part of my guard."

Kai felt a spike of nervousness mixed with some relief. On the one hand, Lehi probably wouldn't spend much time in the thick of the battle. On the other hand, any battle could turn bad, and Kai hadn't earned the place of a member of the high captain's guard. He wasn't skilled or experienced enough, hadn't trained with the group, didn't know their tactics or fighting styles. He'd be more apt to make a mistake than save Lehi's life. And what would the other guards think of him?

He made his way back to Vyim and spent the next few minutes checking his bow, the fletching of his arrows, the sharpness of his sword. He kept his weapons well maintained, so there wasn't much to do. Finally, he mustered to where Lehi was making final preparations with his captains, going over strategies and contingencies, reviewing the communication signals they would use with the group of soldiers secreted two miles to the north in another section of forest.

The members of Lehi's guard had formed a loose ring around the group. None of them looked askance at Kai when he joined that ring, so Lehi must have said something to them. He sidled over to a tall, solidly muscled man.

"I'll follow your lead," Kai whispered to him. "I don't know what I'm doing." It was a frank admission, and he hoped the man appreciated his honesty.

He acknowledged Kai with a dip of his head. "Don't worry about it. We'll keep you safe."

So, that was it. Moronihah had asked Lehi to keep Kai safe during the battle. Kai felt somewhat relieved, but also embarrassed. He buried his shame and said, "Thank you." Then he settled a pace away in their protective circle.

Ten minutes later they were moving. Two skirmish scouts had just returned, one reporting he may have been sighted. Lehi scowled at the guilt-ridden soldier, but then set his captains in motion, along with several runners, and the camp began to limber up like a large beast that had been lying down and needed to shake out its muscles—only this beast was a hunting cat with sharp claws and long fangs.

Kai jogged to keep up with Lehi and his guards, weaving through the trees toward the line where the wood ended. When they broke out of the trees, it signaled the entire army to move forward at an easy lope. Nephite and Lamanite horns began sounding from all directions, and Kai felt the rising tension and dreadful excitement of the upcoming clash. Fear mixed with determination, and even though he knew it wasn't likely he would see much action, he felt a oneness with the other members of the army, most of whom would bear the brutal brunt of battle.

"Kihoran, beside me!" shouted Lehi. Kai detached himself from the ring of elite guards and moved up to jog beside Lehi. Then another horn sounded, and everyone started walking. Kai knew that horn signal, but he was so distracted he stumbled and nearly fell before getting back into position, embarrassment flushing through him.

Thankfully, Lehi didn't remark on his clumsiness, instead pointing up ahead. "See, son, they know it's us. They see my banners. Their idiot general is already trying to prepare a path for his retreat, around the south side of the lower bluffs. I didn't expect him to do that. Coriantumr didn't strike me as the cautious or cowardly type, especially after he took his entire army on this foolhardy adventure." He shook his head in derision, but he didn't seem disappointed, and he didn't shout out any new orders.

A minute later they started jogging again at the proper horn sound. Kai was paying attention this time. After another minute they walked again. Ahead, the men in the Lamanite lines—who had been marching forward at a steady pace, horns blowing and drums beating—suddenly stopped. A parley flag popped up near the middle of the line.

Lehi roared in laughter. "A parley flag. Rich, that is. He can't possibly think I'm as dumb as he is." He turned and signaled with a series of hand gestures to the horn blowers a short distance behind him. Then he clapped Kai on the shoulder. "Keep walking, son, and be ready to run."

Confusion shivered along the Lamanite lines, since the Nephites hadn't halted their advance. The distance between the two sides continued closing, leaving only about two hundred paces. Horns sounded from an area deep behind the Lamanite lines, and someone waved the parley flag frantically. At a hundred paces, the Nephite horns responded, and the Nephite lines surged forward. Lehi held out an arm as Kai was about to start running, then held up five fingers, counting them down to zero.

Then Lehi and his guards ran, aiming for the area in front of the parley flag. Presumably, thought Kai, General Coriantumr would be in that vicinity. If Lehi's men could break through the lines and engage Coriantumr, the battle might be exceedingly short. The members of Lehi's guard were his best warriors, the men forming the middle of his lines only slightly beneath them.

The Lamanite lines didn't break quickly, though, given their superior numbers. The battle became fierce, the air filling with the sounds of clashing metal, men screaming and cursing, bodies thudding to their mother earth. After a few minutes, Lehi took his group back several paces to observe, then started sending and receiving runners with messages. Nephite horns carried their own directives, but they didn't always blow standard patterns—Lehi had created some unique sequences. Maybe he even varied them periodically, to make sure the enemy never learned them.

Lehi had troops in reserve, including some cavalry, and he began to deploy them to press advantages. The Nephite lines didn't seem to be bowing anywhere, but fragile spots appeared in the Lamanite lines. Lehi pounded on those weak areas, even running up close to one of them and bellowing for his men to press harder. They responded, and soon there was a break, and then another, and a few of the Lamanites began to fall back, uncertain what to do. The Lamanite horns blared new notes, and Kai observed the beginning of an ordered retreat, covered by volleys of arrows that didn't fully clear the Lamanite lines. Dozens of Lamanites fell from those arrows, which they couldn't see coming, while only a few of the Nephites were struck.

At that point, Lehi surprised Kai yet again by wading into the fray with his guards. He must have known the Lamanite archers had begun their own retreat, and perhaps he wanted to punch all the way through and reach some of them before they could reform in a different location. Kai gripped his sword tightly as Lehi's guards engaged Lamanite spearmen, showing off their superior strength and skill as they cut the Lamanites down and drove forward, buoyed by the unconquerable will of their brilliant and determined leader. Kai looked for opportunities to bring his own sword to bear, but so great was the guards' proficiency that no enemy got past them. In fact, many Lamanites turned their backs and ran, especially when the rest of Lehi's troops rallied forward and shattered the remainder of the line, smashing into one of the archer groups as well. The parley flag had disappeared, most likely overrun.

Kai expected the Nephite soldiers to pursue the Lamanites at full speed once the Lamanite archers had been diminished, but Lehi issued new orders, and the horns sounded a normal walk. Then, Nephite archers began to harry the fleeing Lamanites, and Kai soon stepped over scores of men felled by

Nephite shafts, some of whom still moaned in pain. Lehi's troops ignored the wounded men for the moment, except to make sure they had no weapons.

Kai strained his focus toward the narrowest part of the river, where the broken bridge slanted awkwardly into the strong spring current. Lamanite warriors already on the other side fled south around the bluffs, or climbed the bluffs to get over them. Some still swam across the river or pushed the few pontoon barges, frantic to make their escape. A feeling of elation blossomed in Kai's chest. The Nephites had stopped the enemy. The Lamanite army hadn't reached Bountiful, hadn't endangered his family. Lehi and his men had done it! Again!

Kai felt primed for a full-scale pursuit, his adrenaline flowing, his sword arm ready. And then he heard the horns again. The Nephites halted and walked backward, reforming their lines until they resembled a shallow arc around the battlefield. At the point from which they had started their charge, they stopped. Wounded Nephites were tended in place or carried away to where the field medics could better attend them. A few of the wounded Lamanites pledged never to fight against the Nephites again, in exchange for the binding of their wounds. Those who refused to make the oath were the last in the triage. Over a thousand Lamanites had surrendered, offering the same pledge. Lehi and his captains accepted all such oaths.

Kai finally worked up the courage to ask, "Why are we letting them go? Won't your men be disappointed?"

Lehi turned his head and gave Kai a mildly reproving look, one eyebrow cocked. "We won. We fulfilled the orders from our chief captain. That's what my men care about. And they trust me to make good decisions. I think I've earned that trust. By the way, did you see the men hiding atop the bluffs when you were studying the landscape earlier?"

For the third time that day, Kai felt embarrassed. "No, sir, I didn't."

"General Coriantumr isn't quite as dumb as I've called him. He had a sizeable, well-concealed strike force up there to protect his rear, and probably a large reserve behind it. That parley flag was also a trick to allow him to get more troops across the water and possibly reposition some of those reserves for flanking attacks by covertly crossing them farther up or down the river. Men like Coriantumr don't honor oaths, by the way, under a parley flag or not.

"After we sent his first wave running, I didn't attempt to cross the river, as he surely hoped I would, and now he's in a quandary. He knows he has Nephite armies between him and Bountiful. His plan to get there before significant resistance formed against him has failed, and he realizes we know his intent. He has a lot of men feeling panicked, too, and while they still outnumber my army, they're in a strange place with no help immediately available to them. Do you know how hard it is to deal with thousands of panicked soldiers?"

Kai shook his head.

"Yeah, neither do I, but it has to be a nearly impossible situation. I predict they'll start marching this very night back to Zarahemla, hoping to get there before we can chase them down or any other Nephite armies can find them. I wouldn't do it if I were him—I'd make a new plan and try to punch through—but I'm not sure how much control Coriantumr really has at this point. My guess is he's a Zoramite, and he's nastier than a wounded she-lion, but he's just one man, and not even a Lamanite himself. That always makes me wonder."

He returned his gaze to the ongoing efforts to tend to the wounded, every one of whom, based on the stories, he would personally visit before the next morning came, friend and foe alike.

"Wonder what?" Kai asked.

Lehi frowned. "Why the Lamanites keep falling under the idiotic sway of our dissenters. Why do they make our traitors their leaders? Why do they bleed and die for these selfish, self-righteous bullies?" He gestured toward the blood-soaked battlefield with a powerful, battle-scarred arm. "Most of these Lamanite soldiers—some of whom could barely be called that—didn't want to be here. So why *are* they here? I'm afraid it's a puzzle I might never figure out. But it sure makes me angry." Fire burned in his eyes as he gazed at Kai. "We lost some good men today, Kai. Faithful men. Men whose families will suffer greatly for their loss. These wars are Satan's greatest joy. I despise war, and I despise Satan, too, at least as much as he despises me."

CHAPTER 12

And because he hath done this, my beloved brethren, have miracles ceased?
Behold I say unto you, Nay; neither have angels ceased to minister unto
the children of men. For behold, they are subject unto him, to minister
according to the word of his command, showing themselves unto them of
strong faith and a firm mind in every form of godliness.

MORONI 7:29-30

Lehi was right. By the morning of the next day, scouts reported the Lamanites making a beeline back to Zarahemla, traveling throughout the night. Lehi ordered his men to prepare to march immediately and sent messengers to take word along the southern roads—and ultimately to Moronihah—of the outcome of the brief battle and where the Lamanites were heading.

As Kai readied Vyim to depart, one of Lehi's aides approached him, the same one as before. He saluted, then handed over a small piece of parchment. Kai read it, then gave him a questioning look.

"He's sure," said the man. "He just wrote out the orders this morning."

"All right, thank you. Where can I find Scout Amon?" He had mixed feelings about working with Amon again.

"He was with the northern group. He'll meet you at the bridge. The main body of the army will march for the main road farther north."

The man jogged off, and Kai finished his preparations. By the time he had mounted Vyim, soldiers were already assembling in their assigned areas of the formation, their captains shouting orders and answering questions. He learned that a small group of men would take the wounded to Bountiful in wagons or on litters; they planned to leave later that day, but since more wounded Lamanites had been brought in during the night, they could end up being delayed.

Not far from the collapsed bridge, Kai found Amon in his saddle, staring across the still battlefield. Lehi's southern group was already crossing the road, heading north. Amon gave Kai a neutral look as he approached.

"So, you and me again, huh? And Lehi put you in charge?"

Kai shook his head. "No, he didn't. We have a specific set of orders, and once we get to Bountiful, we split up. He gave me an individual assignment after that." He almost said Amon could lead until then, but he decided against catering to Amon's juvenile attitude. Hadn't Kai's plan to steer the Lamanites south worked? And so what if Lehi liked him? He wasn't even a permanent part of Lehi's army.

"I have a separate assignment, too," said Amon, chin lifted. "So, I guess we should get to it. We can head straight for that gap between the forest and the bluff … if that's okay with you." The sarcasm was faint, but still hard to miss.

"Why wouldn't it be?" Kai asked, openly challenging the sarcasm.

Amon didn't respond, just kicked his horse into a trot. Kai followed at a distance of twenty paces, per his training, picking his way among the flotsam of battle along a slightly different path than Amon took. Only a few arrows protruded from the ground or lay in the grass, and those were cracked or missing fletching. The good arrows had already been gathered by a scavenging party sent out by Lehi. They had collected spears, swords, and pieces of armor as well.

Instead of proceeding to the lower ground of the gap, Amon turned up the hill toward the bluffs. Kai didn't question him, just followed while increasing the distance between them. Lehi had spotted Lamanites at the top of the bluffs before the battle; there was a chance some had remained to see what the Nephites did.

But Coriantumr hadn't left any men on or near the bluffs, and the air was eerily still.

Amon stopped halfway across, letting Kai catch up. "Sorry, I changed the plan," he said, the sarcasm thicker.

"And it was a good idea," countered Kai. "Why would I complain about a good idea?"

Amon turned and almost sneered. "Maybe because it wasn't yours?"

Kai stared at him, tempering his rising anger. He didn't stop himself from swinging at the root of the tree, though. "So, what is it you really don't like about me?"

Amon rested his hands on his mount's withers and gave him a condescending look. "How old are you? Nineteen? And—"

"Twenty-two."

Amon leaned back. "Oh, twenty-two, pardon me. So, with all that 'extra' experience, it's no wonder you show up and Lehi puts you in charge of one of the most important scouting missions in the last twenty years. And then you take a risk without telling any of the rest of us."

His look of smug accusation grated across Kai's mind. Amon had never accepted him as the leader, even though he supposedly trusted Lehi, who had made the decision.

"So, why didn't you ask Captain Lehi about it? Or better yet, lodge a complaint?"

Amon laughed. "I would have been demoted. Yeah, you would have loved that."

Kai's tone became more serious; their bickering was getting ridiculous. "Don't you realize what's going on?" he asked, his eyes demanding a genuine answer.

"The same thing that's always going on," replied Amon testily. "The Lamanites attacking us, killing us, taking prisoners."

"It's more than that," said Kai. "Moronihah called me to Zarahemla after Pahoran was murdered. All these events are linked. There's another group, called the Gadiantons, coordinating with the Lamanites, trying to overthrow the government and put us all in bondage. Yes, it's been attempted before, but not even during the Great War did they get so close. Zarahemla had never fallen to the Lamanites—until now—and they had help from the inside. We may have turned Coriantumr back from Bountiful, but we're still in grave danger. And by the way, Moronihah sent me here over Helaman's objections."

Amon's face morphed in strange and troubled ways as Kai spoke, and at the mention of Helaman a look of slight awe, tinged by shame but still sprinkled with resentment—and probably jealousy—manifested itself. He turned his head away.

Kai waited several seconds for Amon to say something, but he ultimately refused, instead urging his horse forward and then picking a path down the steepest portion of the western hillside. Kai let him go, following again at an appropriate distance. At the bottom of the hill, they encountered the trail of the retreating Lamanite army—crushed grass, thousands of footprints, ruts left by wagon wheels, and countless blood stains. Occasionally, they found the body of a man who had succumbed to his battle wounds; the Lamanites were in such a hurry they hadn't paused to bury or burn any of their fallen.

Soon, the trail merged with the main road from Bountiful. After following for another ten miles, as prescribed by Lehi, and finding nothing unexpected, they set a message marker for Lehi's army and turned north off the road, angling northeast toward the place where they had ambushed the Lamanite scouts—and where they had left two of their number. Amon begrudgingly asked Kai to take the lead, since Kai knew the area better, and they quickly found the spot. As they dismounted near the trees, one of the scouts emerged, a broad smile on his face.

"You're back! We thought you'd abandoned us." He was joking, and Amon smiled.

"We should have, Matthias," Amon said. "You're dead weight. Where's Mezrahir?"

Matthias hiked a thumb over his shoulder. "He's back there with Ashtenoth, the Lamanite scout." Amon's jaw dropped. Kai's almost did, too.

"He's alive?" asked Amon in amazement.

Matthias shrugged. "I'm shocked, too. I'll let you ask them about it. Come on." He turned and started hiking into the trees.

Kai and Amon dismounted and followed, leading their horses. About fifty paces in, they found Mezrahir and the Lamanite, Ashtenoth. Both sat on large rocks, using their knives to carve pieces of wood into useless and unrecognizable shapes.

Upon seeing that the Lamanite had a knife, Kai stopped, tensing. A split second later, so did Amon. Matthias just walked up to the other two and announced their arrival, as if everything were normal. Kai and Amon moved forward again, slowly, dropping the leads of their horses.

"Explain," demanded Amon, staring at the knife in the Lamanite's hands. Ashtenoth seemed to realize the discomfort he was causing and set the knife and his piece of wood on the ground. Then he stood, raising his hands to shoulder height.

He's standing, Kai thought in awe, with no sign of debilitating wounds.

"I know this looks strange," Ashtenoth said. "Maybe . . . maybe Mezrahir can explain better?"

"Yes, Mez," said Amon, his mouth still half agape. "Please explain."

Mezrahir smiled as he stood. He seemed to relish Amon's discomfort. "Well, it's pretty simple. You guys left, and Ash here was sure he was going to die, so he started asking us questions about what to expect on the other side. We told him, and he asked more questions—about God; about Jesus Christ, whom the Anti-Nephi-Lehies had left Lamanite society to follow; about how we Nephites are so often preserved in battle. And then . . . at one point he asked if we could pray for him, and Matt got bold and told him we might even be able to heal him."

"He was less astonished at that idea than I expected," added Matthias.

"So we blessed him," continued Mezrahir, "and by the next morning, he was healed. He barely even has scars. And he wants to be baptized."

"And I want to bring my family here," said Ashtenoth, his look one of humility and pleading. "That's possible, right?"

Kai looked at Amon, who returned his gaze and then stared at Matt and Mez, clearly uncertain how to respond to that request. It was Kai who finally answered. "Of course it is."

A worried look suddenly painted Ash's face. "Wait, you won, right? Coriantumr was defeated?"

Amon took a step forward. "We kept him from continuing to Bountiful, where Kihoran is from." His tone made it sound like he and Kai were fast friends. "But he still has a large army, and he's marching back toward Zarahemla."

"And the other army?" asked Ash, still sounding worried.

"The city has been reinforced, and as far as we know, that other army hasn't attacked, because Coriantumr didn't make it. Kihoran and I are going to check that out, though, by order of Captain Lehi."

A look of relief washed over Ash's face. "Praises be to God," he said, raising his arms as he dropped to his knees, face aimed heavenward, an actual tear leaking from the corner of one eye. Neither Kai nor any of the other scouts had an immediate response. After a few moments, Ash regained his feet, pegging his gaze on Amon, his voice earnest. "I hope Coriantumr is surrounded and destroyed … though I, um … hope not too many of my brothers have to die because of his evil, and that of our king." Another tear escaped.

"Well, this calls for a celebration!" exclaimed Mez. "I'm sure we can find some game to hunt, and now we can build up a fire and have a serious feast."

"We can't stay," said Kai, stepping up next to Amon. "Our orders are strict. You can celebrate if you want, but then you are to ride for Bountiful and report to the ranking captain there. We have more scouting to do."

It felt as if he had thrown a wet blanket over a fire, and Mez and Matt became more serious.

"Of course," said Matt. "This isn't over yet. We'll get moving immediately. We only have two horses, but it still won't take us long to reach Bountiful. Maybe we'll see you there?"

"I hope so," said Kai.

"Wait, where will I go in Bountiful?" asked Ash. "Will they put me in prison?" He seemed bravely determined to accept his fate.

Matt shrugged. "Maybe, until you can come before a judge. But I'm sure it will work out."

An idea came to Kai. "When he's free, help him find my parents—well, adoptive parents—Gideon and Ishara, in the southeastern district of the city. They'll be able to help."

Ash looked at him gratefully. "Thank you, um …"

"Kihoran."

"Kihoran. I have hope—more hope than I've felt my entire life. God is good. I'm glad he sent me to all of you."

"So we could shoot you," said Mez.

"And then heal you," added Matt.

"And then ship you off to a strange city that produces odd people like Kihoran here." Amon accentuated his quip with a slap on the back of Kai's shoulder, again as if they were long-time friends.

The gesture felt awkward and fake, but Kai didn't complain.

Several hours later, Kai and Amon passed a few miles to the north of Bountiful, executing a standard scouting pattern. They hadn't seen any signs of potentially hostile activity, so they turned south, arriving at the city a short time after nightfall to report in.

Captain Orihon commanded the garrison at Bountiful. Kai had met him a few times, and he seemed highly competent. He had employed his own men and the reinforcements from Lehi in building additional defensive structures around the city and atop the walls. When Kai entered his office in the Hall of Judgment, Orihon informed him he was just about to leave for home to get a hot meal and some rest. He had already received the latest intelligence reports from Lehi.

"I'll take your report in the morning, Scout Kihoran. There's nothing urgent in it, I presume?" He stood behind his desk—a solid permanent piece crafted by fine Nephite artisans.

"No, sir. I'd like to leave before first light to scout the army across the eastern border, though. I'm familiar with many of the peoples to the east."

"No need, soldier. We've been speaking with some of their representatives, listening to their excuses and offers of assistance. The Lamanites have faded away to the south. I don't think they're returning, but we're keeping an eye on them. By the way, Lehi asked me—no, ordered me—to tell you to go see your family. He wants you to spend an entire month with them. Yes, that's a change in the orders he gave you. He says Moronihah and Helaman will then want you back in Zarahemla. I wish he would have told me a little more than that."

Orihon paused, letting the implied question linger. Kai related to him the short version of his months-long story, including mention of the attempt on Helaman's life, but he downplayed his own involvement.

The captain gave him a broad grin. "Well, soldier, you've made Bountiful proud. Of course, we can't tell anybody, but *I'm* certainly proud. Now go home. Get some well-deserved rest. You can deliver your scouting report on parchment tomorrow, and I'll review it."

Kai felt odd leaving the building without a new assignment … besides the order to go home and rest for a month. A *month!* It seemed … wrong. Men would be fighting and dying over the next month. He wasn't wounded, and he could be useful. Even Amon would receive a new assignment; and now Kai was the one feeling jealous.

It wasn't that he didn't want to spend time at home, of course. He certainly did. But it would feel far better to return after peace was re-established, not when he should be out on the battlefield helping his fellow soldiers. As he drew closer to his house, leading Vyim on foot through the lantern-lit streets, the sense of disappointment didn't subside, even though his excitement to see his parents, his sister, and Siarah competed with it.

His parents. Over the last month or so he'd truly started to think of Gideon and Ishara as such, referring to them as his parents more comfortably with others—and with himself. He was reasonably sure they had no idea he was coming, and he couldn't wait to see the look on Neva's face when she saw him. She would be the first, because somehow she always was.

As he approached the front porch, he realized he should have found a place for Vyim. Some of the neighbors had barns, but he could easily have left Vyim in the garrison stables as well. He had to admit his oversight was partly due to pride. He wanted to show off his horse.

He could tell a lamp shone from the kitchen area. He guessed his family was reading. Gideon and Ishara loved studying scrolls and other texts. His mother liked to write out her thoughts, too, so there were always pieces of parchment in the house with her writing on them.

He didn't bother knocking. He told Vyim to wait and pushed the door open slowly, minimizing the noise. Then he closed the door softly and stopped to listen. They weren't reading. They were playing a game, and he instantly knew which one. In most places, it was called Hunters, but he'd heard it called Breakthrough as well. It was played on a large, flat, etched surface—usually wood, but expensive versions were made of stone or metal. Each player had three tokens, and they could move them along multiple paths, confronting or avoiding non-player enemy blocks as they tried to get to the prize in the middle. The tokens had a maximum combined distance they could move each turn, and at the end of each round, one player, on a rotating basis, could move three of the blocks. There was a chance element to the game as well: a die rolled at the beginning of each player's turn would either grant two additional segments of movement, remove two segments of movement, or allow a free enemy block move. A die roll also determined the outcome of a confrontation with an enemy block—a risky choice which could either move the block to the side or knock the player's token back two segments.

Kai smiled in the darkness near the door as he listened. His mother yelped in glee at a good roll of the die, as his father groaned. All three members of his family became animated when playing this game, even his normally reserved father. Part of Kai wanted to just enjoy watching them, but part of him wanted to join in, even though he'd start out behind.

A second later, it was like someone had tapped Neva on the shoulder, causing her to turn her head in his direction. "Kai, you're home!" She jumped from her chair like a startled rabbit and raced toward him, nearly driving him into the door.

His mother rose and put her hand over her heart, face beaming, eyes instantly glistening. His father got up to stand next to her with his arm around her waist. They waited patiently for Neva to finish her hug, and Kai finally made her let go and stand on her own feet. Then he strode over to his parents and embraced them, Neva joining in.

"It's good to see you, Mother, Father. I'm so glad you're all safe."

His mother started crying. His father squeezed tighter, and they held the embrace for several long moments. Then his mother broke them apart and took half a step back to get a full look at him. She wiped tears from her cheeks as she said, "You look healthy. You weren't hurt?"

Kai shook his head. "I'm fine, thankfully. I don't think I've been in any real danger." That statement was a mighty stretch, but he didn't want her worrying too much.

"You know Lehi beat the Lamanite army, right?" asked Neva, emphasizing her query with a punch to her hand. "Were you there?"

Kai nodded. "I was there, with Lehi and his guards. We defeated them quickly. His men are some of the finest warriors we have, along with the men of Gideon."

"So the Lamanite army is destroyed?" asked his father. "How many men did we lose, and how many prisoners did we take?" Kai knew his father would be concerned first with how many had died or were hurt. That was Gideon's heart.

"It's still a very large army," replied Kai. "They had nearly twice our number, but I'm sure they worried more Nephites were on the way. And they fear Lehi like a plague. They didn't want to face him until after taking Bountiful—and getting reinforcements from across the border."

His father's brow furrowed in alarm. "From across the border? There was another army? We hadn't heard of this."

"You will. Tubaloth convinced a few of the eastern lands to join him, but Captain Orihon just told me that once Coriantumr was turned away, the alliance fell apart, and the Lamanites retreated to the south—um, well, Orihon probably didn't want me to reveal that yet." He scratched his jaw, feeling somewhat abashed.

His father considered the information, then asked, "And what of Zarahemla? We've heard it has completely fallen, but some say a section of the city still fights on, bravely protecting the temple, with Helaman leading them."

An oppressive gloom settled over Kai. He smiled wanly. His mother gasped and put her hands over her mouth.

"Helaman's fine, but Zarahemla is indeed fallen. I saw Helaman just a few days ago, in Gideon, after Moronihah arrived." Ishara let out a long sigh of relief mixed with anguish. It was a peculiar sound.

"How did he escape?" asked his father.

"Well, I guess the best way to say it is the Lord got him out of there before the Lamanite army arrived. Helaman called a special conference in Gideon—*not* Zarahemla—for the saints of that region, and the meeting was held on the morning after the First Day celebrations, so people would have to travel on the First Day. The Lamanites attacked on the second day, early in the morning, after most of the saints had left."

His father's eyes widened in amazement at first, but then he gave a firm, knowing nod. "Those who heeded the Lord's prophet and sacrificed some of the celebration were spared. Like you."

That was a dicey point, and there were nuances he couldn't go into with his family. "Actually, I was in the city when it was attacked." His mother gasped again, swaying slightly. His father's arm returned to her waist. "I still had an assignment to fulfill. I was able to hide, though, with Vyim, and I saw Coriantumr kill Chief Judge Pacumeni. Then, with some help, I was able to escape. I went to Gideon, and then I was sent here."

"Who's Vyim?" asked Neva. "That's a funny name."

"Oh, right," said Kai. "I didn't tell you. He's my horse. He's standing just outside the front door. I haven't . . . um, stabled him for the night yet."

He could tell Neva wanted to rush out and see him right away, but she glanced at their parents, probably sensing they still had questions.

"You said you spoke with Helaman?" asked his mother. Wonder fluttered at the end of her tone.

"Yes. I've spoken with him a couple of times. We uncovered a plot in Zarahemla to assassinate him, and the murderer was stopped. I also met one of the two thousand. His name is Dan. He's one of Helaman's guards." He felt like he was boasting, trying to impress his parents.

His mother suddenly wrapped him in another hug. "Oh, my goodness, son, you've been through a lot in such a short time. I'm even more grateful you returned to us safely." She didn't let go, and his father joined in again. Kai waited for Neva's arms to complete the family hug, but instead he heard her nearly bouncing on the balls of her feet. He grinned as he let go.

"I love you all." He smiled at Neva. "And you really, really want to see my horse, don't you?"

She narrowed her eyes a little, and he realized he had just spoken to her as if she were a young girl rather than a young woman. It struck him that she was now almost eighteen, though she looked younger, at least to him. He would never dare tell her that. She finally folded her arms and smirked. "Yes, big brother who's been meeting with all these famous people. Yes, I do. I'll probably like him better than I like you."

Kai laughed, then waved for them all to follow as he walked out of the kitchen and through the front room. He exited the house, stepping to the side to let everyone by, holding out an arm toward Vyim, who nibbled on some hardy grass growing between their house and the street. Vyim raised his head, chewing placidly, taking them all in.

"This is Vyim," he announced. "Probably the fastest—and smartest— horse in the world."

Neva approached Vyim tentatively, holding out an open hand toward his nose. Vyim didn't react at all. "He's big," she said, "and gorgeous." She turned to look at Kai. "And he's really yours? How could you afford him?"

"Well," Kai said, scratching his head. "I'm not exactly sure how it all happened. He used to belong to the army, and now ... well, now he's mine. I think. Well, I'm pretty sure."

"So you did a little more than what you've told us so far," commented his father with raised brow.

Kai shrugged. "It worked out. And I really, really wanted Vyim. Oh!" He held up a finger toward Neva. "A friend of mine bred him with several mares. I might be able to get one of the foals. If so, that foal is yours."

Neva's face went blank at first, but then lit up like the full moon. "Really? You mean it?" She jumped up and down several times—like a little girl— but then regained her composure and continued primly, "Thank you, Kai. I hope it works out."

Kai chuckled. "I'm pretty sure it will. Although—" His shoulders sagged as a dark cloud billowed into his mind, his smile disappearing in a flash. "That friend lives near Zarahemla. I don't know if ..." The gloom deepened as he thought of Aaron and Nalani and their children. Their farm was only a few miles north of the city. Had the Lamanite army raided it on its way out? Had the Lamanite garrison that remained pillaged it? He wished he could jump on Vyim's back that instant and fly to Zarahemla to check on them. He said a silent prayer instead.

"Oh," said Neva, her face saddening. "I'm so sorry. I hope they're okay. I don't care about having a horse. That's selfish when people are dying all across the land." She started crying, and probably without realizing what she was doing, she wrapped her arms around Vyim's neck and leaned into him. He lowered his head, cradling her back.

Kai and his parents let the moment linger, and then Kai had an idea to cheer her ... and him, too. "Do you want to come with me to show him to Siarah? It's only the third bell of the evening; her parents won't mind. They might even have a place out back to keep him for the night. I can get him properly stabled tomorrow. You can ride him—I'll lead."

Neva turned and lifted her head, sniffling. Then she nodded. "Okay, yes, I'd like that."

Kai pasted on a smile, and then he had another thought—why hadn't he gone to see Siarah first? Captain Orihon had ordered him to go home; had he just locked that order in his head? Would Siarah think he didn't prioritize her? And he was bringing his *sister*. Siarah liked Neva, but Neva's presence might make the situation awkward. His head hurt trying to sort it all.

It was too late to change plans, however, and soon Kai was walking the half mile to Siarah's house, with Neva sitting astride Vyim like an eastern princess. Kai's nervousness lessened as he evaluated his actions further. He had spent only a few minutes with his parents, and then had headed straight to Siarah's house. Siarah would understand; the nation was at war, and he had come home safely from a battle. He could tell her more about Helaman, too, and some of his adventures—not all of them, of course, and not many of the details. He briefly wondered whether Ara was okay. She and her friends had taken a grave risk for him.

When they arrived, Kai patted Vyim on the neck and dropped the lead to approach the door. He knocked softly, not seeing any evidence of light through the windows. Vyim whickered softly as Kai heard a faint noise from inside. A few moments later, the door cracked open, and the bleary-eyed face of Siarah's father, Master Thandrum, appeared. His eyes widened as he recognized Kai.

"Kihoran!" he exclaimed in a hoarse whisper, opening the door further. "You're here, and you look well! Come in!" As Thandrum backed up a step, he spotted Neva and Vyim and paused. "Neva, too. And …" He glanced questioningly at Kai.

"That's Vyim, my horse. He can remain there for now, though I was wondering—could he stay behind your house tonight? My parents don't have any room. I'll get him stabled tomorrow."

"Of course, of course. But where did you get a horse?"

Kai took advantage of the opportunity to ingratiate himself a bit with Siarah's father. "Captain Moronihah gave him to me."

Thandrum blinked, staring at Kai, then at Vyim, then back at Kai. "Oh. Well, I'll go get Siarah. She'll be overjoyed to see you. And both of you, please come in." He left the door open as he retreated into the house. Neva dismounted, then giggled as they both entered. It was dark inside; Thandrum hadn't lit any lamps. Kai closed the door quietly.

Soon Siarah emerged from the side hallway. She carried a small lamp, and her pace quickened as she saw Kai. She set the lamp on a small table and then lunged to throw her arms around him, burying her face in his neck.

She started sobbing almost immediately. Kai held her tight, feeling happier than he had in a long time.

She finally leaned her head back, gazing up at him in the soft glow of the lamp. Her hair was a disheveled mess, but she was beautiful. "When did you get back?" She glanced at Neva, and Kai felt a twinge at the question she hadn't asked.

"Just tonight. Captain Orihon sent me home, and then I came here."

She let out another sob, then said, "I'm so happy to see you" before burying her head in his neck again for a second round of crying. Kai snuck a peek at Neva. She shrugged, but she was crying, too. So much crying, and he hadn't even been hurt. He might have a bruised shin and a slightly sprained wrist, but he was whole and hale.

She finally recovered, maintaining her tight hold as she looked up again. "I sent you a letter. Did you get it?"

"Yes. I loved it. I didn't have a chance to send one back. Things have been … well, a little hectic."

She bobbed her head, then shook it slowly. "I can't imagine what you've had to go through. How did Zarahemla fall? Everyone thought it was impossible. I know some king-men briefly took it over near the end of the Great War, but that was just politics."

That incident hadn't just been 'politics,' but Kai didn't try to correct her. "The Lord protected me, that's for sure. I was there when the Lamanites took the city, which was vastly undermanned with most of the troops at the border, and it's a miracle I was able to get away after they destroyed the token garrison. You can thank Vyim—he's very smart and incredibly fast."

"Vyim?"

"My horse, waiting just outside. He's staying here tonight, out back, and then I'll get him stabled."

She blinked, but didn't ask more about Vyim. "You were really in the city when they attacked?" Before he could answer, she added matter-of-factly, "Well, of course you were. That's where Moronihah had sent you, and you're one of his best soldiers. I'm just … I'm so happy you're all right, Kai." A third round of crying began. Kai gently stroked her hair, and soon it seemed impossible she could produce any more tears.

At last she released him and stepped away, making complicated motions with her hands as she calmed herself. "Okay. I'm okay." She looked at Neva again. "It's good to see you, Neva. You must be really glad Kai is home, too."

"Yes. He surprised us. Well, I guess God surprised us."

Siarah laughed out another sob. "He did, didn't he?" She turned her adoring gaze back to Kai, stepping close. "How long do you get to stay this time?" There was a lot more to that question than simple logistics, and Kai hadn't thought that far ahead yet.

"Lehi said a month, so I guess I'm staying a month. Then I'm to return to Zarahemla ... presuming, of course, it's been liberated by then. I'm sure it will be."

"It will be," agreed Neva with a firm nod.

"But you might be involved in more battles," noted Siarah, clearly worried while putting on a brave face.

"Maybe. But the Lamanite general made a terrible mistake by leaving Zarahemla. Moronihah, Lehi, and the other high captains will chew him up. Some of his men are already panicking. I doubt many of them wanted to be here in the first place. A few other scouts and I captured one Lamanite who wants to be baptized and bring his family to live here. He was ..." Kai cocked his head as he recounted the wonderment in his own mind "... well, he was healed by the administration of a priesthood blessing. Or *through* a blessing, I guess. He had a lot of faith. I saw him after the healing, and I know how badly he was wounded. One of those wounds was from my arrow. We were sure he would die."

The room grew quiet. Kai heard a slight shuffling that meant Thandrum and Dinah were listening in.

"Did you have to kill anyone?" asked Siarah softly.

"I'm not sure," Kai answered frankly. "I know I scored some hits from the wall in Zarahemla, but most arrow wounds don't kill a man in armor. And I threw a man back over the edge, but the wall slants, so I don't know how hard he hit the ground."

"So ... you still probably haven't had to kill anyone yet, right?"

They'd had this conversation before. She understood the requirements of his job, but she was one of the gentlest people he knew. She hated that he might have to kill someone, and part of her fear was what it might do to him. Kai understood. He'd been taught in the army that it was a traumatic thing to extinguish the life of another person, even when defending yourself and your family. A good soldier didn't just train physically and mentally, but emotionally as well, to deal with such horrors. A great soldier, Moronihah often said, echoing his father Moroni, trained just as much spiritually as physically, so the Spirit of God could better help.

"Not as far as I know. Hopefully, I'll never have to. Someday we'll have sustained peace in this land. I feel it. An old priest I met in Gideon believes it, too. I just hope it will be in my lifetime."

"Now you sound just like Father," chimed in Neva, teasing. "When did you grow up and become all philosophical?"

A chortle escaped Kai's lips, releasing some tension. "I have no idea." And he truly didn't.

Siarah wanted to spend every minute of the next day with Kai. He saw Gideon and Ishara at breakfast, then bid them goodbye. Neva was still asleep.

Siarah expressed minor disappointment when she learned Kai had promised Neva—and not her—a foal sired by Vyim, but she quickly returned to her cheery self. She loved Kai's horse, and the first thing she asked was if they could go riding. Kai explained they could only ride within the city walls, but she didn't care about that; her only condition was that they not borrow another horse from the garrison stables—she wanted to sit behind Kai with her arms wrapped around his stomach and her head lying against his back. As they rode, he occasionally heard her sigh contentedly. It felt good.

They crisscrossed the city for almost three hours, until Kai stopped at a vendor—his favorite in the city—that sold meat pies. He wanted to remind himself how good they were and compare them to the ones he'd recently tasted in Zarahemla. He helped Siarah to the ground, then jumped down himself. Siarah walked gingerly as they approached the vendor, though she hadn't yet commented on being sore.

Kai ordered two meat pies of the same type—with just as much vegetables as meat, and lots of spices. The man warmed the pies over some coals for a minute, then let the outside cool briefly before handing them over. Kai paid and thanked him, then took Vyim by the reins to lead him for a stretch while he and Siarah ate.

"Vyim might enjoy us walking for a while," he explained, "instead of us both being on his back."

"Are you saying I'm too heavy?" she asked, but he knew she wasn't serious.

"Well, after this meat pie …" he joked, then braced before she slapped his shoulder, which she managed to do just as she was taking a bite of her pie. She was talented.

They walked on, and a few seconds later—after another bite of her pie—Siarah commented, "The Shipbuilder's Gardens will be beautiful this year."

Kai nodded his agreement as he chewed. The gardens always impressed, earning their fame. They were said to fairly represent—at least in some respects—the place called Bountiful where the Lord had commanded Nephi to build a ship with the help of his brothers, who had initially resisted. That story had always fascinated Kai. He wondered what had really happened to Laman and Lemuel when Nephi stretched out his hand toward them. Did lightning fork down from the sky? Did an angel touch them? Whatever it was, it had changed their minds in a hurry. Some army trainers yelled at poorly performing recruits that if they didn't shape up, God would shock them. Kai hadn't heard of anyone ever being shocked for real, of course. And the new soldiers weren't being asked to build a ship capable of transporting people across the Great Sea so they could start a new nation. They just needed to learn to hold a spear properly, or a sword or a bow, and not accidently hurt themselves or someone else. Some trainees believed the threat, though.

As they continued walking and eating, Kai recalled his own training. He was fourteen when he joined. Moroni had recently given command of the armies to his son, though he still served as an adviser. Kai had shown himself to be agile, and he had sharp eyes. His trainers noted he was calm under pressure, too, at least compared to most recruits, so they started him as a scout. Almost three years later, just before Moroni died of a fast-progressing disease at only forty-nine, Kai also became a spy.

Eight years had now passed since his first day in the army, but it seemed like much longer. He had become decently skilled at his job, but he wasn't sure how long he could remain a spy. How could he have a family if he was gone most of the time? Regular full-time soldiers at least had their families with them—even when they moved to a new location temporarily. Militiamen, too, of course. But spies frequently had to leave their loved ones for extended periods. Siarah had him thinking hard about the future, and he was torn. Should he wait to marry her? Should he leave the army? He wasn't entirely confident he could figure it out within a month.

Siarah hadn't said anything directly, but she seemed to know what she wanted, and that was to marry Kai. Without further delay. After they finished eating and got back on Vyim, she led them by Bountiful's temple—twice, including once all the way around it. When they finally dropped Vyim off at the garrison stables near dinner time, she commented, "We'll probably have to get another horse. I need to learn to ride better, so I can help teach our children." She grabbed his hand and squeezed it as she leaned in close.

"Well, if Aaron and Nalani are okay, and their farm wasn't destroyed, within a year I think we can easily make that a reality." He felt another strong spike of worry, praying again for Aaron and Nalani's safety.

They went to his home for dinner, which his mother had spent all day preparing, enlisting Neva's help for much of the time. Neva didn't love cooking, but she was in a better mood about it than Kai would have expected. His father had splurged and purchased some fine cuts of meat, and Neva had found a wide variety of fresh fruits and vegetables, some of which were rare for that season. At least three types of bread cast mouth-watering aromas throughout the house, competing vigorously with the meats. Waiting at the kitchen table for the food to be done, served, and prayed over was excruciating. His hunger chased him like a starving wolf, especially after spending so many days in the field on short rations. The effects of the meat pie had disappeared what seemed like days ago.

"Well, this is indeed a meal of great gratitude," said his mother after Gideon had offered a protracted blessing. Yes, she was going to make a speech. "We praise our Father in Heaven for the safe return of our son." She gazed at Kai lovingly, her eyes glistening. "May he continue to watch over you, Kihoran, as you learn to trust him even more." Her eyes passed across everyone, her face as bright as the noonday sun. "And now, dig in!"

Though stunned the speech had already ended, Kai didn't hesitate. When the first bite of food passed his lips, visions of heaven filled his mind.

His belly was near to bursting by the time he finished. His father had remarked several times how impressive his food intake was, and Siarah somehow seemed proud. Neva made jokes about him the entire time. Their banter felt good. Normal. *Peaceful.* Kai refused to let himself think about the war too much that evening, a feat made easier when Siarah dragged him to her parents' house for desserts. Dinah had spent most of her day baking.

By the time he fell asleep that night—the second night in a row in his own bed—he was nearly in a food coma, but he felt deliriously happy.

Early on the sixth day of his extended leave, unexpected orders came. A loud rap on the front door awakened him. He could hear his parents stirring in their room. Neva slept like a log, so he heard nothing from hers. He got up, pulled on a robe, then went to answer the door.

When he saw the crisply dressed officer's aide standing at attention, he knew something had happened and that he would probably have to leave. The timing was awful; he had decided to propose to Siarah so they could be married before his month at home was up.

"Scout Kihoran, you are summoned to meet with Captain Orihon at the third bell of the day."

Kai nodded neutrally, and the man saluted before leaving. Kai inched the door closed, his mind racing. Had Coriantumr broken out of the Nephite trap? Maybe the other Lamanite army had returned from the south—yes, that was most likely. The city needed to prepare for imminent battle.

His father appeared around the edge of the hallway.

"A message, son?"

Kai gave a half-smile, half-grimace. "Yes, father. I'm meeting with Captain Orihon in less than two hours. I pray it's just another debriefing, but I fear it isn't."

Gideon stepped fully into the room, concern in his eyes. "You're probably right." He sighed. "Oh, I don't know what your mother will say."

"Sure you do," Ishara said, emerging from the hallway to stand beside her husband. "She'll say, 'Go with God,' and she'll pack enough food for our boy that he'll be able to feed the entire army for a month."

Gideon chuckled, then put his arm around her shoulders. "How did we think Kai's visit could really last an entire month, in the middle of a war, when he is so important?"

Kai blushed. He wasn't that important. He'd tried to do the right things, and he'd gotten lucky, that was all.

His mother broke free and moved toward the kitchen. "I'll start preparing some breakfast."

"And I'll be back," said Kai. "I need to talk to Siarah first."

His father gave him a sympathetic look. "I'm sorry, Kai. I know you wanted to stay longer. We love having you home. But I admire your willingness to defend our freedom. I thank the Lord every day for your commitment and courage. I really do. That's not just something a father says." He almost choked up.

Kai felt a lump growing in his own throat. "It will be okay. I promise." He knew a soldier's promise didn't mean much, but he'd said it anyway.

Siarah took the news better than Kai had feared. She reiterated her pride in him, and she gave him three letters, which she said she'd been inspired to write during the night, and which she wanted him to wait a little while to read. One spoke about the past, one the present, and one the future. He didn't have anything to offer in return, but he promised he would write when he arrived at the place of his next assignment, even if it was in the homeland of the Lamanites. He was terrible at making himself write letters, but he was determined this time—and that was a soldier's promise he could keep.

She kissed him before he left, and he nearly melted. He almost convinced himself to march into Captain Orihon's office and resign his position in the army—even give back Vyim if necessary—but he realized quitting wouldn't endear him to Siarah, or start their life together off right. He would disappoint her, his parents, his sister, and himself. He had to do his duty and fight for his people. He must exercise faith in the Lord that it would somehow all work out.

He felt somewhat better by the time he met with Orihon. The captain was incredibly busy, and Kai had to wait almost an hour to see him, but he didn't sense any alarm in all the activity in Bountiful's Hall of Judgment.

"Scout Kihoran," Orihon said as Kai finally entered his office. "Close the door, please."

Kai did so and sat down. Orihon picked up a parchment from his desk and studied it for several seconds. Finally, he looked up. "I was just reviewing your new orders, which arrived last night. Moronihah wants you to report to Sidom as soon as possible, at the Hall of Judgment. You are to dress as a civilian and use an assumed name. Someone there will apparently recognize you." His eyebrows rose slightly. He didn't know Kai was also a spy. Few did. Officially, Kai was part of the Bountiful militia, with experience as a scout, which the broader army sometimes called upon.

Kai gave him a somewhat confused look, acting surprised. In part, he was. *Sidom's government still stood?* "Um … okay. Did he give a name I should use, or say why?"

Orihon shook his head. "No, but it looks like you might become a spy. You're a good scout, I know that. I've seen other good scouts become spies. How do you feel about that?"

Kai almost let the hint of a smile sneak through—very un-spy-like—but he continued to play dumb, adding some uncertainty to his expression as well.

"I … don't know. I mean, what does that mean? I was planning to get married."

Orihon nodded in understanding. Kai imagined he dealt with his soldiers' family concerns quite often. He'd sometimes wondered how much time a captain or high captain committed to dealing with such issues. It was obviously much worse in the aftermath of battles, when families of the slain had to be notified and permanently injured men needed counseling.

"This war will be over soon, soldier. And Captain Moronihah knows how important families are. Your plans might be delayed for a while, but don't cancel them." He winked, or tried to. Like Kai, he wasn't good at it.

Kai gave a sober nod, acting the part of an obedient and trusting young soldier. "Yes, sir. Thank you, sir."

"One other thing," said Orihon, his brow furrowing. "This was also included in the orders." He lifted a folded parchment from his desk, still sealed on the overlap with green wax. "It's a letter from Helaman, addressed directly to you. I don't know if he wrote it himself or had a scribe do it, but it's a great honor. I know you carried critical intelligence out of Zarahemla which helped us save Bountiful, when you were there on merchant business. Helaman recognizes such things, as his father did. Thank you, soldier."

Kai took the letter and stared at it a moment. "I was just doing my duty, sir. Others in my place would have done the same."

"Yes, some would have, but not all. Take your horse and one other. Travel fast, and let the Standard of Liberty guide you."

Kai stood and saluted, thanked Orihon again, and exited the office. Five other people waited outside to see the captain. Kai cringed at what it would be like to sit behind a desk most of the day. Part of him was glad he was about to travel again, even though it meant leaving for a while. He had Siarah's letters, and he would keep his promises.

He found a quiet hallway in a distant part of the building and sat on a small bench to read Helaman's letter. He had thought about waiting until that night, after he'd put a few miles behind him, but his curiosity grew with every passing second.

He opened it and began to read.

My friend, Kihoran of Bountiful,

The Lord continues to impress you upon my thoughts. I am grateful, of course, for the service you have already provided to the army, to this nation, and to me personally. I know you don't want public recognition for what you have done. I respect and admire that.

Beyond thanking you again, though, there is more I need to tell you. The Lord has made it clear our paths should converge again, and sooner than I expected. I don't understand exactly why, but I know he does, and I trust him. You are a good man, and I would like to offer you employment in my service and that of my household. It would require you to leave the army, and I have already received Moronihah's approval, if you decide to accept.

You would officially be a personal aide, and not a high-level one, though I will remunerate you as if you were. Unofficially, you will be a member of my personal guard. Part of your duties will also involve functioning as a spy from time to time, particularly in ferreting out the activities of the Gadiantons and the threats they will continue to pose. I must be careful whom I trust. I need God's help in that, and one of the people he has guided me to is you.

I had hoped that with the impending defeat of this latest Lamanite threat, we could eliminate the Gadianton movement as well, but despite my many prayers and pleadings in this regard, the Lord has not assured me this will be so. I think I understand. He will not violate our agency, so we must struggle to convince our brothers and sisters of the true path to peace and prosperity. He will help us do that, but it will not be easy, as I'm sure you know.

Perhaps the punishment meted out on Zarahemla for her perversions and corruption will wake a few people. But we forget so quickly and are so slow to remember! Still, I have hope for many, and our goal is not earthly but eternal.

Please prayerfully consider my offer. I look forward to seeing you in Sidom.

Kai pondered the letter for several minutes, re-reading it three times. How could such a letter be real, and addressed to him? He knew God had helped him over the last several months. He knew he was fortunate to be alive. But now the prophet of the Lord said he needed him. Who could believe such a thing, even if Kai were free to tell them?

He had to accept. There was no question about that. And when he wrote his letter to Siarah, he'd have to ask Helaman what he could include in it. He probably couldn't say anything about the Gadiantons, whom Helaman had just prophesied would continue to be a problem. Imrahiel had wanted him to get close to Helaman, and he had. Becoming Helaman's aide would earn him additional favor with Imrahiel while at the same time helping him protect Helaman. The more he thought about it, the more he realized how perfectly it had all been set up. Not by him, nor Helaman, nor Moronihah, but by the Lord himself.

He finally went to retrieve Vyim and the other horse, as ordered. A gray gelding named Thunder had already been prepared for him, laden with bulging saddle bags. Kai also received a brand new bow, some tough leather armor for his head, chest, arms, and legs, and two spears—an infantry spear and a longer cavalry spear. He stared in puzzlement at the officer who handled the requisitioning.

"I'm supposed to be traveling incognito, as a merchant. All this gear makes me look like a soldier."

"Wear the cloak and cap of a merchant," the man rejoined without a pause, barely looking at him as he completed the paperwork, "and nobody will think you're a full-time soldier. They'll wonder whether you lost a guard, though … maybe to a Lamanite patrol."

Kai should have thought of that. There wouldn't be many merchants traveling at all, and those who did would have guards and be heavily armed themselves. He would earn a few stares for being either brave, foolhardy, or just plain greedy, but few would suspect him of being a soldier, much less a spy.

He thanked the man, then set out for a familiar shop where he could purchase the appropriate cloak and cap of a full merchant. When he entered the establishment—owned by an old woman, Merga, and her husband, Orofin—good friends to Gideon and Ishara—Merga was chatting with a patron. She winked and smiled when she saw Kai, then excused herself and approached him. She grabbed his wrists.

"Kihoran, my love, you look better than I've ever seen you."

He was always uncertain whether she was flirting with him or not. Orofin didn't seem to mind—he laughed at her playfulness sometimes—and she didn't behave any differently whether her husband was present or not.

"Thank you, Mistress Merga. And you look younger than when I was last here."

"Aw, pshh," she said, slapping him on the arm, as she usually did when he complimented her. "You're a sight for sore eyes, though. I'm sure Gideon and Ishara were delighted to see you back."

"Yes, they were. And now I must leave again, unfortunately."

"Ah, well, you've got important business to do. Goods still have to flow, even in the middle of a war." She wasn't one to act surprised—she had seen a lot in her life.

"I need to purchase a merchant's cloak—dark green, if you have it—and cap to match."

She put a finger to her lips and tapped a few times. "Yes, well, I don't have dark green … unless you have time for me to make one?" She glanced out the window where his horses waited.

"No, I'm afraid I don't."

"Well, I have a beautiful burgundy set, very striking, and it would look magnificent on you."

Kai raised his hands, smiling. "You don't have to sell me on it. If that's what you have, I'll take it."

"Wonderful. I'll go fetch it for you." She turned and walked briskly toward the back of the store, passing through a doorway into the room where her and husband, along with at least two apprentices, did their work. She returned in short order, displaying the cloak draped across her outstretched arms, the cap hanging from the fingers of her right hand. He could tell instantly the workmanship and material were fine. The set looked expensive.

"Those are perfect," he said, "but how much?"

She thought for a moment. "Well, we've had this one in our stock for a while. Someone ordered it made and then had to cancel, so I can reduce what we would normally charge. And if you can do us a favor, I can reduce the price even further."

Kai cocked his head. "What can I do?"

"Here, hold these." She passed the cloak and hat to him, then retreated to the work room again. When she returned, she carried a thin, straight dagger, leafed in gold and silver on the pommel and small cross guard. The hilt was intricately wrapped in strips of rich leather, and the blade gleamed. It looked old but well kept; it must have been oiled and sharpened religiously. Its value likely exceeded that of the cloak and hat by a wide margin.

She held up the elegant knife in both palms. "This dagger has been in my family for four generations," she said proudly. "It was crafted by one of the most skilled artificers Nephi has ever produced. Orofin and I have kept it, thinking someday we would sell it to a wealthy collector. That time is now."

Now, in the middle of a war? Granted, the general presumption was that the war would end soon, but it still didn't seem like a great time to make such a sale, especially given the devastation the Lamanites had just caused. The economy would take some time to recover fully.

"Why now?" he asked.

"Well, I know you can keep a secret, though it won't be secret for much longer anyway. Orofin and I, with some of our children who have agreed, are going to migrate north and join some of the others there. We feel strongly it's time for us."

Kai nodded as if he understood, and maybe he was starting to.

"You will be sorely missed here," he noted sincerely.

She gave him her most dazzling grandmotherly smile. "We'll miss being here. But the Spirit has confirmed our plan, and if we can get a good price for that dagger, it will make our journey a lot easier. If you can find a good buyer, we would be very grateful, and you can keep ten percent of whatever you get. Be smart about it. Take your time. We're not in a big hurry. We have faith in you."

Such a compliment from Merga was a high honor.

"Does it have a sheath?" he asked.

Her eyes popped wide. "It does! I almost forgot. We just had a new one made. I'll go get it."

She scurried off again, leaving Kai standing with the cloak, cap, and dagger. Another client—a middle-aged woman—walked into the shop and nodded politely at Kai, her eyes pausing briefly on what he held before she began browsing the goods on display.

Merga returned, handing him the sheath while glancing at the other patron. "Pay us when you return," she said. "And God be with you, Kihoran."

She clearly didn't want anyone knowing she and her family were planning to leave yet, so he thanked her and left the shop, after paying for the cloak and cap.

The cloak fit perfectly, almost as though it were made for him, and it fanned out elegantly over Vyim's flanks after he had mounted. The cap fit well, too. The cloak had two spacious interior pockets, and he placed the sheathed dagger in the left one. With the rest of his accoutrements, he looked every inch the wartime merchant, as the officer had said.

After passing by Siarah's house one more time and being rewarded with another mind-fuzzing good-bye kiss, he began his next journey—this time as neither scout nor soldier, but as a servant of Helaman.

CHAPTER 13

For we labor diligently to write, to persuade our children, and also our brethren, to believe in Christ, and to be reconciled to God; for we know that it is by grace that we are saved, after all we can do. And we talk of Christ, we rejoice in Christ, we preach of Christ, we prophesy of Christ, and we write according to our prophecies, that our children may know to what source they may look for a remission of their sins.

2 NEPHI 25: 23, 26

Siarah tried to be happy. She prayed to have faith. But she struggled not to complain about Kai leaving again. The prophet had called him—should that not be enough to lighten her heart and quell her fears?

Pouring her heart into making clothes helped a little, but not as much as she had hoped. Even the normally joyful labor of cutting and sewing her favorite designs—those for children—reminded her she still didn't have a husband, still had no immediate prospects of children of her own. She had never wanted anything more than to have children with Kai, born in the eternal covenant of God.

She knew what her priorities should be, and having to chide herself about it made her feel worse. The Lord Jesus Christ was her greatest source of joy, and she wanted more than anything to be faithful to him and follow his guidance. She wasn't confused by her desires for Kai and their elusive future … just … frustrated. She often wondered when the Lord's promises would be fulfilled, and in those moments, she reminded herself to practice more patience, even though she sometimes felt like she had been patient enough.

She was working on a dress today—a common dress. It was nothing fancy, nor was it designed for a pregnant woman. She could more easily focus herself when working on a dress like this one.

A knock came at the door to her little shop attached to her parents' home.

"Come in, please," she said without looking up, intent on her work.

The door opened, and someone stepped inside, closing the door behind them. She glanced up after a moment, noting the patron was a well-dressed man, probably in his late twenties, but she hadn't reached a good stopping place yet.

"Just a moment," she said.

"Take your time," the man graciously replied.

When she finally turned her attention to him, he smiled and bowed. "You are Siarah, I presume?"

"Yes, I am. I make clothes for men, women, and children. I offer design services, too. What are you looking for?"

The man raised a hand. "Sorry, I'm not looking for clothing, although …" his eyes scanned a few of the items displayed in her shop, then rested again upon her "… it appears you are quite talented. I'm trying to locate a friend, someone I met a short time ago in Zarahemla. He's from this area, and he's a merchant scout. His name is Adonihah."

She gave him a startled look. "Oh. Yes, well, I know him, but he's not here. He was called away on business." Her mind started spinning around Kai's two identities. This man knew him as Adonihah, but if he was here in Bountiful asking about him, he would soon learn Kai's real name. Would that matter? Could it put him in danger? She had no idea, which terrified her.

"Indeed. I spoke to his employer already, and his parents, who directed me to you. Would you happen to know where he is headed? You are betrothed, or nearly so, is that correct?"

She felt her face flush, and for more than one reason. "Well, um, yes. He doesn't tell me everything about his … um, business … but I know he's headed for Lehi, then probably to Zarahemla again."

It felt strange to lie like that, even to a stranger, yet it was also thrilling. She thought that must be how Kai felt every day as a spy. But she also wondered whether the man could tell she was lying. Some people were expert at discerning lies—by tones, facial expressions, or gestures—and she was *not* an experienced liar. Should she have lied at all? What if this man was another spy for the army, and he needed to get in touch with Kai?

"Are you okay?" he asked.

"Sorry," she said, "I haven't been feeling too well. Is . . . is there a message you wanted to leave for him?" She was convinced he knew she was lying, but he didn't let on.

"No, thank you. Lehi, you said?"

"Yes, I'm sure that was it. It's such an interesting city, though I haven't been able to visit it myself yet. I want to, though." She realized running her mouth probably gave the man another indication she was lying.

"That seems odd, unless he thinks the Lamanite army Coriantumr sent north has been pushed back already. He's braver than I am." He chuckled, but it seemed forced. Was he bluffing? Siarah felt a spike of nervousness, but she tried to cover it with her genuine concern for Kai.

"So you believe he'll be in danger?" She half stood, then sat back down, placing her hands on her mouth.

"I'm sure he'll be fine," the man said reassuringly. "I suppose I'll need to wait until he arrives in Zarahemla, once it is liberated. I had hoped to find him here. I had some business to transact nearby, and I brought other items I thought Adonihah would find interesting . . . but alas, it was not to be. Thank you, Miss Siarah. I wish you both well." He bowed elegantly, then left.

For several minutes she contemplated the man's visit, frozen to her chair. Why had he come? And who was he? She hadn't even asked his name. Ha! That was more proof she would make a horrible spy. She put aside working on the dress. Procrastinating would cause more stress later, but she was worried about Kai *now*. Part of her wished he had never told her he was a spy.

Perhaps she should write Kai a letter with a detailed description of the man. Maybe it didn't even matter that she hadn't asked for the man's name; if he were dangerous, would he have given her his real name? She could ask Captain Orihon to dispatch a scout to deliver the letter. She might have to exaggerate the urgency a little, but she told herself that would be fine. The more she thought about the odd visitor, the more unsettled she felt. Kai needed to know.

Kai traveled fast, as ordered, but not as fast as when he'd left Gideon to carry Moronihah's orders to Captain Lehi. He had plenty of time to think, given the distance to Sidom. He passed several refugee families on the main road. Most traveled east toward Bountiful, but a few aimed west, returning to what might be left of their homes and livelihoods along the path of Coriantumr's desolation. Word of Lehi's great victory over Coriantumr had spread fast, and Kai started hearing fragments of news regarding other battles, every one of them a victory for the Nephites.

It was dangerous to trust all he heard, though. People wanted to believe the Nephite armies were victorious, so they tended to share stories reflecting that hope. It wasn't until late in the second day out that he flagged down a pair of mounted messengers on their way to Bountiful. The news they shared was far better than expected. From their reports and what they had heard from a few army scouts, it seemed clear the Lamanites were still in full-scale retreat, desperate to get back to Zarahemla. They would never reach it. Moronihah had already placed a large army along that path, while other armies, including Lehi's men, harried the Lamanites from the north, south, and east.

Kai's mood brightened considerably after that conversation, and he slowed his pace slightly. He would learn more when he arrived in Sidom, and hopefully the trend would continue to be good.

As he passed close to the place where Mistress Havah's inn stood, he recalled his harrowing prior visit to Sidom. But he wasn't worried about Mistress Havah—not when he would be meeting with Helaman among such a visible army presence. Two large camps had sprung up near the city's walls, each holding at least a thousand soldiers. He passed through the large eastern gates of the city without issue, though the bulked-up guard force at the entrance made it clear the city leaders would brook no trouble.

He proceeded straight to the large, stone-built Hall of Judgment near Sidom's center. It wasn't uncommon for merchants to show up there, especially ones who had lodged complaints against other merchants or had been accused of running afoul of the law themselves. He secured Vyim and Thunder out front before approaching the guards at the doors. He showed them his summons from Helaman, and they allowed him inside.

He sought directions from three different people before a young woman finally directed him to the room where Helaman was meeting with some of the priests and judges of the city. Kai asked the guard at the first door to let Helaman know he was there, and then he waited, finding a bench on which to sit.

Twenty minutes later, another guard summoned him inside, where he found Helaman and several of his guards—including Dan—sitting along the outer edge of a series of tables arranged in a large circle in a massive chamber with a high domed ceiling. Kai counted more than thirty priests and judges seated around the circumference, a few with their own guards standing behind them. Most of the judges were men, but two women stood out. Though they were becoming more common, Kai had only met one female judge in his life, in Bountiful. She happened to be Gideon's favorite niece, though she was considerably older than Kai.

Helaman stood, nodding a greeting at Kai before addressing the priests and judges. "Let us pause here for lunch. We can resume in two hours."

Kai stepped away from the doorway as everyone in the room, save for Helaman and his guards, began to exit, both through that door and another one farther down. A few of the leaders glanced at Kai, some with more than mild curiosity. They didn't know him, and he could tell that bothered them. He could imagine how many people would be tasked over the next few hours with finding out who he was.

He was so busy watching everyone leave that he didn't notice Helaman approaching him. After the last person had left and the doors were closed, Kai turned to see Helaman standing just a pace to his left, hands folded calmly in front of him. He looked more and more like a judge himself.

"It's good to see you alive and well, Kihoran. Thank you for coming, and so quickly."

Kai gave a short bow. "I was surprised to get your letter."

Helaman laughed lightly as he gestured toward the table where he had been sitting. Two of the guards positioned a pair of chairs so Kai and Helaman could sit facing each other with no tabletop in between. Kai glanced at Dan, who stood a few paces away, watching the doors. Dan smiled, nodding his own welcome.

After they sat, Helaman asked one of the guards to arrange for lunch to be brought in for all of them, and then he turned his attention to Kai.

"Your family is well, I hope?"

"Yes, thank you. I'm grateful they were never in real danger."

Helaman sighed. "Well, it was a close thing, wasn't it? I'm not sure how many commendations one man can earn, but we owe Captain Lehi several more. You as well."

Kai shook his head, face reddening. "No, I did my duty, and I got some lucky breaks, that's all."

Helaman's deadpan look mixed incredulity with mild rebuke. "It's good to be modest, Kai, but not dishonest. You showed courage, determination, and faithfulness. 'Lucky' breaks more commonly happen around people who do so."

"I'm sorry," said Kai, lowering his eyes, not knowing what else to say. He also noted that Helaman had called him Kai for the first time.

"No apology necessary. And I didn't bring you here just to thank you. First, though, I do want to know more about your family. Who are your parents?"

Kai hesitated. Helaman probably already knew the answer—at least the basic one.

"I'm not sure. I was orphaned when I was six and my sister Neva was only one. My parents had joined the king-men trying to overthrow the government, and they disappeared. Neva and I were eventually taken in by a couple named Gideon and Ishara from Bountiful. They've been my parents since then. I am who I am because of them."

Helaman's gaze intensified, his expression solemn. "Your birth parents never came looking for you?"

Kai shook his head.

"And you know what that probably means."

Kai hesitated, then nodded. They had either died in the battles with Captain Moroni's armies or fled to another land, leaving their children behind in either case, two of many. The orphan population had swelled during that time.

"When were you baptized?"

"I waited until I was thirteen. Neva and I were baptized together."

"And then you joined the army at fourteen?"

"Yes. It was the year after Moronihah took over the command, though his father still advised him."

"I remember. I was nineteen. My father had only recently resigned his position in the army, and he finally came home." His lips curled into a warm smile as he stared at a spot beyond Kai's shoulder. "I still remember the look of pure joy on my mother's face when he stepped through our front door." Tears welled in his eyes, and he focused again on Kai. "Gideon and Ishara must have felt the same when you returned."

Kai sniffled, feeling suddenly emotional. "Yes. It was a happy reunion."

Helaman took a deep breath, letting it out slowly. "Well, I wish we didn't need such reunions, nor all the distress which precedes them. I worry how we can continue to endure the calamities of war. But I also fear we're incapable of abiding the prosperity of peace. We forget so easily how good the Lord is to us! And then we ignore him, arrogantly believing we are in full control."

Kai stared at his hands in his lap. Images of Zarahemla's fall flooded his mind. Proud, invincible Zarahemla. Wealthy, erudite Zarahemla, with her tall towers reaching greedily toward the heavens. Perhaps that assessment was too harsh, but he had learned more in the last year than in all his previous years combined, and he suspected his evaluation of Zarahemla didn't capture the fulness of her vanity.

He finally lifted his head. "How is your family?"

Helaman seemed taken aback for a moment, but then gave a broad smile. "They are well. I have an amazing wife. Her name is Jerena, and she's from Manti. My mother and her mother sometimes help with the children. They've adapted to our temporary life in Gideon. And the people of Gideon, Kai! They're wonderful, as I'm sure you know."

"I do." Kai fondly recalled his time there, especially with Shemnilom and the militia.

"I appreciate you asking about my family. Our food will be here soon, and I'm sure you're hungry, so perhaps we should discuss my invitation."

Kai sat up straighter, pulling the letter from his tunic. "I accept." He didn't need to dress up the words.

Helaman beamed. "Wonderful! I had hoped you would, but I couldn't be sure. I presume you can start today?"

"Yes, sir."

"Please don't call me sir. Helaman is good, or brother. Dan calls me brother because he used to call my father … well, 'Father.'" He chuckled.

"Very good, um … Helaman." He had almost added an honorific before it, by habit.

"Thank you, Kai. It's all right if I call you Kai, right? I didn't ask earlier."

"Either one is fine."

"Perfect. Kai it is, though sometimes I'm sure I'll slip into the formal without thinking." He shrugged. "Now, we may be returning to Zarahemla quite soon, and you're probably wondering why I'm meeting with some of the judges and priests here in Sidom."

"Well, yes, but it's not really my place to ask." Kai was curious, but he didn't think he needed to know.

"Ah, but it *is* your place. You're one of my aides now, remember?" Helaman winked. "As you know, we're without a chief judge again. I've been speaking with these leaders—some of whom aren't from Sidom, by the way—about some good candidates. The process has been interesting, to say the least. Tomorrow I'll gather with judges from Bountiful and other eastern cities. Many are coming."

"Will you be one of the candidates?" asked Kai. He knew Helaman had said he didn't want that, but to Kai he seemed as likely a candidate as any other. Moronihah was, too, along with Chief Judge Antonihah from Gideon.

Helaman frowned slightly, then sighed. "I don't really want to be, but the Lord doesn't seem to want to let me off the hook this time. I guess we'll see."

Just then the door opened, and a city guard stepped into the chamber, followed by an older woman. Kai jumped to his feet, hackles up.

"You know Mistress Havah, I take it?" Helaman sounded only mildly surprised. Kai looked at him and nodded, feeling somewhat abashed at his alarmed reaction when all the other guards were calm. Helaman stood and faced Mistress Havah, whose eyes locked on Kai briefly before she smiled at Helaman and gave a small curtsy.

"Mistress Havah, welcome. You're just in time for lunch. It appears you've met Kihoran of Bountiful, my newest aide."

She tilted her head, gazing at Kai. "Adonihah. You are a brave and fortunate man."

"Or Adonihah," said Helaman with a chuckle. He either hadn't noticed the mystery hanging on her last words or was ignoring it. "I clearly have much to tell both of you … and to thank you for again. Sidom is still free because of you, Mistress Havah. And I'm still alive because of you, Kihoran. Please, come and sit. We can talk while we eat."

Ara could tell the Lamanites were growing nervous. Word should already have come back that Bountiful had been taken and the Nephite nation teetered on the verge of collapse. She had overheard more than one of the Amalekite and Zoramite captains bragging about how they would handle the surrender negotiations, and predicting what rule over the Nephites by King Tubaloth would look like. They also claimed they would make Zarahemla far greater than the Nephites ever could—that the entire world would fear the new Lamanite empire.

But no Lamanite messengers had come—from anywhere. The captain in charge of the city's Lamanite garrison—an emotionally flammable Amalekite named Gulharidan—had finally disobeyed orders and sent scouts in all directions. None had returned, and more than a month had passed. Ara happened to be cleaning the appropriated chief judge's home—an assignment Imrahiel had arranged in order to keep a closer eye on the captain—when Gulharidan finally exploded in a meeting with several of his lesser captains, illogically blaming them for the demise of the scouts. The resulting inferno frightened even her father and Imrahiel, who had arrived to advise the captain on matters of security inside the city.

As far as she could tell, her involvement in Adonihah's escape remained a secret. Neither her father nor Imrahiel seemed to be aware he had been trapped in the city. The Lamanites knew someone had escaped, but not who, and they were only mildly suspicious of the women who had demanded to bathe in the river and distracted the guards, viewing the escape as an action of opportunity. A few of the women had been brought in for questioning, the real purpose of which was to intimidate them into providing favors to various Lamanite captains, plus Imrahiel and others … including, she thought in disgust, her father.

At home a few days later, Ara was preparing breakfast when her father and Kishkumen entered the kitchen. They had been out all night and looked haggard and unhappy. They slumped into seats at the table, resting heads in hands and closing their eyes. Neither had acknowledged her, or the strong smells of eggs and thick strips of meat cooking.

She glanced at them occasionally. They didn't say a word, not even to each other, and their eyes remained closed. Ara allowed herself a small smile. They had allied with the Lamanites to overthrow the city, and the Lamanite general had deviated from the agreed upon plan. Had they truly believed they could control the actions of King Tubaloth and his senior captains? Had confidence in their 'superior wisdom' begun to shatter, or did they just consider the Lamanites too dumb to bow to their intellect?

She finished cooking and carried two plates of eggs, meat, and bread to the weary men. At first it appeared they had fallen asleep; neither made any movement when she set the plates down. After a few seconds, though, Kishkumen cracked open an eyelid and spied the food. He took a deep breath and fully opened his eyes, leaning back as he slid a plate in front of him. He looked up at Ara.

"How did you know we were coming?"

"I didn't." She shrugged, shaking her father's shoulder gently. He finally roused, taking a moment to recognize the food.

"Hmmm." Kishkumen forked a bite, chewing slowly, dark eyes locked onto something in the distance only he could see. His presence was like a brooding, murky vastness that made Ara shiver. She would sooner die than marry such a man.

Her father just stared at the food, wobbling slightly.

"What is it, father?" she asked, a little annoyed at her concern for him.

He glanced up at her, eyes not yet fully focused. He looked like an apparition. "We may have to leave here soon, though I'm not sure where we'll go."

Kishkumen slapped a hand hard on the table, causing Ara to jump. "We've been through this a thousand times. We are *not* leaving! If Moronihah arrives with his armies and the Lamanites give up—which they will—we are ready to eliminate any of the Lamanite leaders who know us by face or name. I myself will take care of Gulharidan."

"Just like that?" Her father snapped his fingers—or tried to—clearly irritated.

"No," growled Kishkumen. "We've planned it all out. Everyone will do their part, even the weak ones like you." His growl had become a sneer. Ara had seen Kishkumen speak with authority to her father before, but she had never witnessed such condescending derision from him. She waited nervously to see how her father would react.

Nahom stared for a time at his food. Then he asked, "What will the Lamanites do to the population of the city—including us—when they see their situation is hopeless?"

Kishkumen glared at him. "They don't have the men to do much of anything, and their morale falls by the hour. After they surrender, they'll plead with Moronihah for mercy." Thick disdain curled around his voice like black smoke; whether it was aimed at the Lamanites or Moronihah, Ara couldn't tell. Probably both.

Her father's face went blank for a moment, but then he nodded. "Oh, yes, I remember we already reasoned that out. You're right. And I'm so tired." He stared at his food again, clearly defeated. "Who made us breakfast?"

"I did," said Ara, raising her hand. Her father blinked at her as if she had just materialized out of thin air.

"Oh. Thank you, daughter." He had actually expressed gratitude. He really *was* tired.

She turned her attention to Kishkumen. "So, how many Lamanite captains are you planning to kill?"

He ignored her, and that was probably the better outcome.

Kai struggled to process his astonishment as he crested the hill and viewed the massive number of prisoners organized into large groups in the broad prairie below. He pulled Vyim to a halt and stared, Thunder nearly bumping into them. He traveled apart from Helaman's main retinue and the small army of about five hundred men tasked with protecting him on his return to Zarahemla. He spied them about a mile ahead, passing to the north of the prisoner groups. Kai hadn't needed to separate himself from the company, but he was a scout, and he felt more comfortable that way. Dan had offered to join him.

"How many, would you say?" asked Dan, pulling up next to him on a rangy roan.

Kai took some time to survey the area and do the rough calculations in his head, as he'd been trained to do. "Each group is about six hundred men, and I count twenty-five groups. That's fifteen thousand Lamanite prisoners … hmmm … being guarded by about three thousand of our soldiers, near as I can tell."

Dan whistled. "That's an awful lot of prisoners, but they look beaten down, and I doubt they have any of their captains. Moronihah would have taken all the surviving officers."

Kai continued to study the desultory gatherings of unarmed Lamanite soldiers sitting and lying on the ground. He and Dan had crossed the battlefield a few miles back. Moronihah had smashed the Lamanites from all directions. And he had killed Coriantumr—that message was spreading far and wide. From initial reports, only about five thousand Lamanite soldiers had escaped the trap and fled toward Zarahemla. Moronihah now pursued them … all that remained of Coriantumr's grand army.

"I agree. These men have no fight left in them."

"And no desire to be here … or probably *ever* return."

Kai nodded. Then his head jerked slightly to the right. Helaman's column had turned south, heading toward the prisoner groups. He breathed in sharply. "What is he doing?"

Dan moved his horse up a couple of paces, as if that would significantly improve his view. "I don't know," he said, concern evident in his voice. "But I need to be there." He kicked his mount and started it galloping down the hill. Kai followed at a trot, suddenly wishing he didn't have a pack horse to worry about. He was tempted to leave Thunder behind several times, but he observed closely the behavior of the Nephite guards. While surprise at Helaman's approach rippled through their ranks, Kai didn't witness any panic, and the prisoners themselves showed no signs of imminent activity. They probably had no idea yet what was happening.

Helaman's army stopped at the perimeter of the fenceless prison camp, and then Helaman and a small group of guards and aides—no more than thirty in total—continued forward, pausing only briefly so Helaman could speak to one of the guard captains. Dan reached him during that conversation, which ended quickly, after which they approached the nearest group of prisoners.

Kai's gut clenched, his mouth going dry. He had just passed the first group of guards on the east, telling them he was part of Helaman's escort. He urged Vyim and Thunder to a faster trot, Thunder's baggage bouncing wildly. Surely the prisoners would figure out quickly who their visitor was. They could rise up en masse at any moment, even without weapons, and attack Helaman, despite knowing their Nephite guards would likely cut them down. Kai warily watched the prisoners as he progressed, but their eyes remained devoid of interest, their demeanors dejected or dull. Strangely, he saw no resentment or hatred.

By the time he reached Helaman, the intrepid high priest had moved on to a second group of Lamanites. Kai dismounted, handing the reins to one of the prisoner guards. He wanted to ask Helaman what he hoped to accomplish, but it wasn't his place. He stayed within a few feet of him, watching and listening, hands itching for dagger and sword.

"You've seen we are not a cruel and heartless people, as your leaders claim," Helaman stated to a group of about two hundred who could hear him clearly. "Those who dissent from us are usually selfish and bitter. They seek wealth and domination, and they are willing to use your blood to obtain it. Captain Moronihah and I have agreed that you may depart our lands in peace after making a solemn covenant never to come to war with us again. These guards will escort you to the border. If there are any who wish to stay, or who wish to retrieve their families and return, we will hear your requests. You are our brothers. We welcome all who are willing to obey our laws, work diligently, and live in harmony with us."

The prisoners offered no verbal responses, but many exchanged looks of thoughtfulness and relief. The vast majority, Kai was sure, just wanted to go home. Some few would want to join the Nephites, as had happened on several occasions in the past. None showed any signs of wounded pride. Helaman had delivered his message perfectly.

After asking those two hundred men to spread the word within their group, Helaman moved on to the next group, and then the next. He stayed longer with some groups, answering the few questions that came up. One of them was, "Why are you doing this?"

His response was simple and sincere. "As I said, we are brothers, children of the same God who loves us equally. Your leaders have tricked you. I urge you to learn the truth, for yourselves. Don't allow them to fool you again. War is hell, and most certainly not the answer to our disagreements."

As they moved along, Kai felt the Spirit more powerfully than he ever had. It was difficult to believe that men who less than a day before had sworn to kill the Nephites in a murderous rage now sat meek as lambs and listened to the words of a prophet. Yes, they were mentally and emotionally drained, but they seemed to soak in Helaman's presence, many of them perking up, looking like real men again.

That energy brought its own dangers, of course. Men who suddenly felt alert and strong could revert to their prior purpose. As Kai's nervousness grew, he felt the Spirit less. He tried to inch closer to Helaman, barely resisting the temptation to suggest they shorten their visit. Helaman had already spoken to enough of the prisoners; they could finish spreading the word among themselves, or the guard captains could. Why take unnecessary risk?

As if Helaman had read his mind, he stopped and considered Kai, pure joy illuminating his features. "It feels good to do the Savior's work today, does it not, Kai?" He grinned broadly before turning and starting forward again, leaving Kai to nod a mumbled response and obediently follow.

Fully three hours had passed before Helaman finished with the last group, and then he began to wend his way back through the prisoners. Kai's nerves lit up his mind again. The first few groups Helaman had spoken to had been given significant time to think, and thinking prisoners were always dangerous. Kai reminded himself the Lamanites had been promised freedom. He fervently hoped they had latched onto that promise, that they fully believed it.

It seemed a miracle to Kai when they finally attained the relative safety of their small army escort. Kai retrieved his horses from a different guard as they approached. When Helaman reached his horse, he stopped and turned, his gaze pausing on Kai only briefly as he addressed all his aides and guards. "I remember the efforts of my father and Captain Moroni to preserve life as much as possible, even the lives of Lamanites who had attacked us without provocation. We are all alike, children of God." He gestured toward the groups of prisoners. "We know he can perform mighty miracles in the lives of these men and their families. Someday we will all be able to live in peace. I don't know when that day will come, but every seed we can help the Lord plant has the potential for a limitless eternal harvest. We must try, whenever and however we can." He paused, breathing deeply, and then mounted his horse, waiting while the others in his retinue did the same.

Kai was the last to mount up. He paused again to study the sea of Lamanite faces. Almost all focused intently on Helaman, some with neutral looks, but most with reverence and admiration. The scene imprinted deeply on his mind, and he wondered again why he had been chosen by the Lord's prophet.

Nalani was dead. It wasn't surprising—so many had cruelly died in the brief, pointless war—but Kai still struggled to accept it. Aaron, the children, and the farm had been untouched, which made Nalani's death seem unreal. Aaron told him she had been away, helping a neighbor a few miles to the south who had gone into labor. The woman's husband had refused to let the Lamanites enter their home, and they had all been slain, even the newborn child. Kai wished there were a way to track down the Lamanites who had done it, but perhaps the Lord had already taken care of proper justice in the battles that had followed. He hoped so.

It bothered him deeply that he might have seen those Lamanites sitting calm and safe while Helaman told them they could all go home, with no punishment whatsoever. Yes, there was mercy in that offer, but where was the justice? Both principles mattered. He tried to tell himself all would be made right in the end, as God promised, but it was hard to believe, especially as he witnessed the lamentations of his friend.

Aaron took him out to show him the foals sired by Vyim—two colts and a filly. They appeared healthy and were growing strong. It was too late to breed Vyim with any of the mares that year, but Aaron didn't care anyway. He asked Kai which foal he wanted, but Kai had no desire to make that choice yet. They still needed to be with their mothers, anyway.

He gathered with Aaron and his children—Joseph, Meren, and Adonai— for a somber meal before he entered the newly liberated city. Young Adonai, just four years old, asked when his mother was coming home. Instead of trying to explain it to him again, Aaron just said, "Hopefully soon," before hiding his eyes behind his hand.

"I'm leaving the merchant scouts," said Kai, trying to change the subject. "I'm going to become an aide for Helaman, if you can believe that."

Aaron wiped his eyes and smiled. "I *can't* believe that, as a matter of fact. How in the world did that happen? Wait, did you arrive here with him?"

Kai nodded. "Yes, but I asked if I could come here first to see if you were all … safe." So much for changing the subject.

Aaron cleared his throat, trying to shake off his emotions. "Well, he must have seen something in you. I'm not sure what, though." He tried to laugh at his joke, but it came out halfway between a croak and a groan.

Kai swallowed hard. "I'm sorry," he said, feeling the sincerity of the sentiment throughout his body. "If there's anything I can do, let me know. I can leave Vyim here for a while, if the kids would like that. The pack horse, too, could stay … well, after I take him to the city and unload him. His name is Thunder. And maybe …" He had thought to mention that perhaps Helaman could visit, but he couldn't make that kind of promise without knowing he could keep it. Helaman was already surrounded by thousands of people who needed comforting. He and the priests and teachers, along with the women leaders, would be extremely busy over the next several months.

And then there was the issue of the judgment seat. Aaron had apparently thought about it as well. "So, do you think Helaman might agree to be the next chief judge?"

Kai shrugged. "He hasn't spoken much about it with me, but … I think he's willing now. He's already met with judges and priests from many cities. I think they all want him to. And I doubt the people will choose anyone else if he accepts."

"That's good to hear." Aaron seemed buoyed by the news. "Is it true he and Moronihah let all the Lamanite prisoners return to their lands?" Kai couldn't immediately tell how he felt about such a scenario.

"Yes, but very few of their captains survived. In fact, some of the Lamanites who surrendered had already executed their captains. Nephites killed Coriantumr, though."

"That's good, at least." Aaron stared at his food. He'd only taken two bites.

"A few of the Lamanites might return and join us," added Kai, though he wondered how that statement might be received by a man who had just lost his wife to them. "They could join the Ammonites first. It might help ensure we don't have to battle the Lamanites again soon." He thought of Ashtenoth, the Lamanite scout who had been healed and converted—he hadn't remembered to check on him while in Bountiful.

Aaron grunted. "I have my doubts. Tubaloth is still king. If they could get rid of him, maybe I could believe it."

He had a good point. Kai wondered if something *could* be done about Tubaloth ... something of which the Lord would approve.

Aaron insisted Kai take Vyim and Thunder with him, so he rode unhappily into the city through the Grand Gates—the same he had used on his first entry to Zarahemla, the same by which he had escaped. He let his eyes linger on *Jacob's Rest* as he traveled along the Path of Mosiah, contemplating the mixed memories. It felt strange not to enter the inn and find his room. *His* room. He almost laughed aloud at the thought. He'd hardly spent any time in it!

More memories flooded back as he entered the Santorem, on his way to Helaman's home. He knew many eyes had seen him, and some of those eyes reported to Imrahiel. He wasn't sure he was quite ready to re-enter the game, but he had to. The Lamanites may have been expelled, but some of the Nephites were worse.

A broad lane next to Helaman's house led back to a large barn, with a small pasture extending from one side. After seeing to his horses, Kai checked in with the pair of guards at the back door, waiting while one slipped inside to report his arrival. There really should be three guards, he thought, so if one left, two would remain. Maybe he could talk with Dan about it.

As if that thought had summoned him, Dan arrived with a hearty greeting. They passed immediately into a sizeable room with benches and pegs on which hung cloaks, hats, and even ropes. Shoes of various sizes and types lay scattered underneath the benches. Dan was quick to inform him they didn't wear shoes in the house. Kai had heard of that rule—it was much easier on rugs, and it also cut down on noise—but he'd never been in a house that enforced it, not even High Judge Zerahir's.

Dan proceeded to give him a tour. He showed Kai the large front rooms that could be used for meetings, the formal dining room which wasn't quite as large as Zerahir's, the ample but currently understocked kitchen, a playroom, a music room, and the living quarters. The house was clean, but signs of children manifested from time to time—a stocking peeking out from under a piece of furniture, a toy left in a corner, the residue of something spilled. Dan explained that most of the Lamanite captains believed Helaman's house was cursed, so it hadn't been despoiled by trespassers or tenants. They would have eventually burned it down, of course.

He stopped Dan during the tour of the living quarters, which were upstairs.

"I haven't seen any place large enough to house guards."

Dan smiled. "That's because none of the guards live here. Helaman insists that when we're not on duty, we're at home with our families, and we're all happy about that. He and Jerena don't have live-in servants, either. They hire help for some of the cooking and cleaning, and tutors, too, but none of those people stay here."

"Oh," said Kai, wondering if he would be staying at *Jacob's Rest* after all, at least temporarily, and if he could afford it.

"You're the lone exception," said Dan with a wink. "Helaman knows you don't have a home here, so he's prepared a room for you, downstairs, next to the mud room where we entered. I'll show that to you now. It was used for storage."

"What about his aides?" asked Kai.

"They're rarely here," replied Dan as he led him along a hall toward some stairs. "He meets with them at the temple, or in some of the synagogues, but when he comes home, he wants to truly *be* home, with his family. I suppose that might change a little if he becomes chief judge, though."

Kai pondered that as he followed Dan down the stairs and they wound their way toward the back of the house again, to a corner that looked like it housed not one but two storage rooms. They entered the one with two exterior walls.

"And here you go," said Dan with a flourish, sweeping an arm around the small, musty-smelling room with two windows, a narrow bed, two chests, a chair, and a table, on one end of which sat a wash basin. The nearest privy was on the other side of the mud room.

Kai stood still for a moment, taking it all in. "It's wonderful," he finally said. "I . . . didn't expect this. I can't believe I'll actually get to live here, with the prophet and his family."

"I know," said Dan, slapping him on the back. "All of us are a little jealous, though we still wouldn't trade it for being home with our wives and children." He immediately looked apologetic. "Sorry, I'm not teasing you for not being married yet, but . . ."

Kai laughed. "It's okay. I had planned on getting married soon, back in Bountiful, but then Helaman's letter came, and, well, it didn't feel right to rush it. It'll work out, we just have to wait a little longer."

Dan clapped both hands on Kai's shoulders, his face beaming. "Well, she's a lucky woman. I'm sure you'll get it all worked out soon. What's her name?"

"Siarah, and thanks. I need to make sure I write her. She's probably already written me three dozen letters that will catch up to me here."

"Yes. Good man. Write to her. I'll even make it one of your official duties." Dan winked again. Kai was grateful to know him.

A portion of the populace in Zarahemla resented the faithful Christians who had left the city just before the Lamanite assault. A rumor even circulated that Helaman and Moronihah had tricked the Lamanites into attacking Zarahemla, knowing they could then crush the Lamanite army while eliminating political enemies at the same time. Kai didn't understand how people could believe such nonsense about genuinely good, brave people like Moronihah and Helaman. It made little sense, but he felt the tension in the streets as he walked to the temple with Helaman for the first time the next day.

Fortunately, few truly gave the rumors much credence. Or so Dan reassured him. Moronihah wasn't popular for leaving Zarahemla's garrison so weak, but King Tubaloth's reputation for being just as bold but less mentally stable than his father and uncle was well-earned. It wasn't surprising he had plunged an army, unsupported, into the heart of Nephite lands. And Coriantumr's strategy to get his men near the capital, while clever, had also been lucky: they had come through the lightly-populated and under-patrolled west, using nighttime marches in small groups and daytime conceal-in-place schemes in pre-scouted locations, though they still should have been spotted. That approach was unlikely to succeed again, especially at such scale.

Many Christians who had ignored Helaman's invitation to the conference in Gideon sought forgiveness for their indifference to his counsel. They had suffered as much as any other group in the city, primarily with the loss of husbands, brothers, fathers, and sons in the garrison and militia. Christian women had suffered the most, though. Any advent of battle and its immediate aftermath cultivated bad behaviors, but Christians were a favorite target for Amalekite and Zoramite captains, dissenters from both the Nephite nation and its most popular religion. They found it easier to look away—or even participate—when the victims were Christians. It was pure evil, and it made Kai's blood boil.

"You're sure you don't want more protection or a faster mode of travel?" he asked Helaman as they neared the entrance to the temple grounds.

Helaman stopped. He turned and studied various people going about their day, some of whom acknowledged him with a small bow before hastening on. Then he directed his eyes to the rising courses of the temple structure. "Yes, I'm sure, though I'll always listen to good counsel from the Lord, through whomever it comes. Don't worry so much about me, Kai. Our focus must be on how we help our people heal from this attack and become stronger. Many hearts have been broken, both literally and figuratively. Thousands died here, and thousands more during Coriantumr's rampage toward Bountiful. I will soon travel along that route to offer what comfort I can to those returning to rebuild, once we can gather a large enough caravan of food and other supplies."

His gaze swept across the four advisers—including Kai—and six guards he had brought with him. "Come. We must begin this journey by seeking knowledge from the Lord in his holy temple."

With that, he turned and began ascending the first set of steps leading up to the great courtyard, lined with stout but elegant pillars on all four sides which were topped by a narrow, crenelated walkway. The Lamanites hadn't done much damage to the temple, probably believing they had ample time to pillage and defile it—perhaps even destroy it completely. But they had held many mocking ceremonies in front of the temple for all to see, even sacrificing a few pigs and blemished goats. The thrill of the show must have overcome any fears of being cursed.

After passing between two pillars, Kai let his eyes rest again on the splendor of the temple itself. Though the same size as Bountiful's, it looked grander. More goldwork decorated the front pillars and massive bifold doors. The carvings on stone and wood were more ornate, as were the oxen bearing the molten sea, the horns around the altar, and the ramp leading up to it.

Kai didn't know what to expect next. He thought Helaman might go into the Holy Place alone, or with a few of the priests, but instead, he angled for the main door to the outer rooms on the south side. Kai followed with the others as they ascended the winding wooden staircase to the top floor, which was the widest. Many of the outer rooms were used for storage—and the Lamanites had indeed ransacked them—but the top floor on the south side was split into two large rooms, where the high priest and the priests could hold council, make decisions, and learn from each other and the Holy Spirit. The room they entered was bare of chairs, so they sat on cushions. A dozen priests had followed them inside, taking their places near the front of the room, facing Helaman. Kai sat along the interior wall, between slanted shafts of sunlight entering through the narrow windows.

Helaman welcomed everyone, then invited one of the priests to offer a prayer and invoke the blessings of the Lord upon their meeting. Kai still felt astounded at the amount of praying that happened around the prophet.

The first order of business was a report from two priests and one of Helaman's aides on the preparations of the relief caravans. That discussion took nearly an hour as people asked questions, resolved issues, and accepted assignments. Next, Helaman asked various priests to report on the welfare of the saints in several cities around Zarahemla, as far away as Gideon. Kai paid closest attention to the report on Gideon, though it was quite bland given that the land of Gideon had been completely spared.

Then Helaman wanted to know what was happening among the saints in the city of Zarahemla. Two priests had prepared reports on that topic. One of them, a slender, long-bearded, older man named Jethro, stood and began speaking.

"Many of the saints who traveled to Gideon took extra provisions with them, not knowing exactly why. That has been a great blessing, along with aid sent from the saints in Gideon and surrounding lands. This life-saving assistance is being distributed to Christian and non-Christian alike, according to those who have the most need first.

"Some of the saints feel extremely guilty for having ignored the call to the conference. Some lost loved ones, and others endured extreme hardship and abuse under the Lamanites. Many have requested rebaptism to help them more fully dedicate themselves to Christ and be forgiven. Some have called for additional blood sacrifices to be made at the altar once suitable animals can be found and gathered. One man even approached us and—" he hesitated for a long moment "—offered himself as a sacrifice, hoping it would redeem his family. His wife was forced to be a consort to one of the Zoramite captains in the city."

The man paused, and Kai witnessed in Helaman one of the saddest looks he had ever seen come across a person's face.

"What did you tell him?"

Jethro mirrored Helaman's expression. "I told him the Lord would never countenance such a thing. I tried not to be too harsh, though he had uttered clear blasphemy. I spoke with him for more than an hour, trying to understand better what he felt and why. None of us—" he gestured at the other occupants of the room "—had to endure life under the brief occupation, though we have all seen difficult things."

Helaman's eyes glistened. "Thank you, brother Jethro. You ministered to that man as the Lord would have. You listened, and you cared. How are he and his family now? Who else can assist them in their physical and spiritual recovery?"

Jethro bowed slightly. "We have assigned two brothers and their wives to check in on them from time to time and report back to us if more specific help is needed."

Helaman nodded. "That is good. Now, about rebaptism." His eyes wandered the room as he gathered his thoughts. "There have always been those whose names should be removed from the records of the church for various reasons. Some may fall into that category now, in which case a rebaptism becomes a possibility for them upon the recommendation of their local priest and council. We will need to discuss what guidelines to give the councils, though. This discussion will likely take the rest of the morning."

An hour into that topic, Kai wondered how much longer he would be able to stay awake as the room became stuffy. He wasn't used to this kind of role, and he had no inputs or insights to offer. Thinking of himself as a guard helped a little; protecting the prophet was a noble duty, and he could be a valuable asset even when attending meetings that surpassed his skill and understanding.

When the lunch hour arrived, they descended to the floor below, where a light meal had been set out for them. Kai wasn't very hungry, so he partook sparingly. Shortly before they were to return to the meeting room, Helaman approached him.

"You're excused from this afternoon's meetings, Kihoran," he said. "I know you need to get started on other things, and some of those, I'm sure, will take you late into the evenings. Perhaps we can speak tonight, or in the morning, about how to rotate your schedule without raising too many suspicions."

"Yes, Helaman." Kai should have been elated at escaping more meetings, but he suddenly felt the weight of his tasks again. He was more than a simple guard. He was a spy, the secretive new servant of Helaman, and he had much work to do.

He didn't expect that work to begin on his way back to Helaman's house. Ara ran toward him as he approached the Santorem, popping out of nowhere, as usual. He halted, but she didn't, forcing him to brace and catch her. As she held him tight, he felt glad Dan wasn't there to see it.

"Oh, Adonihah, I thought it was you I saw earlier, but I couldn't be sure." The words were half-muffled in his shoulder.

He squeezed back, politely. "It's Kihoran, or Kai."

She released him, backing up a small step, hands falling to her sides. Confusion filled her eyes. "What?"

"My name," he said. "It's not Adonihah. It doesn't matter anymore. I'm not sure how much it ever really did."

"Oh." He couldn't tell whether she felt hurt or not. "So, Helaman knows your real name, too? And you're one of his aides ... or guards? Now I'm certain it was you I saw with him this morning."

Kai nodded. "Yes, I'm an aide. That's what Imrahiel wanted, right?"

A shadow passed across her face. "He is evil."

"He's still here?"

"Yes. He—" She glanced around quickly, but nobody was close enough to overhear. "He had some of the Lamanite captains killed right before Moronihah arrived."

Kai grunted. "That makes sense. He wanted to save himself. If those captains had been captured and questioned, he'd already be hanging."

She shivered. "I don't want to have anything to do with him, or my father, or any of them. But I'm trapped."

Kai felt a sharp twinge of pity for her. She had taken more than the first set of oaths with them.

"Walk with me?" he said, conscious of how conspicuous they appeared standing in the middle of the street. She grabbed his arm, and they started toward the entrance to the Santorem. It seemed like only days had passed since they had last approached it together—that is, until they passed the first scorched home, half of it lying in rubble and ash.

"All the women who helped me escape are okay?" he asked.

"Yes, mostly. Some of them … well, they did what they needed to survive." She turned her head away for a moment. Kai didn't have to ask.

"And you?" he asked more softly.

He saw a tear begin to fall. "I was okay. My father protected me, though I'm ashamed to say that now."

"Oh." He was grateful she was alright, but he felt troubled about … well, everything.

"There's a rumor Helaman will be the next chief judge. I'm not sure how long it'll take to set up the election, but I know Imrahiel isn't happy about it. You're in a dangerous place, Adon—um, Kai, so close to him."

"I know. But it's where I'm supposed to be."

She pressed into his side briefly. "So brave." The admiration in her voice filled him with warmth and courage, followed by resurfacing guilt.

"Maybe we can work together to protect him," she said, suddenly cheery. "I can be helpful." She pulled him to a stop and turned toward him. "You know what? Us being a couple will be perfect. Imrahiel will think he can use both of us, sometimes even asking us to spy on each other. But we can really be working against him."

Kai started them walking again, trying to look pensive. He didn't really have to try—his mind was going berserk. He'd known he'd have to interact with Ara if she were still in the city. Her father was too significant a player among the Gadiantons, and if he tried to get information from Imrahiel by himself, he'd get played, no matter how much interesting intel he could provide to the man.

He finally bowed to the inevitable. It wouldn't be easy. "I think you're right. And I'll do whatever it takes to protect Helaman." He hadn't intended to inject so much cold steel into his voice, but his commitment was tempered deep.

When they neared Helaman's home, Kai prepared to bid her goodbye and set up a time to discuss plans when she said, "Can I come inside? You can vouch for me, and we can start planning."

"Um, sure, I think so," Kai said, almost stuttering. "I actually have a room in the house ... though that's not where we're going."

Ara made a show of pretending to be disappointed, which was both confusing and distracting. After talking with the guards at the front and entering the house, he took her to the music room, which was at present unoccupied. She spent a few moments examining the musical notations on the walls, along with the instruments—some wind, some string, but no percussion.

When they sat, she adjusted her chair to be angled so they were partly facing each other, with one of her knees touching his. She seemed about to kiss him, but she didn't. Instead, she grabbed his right hand in both of hers and said, "You were going to teach me about being a Christian, remember?"

"I was?" he replied before that memory blossomed into existence. "Oh, yes, I was."

"Good. Can we start now?"

Kai swallowed. He couldn't remember being more nervous or unprepared in his life.

CHAPTER 14

*And now, my sons, remember, remember that it is upon the rock of
our Redeemer, who is Christ, the Son of God, that ye must build your
foundation; that when the devil shall send forth his mighty winds, yea,
his shafts in the whirlwind, yea, when all his hail and his mighty storm
shall beat upon you, it shall have no power over you to drag you down to
the gulf of misery and endless wo, because of the rock upon which ye are
built, which is a sure foundation, a foundation whereon if men build
they cannot fall.*

HELAMAN 5:12

Many weeks passed before Kai was able to have his first meeting with Imrahiel since the invasion. Kai had spent several of those weeks traveling with Helaman and the relief caravans, which had gathered from north and south, converging at various points along the path of what many were calling 'Coriantumr's Folly' or 'Tubaloth's Stupor.' The trail had been filled with heartbreaking encounters, akin to the sorrows of the Great War, but Kai had also beheld thousands of Nephites rallying in faith, especially when they saw and heard Helaman, their beloved young prophet. He ministered individually to as many as possible, wearing himself out day after day.

Two weeks after their return, Imrahiel finally summoned Kai, through Ara. It was clear he harbored strong doubts about Kai—Ara reported he had told her that directly. Kai had almost sought him out, but decided the time wasn't yet right. In the meantime, he had plied many of his merchant contacts again—those who had survived the fall and occupation. Chemish, sadly, hadn't. Jorash and Nezariah, whom Chemish had suspected of treasonous activity, had actually gained influence in the city, especially after putting out false stories of their courageous 'resistance' against the occupiers. It wasn't difficult to verify their tales as self-serving propaganda, but most people had more pressing things to worry about than checking noble boasts.

It felt eerie walking into the fancy pottery shop and toward the back sitting room, which looked largely the same, despite so much having become clearer. Kai's discernment had improved. He had spent most of his life stumbling through varying levels of fog, most of which had recently been burned away by a blazing sun. He comprehended how evil Imrahiel was. The dichotomy between Helaman and Imrahiel matched the difference between the brightest day and the darkest night.

Imrahiel had acquired a new chair for himself—taller, fancier, and plusher, with gold leafing and intricate designs. Kai guessed he had plundered it from the Hall of Judgment. Or perhaps it had belonged to one of the Nephite nobility. Many of them had been imprisoned, and several executed for not swearing fealty to King Tubaloth fast enough, even though the Lamanite monarch's purported aim had been a 'unity' government. Gideon and Ishara had taught Kai that duplicitousness was ever the hallmark of those who lusted for power, but over the last several months he had internalized that truth.

Imrahiel gave a condescending smile as Kai entered the sitting room. Kai didn't wait for permission to sit in his customary chair across from Imrahiel; he tried to seem in control without appearing pretentious. It was a narrow line.

Imrahiel studied him for several seconds, apparently attempting to unnerve him. Kai needed this meeting to be productive, so he finally let it seem Imrahiel's intimidation had worked, saying, "I haven't violated my oath, if that's what you're going to ask."

Imrahiel just nodded, continuing to examine him, his smile becoming sinister.

"And I'm close to Helaman now. I'm one of his aides, and I even live at his house." He made sure he didn't sound too desperate to please. Another fine line.

Still, Imrahiel didn't speak, and Kai began to feel real anxiety—not because he feared Imrahiel, but because of how badly he wanted to protect Helaman from the Gadiantons.

"I can get you some information," Kai offered. "Just tell me what to look for."

Finally, Imrahiel spoke. "It is not for you to demand I tell you anything."

It was a ridiculously haughty and nonsensical response, but Kai tried to appear contrite. "I understand."

Several more seconds passed, which Kai spent staring at the floor, his mind seeking to anticipate various traps.

"You say you have not violated your oath, young Adonihah, also called Kihoran. I hope that is true. You will have to prove it. But let's start with a report on Helaman's campaign tour through the heartland."

"Campaign tour?"

Imrahiel chuckled, venom dripping from his voice. "Yes. That's what it was. He wishes to become the next chief judge, and that election will likely occur in the next two months. There isn't anyone who can seriously challenge him at this point, especially not after he led that relief caravan."

Kai nodded slowly. "He's spoken several times of his desire to be chief judge." That statement was true, from one perspective. Helaman loathed the thought of being chief judge, but he yearned to help the Nephite people, and he had come to realize he could better do that through the chief judgeship, with the Lord's guidance. Kai had witnessed sensitive personal moments in Helaman's struggle with the seeming inevitability of the additional mantle of leadership. Imrahiel was blind as a day-old mole ... and so arrogant about it.

"He's even more selfish than his father," proclaimed Imrahiel, voice laden with disdain. "War hero. Pshaw. All those stories are embellished. He sought glory and wealth, and he got both."

Kai bobbed his head as if in fervent agreement. "Helaman's home is one of the nicest in Zarahemla. If he becomes chief judge, he'll demand even grander."

"He *will* become chief judge," corrected Imrahiel, "but we can't allow that to stand for long. The Lamanite invasion was a tragedy, but at least it gave us the opportunity to start over without some of the corrupt elites who ran everything in this nation. The Lamanites would have executed Helaman if they had caught him here, you know."

Kai could see malevolent longing—and severe disappointment—in Imrahiel's eyes. Murdering the Christian prophet had been part of the plan, of course. They would have also needed to get rid of Moronihah eventually, but there had surely been a different scheme for that. Kai wondered whether the plan for Moronihah's demise had been foiled or was still in place. He would talk with Dan about what they could do to protect the chief captain, too, especially when he was in the city.

"How … I mean, what can I do to help? I know we can be stronger without entitled people of 'pure' lineage like Helaman allowed to lead." He had rehearsed that line and delivered it well.

Imrahiel gave him a scrutinizing look. "Well, you and Ara have been seeing each other, correct?" He made it sound as if he wasn't sure; also as if he hadn't ordered her to get close to him.

"Yes."

"And she has visited Helaman's mansion several times with you?"

"Yes."

"How does Helaman's wife feel about her? Would she perhaps hire her for some of the work around the house? That is, if we can arrange for some of the other help to withdraw?" That sounded ominous, and Kai almost swallowed.

"Perhaps. Jerena does like Ara."

"Good. Then find a way to let Helaman know Ara is looking for new employment. I'm sure he'll tell his wife, and if it is as you say, we may be able to get Ara inside and more closely into his wife's confidences. There are certainly things Helaman doesn't tell his wife, but other things he probably tells *only* her. We need as much information for our planning as possible."

The words 'our planning' sent a shiver down Kai's spine; it wasn't hard to guess what they indicated.

"I will," promised Kai, again acting enthusiastic. "Do you—do you want me to tell Ara about this?"

"No. I will tell her myself tonight."

Kai wasn't sure he had meant to add the word "tonight"—Imrahiel was exact with his words, and he wouldn't have needed to tell Kai when exactly Ara would know. A thought began to form in Kai's mind, but he would need more information from Ara to complete it.

"So, what did he say?" Ara perched on the edge of her chair in the children's playroom, hands fidgeting. Helaman's family was using the music room today; two of the children created a cacophonic racket under the patient tutelage of a teacher. Ara was already at the house when Kai returned from his meeting with Imrahiel.

"He's going to tell you tonight," Kai answered. "Are you meeting him?

Ara thought a moment. "My father told me he'd have visitors tonight, but I haven't been invited to anything. He won't let me join in on any of the discussions. He trusts me less than Imrahiel does."

"Because you've revealed more of yourself to him than to Imrahiel. Will your father betray you?"

"No, I don't think so. But I'm being more careful around him now."

"Good. So, Imrahiel will be there tonight, and he'll find a way to speak with you."

"I suppose so, yes."

"Is there anyone Imrahiel fully trusts?"

"Gadianton. And Kishkumen."

"Kishkumen?"

"You saw him in our kitchen once. The one who wants to marry me. Tall, aloof, always angry. A real gem." Kai remembered. The man who had killed one of Moronihah's spies.

"Do you know where they live?" he asked, keeping a check on his anger.

Ara nodded. "Kishkumen, yes. Not Gadianton, though. He's the most secretive man I've ever heard of. I'm not even sure I've seen him in person, even though he ran for chief judge. Why?"

"Well, while you're hopefully meeting with Imrahiel tonight, I think I'll do a bit of scouting around Kishkumen's house. Don't worry, I'll be in disguise. Maybe that limping workman again?"

She rolled her eyes. "Yeah, that was spectacular. How about a law officer? I'll bet Helaman knows someone who could get you a uniform and one of those official-looking cudgels."

Kai's eyes widened as he thought about it. "That's a brilliant idea. Officers usually travel in pairs, but the force is depleted. I've seen plenty of one-man patrols. I should be able to make that happen, but I need to head to the temple first and find Dan—he has the right contacts among the officers. Then I'll come back here and wait until full dark."

He got up to leave, but Ara pulled him back down. "Wait, what is Imrahiel going to tell me?"

Kai glanced at the open doorway and lowered his voice, though the 'music' from the other room made it impossible for anyone to hear them. They could barely hear each other, even with their heads close together.

"We'll try to get you a job here, in the house, and he wants you to befriend Jerena, get her to share things about her husband's activities. You know, standard spy stuff." He smiled, almost winking but catching himself.

"He doesn't trust either of us, does he?"

"Nope. But what choice does he have? He's desperate, Ara. And desperate people make mistakes."

With Dan's help, it wasn't difficult to procure an officer's uniform. Sadly, the law offices had plenty of extra uniforms on hand. Many officers had tried to resist the Lamanite occupation in one form or another. Most had been executed. Kai even acquired a cudgel, though it was a larger, military-style model recovered after the brief battle of liberation. With the officer's cap pulled low over his eyes, a few expertly placed smudges of color on his cheeks, nose, and chin, and three extra shirts wrapped around his belly, he looked like a different person, especially at night.

He added a slight limp to his persona as well. He was good at pretending to hobble along, and limps were effective, no matter what Ara said.

Helaman hadn't arrived home by the time Kai left, two hours after dusk, but Kai told Jerena he hoped to have important information he could share with her husband in the morning.

For the next two hours, he patrolled the area around Kishkumen's house slowly and methodically, using his fake limp to take his time and avoiding pools of light from the torches in the streetlamps.

He found one other person watching the area: a man who appeared to be drunk but wasn't, sitting in the mouth of an alley. Kai wondered if there were any roof watchers as well. Kishkumen was evidently an important person, so it made sense he would have security around his house. After pondering a few minutes on what to do, he finally decided to plop down at the front of a building next to the alley where the fake drunk man sat. He felt strongly that was where he should wait, though he couldn't articulate why.

He dropped his chin to his chest and pretended to sleep, not even glancing toward Kishkumen's house. For the first few minutes, he could hear the other man rustle around occasionally, certain he was aware of him. For the next several minutes, he didn't hear anything, besides periodic traffic in the street.

He was about to get up and leave the area when the fake drunk stumbled to his feet and shuffled slowly toward him. It sounded like he was dragging a leg, which was a nice touch. Kai stayed calm, keeping his breathing slow and even. The man stopped when he reached him, and several seconds passed. Finally, Kai felt a small shake of his shoulder.

"Hey, officer, what you doin' here?"

Kai pretended not to be affected, so the man shook him a little harder and repeated his slurred question.

Kai jerked as if suddenly waking, bringing both arms up in defense, one with the cudgel. The man took a startled step back, using reflexes no drunk man possessed. Kai blinked at the man a few times. "What? Who are you?"

"I'm just … passin' through, officer," said the man, swaying a little but catching his balance.

"And you're drunk," said Kai testily. "Go home. I need to rest."

"Ain't got no home," said the man, who then fell against the front of the building and slid down into a heap.

"Then go back to the alley," said Kai, making sure he sounded annoyed.

"You saw me there?"

"Of course I saw you there."

"Oh. So what you doin' here?"

"Resting, I said. My shift's over. I'm tired. I don't have much of a home, either, so go away or I'll arrest you."

"Lamanites?" the man persisted.

"Yeah."

"Murderin' barbs. Helaman helped 'em."

"I doubt that."

"Why wasn't he here? You thought about that?"

"My wife and I should've left with him."

"You Christian?"

"I guess," said Kai, letting the man try to set his hook.

"Somethin' happen to your wife?"

"She's probably dead, but I don't know for sure yet."

"Sorry," said the man. He sniffled as if he was about to start crying. Another nice touch. "It was Helaman, though."

Kai didn't respond immediately the second time the man posed the accusation. He just glared at him as if thinking it over. Finally, he said, "I'm not interested in conspiracies."

"Ain't no conspir'cy. I know some guys who know the truth."

"Yeah, I'll bet you couldn't say that to me when you're sober. Maybe I *should* arrest you." He made it sound like an empty threat, like he was wavering because of the man's claims.

The tone and tenor of the man's voice transformed as he repositioned himself. "I *am* sober, friend." Now Kai was getting somewhere, and it seemed a miracle. "Some of us know the truth, and we keep an eye out for each other."

Kai looked around. "So you're faking. Who are you watching out for around here?

The man shook his head. "I can't tell you that. But we need another ally on the inside with the law officers."

Another ally? Kai shouldn't have been surprised. "Why? What good does that do? The Lamanites were defeated and Helaman's back. He'll be the new chief judge. And things will go back to normal for most people."

"But not for you and me, right? I've suffered losses, too, and it's because our leaders are fools and thieves."

"And the solution is?" Kai mixed challenge and desperation in his tone.

The man didn't hesitate. "The common people take back the government, and we put someone in charge who actually cares about us."

"Like a king?" asked Kai, letting doubt creep into his voice. "That's been tried. Many people died."

"Things have changed. This Lamanite invasion was bad. Real bad. People want to see something different. Helaman is more of the same. You watch. He'll propose building a palace for himself."

"Wouldn't a king do that, too?"

"Not a good king."

Kai pretended to think it over, then nodded as if the man had a point. "I doubt I could be of much help. I'm fairly new, and of low rank."

"Doesn't matter," countered the man. "In fact, it's better. You know how much we need to do this. You haven't been corrupted by perks and privileges. And you have the memory of your wife to guide you."

The man had taken a risk there, but Kai might have done the same in his place, if he were desperate. He looked away, across the street, appearing to consider the opportunity seriously.

He finally fixed his eyes on the man again. "Okay, but how do we do it without hurting too many people?"

The man took on a grave expression, seeming to sympathize. "There are ways. We've been planning. The law officers will be important, especially the patrol officers like you. It will take a while to get everything in place, but when the time comes, we can make the transition smoothly."

"So … what do *I* do?"

The man took a deep breath, clearly excited. "Find out, without being too obvious or giving anything away, which other patrol officers can be convinced to help us. It won't be easy, and you'll have to be careful. What's your name, by the way?"

Kai couldn't believe it had been so easy to fool the man, though part of him was still wary of a trap. "Giron. Is there a contact I should work through? Can you give me a name, or should I just come back here and report to you?"

"I can't give you any names yet. But trust me, they're working on the same things. At some point we'll ask you to start cooperating. Just be patient. Return to this street every few days. Salvation is coming."

Kai closed his eyes, his breathing shallow and reverent. "Salvation, yes. You're sure we can do this?"

"Positive. We're closer than you think. Have faith."

Kai wanted to ask, "Faith in what?" but he refrained. It was time to return to Helaman's home, after making sure he didn't have a tail. The night had gone much better than expected.

———

"So now you have a *third* name?" asked Dan incredulously.

Kai shrugged, glancing between him and Helaman. It was early morning, and they occupied comfortable chairs in Helaman's study.

Helaman smiled. "And you made yourself a member of the law officers of Zarahemla. I doubt I could have been a spy. I'm not much of a soldier, either, unlike my father."

Dan chuckled. "Your father wasn't a great warrior, but he was a strong leader and a fearless, hell-chasing general. A great man, too, of course. The Lord's prophet."

Helaman's eyes took on a faraway look. "When he died, I wasn't ready for the role of prophet, but I can feel the Lord helping me, every day. I hope you feel his strength, too." He let his gaze rest upon Dan and Kai in turn, waiting until each nodded.

"I'm not sure why I engaged with the man the way I did," Kai said, "or even why I sat down there. I'm sure the Spirit guided me." He rarely spoke like that, but he couldn't deny what he had experienced.

"You did well," said Helaman. "Given all the chaos, we can easily get you on the records as a law officer. In fact, we could have you assigned to special projects, right Dan?"

Dan gave a pensive nod. "I don't see why not. The request shouldn't come from you, though. I know someone who can make it happen, and it will look normal—well, as normal as we can get at the moment."

"Good, then it's settled." Helaman turned again to Kai. "When do you check back in with your contact? He didn't give a name, did he?"

"No. I asked him his name before I left, but he just grinned and spit. I'm supposed to check in every few days, somewhere in that same area, at about midnight."

"Well, stay vigilant, my friend," said Dan. "These are dangerous people."

"I do remember they tried to kill me once," Kai deadpanned. "You were there."

"Yeah, sorry." Dan gave a somewhat abashed smile, which looked odd on him.

Kai stared earnestly at Helaman. "Why can't we just arrest Imrahiel now? You have two witnesses to their plans to kill you—me and Ara. We could arrest her father Nahom as well, and perhaps he could become a third witness."

Helaman frowned. "I wish it were that easy. Maybe if Moroni were still here it would be. But we have two problems. First, we can't be sure how most of the judges would react, and even if I were already chief judge, the lower judges could prevent me from ruling on a case involving me directly—I'm obviously biased when it comes to threats against my own life. Second, Ara's father probably won't talk, not unless we torture him, and we won't do that. The only members of Gadianton's group who have talked were low level, and every one of them ended up dead—two while they were being held in prison. The Gadiantons have strong benefactors within the government, their influence oversized across society. We would almost need to catch them in the act of trying to assassinate me to turn enough support away from them."

He cleared his throat, seeming uneasy. "On the other hand, I worry about how much we seem to be appeasing them in the name of peace, compassion, and unity, because we're afraid of how violent they'll become if they don't get their way. That's yet another reason I wish my father and Moroni were still here. They had strong solutions to problems like these. They had better instincts and more courage, too."

Kai couldn't fully fathom all of that, but he inclined his head as if he understood. He trusted Helaman, maybe more than Helaman trusted himself. Dan, too.

"Oh," he said after a few silent moments, "I almost forgot. When I met with Imrahiel today, he asked me to help secure Ara a job here, doing some of the chores. I know you don't bring much help in, but I said I would try. He wants Ara and Jerena to become good friends, so that maybe Jerena will give her useful information she can pass along."

Helaman tilted his head, thoughtful. "He *is* thorough, isn't he? And I can do better than that. We could use additional help with the children, especially when Jerena needs to meet with some of the sister leaders in the church. That will make Imrahiel happy, wouldn't you say?"

"Yes," Kai agreed, "but let's wait a week. Then Ara can tell Imrahiel about it. If it happens too fast, it'll look suspicious."

"Speaking of suspicious," said Dan, "are you a hundred percent sure you can trust Ara? I like her, I do, but she's officially part of their group."

"Technically, so am I," noted Kai. "But you're right. I need to be careful. I'm pretty sure I can trust her, but I can't be completely certain."

"Have you prayed about it?" asked Helaman, fixing Kai with a solemn stare.

Kai's face heated in embarrassment. "Well … um, no, I guess I haven't. I'm sorry. I should. I mean, I will."

"It may take more than one prayer," added Dan. "A lot more. Heavenly Father helps us, but he makes sure we get to do our part, for our own good. So be diligent about it. And patient."

Kai felt like he was ten years younger, being lectured by Gideon and Ishara. Unlike then, however, he didn't experience the same resentment or entrapment. The gentle chastening pricked his pride, but what justification did he have to complain about it? The situation was deathly precarious, and they needed help to figure it out. He almost wished his parents were in Zarahemla with him. Their wisdom and faith would be helpful.

"Thank you. I will." A sudden sense of peace washed over him. Perhaps an answer would come more quickly than he thought. Or perhaps not. Either way, he promised himself he would be diligent and patient.

CHAPTER 15

"I'm nervous about tomorrow." Ara bit her lip, staring out the window of the music room in Helaman and Jerena's house. Many months had passed. The new year had come again, the festivities in Zarahemla having taken on a much more subdued tone. Too many people were missing, and the city still labored through its shame as it struggled to recover.

"Me, too," said Kai. The election had been delayed significantly by the high judges, to allow people affected by the invasion time to focus on rebuilding, but tomorrow the results would be announced. Anticipation throughout the city was meteoric, despite the often belligerent and bare-knuckled politicking. The Gadiantons had done their best to spread every sort of rumor imaginable. Some of those rumors were partially based on information Kai and Ara had provided to Imrahiel. Helaman's responses were always calm, well-reasoned, and sincere. Even if Helaman hadn't been able to anticipate some of the rumors, Kai was convinced nothing could have knocked him off-kilter or seriously sullied his reputation. That drove Imrahiel mad.

Once Helaman's name was announced as the winner—as every survey said it would be—the Gadiantons would attempt to assassinate him, perhaps the very same day. Kai and Ara had confirmed the continued development of those plans, though details were frustratingly difficult to uncover, even with Kai officially working part-time as a night-shift law officer in disguise. He hadn't yet been asked to take the second set of Gadianton oaths, and that was a blessing, but it meant he had less access to information.

Despite his constant worries over Helaman's safety, things had seemed to slow down for Kai over the last few months, so he didn't feel like he was always treading water in his new role. He had written three letters to Siarah and received more than three dozen in return. Jerena passed them to him when Ara wasn't around. He didn't feel comfortable inviting Siarah to Zarahemla yet, of course; things would soon be coming to a head with the Gadiantons, and he had to keep up the subterfuge of dating Ara. They had already eaten in every decent restaurant in the city, on both sides of the walls, and Vyim and Thunder got plenty of exercise.

That largely pleasant pause was surely about to end.

Ara turned her gaze to Kai. "My father has been more secretive than usual the last few days. He won't tell me anything; he just keeps reminding me to keep my oaths." She shivered.

"You've already broken them, including showing me some of the advanced signs."

She shook her head. "I don't care anymore if they kill me. Well, not like I used to." She reached over to grasp his hand. "What you've been teaching me—and Jerena, too—is like warm sunlight on the perfect spring day. It has changed me, Kai. I've been reading the scriptures. And remember those letters from Helaman I copied from Zerahir? They fill my soul with joy. Part of me recognized the truth then, but I didn't know how to open that door. You helped me."

He wasn't sure what to make of her impassioned proclamation. He'd been praying for months about whether he could fully trust her, but no clear answer had come. Was her claim of spiritual awakening the answer, or at least part of it? Oddly, and thankfully, she hadn't pressed him on their real relationship, perhaps waiting until their joint mission was complete. She kissed him occasionally, however, and he didn't have to pretend to enjoy it.

"And you've helped me," said Kai, trying to blunt the compliment. "Imrahiel still has at least a little trust in me. I know getting you a job here pleased him. And it was your idea to tell him I had disguised myself and used another false name so I could infiltrate the law officers while also secretly helping to protect Kishkumen. That was brilliant. Even though he hadn't approved it beforehand, he liked it, and I wouldn't have thought of it."

Ara looked down, blushing, which Kai knew was hard to fake. "I don't know about that, but … well, it just seems like my mind is clearer now, and sometimes ideas come from nowhere." She lifted her head, an earnest pleading in her eyes. "Do you think God is starting to forgive me? Have I found some favor in his eyes?" Uncharacteristically, she removed her hand and sat primly, eagerly awaiting his answer.

"Yes, I do believe that." He felt as though he really did. "And it will continue if you keep trying."

"I know." She lowered her head again. "It makes me wonder what more I can do. How can I help protect Helaman, Jerena and their children? I'm almost positive the Gadiantons will make the attempt tomorrow. I know Helaman will have extra guards, but *they* know that, too. What are we missing?"

Kai had been thinking hard on that question. He and Dan and several other guards had discussed it at length for many weeks, preparing for the eventual day. Helaman didn't want a lot of soldiers in the city so soon after the citizens had been terrorized by soldiers, albeit Lamanites instead of Nephites, but the guards and aides had prevailed upon him to allow a few more. They had worked out plans with a pair of captains on how to strategically position two hundred troops along Helaman's processionary route from his house to the temple, where he would accept the oaths of duty.

The house was secure, too, including the roof. Unless the Gadiantons came with a small army, they stood no chance of getting in during the night or in the morning before Helaman departed. The temple itself was the most secure and least likely place for an assassination attempt. Even the best bowman wouldn't be able to get close enough for a reliable shot.

Kai shrugged. "We're as ready as we can be. Whatever they try, we'll stop it."

Ara stared at him for several seconds, obviously still searching for other possibilities. Finally, she breathed heavily and said, "Yes, I think you're right. We've done all we can. As Jerena would say, "It's in God's hands now." Though there's one other thing we can try."

"What's that?"

"Can we pray together, for Helaman's safety?"

Kai felt a jolt. They had talked a lot about prayer, but hadn't said any prayers together, not when it was just them. He couldn't object. Given what lay ahead, every prayer was needed.

The day dawned overcast, the skies misting and drizzling the first few hours. Helaman's procession was scheduled for the beginning of the fifth hour, following the custom that the chief priest of the Christian church, who had so much influence in Nephite society, make a respectful and humble journey from his home to the temple. There, he would welcome the new chief judge of the people, extend his loyalty and support for peace and order under just laws, and publicly encourage the popularly elected judges to impartially enforce those laws.

Today's procession would take on a different aspect, of course. Not since Alma the Younger had a single man filled the offices of chief judge and high priest. Alma had handled both for eight years, then concluded it was too much, giving up the chief judgeship to Nephihah. Though just thirty-three years had passed, so much had happened since that time. Kai hadn't ever known anything but secular chief judges in his life.

A few minutes before departure, everyone formed up on the street outside the house. Kai stood to Helaman's left, with Dan on the right, other guards forming a tight circle around them. Kai scanned the rooftops again—nothing.

"Relax," said Helaman to Kai. "All will be well."

"I'll try," he responded.

Helaman laughed lightly. "And you'll fail. It's all right. By the end of the day you can relax. I promise you we'll be fine. *I'll* be fine."

Kai attempted to portray a believing expression. He wasn't sure he succeeded. Helaman took a step toward Dan and spoke to him in a low voice. Kai's ears burned, but he couldn't discern a word. Huffing slightly, he let his gaze pass over each of the other guards. He knew them well, had analyzed each one. He'd even spoken with their families under the guise of delivering a special thank you from Helaman for the service of their sons, husbands, fathers, and brothers. They all seemed dependable and loyal. But what if the Gadiantons had gotten to one or more of them somehow? Persuading someone to believe in their cause wasn't the only way to change behavior—blackmail or threats were often used. Kai had tried to cover those avenues as well, with Dan's help.

Suddenly Helaman turned away from Dan and began his march down the street, the large group surrounding him lurching into motion. No trumpets, drums, or booming voices announced the start of the procession—they just began moving.

Helaman kept a stately, steady pace, his head swiveling back and forth, his dignified aspect accented by broad smiles and occasional waves. A few people lined the streets of the Santorem, but Kai knew the crowds would be much larger and noisier when they left the upper-class neighborhood. Many citizens yearned to see the prophet today and earn his blessing—especially those who had ignored his counsel prior to the invasion.

The throngs outside the Santorem were twice as numerous as Kai had expected, and his nervousness soared. He tried to share a glance with Dan, but Dan calmly assessed his side of the procession, so Kai continued to do the same on his. His eyes darted incessantly over heads and rooftops, scanning for threats. Many people clapped, and some called out Helaman's name. Helaman kept smiling and waving. He seemed to be enjoying himself, and as if the elements agreed that he should, the clouds lifted and thinned, the sunlight growing brighter as they traveled toward the temple.

A few minutes later, Kai spotted a disturbance in the crowd on his side. He tensed, hand moving to the hilt of his sword. But it turned out to be a small group of boys chasing each other and tussling good-naturedly. Their parents tried to get them under control as Helaman passed, and Kai saw at least one mortified look from a mother.

"Let them play!" shouted Helaman, eyes toward the young boys. "The Lord loves little children!"

That encouragement seemed to relieve the parents greatly. For their part, the boys stopped and stared at the prophet with suddenly serious looks on their faces. After the procession had passed, though, they were back to their frenetic fun.

At one point, Kai thought he spied movement along a rooftop, but after staring at the spot for a few seconds, he wondered if it might be a distraction. He did a quick survey of everything else around him. Nothing.

Soon they ascended the steps of the temple, and Kai was amazed Helaman had been right. Nothing had happened. Helaman insisted on taking the last several steps alone, so he could assume his normal place near the high judges and several of the lower judges.

That was it! One of the judges was going to make the attempt. Kai was convinced. He motioned to Dan with a hiss that came out louder than he'd intended. Dan saw the intense look on his face and hastened over.

"It's one of the judges," said Kai, nodding his head in their direction.

Dan gazed toward them, contemplating. "Doubtful," he replied.

"It has to be," Kai insisted. "One of them will sacrifice himself to kill Helaman."

Dan gave him a level look. "Nothing in our research has indicated any inclination toward self-sacrifice among the Gadiantons, especially not elected judges who might be Gadiantons." He lowered his voice. "I don't believe Helaman is in danger, and it's clear he doesn't, either. Calm down, Kai. Watch closely, but be steady."

Kai tried. He regulated his breathing. He mentally reviewed everything he'd observed. But most helpful was just watching Helaman, who even glanced at him a couple of times with a reassuring smile. The prophet was confidence personified, even though Kai knew he felt nervous about becoming chief judge, doubting how well he could perform that role.

One of the high judges stepped forward, a man named Ghealthim who appeared older than any of the hills around the city. His voice carried with surprising strength as he read from a parchment, his words audible across the large courtyard of the temple, packed with multitudes extending beyond the columns and down the broad steps fanning out on the hillside.

"Citizens of the great city Zarahemla and the nation Nephi, your voice has been heard regarding who is to be our new chief judge. Conducting an election in such dire circumstances proved challenging, but you have stepped forward to do your duty as free citizens. We thank you.

"Among the three candidates who put forward their names to become the next chief judge of the Nephite nation, the one who received the most votes, by a large margin, was Helaman, son of Helaman, of Zarahemla."

The people raised a great shout of joy, their cheering continuing for several seconds. Ghealthim extended an arm toward Helaman and motioned him to move to the center of the group of judges to address the crowd. Two scribes suddenly appeared as well, ready to record his words and distribute them everywhere within Nephite lands, and perhaps even beyond.

Helaman didn't exult in his victory; he barely smiled. He still looked confident, but Kai could tell he felt the tremendous weight of the new responsibility. Helaman positioned himself and paused. The crowd finally quieted, until nary a whisper could be heard.

"My brothers and sisters, I am honored and humbled today by the trust you have shown in me, and I feel keenly the responsibilities I freely choose to bear in this office. I covenant with you that I will give all I have—even my very life—to protect your freedoms and uphold our laws without prejudice, guile, or greed. I covenant, too, with God, our Great and Eternal Heavenly Father, that I will promote your welfare always, even if you do not profess him, that I will seek his wisdom to guide and strengthen me, that I will—"

"Tyrant! Son of a murderer!" Kai couldn't immediately locate the man who had yelled, but his hackles rose. Several other people started chanting the same thing, until at least thirty had joined in. A few members of the crowd tried to tell them to quiet down and show respect, but the protesters just yelled louder. Helaman contemplated them with a look of sadness on his face, but Kai couldn't tell what he felt beyond sorrow.

The chant morphed into more vile accusations, and many of the group of thirty threatened violence toward other members of the crowd. The disruptors were mostly men, but a few women had joined as well, all armed with some sort of weapon, though not brandishing them. They didn't represent an immediate danger to Helaman, though soldiers and guards repositioned to respond to any violent actions they might take.

For nearly two full minutes, Helaman observed the group intently. He didn't make any attempt to speak over them, which was impossible anyway. Finally, he looked toward Dan and motioned him over. Dan trotted up the steps, stopping one step below the prophet. Helaman leaned down and spoke to him for several seconds, after which Dan made his way down to the largest group of guards, which included Kai. He also called over the two army captains.

"We are to arrest those disrupting the ceremony and escort them to the main prison, where they will be questioned and held until the end of the day. They have threatened physical harm to the peaceful people around them, and they could be prosecuted for that, but Helaman and the high judges will make that determination later. If any resist, use force to apprehend them. And don't approach any of them unless there are at least two of you for each person. Is that clear?"

The captains and guards nodded.

"Okay, go," said Dan. "Kihoran, you and three guards stay here." He pointed at which three. "The rest, with me." With that, they were off at a jog.

The group of thirty knew something was up, but they apparently thought Helaman's response would be a show of toothless force. As soon as the captains had gathered enough soldiers, though, Dan charged them into the various sections of the group. Some resisted, but they were easily overcome. Within a few minutes, all the protesters lay on the ground with their hands tied and mouths gagged. A handful had tried to escape through the crowd, but the people had stopped them, holding them for the soldiers and guards. There were a few injuries, including to at least one soldier, but it was over. The prisoners were hoisted to their feet, and a pathway opened up as the soldiers and guards led them away through the clapping throng.

Kai looked up again at Helaman, whose expression hadn't changed much. Sadness still dominated, joined by resignation. Kai thought through what Helaman had just ordered. He oft complained of not being as brave as his father and Captain Moroni, of not acting decisively enough. Yet he had made a bold move, surely knowing it would further enrage those who opposed him—especially the Gadiantons—and increase the danger to his own life. Kai's fears rose as he realized how deeply Helaman had meant the oath he pronounced before the disruption.

Quiet returned, and Helaman let the silence deepen for nearly another minute before resuming his speech. "There are those who believe our freedoms to be illusory, or worse, detrimental. They are most eager to force people to follow them, and to control every conversation. They claim their path leads to progress, to fairness, to human dignity, but that is a lie, and it always has been. The adversary of our souls wishes for us to surrender our free will to him and his chosen servants, so that he may more easily work his poison in us. God, on the other hand, bids us to obey his commandments and explains the natural consequences of this world to help us understand the advantages of obedience. He will never force us to follow him. Nor will his true servants.

"I strive every day to be a servant of God worthy of his acceptation. Whether you are Christian or not, it is my duty to serve you at his direction and pleasure, in all fairness and holiness before him. I have pledged my life to the cause of his son, our Savior, Jesus Christ, who is soon to descend to earth. I also pledge my life to the continued peace, prosperity, and progress of this nation. I will uphold and defend our laws, most of which were inspired by God for our benefit, to allow us the freedom to learn, achieve, and grow.

"I love this nation, and I love its people. Your courage and determination through our most recent struggle inflicted upon us by our Lamanite brothers and sisters was most remarkable. I wish you could have a man as wise as my father to lead you. But he has gone the way of all the earth, rejoicing and laboring in heaven now. He and my mother taught me many things, but I still have so much to learn. I ask for your prayers, and your patience. I ask for your faith, too—not just for me, but for each other. I ask you to remember the many blessings the Lord has graciously and lovingly granted us, the many times he has delivered us from utter destruction. I ask you to thank him, unceasingly, every day, for all that you have and are, and to reach out to those around you who suffer, who plead with God for relief.

"He will not compel you to serve one another, either. But he invites you to make that choice, knowing how much it will aid you, both now and in the eternities. Well did King Benjamin say, "When ye are in the service of your fellow beings ye are only in the service of your God." Like King Benjamin, I am an unprofitable servant, but I *am* his servant, and I am yours, too. My greatest hope is that when the final judgment comes, you and I can stand before the pleasing bar of God with our hearts knit together in love and mercy, our minds filled with the joyful contemplation of eternity, our consciences free of offense toward God and our fellow sojourners on this earth."

He paused, and Kai took stock of the crowd. An aura of reverent worship had settled upon them. Some knelt, and Kai felt incredible peace, despite what had happened moments before with the protesters.

Helaman made a quarter turn to his right, looking toward High Judge Ghealthim, who stepped forward and faced him. Ghealthim then administered the formal oath of the office of chief judge, raising his right hand, as did Helaman.

When the oath was complete, Helaman again turned fully toward the crowd and bowed solemnly. When he straightened, the people, who had anticipated the moment, burst into more applause and cheering. Kai caught the beginnings of a full smile on Helaman's face as he raised his hands to wave and bow, then do it again, repeatedly. Several long minutes passed before the crowd quieted down, and after a brief farewell, Helaman turned and walked toward the doors of the temple, alone. Kai and the other three guards hustled to catch up.

Kai had never felt so busy and stressed. While Helaman retired relatively early that evening, celebrations throughout the city lasted well into the night, including all through the streets of the Santorem. No immediate dangers had arisen, for which he was grateful. But he battled waking dreams of Imrahiel, Kishkumen, Gadianton, and Nahom, who posed a constant threat, especially now that Helaman was officially the chief judge.

After a tense next day with little sleep, Kai met the fake drunk near Kishkumen's house late that night.

"I hear you witnessed firsthand the arrests of our people," said the man. A few weeks ago, he had finally told Kai he called himself Mindon.

Kai nodded in the semi-darkness. They sat in the alley, where Mindon had a view of the front of the house. "They didn't attack anybody, but Helaman had them arrested anyway. He didn't waste any time, either."

"Yes, his father was like that. We're getting closer, though, Giron. And I've been thinking. You've made some good inroads with some of the other law officers—I've met with a couple of them. If we can get a group of you assigned to security detail in the Hall of Judgment on the same day, we may be able to execute a plan to get inside so we can take over the government."

Kai turned to him. "I think it's possible. I know who does the scheduling, and while he isn't one of us, he's more gullible than most. Is there a particular day you're thinking of, or do I need to arrange one and let you know?"

"The leaders would like it to be within the next week."

Kai could never get Mindon to tell him who 'the leaders' were, and he never asked directly. Perhaps Mindon didn't know. Information was highly compartmentalized among the Gadiantons—one reason it was so hard to identify them and gather hard evidence. It was also a chink in their collective armor.

"That's fast."

"We need to set aggressive goals."

Well, the Gadiantons were definitely goal-oriented, though usually more patient. Helaman's assumption of power had them spooked. Setting up the trap would be the easy part. He still wasn't sure he was ready to execute it, but he would have to be. He hoped Mindon couldn't hear the churning in his gut.

"All right," Kai said after a few moments. "We'll try for five days from now. I'll let you know if something happens and it can't be arranged."

"Don't just try," said Mindon, dark fire dancing in his eyes. "Do it. Whatever it takes. This is our chance."

CHAPTER 16

*Yea, and it came to pass that the Lord our God did visit us with
assurances that he would deliver us; yea, insomuch that he did speak peace
to our souls, and did grant unto us great faith, and did cause us that we
should hope for our deliverance in him.*

ALMA 58:11

Dan grasped Kai's shoulders. Nearly a week had passed, and everything was set. "Don't worry. Everything will look normal. We won't tip them off."

"I know, but I'm worried this isn't the right approach. The priority is to protect Helaman. Why would we let *any* of them in? Why not just run the security protocols we have and keep him safe? We have enough men, plus sufficient evidence to arrest Mindon."

Dan shook his head. "We've talked it through with Helaman. We need to be bolder. We must let them make an attempt, and catch them. You heard him. He's not afraid to die. Neither am I. We must eliminate the Gadiantons, for the good of the people."

"They're like locusts. How can we eliminate them?"

Dan gave him a sober look. "I don't know for sure. But we must try. And keep trying."

Dan's determination gave Kai little comfort. Sometime that day or evening, the Gadiantons would again attempt to assassinate Helaman. The thought made Kai sick; he had come to love Helaman and his family. Ara had, too.

As if he had called out her name, she rushed up to them as they stood near the back entrance to Helaman and Jerena's home. She must have come through the gardens. "It's Kishkumen," she said breathlessly.

"He's the assassin?" asked Kai.

"Yes, I'm positive. My father didn't know I was listening from my room, with my door cracked open. It's him. He's the one who killed Pahoran, too."

Kai looked at Dan, whose face had darkened, then back at Ara. "Do you know when?"

She shook her head in frustration. "Probably in the late afternoon, and they might try to kidnap Helaman instead of kill him. They know how much the people love him. Killing him might work against them, while holding him hostage is … helpful to them, I guess? I don't understand exactly how. My father argued about it with someone whose voice I didn't recognize. Imrahiel was there, too. I don't know their final decision, because they left before it was resolved, but they're moving forward." She gazed anxiously at them, wringing her hands. Kai had never seen her this worried.

"Thank you, Ara," said Dan sincerely. "This is helpful." He turned to Kai. "This assassin is very skilled, and they might have help on the inside we haven't uncovered, but I don't think our disposition changes. We're still ready, agreed?"

"Yes," Kai said after only a moment's hesitation, surprising himself. "But I'll find excuses to range into different areas of the building. I need to be active."

Dan thought about that a moment, and then nodded. "Follow the Spirit, Kai. Let him guide you. That's our primary advantage."

Ara nodded her strong affirmation of that statement and finally stopped wringing her hands.

"I will."

The day of business passed slowly at the Hall of Judgment. Helaman attended multiple meetings, with little time to himself to study or plan. Kai had heard him comment about the steep learning curve he faced, and that the issues confronting the nation weren't going to pause while he got up to speed. Kai felt for him, but he couldn't waste time worrying about that.

Instead, he acted like a harried aide—which he was—delivering written and verbal messages all over the sprawling, interconnected building complex. Most of the errands were fake. He needed to be as many places as possible, watching for Kishkumen or any others who looked suspicious.

Late afternoon passed, and the sun set, though Kai couldn't see it. He had gone to the basement, ostensibly to retrieve various records Helaman had requested. The basement hallways weren't even busy during the day, but now they echoed with emptiness. He had just turned a corner when he spotted a man emerging from a short hallway leading to nothing but a pair of storage rooms. Was there an underground entrance Kai didn't know about, or had the man been hiding?

The man turned and locked his dark eyes on Kai. It was the man from Nahom's kitchen, and the street near the warehouse. Kishkumen.

Kai nearly tripped as he halted. After checking behind him, he flashed a sign he had been taught as part of the first oath. Kishkumen recognized it and gave a slight nod, looking somewhat surprised, then motioned Kai to approach. Kai complied, stopping two paces from him.

"I've seen you before. Who are you?"

"Kihoran. I also go by Adonihah. I am one of Helaman's servants, and I report to Imrahiel."

Kishkumen grunted, but he seemed pleased. "Do you know who I am?"

"No," Kai replied, shaking his head, "but I see the bracelet you're wearing, and I was told to help whoever wore such a bracelet."

Kishkumen glanced casually at the bracelet, woven with blue and purple cords and tied with black thread. "Good. I presume you know these buildings well. I can't afford to get lost in this maze."

"Yes . . . yes, sir, I do. Where do you want to go?"

Kishkumen studied him a moment. "Give me the second sign."

What a blessing Ara had shown it to him. Satisfied, Kishkumen nodded. "Helaman should be in his office, right? He's still here?" A hint of worry laced his voice.

"Yes, I think so. You want to go there? It's on the third floor."

Kishkumen nodded sharply. "Which way?"

Kai pointed straight ahead, and Kishkumen started moving quickly, motioning for Kai to walk beside him, on his left.

"If anyone asks, Helaman sent for me, and you're just bringing me to him. Tell them I'm an emissary, but that you can't give my name or title. People know Helaman and Moronihah have spies; they'll let it go. Even the guards won't fuss much." He seemed confident, and he hummed with dark energy. Kai could have sworn the lanterns flickered as he passed, and not from the stirring of the air.

Kai led him through two turns and up one flight of stairs before he spoke to him again. The main floor sat deserted now, too, except for the occasional law officer or guard.

"It's finally happening," Kai whispered. "This will bring it all down."

Kishkumen didn't look at him, but his jaw clenched. "Yes, it will."

"Do you … do you need my help? Helaman will have at least one of his personal guards. Maybe I could distract the guard while you … capture him?"

Kishkumen didn't answer for nearly a minute as Kai led him across a courtyard and through another doorway, then down a long hallway and up another flight of stairs. Most of the lower-level judges and their staffs occupied the second floor, and they had already gone home.

"I'm not going to capture him," Kishkumen finally said. "I will kill him. The murder will be blamed on High Judge Zerahir, who will be found hanging at his house." Suddenly he stopped and turned to Kai. "Why am I telling you this? You will forget what I just said; if not, you will hang, too. Understood, Adonihah?"

Kai nodded obediently, doing his best to appear subservient.

"Good. Your job is to get me to Helaman's office, nothing more. Introduce me to the guard, get out of the way, and I'll kill him first. Helaman is a whelp. Executing him will be easy."

They continued walking, but Kai's mind sprinted. Kishkumen was larger, stronger, and more experienced at killing than he was. Kai hadn't, to his knowledge, ever slain a man. Maybe one of the Lamanites he'd battled had died of his wounds, but launching arrows from a distance or bull-rushing a surprised man over a wall was different than face-to-face combat.

Kai debated whether he should wait until they approached the door to Helaman's office. Would he and the guard be able to subdue Kishkumen, or would Kishkumen incapacitate or kill them both? Dan had other guards hidden nearby, but they might not be fast enough. And what if the posted guard had been compromised? Kishkumen certainly wouldn't tell Kai about that.

He couldn't let Helaman die; he *wouldn't* let Helaman die. A clear thought came to him, as if rising from a brilliant mist: to protect the prophet, he would have to surprise Kishkumen. A plan quickly formed in his mind. He surmised that when they turned to ascend the stairs to the third floor, Kishkumen would naturally look up. Kai had a knife—the dagger from Merga—hidden under his tunic, and he could stab Kishkumen in that moment. He would have to be fast—extremely fast. And accurate.

His heart thumped like clashing thunderheads as they approached the stairs. He could feel Kishkumen's anticipation growing as well. That was a good sign—it meant Kishkumen was focused on his plan, paying less attention to his guide.

As expected, Kishkumen looked toward the top of the stairs as they turned to begin climbing.

In a flash, Kai had the dagger in his left hand. He gripped it hard, then stabbed upward into Kishkumen's torso, just below his ribs, using his right arm to lift Kishkumen's left arm out of the way. In a surreal instant, he felt the tip of the knife pierce Kishkumen's heart, and then he withdrew it and stepped back, ready for any reflexive resistance.

Kishkumen spun his back against the wall, staring at Kai with a look of affronted shock, one hand covering the wound while the other tried to reach for his own knife. His hands were slow and shaky, though, his voice feeble as he tried to utter a curse. Within seconds the light in his eyes began to fade, and he slumped to his knees, then onto his side on the stairs. His last breath rattled from his throat, and he became still, glassy eyes locked onto Kai in an expression of eternal rage and horror.

Kai stood frozen and confused as he watched Kishkumen's last moments. He had just killed a man, up close and in person. The gory scene made him feel like retching, but part of him wanted to rejoice, to exult in the victory. The man who had killed Pahoran, and planned to kill Helaman, was dead. He was *dead*; he wasn't coming back. And Kai had accomplished that, with the Lord's help.

His mind lurched back to normal activity, and after one last look at Kishkumen's body, he bounded up the stairs to the third floor, running with Merga's bloody dagger as if angry Lamanite soldiers chased him. When he made the turn into the hallway leading to Helaman's office, he finally slowed to a fast jog, not wanting to alarm the guard.

The guard was now Dan. Before Kai halted in front of him, Dan had already assessed the knife, the blood on Kai's hand, arm, and clothes, and his shortness of breath.

"What happened?" he asked, drawing his sword and glancing beyond Kai's shoulder.

"The assassin is dead. I have to tell Helaman."

Dan blinked, face both shocked and grim, then opened the door and entered the office, Kai following.

Helaman stood behind the desk, his brave mien more than a front, Kai knew. His eyes dropped to the blood-dripping knife.

"It was Kishkumen, like Ara said," blurted out Kai. "I killed him at the bottom of the north stairs. And we know where he lives."

Helaman nodded somberly, then looked to Dan. "Mobilize the teams. We need to take as many of the Gadiantons as we can, tonight, including Gadianton himself." His expression oozed calm, confident leadership, but his voice still quavered a little.

"Right away." Dan turned and left the room, sprinting down the hall and shouting for two of the hidden guards to converge outside Helaman's office.

Helaman looked again at the knife in Kai's hand, which drew his own eyes down to the deadly instrument. He had almost forgotten he still held it. A drop of deep-red blood tumbled from the tip, splashing onto the wooden floor. Without thinking, Kai wiped the dagger on his breeches, first one side and then the other. He stared at it a moment longer before placing it gently on Helaman's desk and sitting heavily in a chair. His adrenaline suddenly faded, replaced by exhaustion and anxiety.

Helaman sat, too, a troubled look on his face.

"It is a terrible thing to kill a man, even when he is trying to harm you or your family, even when you are justified."

Kai nodded, feeling numb. He didn't stare at the knife, fixing his gaze instead on Helaman's robes of state, blessedly free of blood.

"Thank you," said Helaman softly.

Tears came unbidden. Kai started to blink them away, but he knew it was pointless. He let them come.

"Jerena thanks you, too. And our children. And my mother, of course. You've done a great thing, Kihoran. Or I should say, *another* great thing. Your nation could never adequately repay you. Nor could I. The Lord can, though."

He let the silence linger, and Kai finally met his eyes. "It was my duty . . . and my honor, something I needed to do." He didn't have any other words.

Helaman's smile burned away most of Kai's tears. "Would that all of us performed our duty, in truth and righteousness. The world would be a different place, my friend and brother. It could finally become like the city of Enoch."

<hr>

Kai didn't participate in the many raids on the Gadiantons conducted across the city over the next two days. He stayed with Helaman and his family. The most immediate threat had been eliminated, but others might be lurking.

He carefully absorbed the reports coming in every few hours from Dan and others. Dozens of Gadiantons were captured, eventually including Mindon, but the raids failed to apprehend the most senior members of the band. Gadianton, Imrahiel, Nahom, and others suspected of working directly with Kishkumen had disappeared mysteriously, as if they had a secret escape route. Neither the gate guards nor the army patrols had seen anyone matching their descriptions, nor any significant groups of people leaving, reporting only normal foot, horse, and wagon traffic. The disappearance of the band's leadership puzzled and frustrated Moronihah, Helaman, and Dan. Kai, too, though he still felt somewhat numb.

The next day, Kai participated in the questioning of Mindon, in the main prison in Zarahemla. The mock drunk sat on a rough wooden bench against one wall of a large holding cell, shackled hand and foot and dressed in plain gray clothes. He glared at Kai as he, Helaman, and Dan entered the room and took chairs on the opposite wall.

"You're a liar," he spat at Kai.

What a terribly uninventive accusation. "So are you," Kai responded.

"I will—"

"You will do nothing," said Dan, his tone hot steel. "You will answer our questions, and that's *all* you will do."

Mindon shifted his malevolent gaze to Dan. "And you're going to make me answer them? Torture me, maybe?"

Helaman shifted in his seat, and everyone's focus turned to him.

"We won't torture you. Were our roles reversed, I know you wouldn't hesitate to torture me, but that's because you follow a different master. Now, first question: how many guards protected Kishkumen's house, besides you?"

Mindon stared back defiantly. "It doesn't matter. You haven't caught any of them."

"We've caught one so far," said Dan, "but he's not in any shape to talk yet."

Mindon's eyes narrowed. "I don't believe you."

Dan's eyes flashed fire. "I don't care if you believe me. Others escaped. You might avoid execution if you can tell us where they've gone. It appears most of your group have abandoned the city. They clearly planned for the possibility of Kishkumen's failure. Where would they rendezvous?"

Mindon spat on the floor. "I'm not telling you anything."

"Then you'll most certainly hang," said Helaman.

Mindon laughed. "Ha! You don't have any real evidence against me. By your precious laws you'll eventually have to let me go."

Helaman gestured toward Kai. "We have a key witness. Other people saw you in the same place Adonihah found you, including two women who saw you together, on multiple occasions. We have enough evidence. None of the high judges will object, nor will enough of the lower judges."

"How does tomorrow morning sound?" asked Dan. "For your hanging?"

Mindon spat again. He looked nervous now, but he still showed defiance. "You don't frighten me, Lamanite traitor. Yes, I know who you are. And I'll appeal for a public trial."

"Denied," said Helaman coolly. "This might be a waste of time, but you will receive one last witness that Jesus Christ is the prophesied Messiah. He will soon come to earth, and after he has fulfilled his mission, he will visit this people, as promised. He loves you, and he bids you remove the chains around your neck and come unto him so he can heal you. You can, if you will. Exercise faith in him, and he will make you strong enough. The choice is yours."

For a fleeting moment, it seemed Mindon had been moved by Helaman's words. But spite and disdain snapped back into his eyes.

"Nice try. I won't fall for your witch's tricks. Set me free now, or my brothers will return and finish the job."

"You've just threatened the chief judge," said Kai coldly. Mindon leered at him, but Kai stood, and Mindon's evil smile turned sickly. "You know what I did to the last man who threatened him, to make sure he couldn't carry out his plans." He took two steps toward Mindon, surprised that neither Dan nor Helaman tried to stop him. He unsheathed Merga's dagger, holding it steady at his side, point toward Mindon. "This is the knife that slayed the invincible Kishkumen. He was zealous, overconfident, and careless. Like you. The chief judge has rightly said we will not torture you. We can only offer you choices … and every choice has a consequence." He took a step closer, and Mindon pressed his back against the wall, fear flashing in his eyes.

"My good friend's wife died in the Lamanite invasion you helped facilitate," Kai continued, his voice now ice. "They had three young children whose mother was unjustly torn from them. Their story is one among thousands. In your mad quest for power and authority, you bathed this country in blood, unleashing untold suffering. If I were to kill you right now, could I be blamed, even by God? Would not my friend's wife declare for me? Would not High Judge Zerahir, murdered to make it appear he was Helaman's assassin? Would not thousands of others?"

The point of his blade nearly touched Mindon's chest, his face hovering mere inches from Mindon's own. He felt neither anger nor hatred, but a strange calmness. He had no desire to kill Mindon himself. He just wanted Mindon to know he deserved his death, which would be executed under the laws of the land. He knew Mindon wouldn't repent, wouldn't help them in any way. Maybe one of the others would, but they hadn't captured anyone else of a high enough level to matter much. The Gadiantons had made good their escape.

The fear slowly faded from Mindon's eyes. He glanced at the knife point, then licked his lips. "Go ahead then. Kill me. I will curse you and all your family from the grave."

Kai straightened and laughed, the sudden burst of mirth seeming to startle Mindon more than his knife had. He sheathed the dagger as he took a step back. "No, you won't. But perhaps Kishkumen will curse you for helping me. Will you be able to prove to him you didn't do it wittingly? You'll meet him soon. Are you ready?"

With that Kai abruptly turned and left the room, closing the door firmly, leaving Mindon no chance to respond. He waited a short distance down the hall for Helaman and Dan to emerge, which they did a few minutes later. They walked slowly toward him, speaking softly with each other. When they got close, Helaman looked at Kai and smiled.

"That was quite good, Kai. I was impressed. Apparently, so was Mindon. You rattled him, and we tricked him into giving up a couple of names we hadn't known before. Dan will seek them out shortly, or at least speak to their families if they've left. Maybe it wasn't much, but it was something. Come, I'm hungry. I'm sure we can find some lunch."

Kai rose, and the three headed for the stairs that would lead to an exit from the prison. Kai had been pondering something, and it seemed a good time to bring it up.

"Sir, can I return to Bountiful?"

"Helaman."

"What?"

"Not 'sir.' Helaman. Remember? Or brother."

"Yes, sorry, I still sometimes forget. I'd like to return home … and possibly get married."

Helaman smiled broadly. "I have more work for you here. You are extremely valuable. A 'profitable servant,' as the Lord might say." Kai's heart sank, but Helaman continued. "However, I can arrange for your family to come live here, if they're willing. Including … Siarah, is it? I will pay for everything. I could also ask Moronihah if he'd be willing to station your adoptive brother, Jevrael, here. He's still at the border."

Kai's heart swelled with hope and promise at Helaman's magnanimous offer. "That would be wonderful, yes. Thank you. Can I send my parents and Siarah a letter today with your offer?"

"By the swiftest messenger, and with the funds they will need to move here. If I could cast my voice hundreds of miles to proclaim it, and also place the funds right in their pockets, I would do it right now." He laughed lightly.

"I very much look forward to meeting your parents, Kai, and your sister, and your betrothed. I'll make sure they receive a proper welcome when they arrive."

Ara's mind spun in ever-accelerating circles, while her heart seemed to beat slower. She wasn't sure what to think or feel. Jerena had just told her Kai's news. His official engagement. Jerena had tried to comfort her. Ara and Kai couldn't have spent so much time together, 'pretending' to be a couple, without Jerena realizing Ara was in love with him.

And he would soon marry another woman.

How was it possible? Ara had prayed many times for the Lord to help her repent and prepare so he would approve of her marrying Kai. And she had felt like he *was* helping her. Jerena had explained how the Lord didn't interfere with people's agency, and Kai had his freedom to choose, but that explanation felt hollow and cold.

It didn't seem fair. Her father had tried to push Kishkumen on her many times, and despite him being an evil man, she had almost given in more than once. Then, she had found a man she truly loved, a man of faith and goodness, and he had helped her find the light missing from her life. He was part of that light. And she couldn't do anything to keep him. Could she? No—she loved him, and she respected him too much.

Where could she go, then? She couldn't stay at Helaman's any longer, not when she would see Kai so often. Not when she would have to act as if everything were normal and fine. She couldn't even stay in Zarahemla.

She finally asked Jerena to help her get to Gideon with what few possessions she had from her father's house. Her sister owned the house now, and when Ara had tried to explain to her what their father had done, she had laughed it off. She was a silly woman, and always had been. Their father had never tried to bring her into his darker, more serious schemes for that reason. Nahom had taken Ara's little brother with him. She doubted she would ever see either of them again.

She had wavered on the choice of Gideon. On the one hand, that city would remind her of Kai, since he loved and admired the people so much. On the other hand, that love and admiration told her those were probably the people she needed to be with most. They could help her, and maybe she could help them, too. Someday. If she didn't prove too weak.

She thought about leaving Kai a short note, but in the end decided against it. She would find new hope in Gideon. Jerena had promised it, solemnly, and had even prayed with her before saying goodbye. And so Ara left Zarahemla, feeling alone, but at least having a place to go and the faint outline of a purpose.

EPILOGUE

Wherefore, we search the prophets, and we have many revelations and the spirit of prophecy; and having all these witnesses we obtain a hope, and our faith becometh unshaken, insomuch that we truly can command in the name of Jesus and the very trees obey us, or the mountains, or the waves of the sea. Nevertheless, the Lord God showeth us our weakness that we may know that it is by his grace, and his great condescensions unto the children of men, that we have power to do these things.

JACOB 4:6–7

In the year of Kai's birth, Amalickiah initiated the Great Rebellion. A few years later, the king-men arose and attempted to overthrow the government, suffering an ignominious defeat at the hands of Captain Moroni which orphaned hundreds of children like Kai and Neva. Later that same year, the Great War began, lasting more than six years.

Nearly a decade of relative peace followed the end of the Great War, but many Nephites left the country, weary of war and believing the peace couldn't last.

They were right. Kai had just turned twenty when the Lamanites under King Tubaloth invaded and were soundly defeated. But Coriantumr's recent overthrow of mighty Zarahemla exposed again the fact that inner turmoil and disobedience to God's commandments among the Nephites always proved far more dangerous than any external foe. Kai had now witnessed that reality firsthand; a Nephite had assassinated Chief Judge Pahoran, and then almost killed the prophet, Chief Judge Helaman.

How long could the peace last this time? Helaman preached optimism, but he was also a realist. He didn't promise perpetual peace—not in the way the world commonly viewed peace.

Kai asked him, at he and Jerena's home, after a satisfying and peaceful dinner. Ara no longer attended any of their family meals, or worked in their home, and Kai hadn't been able to find her at her house, but Jerena had assured him she was fine.

Helaman repeated Kai's question. "How long will peace last?" He pondered a moment. When he answered, his eyes radiated the wisdom of his father, the Elder Helaman.

"Truth is a sword, Brother Kihoran." Whether he called him Kai or Kihoran, Kai always felt deeply respected by the prophet, but especially when he added the term 'brother.' "All people sin against the truth, and it cuts them. They react to that pain. Some react worse than others, even when they've been clearly taught the origin of life, the joyous opportunity for repentance and redemption in Christ, and our true heritage as children of a loving God who prepared themselves diligently to come here and embark upon the next phase of our progression.

"This is a fallen world, a seemingly cruel realm, a great testing ground. Sometimes, it is difficult to remember that the purpose of our existence lies in immortality, not mortality. Our struggles to survive and thrive on this earth mean nothing beyond what they can teach us about faith, love, determination, and kinship. We take these attitudes and hard-won knowledge with us when we die, and nothing else.

"Will peace last? That is, above all, an individual question. Peace will persist eternally for every person who places their faith and trust in the Lord, and who exerts themselves in serving God and their brothers and sisters, diligently and consistently. They discover *his* peace: the Savior's peace. They might die a most horrible or violent death on this world, but they will die in the arms of his love. And they will be welcomed back home in perfect peace and great glory.

"My priority is to prepare men's and women's hearts for peace. Anyone—everyone—can achieve it. I have great hope that many will. Their individual exaltation is priceless. Of course, I realize, as does our Heavenly Father, that many will fail to accept and cultivate the Lord's peace, the true peace that leads to all peace. That means the plague of war will continue. Famines and other natural disasters will also come—sometimes because these trials are the only way to remind us of the path to true peace.

"Do not fear, Kai. God is faithful. He sees the end from the beginning, and his plans cannot be foiled by men, even when it seems to us that they are. He sees not just our world, but many others. He sees not just our time, but all time, for it is one eternal round to him. He sees not just our present state, but our eternal potential as his sons and daughters, who can become powerful beyond our ability to comprehend. He sees not just this fallen existence, but the eternities that will follow. He loves us more than we could ever know. He proves it, every day, in so many ways, large and small. I've only recently come to feel like I'm beginning to understand it, along with all its implications.

"You have a happy road before you, because you have chosen Jesus Christ as your guide. I don't know what challenges you will yet face, but you will not confront them alone. If you learn to fully trust the Lord, and if you heed his counsel so he can trust you in turn, you will *always* have peace."

Kai felt like a column of light had descended from heaven to surround them all—Kai, Helaman, Jerena, and their children. He wanted to ask Helaman to write down what he'd just said, so he could memorize it word for word and repeat it to himself often. But he knew Helaman's response would be to tell him to study the scriptures, for all of it could be found there.

"Thank you, Helaman. I know you're right, and I'm amazed at how many miracles have brought me to this place."

"You've been the Lord's hand in miracles yourself," said Jerena. "Helaman is planning a big celebration for you, for saving his life—probably all our lives."

Kai had heard whisperings of the celebration, and he didn't desire it.

"If it's okay with you, I'd rather not be recognized or celebrated. Can you say you don't want to reveal the person's name for their own safety? You could tell everyone it was a servant in the right place at the right time, the Lord using a weak thing to accomplish a greater purpose. Would that work? It's true. Some know who I am, but eventually, if the official histories don't record them, their stories will just become rumors, which will eventually fade to myths and then disappear altogether. Hopefully."

Helaman sat back and clasped his hands, a slight smile tugging at his lips. "Whatever you wish, Kihoran. At this point, I can't deny you anything. Well, except for leaving my employ, at least for a while." He winked at Kai, then shared a smile with Jerena.

Kai smiled, too. "Thank you. I like it here, more than I thought I would. I have to admit, though, that someday I might like to go north and see what it's like for our people there."

Siarah stared at Kai's letter. He had finally sent another one—he was truly horrible at sending letters—but what it contained seemed almost too amazing to comprehend. Reading it again by candlelight had augmented its mystery and power. She couldn't fathom that he had killed an assassin trying to murder Helaman. And now Helaman had offered to move Kai's family—and her—to Zarahemla. What about her own family? She instantly dismissed that thought as selfish, ungrateful, and disrespectful to the prophet. Truth be told, they were better off than Kai's family, so they could probably move themselves if they wanted to, though Kai hadn't mentioned them.

She could forgive him that, of course. He was a hero. In fact, she was sure he would become one of the most astounding and noble legends of all Nephite history. Her whole body tingled with pride for him, and she thanked the Lord every hour—every second!—for what this news would mean for their future. Kai implied in his letter that he didn't want the accolades, even going so far as to ask her not to tell anyone what he'd done, for safety's sake.

But the honors and privileges were his. Kai had earned them, and together, Siarah and he could use them for good. She rose from her work chair, holding the letter to her breast, then turned and cocked her head as a soft knock sounded at her shop door.

END OF BOOK 1

ABOUT THE AUTHOR

M.D. HOUSE is a recovering corporate cog. As an author, he started out writing science fiction, but became fascinated with the stories of Barabbas, Cornelius, and the Apostle Paul, among others, which has led him on an amazing and faith-affirming Christian fiction writing journey. He still writes clean, faith-based science fiction, with some fantasy coming soon as well. You can learn more about him at mdhouselive.com.